DOWN

Floodgate

Glenn Cooper

Down: Floodgate

Cover Art and Cover Design by Sherwin Soy
Author photo by Louis Fabian Bachrach
Formatting by Polgarus Studio

Note: American spelling is used throughout
except when referring to specific British places and titles.

1

Half the boys were standing ankle-deep in muddy pond water. The other five were a few feet away on boggy land. None of them said a word until Harry Shipley, the youngest by almost a year, a boy prone to panic attacks in the best of circumstances, began to blubber. He was the only thirteen-year-old, officially too young for the form, but academically too advanced to have been held back.

"Not now, Harry," Angus ordered, searching the bleak landscape for anything familiar. "Not a good time."

Angus Slaine was head boy of the Year Tens at Belmeade School. He was tall for his age, devilishly handsome with an angular face and longish blonde hair. Glynn Bond, his best friend, was the first to slosh out of the water. Angus followed and Glynn offered a hand.

"What the fuck?" Glynn said. He was a muscular boy with a solid wrestler's body and a low center of gravity.

Angus removed his loafers and emptied them. "Is that a question or a statement?" he asked of Glynn.

"I want to know what's happening," Glynn said, emptying his own shoes.

Boris Magnusson's mouth was stupidly open. "We all do," he said.

Harry was pulling at his loose woolen trousers that had slipped halfway down his backside. Between sobs he announced that his belt buckle was missing.

"Shut up, Harry," Angus snapped. "I won't say it again. Would you three stop looking like wankers and get out of the water?"

The boys obeyed and joined the others on the soft grass. There, the lot of them tried to make sense of what had just occurred. They had gone back to their dormitory to change out of their PE kits into school uniforms for maths class. It was their first GCSE year and although exams were a year away the pressure was mounting, particularly for the weaker students. It was Belmeade practice and part of the mystique of the elite boarding school to push the boys to sit the exams at the end of Year Eleven. Boris and Nigel Mountjoy were struggling academically and it had fallen to Angus to try to sort them out. The answer had been staring at him in the form of Harry's pimply, rodentine face. Annoying Harry. The maths whizz. The one they called Shitley, the boy every pupil wanted to punch. Angus made a tacit deal: Harry would tutor Nigel and Boris in exchange for his protection, and the arrangement had stuck. They were about to leave their dormitory with five minutes to spare, more than enough time to cross the green, run up the stairs, and find their desks in Mr. Van Ness's classroom, when, in an instant, they were in a clearing surrounded by woods, half in and half out of a scummy pond.

Danny Leung asked the others if their uniforms were as messed up as his. He was the ultimate outsider who had worked himself into a position of respect by dint of his mad footballing skills. His father was the cultural attaché at the Chinese embassy. When Danny enrolled at Belmeade as a junior boy, Angus's father had made the casual remark at the supper table that Mr. Leung was probably a spy and Angus had duly reported the gem to his mates. Danny was henceforward, Red Danny.

"It's more than my belt buckle. My zipper's gone, my buttons are gone, my tie's gone missing."

The other boys had the same wardrobe problems.

Craig Rotenberg asked if all of them had eaten porridge for breakfast.

"What kind of stupid question is that?" Glynn asked.

"It's not stupid," Craig said. "Maybe we were drugged. Maybe we were knocked out and taken out of school."

"I didn't have porridge," Nigel said.

"Me neither," Danny said. "I hate porridge."

"It doesn't mean we weren't drugged," Craig said.

"Natural materials." They all looked at Harry who repeated it more emphatically. "Natural materials."

"What are you going on about, you git?" Nate Blanchard asked angrily.

"Our shirts and socks and underwear are cotton," Harry said, sniffing back his tears. "Our blazers and trousers are wool. Our shoes are leather. All the metal bits, the plastic buttons, the polyester ties, that's what's gone missing."

"Who the hell cares about our clothes?" Boris yelled. "Our entire bloody school's gone missing!"

"We'll need to have a look-about," Angus said, sweeping his arm at the encircling woods. "There's bound to be someone around."

"How're we supposed to keep our trousers up?" Boris asked.

Kevin Pickles was a lad who had long compensated for his short stature with a rapier wit. Making other boys laugh was a damned sight better than being called gherkin. He had wandered away from the group and was now calling to them from tall grass halfway around the pond.

"How much will you give me to keep your willies from showing?"

"What did you find?" Danny called back.

Kevin held two fishing poles high over his head and ran back to join the others. Angus inspected them and declared them to be rubbish. They were hardly more than long, whittled branches with lengths of crude line tied to the ends. The barbed hooks, complete with writhing worms, were carved from bone.

"Let me see one," Glynn said, taking a rod and inspecting the line. "What's this made of? It's not nylon."

Stuart Cobham was the fisherman of the group. He snatched the rod from Glynn's hand, passed the line through his pinched fingers and said, "I think it's gut."

"Gross." That from Andrew Pender, a pale, willowy boy who counted on Harry to be the principal recipient of derision.

Stuart tested the strength of the line and declared it perfectly adequate for its proposed task.

"We don't have anything to cut it," Nigel said.

"Sure we do," Stuart said, putting the line in his mouth. He bit down and used his lower teeth as a saw until it cut through. In several minutes they each had several inches of line to cinch up their belts and some of the boys secured flapping shirts too.

Angus was aware that everyone was waiting for him to choose a direction of travel. He looked around for inspiration. The sky was a featureless pale shade of gray. The woods surrounding them looked more black than green. There was a light breeze carrying a hint of a bad odor.

"That way," Angus said.

No one asked him to justify his decision. They followed him through the meadow in a loose scrum. Glynn drew alongside him.

"There's got to be an explanation," Glynn said.

"Maybe we're being punked," Angus replied. "Maybe it's a TV program."

"I don't see any cameras," Glynn said.

Harry was crying again.

"Do you want me to shut him up?" Glynn asked.

Angus didn't answer. He was pointing at something on the ground. "Look at that," Angus said.

Stuart was employing one of the fishing rods as a walking stick. He used it to part the grass where Angus was pointing. "I think it's blood," he said.

"I think you're right," Angus agreed. "There's more over there. There's a trail of it. I think it goes into the woods."

"We should be careful," Glynn said. "We need weapons."

"What do you think's going to happen?" Boris asked in a mocking tone. "Are you scared a polar bear's going to pop out like in *Lost*?"

"Try not to be a complete prick, Boris," Angus said. "Everyone stay sharp. If we are being punked and filmed our reactions will be on YouTube until the day we die. You'll never, ever get laid if every girl on the planet sees that you're pathetic wankers."

The meadow grasses gave way to a trampled-down path through a thicket of brambles. Just beyond lay a dense forest. Walking through the thicket along the path, Glynn's jumper caught on thorns. He pulled away and left a small patch of Belmeade blue behind with a bit of gold embroidery, part of the S in School. Once inside the wood, the canopy blotted out much of the thin daylight. Tall pine trees creaked in the breeze. The forest floor was a carpet of needles, ferns, and large, flat mushrooms. Angus lost the blood trail but found it again with dots of crimson on a creamy expanse of fungus.

The boys were walking in silence. Even Harry was quiet but his prominent Adam's apple bobbed up and down with each wooly-mouthed swallow.

Angus stopped and turned to signal the boys to stop too.

They all heard it. A low moan.

Danny picked up a thick stick and some of the others followed suit. Ahead was a naturally fallen tree, its massive trunk and roots lying on the ground.

Here's where the sixth-form boys are going to get us, Angus thought. They'll be springing up, filming us with their mobile phones and having a good old laugh at our expense. Don't let them make us look foolish.

He took a deep breath, walked up to the tree trunk and slowly leaned over it.

"Shit!"

The other boys recoiled at his cry but Glynn, suspecting a ruse, clapped Angus on the back and looked over himself.

"Jesus."

A gaunt young man was looking up at them with pleading eyes. "Help me."

"What is it?" Nigel called out from the rear.

"He's hurt," Glynn said. "He's hurt bad."

The other boys slowly came forward, almost too scared to look. They lined up on their side of the tree and forced themselves to look over. Kevin was too short and had to hike himself onto the log.

"We should help him," Stuart said.

Angus found the courage to speak to the young man. "What happened to you?"

"Rovers," he rasped. "Gut-stabbed."

"You're stabbed?" Glynn said.

The man took his hands off his abdomen. His intestines were visible through the gaping wound.

Several of the boys dropped back a few feet. Harry threw up.

"We need to get you help," Angus said. "Which way is help?"

"Are they still about?" the man panted.

"Who?"

"The rovers."

"I don't know what you're talking about. We didn't see anyone else."

The man said, "At least I won't be eaten."

"Did he just say eaten?" Danny asked Craig.

Angus began to climb over the log. When Glynn asked what he was doing he replied, "Let's just see if this whole thing's staged. He's probably trying to frighten us with a sack of sheep guts."

Glynn followed and the two boys kneeled at the man's side.

"Christ, it's real," Angus said, when the man moved his hands away. He turned his head and gagged at the man's rank odor. "It's fucking real. What the hell is going on?"

"You got any water, friend?" the man asked.

"No but we can try to bring you some from the pond," Glynn said.

"I haven't seen you before. Which village do you hail from?"

"We're at Belmeade School," Angus said. "Well we were."

"You're too young."

"Too young for what?" Stuart said from the other side of the log.

"Did you see my mate?" the man said. "When the rovers come we hoofed it. They got me but I hope my mate got free."

Danny noticed something off to the right. A patch of dark blue on the forest floor.

While the boys were debating how they were going to bring water to the man they heard Danny calling. “Guys, I think you need to come here.”

There was a blue cap lying next to a man’s head. The rest of the body was several feet away on bloodstained pine needles.

Transfixed by the horror, the boys looked into the head’s staring eyes and then those eyes blinked and the dry lips moved.

Most of them screamed.

They ran back to the gut-stabbed young man.

“Your friend’s dead!” Angus shouted.

“He’s not dead.”

“Tell us where we are and what’s going on,” Angus demanded. “We won’t help you unless you tell us.”

“You don’t know?”

“We have no idea, all right?” Glynn yelled at the top of his lungs.

“You must be new ’uns,” the man rasped. He managed a short painful laugh. “Well let me be the first to welcome you to your new home. Welcome to Hell.”

2

Ben Wellington spent most of the brief helicopter ride from Dartford to Whitehall on his mobile. On the bench across from him, Emily Loughty and John Camp were too numb and exhausted to do anything but stare out the windows at the sprawl of greater London. They hadn't seen the sun in a month and the glare stung their eyes. Phone to ear, Ben silently offered Emily his sunglasses but she shook her head. The yellow light, though painful, was too precious.

Shortly before touchdown he pocketed the phone and said, "The cat's well and truly out of the bag."

"People know?" John asked.

Ben told them about the physics blogger Giles Farmer and his article which had primed the pump a day earlier. It was titled, *The Mystery of the Massive Anglo-American Collider: Have We Opened a Nasty Door to Another Dimension?* Any possibility of falsely rubbishing Farmer's story had now collapsed under the hysteria surrounding the mass disappearances and intrusions along the path of the tunnels of MAAC, the Massive Anglo-American Collider.

Police and army units were responding to a "series of incidents" as the government was characterizing the evolving situation, but there was a clamor, rapidly approaching hysteria, for answers. Farmer was all too willing to go before the cameras from the stoop of his bed-sit in Lewisham and from this soap box he was challenging the authorities to come clean.

"Farmer says he knows you," Ben said.

"I remember him," Emily said. "We talked a few times on the telephone. He was bright but on the fringe." She shook her head then continued, "Well, maybe he was more clever than me."

"Do you want to see his article?"

"I don't have the strength for it at the moment."

"He says he spoke to your father."

"Christ. I need to call my parents and let them know we're safe. They must be frantic."

"Can she use your phone?" John asked.

Ben passed it over and she had a brief, tearful chat with her mother. Emily told her that Arabel, Sam, and Bess were all in good health and that arrangements were being made to fly them to Edinburgh. She'd be up when she could but she had work to do and yes, it had everything to do with the problems they were watching on TV.

"I didn't know what I could tell her," Emily said, handing the phone back.

"I'm afraid I have no advice," Ben said. "The prime minister will have to make a statement soon but not before the Cobra meeting."

Ben shook his head at the list of texts accumulated in the last few minutes.

"What?" John asked.

"One of the missing boys from the school in Sevenoaks is the son of the Secretary of State for Defense, Jeremy Slaine. He'll be in attendance at the Cobra meeting."

John let out a weary, "Wonderful."

With the landing pad at Whitehall in sight, Ben's phone rang. "My wife," he muttered. "No, I won't be able to return home," he said to her. "I'm just about to meet with the prime minister. Did you get the girls from school? Good. Keep them inside and lock the doors. I'll be home when I can. Yes, I know. I'm sorry. I'll ring you back in an hour or so." When he finished he said, "In times of crisis, I always seem to be placing job over family. Not my finest moment."

When they entered the crowded Cabinet Office Briefing Room A at Whitehall John saw people wrinkling their noses the way he had sniffed at Hellers. It dawned on him that after a month without a good wash, he and Emily probably smelled as rank as the dead. Ben had briefed them that the entire cabinet was going to be in attendance along with a host of military, police, and civilian advisors. The front of the room displayed video feeds of the main TV channels and CCTV footage from around London. The PM's principal private secretary scanned the conference room and picked up a telephone. "Tell him we're ready," he announced.

When Prime Minister Peter Lester entered he went straight for John and Emily, insisting they remain seated.

"We're so grateful you made it home safely," he said, doing an excellent job of appearing to ignore their aroma and grime. "It's good of you to come here directly from your ordeal. Would you like something to eat or drink?"

They both said "coffee, please" simultaneously which briefly lifted the pall in the room. Everyone chuckled except for Jeremy Slaine, the secretary of state for defense, who looked as if his head might explode from incandescent rage.

The PM took his place at the head of the table and pointed at Ben. "Mr. Wellington, I believe you're in the best position to brief us on what happened this morning at Dartford. And by the way, in George Lawrence's absence I've made you acting DG of MI5." He offered a terse congratulations but Ben swallowed hard at the news and looked shaken.

Ben began with a bald recitation of the facts. The planned MAAC restart had occurred at 10 a.m. and after the collider reached full power, the automatic shutdown mechanism had seemingly kicked in within the planned few nanoseconds. He couldn't be sure of the timing because the control-room personnel had vanished. The missing personnel included a number of VIP observers, namely the UK energy secretary, Karen Smithwick, the US energy secretary, Leroy Bitterman, George Lawrence, head of MI5, Campbell Bates, the director of the FBI, Anthony Trotter, the assistant chief of MI6 and acting head of the MAAC, and some twenty MAAC staff members including Matthew Coppens, the acting head of the

Hercules Project, Henry Quint, the former director of MAAC, David Laurent, a senior scientist, and Stuart Binford, the lab's head of public relations. In addition three MI5 agents guarding the control room were caught up.

The tally on returnees was a happier story but not without tragedy. Of the eight civilians who had disappeared a month earlier from an estate at South Ockendon, Martin Crandall, Tony Krause, and Tracy Wiggins had survived and were receiving medical evaluations. Four members of the same family of builders had all perished. And one woman, Alice Hart, a council electrical inspector incredibly had elected to stay behind in the other world.

Of the Dartford victims, he was pleased to report that all had been rescued. Emily's sister Arabel, her two children, and Delia May, an MI5 analyst, were also in a reasonable state of health receiving medical attention.

Two of the rescuers, Emily and John, were before the committee. Trevor Jones had insisted on accompanying Arabel Loughty and her children to Edinburgh. An MI5 jet was standing by to transport them from Stanstead when they were released from medical care. And lastly, Brian Kilmeade, the medieval weapons expert, who by all accounts had acted with exemplary skill and heroism, had also made the incredible decision to remain behind.

Ben then turned to the current and evolving crisis. He apologized for the lack of details but promised to update the committee in a few hours when more would be known. As far as he had been made aware, an entire class of Year Ten boys had disappeared from their dormitory at the Belmeade School in Sevenoaks and an undetermined number of souls were missing from the town centre in Leatherhead and a housing estate in Upminster. A large number of aliens, or Hellers as they were being called, were rampaging through Leatherhead with smaller numbers at Sevenoaks and Upminster.

"And finally ..." Ben said.

Jeremy Slaine hit the table with his fist and interrupted him. "I can no longer sit in silence," he fumed. "My son, Angus, is one of the boys who's gone missing. Are you aware of that?"

"I am, sir," Ben said. "I'm very sorry."

"Sorry won't cut it, will it? What I cannot understand and what I find utterly incomprehensible is that the majority of this cabinet was kept in the dark about this affair until yesterday." He gave the prime minister a withering look and said, "Peter, that was inexcusable. If we were not in the midst of a crisis I would resign immediately."

"I do apologize, Jeremy," Lester said. "I take full responsibility for the information blackout. We desperately wanted to contain the story as a matter of public safety. We wanted to avoid panic at all costs and were cautiously optimistic we could contain this. We were wrong. I assure you, we will do everything possible to retrieve your son and his classmates."

"I believe it was the height of irresponsibility not to mothball MAAC at the first sign of trouble," Slaine said. "We must now reap what you have sown."

"With twenty-twenty hindsight, I might have come to the same conclusion," the prime minister said. "However, brave people, like Dr. Loughty and Mr. Camp, risked their lives to save innocent parties, and we did not wish to abandon them."

The Home Secretary, Margaret Beechwood, in an obvious attempt to diffuse the awkward row, said, "Mr. Wellington, you were just about to conclude your remarks, I believe."

"Yes, Madam Secretary," Ben said. "I was saying that there was one more item to report, in some respects the most extraordinary in a sea of extraordinary events. There was one more individual who arrived here with our people at Dartford. He is someone known to all of us, a former monarch of England. We have in our custody King Henry the Eighth."

The room erupted with the clamor of a dozen voices and the prime minister had to raise his hands and ask for quiet.

"I've been aware of this for only an hour or so," the prime minister said. "Suffice it to say it adds a rather bizarre and urgent element to an already bizarre and urgent crisis."

"Has the queen been notified?" the home secretary asked.

"The palace has been briefed about the general nature of the crisis but no, we haven't as yet disclosed King Henry's arrival. We feel we need to satisfy ourselves that this man is who he claims to be."

John piped up, "He's Henry the Eighth, all right. Believe me."

"I'm not suggesting you're wrong, Mr. Camp," the prime minister said, "but we need some kind of independent verification before we present him as such to the queen."

"Before I went over," John said, "we commissioned a Henry expert, a Cambridge history professor, to help me profile him. This guy, Malcolm Gough, has already signed the Official Secrets Act."

"Margaret," the prime minister said to the home secretary, "could you arrange to get this professor down to London straight away and arrange for a secure location for him to interview our—what shall I call him—our visitor?"

"If I may," Slaine interrupted, "this is a sideshow. People's lives are at risk in London. I understand there have already been casualties. My son's life is at risk. Might we address these issues?"

"Yes, let's move on, as Jeremy suggests," the prime minister said. "Margaret, would you brief us on the ongoing police operations?"

The home secretary passed the baton to the commissioner of the Metropolitan Police who asked his assistant to pull up CCTV footage from Leatherhead.

Sir Evan McPhail rose and went to the front of the room. "The home secretary has asked us to coordinate a response with the home county police departments affected by this invasion. In Leatherhead we have supplemented the resources of the Surrey Police with a number of armed tactical officers and armored vehicles. This CCTV feed is from Church Street in the town centre."

"It looks deserted," the prime minister said.

"What is that?" the deputy prime minister asked. "Is that a body?"

"It's deserted now," the commissioner said. "And yes, I believe that is the body of a member of public. Here is footage from ten o'clock this morning."

Men were streaming down the street, running wildly and chaotically, attacking people with their fists and feet. One of the men appeared to stomp and kneel over a man where the corpse would later be seen.

"Rovers," John said quietly. "Lots of them."

"What are you saying?" the secretary of state for health asked.

"They're the worst of the Hellers," John said. "They're gangs of completely vicious outcasts. They terrorize the rest of the population. They're also cannibals."

"Christ almighty," the home secretary said. "Is that what's happening there?"

"It looks like he's taking some flesh," John said. "Do you know how many of them came through?"

Sir Evan replied that a preliminary and rough estimate from CCTV and eyewitnesses pegged the number in excess of fifty.

"Where are they now?" John asked.

"We're not sure," the commissioner said. "Here is a live image from a police helicopter over the town centre. As you can see the streets are empty. Residents have heeded our TV, radio, and loudspeaker warnings to stay indoors. It is possible that these rovers as you call them have also taken shelter within structures. The area has been cordoned off and we are discussing how best to enter and clear it. I will have an operational plan from my field officers and the Surrey police shortly. We are concerned about the volatile mixture of armed police and civilians. We want to avoid collateral casualties if at all possible."

The home secretary asked, "Mr. Camp, on the footage we've seen, these rovers don't look all that different from members of the public. How can the police distinguish them?"

"From a distance, it won't be easy," John said. "Their clothes are pretty rough but they could be in people's houses right now, doing what they do, stealing food and clothes. Up close, you can smell the difference."

"Did you say smell?" the commissioner asked.

"They smell like meat that's gone off," John said. "They think we smell uncommonly fresh. You could probably get police dogs to alert to the scent. We could get an article of clothes from King Henry to train them up."

"It's a good idea. I'll get that done," Ben said.

"We'll need to know what our rules of engagement are," Sir Evan said. "By this I mean will we have the green light to shoot to kill?"

"My understanding is that they are already dead," the deputy prime minister said.

"Do you hear how ridiculous that sounds?" Slaine said. "They're running around killing innocent civilians. Of course we should shoot to kill."

"Can they be killed?" the prime minister asked. "Mr. Wellington, I believe you had some experience apprehending some of them in Suffolk recently."

"I'll steer clear of semantics," Ben answered. "They can be killed. What's left are corpses that seem like any other corpses. What happens to them beyond that, I wouldn't care to speculate."

"Mr. Camp? Dr. Loughty? What do you think?" the prime minister asked.

Emily asked John to comment. "We don't have any direct experience with that," he said. "I'd guess after they are killed they'd wind up back in Hell but it's only a guess."

Slaine said, "So they can be shot and they can be killed. The army is far better positioned than the police for exercising lethal force. We should be deploying the army into the affected areas with immediate effect."

"With respect," Sir Evan said, "with the Metropolitan Police supplementing the county police departments, we have an adequate armed presence to deal with the situation. The police are trained to work in domestic population centers and mitigate civilian casualties. I'll be the first to request the assistance of the army if we are in danger of losing control of the situation."

Before Slaine could come back at the commissioner, the prime minister said, "I'll take your suggestion under advisement, Jeremy. This committee will be in perpetual session until the crisis has been resolved. Margaret and Sir Evan, I'll require an update on police activities in one hour's time. And by the way, if you capture these Hellers where will you be holding them?"

"We plan to use our holding cells at New Scotland Yard," Sir Evan said. "We're presently clearing them of conventional prisoners."

"Very well," the prime minister said. "Now, I'd like to ask Dr. Loughty a few questions."

Emily nodded and finished her coffee.

"Every time the collider has been reactivated the situation seems to have worsened. Is that also your view?"

"I'm afraid I'd have to agree," she said. "We're seeing increasing instability in areas, nodes if you will, along the architecture of the MAAC tunnels. To date we've had points of inter-dimensional contact at Dartford, South Ockendon, Sevenoaks, Upminster and Leatherhead."

"Did we have a problem this morning at South Ockendon?" the prime minister asked.

The home secretary said she was unaware of any unusual activity there.

"It's impossible to say why some areas are affected and others not," Emily said. "I'd need to spend time analyzing the data. Right now the Dartford lab has been quarantined so I won't have a way of accessing computer systems and obviously I can't speak with my key department heads as they have disappeared. If we can get the assistance of scientific staff at the LHC, the Large Hadron Collider in Geneva, perhaps I can safely tap into the servers and access key data."

The deputy prime minister, a heavyset man whose wide forehead was beaded with sweat despite the air conditioning, raised a finger and asked, "If we permanently shutter the collider and apprehend all these Hellers, will that be the end of it?"

Slaine almost jumped out of his chair but the prime minister insisted that Emily be allowed to answer the question.

"Perhaps, perhaps not," she said. "I'd prefer not to be so wishy-washy but there's no scientific precedent for what's happening. The best case scenario, which would of course be a tragedy for the people who were transported to the other dimension this morning, is that in the absence of further collider activity the problem will be cured and future dimensional transfers will cease. However, I can't guarantee there won't be spontaneous instability at current nodes or new nodes. Until we have a better handle on that it's prudent to quarantine all known nodes."

"Has that been done?" the prime minister asked.

"At Dartford, yes," Ben said.

"Consider it done elsewhere," the home secretary said, picking up a telephone.

Emily said, "My understanding is that in my absence an expert panel of physicists was convened and failed to come up with a solution. I'll need to speak with these advisors urgently. However, we did make contact with the world's greatest expert in strangelets, the exotic particles we believe are at the heart of this phenomenon."

"Who is that?" the prime minister asked.

"Paul Loomis, the former director general of MAAC."

The prime minister nearly shouted. "Excuse me, but Dr. Loomis is dead."

"We found him on the other side."

It occurred to John that Emily had been assiduously avoiding calling a spade a spade. Maybe Hell sounded too unscientific to come out of her mouth. He kept quiet.

"If you recall, he did murder two people," Emily added. "This undoubtedly explains his presence."

"Too fantastic for words," the prime minister muttered.

"In any event," Emily said, "Dr. Loomis insisted he knew how to solve the problem."

"And?" the deputy prime minister said.

"Unfortunately we were separated before he could tell us."

"Well that's no bloody help, is it?" the home secretary said.

"No, it isn't," Emily said.

"We're prepared to go back and find him," John said. "And while we're there we can try to rescue as many people as possible."

"But that would mean firing up the collider again," the prime minister said. "That sounds most unwise."

"My son is over there!" Slaine thundered.

"Jeremy yes, I'm sorry. We're making no decisions today. You'll appreciate we have to take into account the safety of not only your son and his schoolmates but potentially millions of people."

"Dr. Loughty, as soon as you get some rest and a meal, I'd like you to liaise with scientific colleagues in Geneva and elsewhere and keep me informed."

"Of course."

"Now, what instructions should we give the populace?" the prime minister asked. "How much can we and should we say? This is more than an issue of public safety. We have matters of faith and spirituality to consider. We may be speaking about physics and extra dimensions but we also have fundamental religious matters at play. Surely we'll need to consult with the Archbishop of Canterbury, the Vatican, Muslim, and Jewish leaders. Craig," he said to the deputy prime minister, "please lead this discussion until I return. President Jackson is standing by at the White House for a briefing."

"We wouldn't be in the soup if they'd built the bloody thing in America," Slaine said bitterly.

On his way out the prime minister placed his hand on Slaine's shoulder and said, "Yes, Jeremy, you're certainly right about that."

3

Thomas Cromwell, faithful advisor to King Henry VIII in life and in death, could only stare in disbelief.

It wasn't the gaggle of blinking strangers a hundred paces away that seized his attention. It was one small item, a knife lying in the muddy road. An instant earlier, John Camp had been holding that knife to his monarch's throat and now Henry was gone, along with Camp and his entire party of Earthers.

Duck was the first to speak. He cried to his brother, Dirk, "My Delia's gone! And the children. All of them, gone."

"Well, it's best for them," Dirk said. "They were in for it. You don't take the king prisoner and hope to be spared. But that load of new 'uns over there. They're up shyte's creek."

A moment earlier, Solomon Wisdom had been worried that an angry John Camp would demand his head in exchange for his treachery but now he seemed intent on his next challenge. He greedily eyed the strangers and muttered to himself that in the presence of Cromwell there was no way to monetize the rich bounty of all these new arrivals.

"Seize them!" Cromwell ordered, and the soldiers slopped double-time down the muddy road, brandishing swords and pistols.

The gaggle of bewildered MAAC employees and their VIP guests were too scared to do anything but stand fast. There were twenty-five of them. The men had fared better than the eight women as to clothing. Although they were missing plastic buttons and metal zips they could keep their modesty intact by holding onto jeans or suit trousers with both hands. The women with skirts had to choose whether to hold them up or clutch their blouses until they figured out how to do both with one hand on each garment. Some of them looked for missing eyeglasses and one young man said something about a painful hole in one of his teeth.

With the soldiers fast approaching, Stuart Binford, the head of public relations for the laboratory managed to say, "Are we where I think we are?"

Leroy Bitterman, the US energy secretary, looked down at his ample belly spilling from his open shirt and suit vest and said, "I'm afraid so."

Karen Smithwick, the UK secretary of state for energy, reached for her absent necklace before realizing her bra was open. She grabbed at her silk blouse and began to cry. Bitterman used his free hand to touch her on the shoulder.

The captain of the guard, seeing that there would be no fight from this lot, ordered his men to surround them.

"Who is your leader?" he shouted.

The senior members exchanged glances. George Lawrence, the head of MI5 and Campbell Bates, the American FBI director, both hoary men, were about to claim the mantle when Anthony Trotter, the assistant chief of MI6 and acting head of the MAAC, declared that he was. As he did so he felt in vain for the pistol he always carried in a shoulder holster.

A leering young soldier got too close to Brenda, one of the female technicians prompting her to cry out in alarm. David Laurent, a French senior scientist, protectively stepped in and the soldier cocked his pistol.

Trotter addressed the captain pugnaciously, "Don't you dare touch any of my people. Do you understand? Are you the man in charge here?"

Cromwell was making his way through the mud. He called out, "I am. What is your name, sir?"

"Anthony Trotter. Secret Intelligence Service."

"Are all of you among the living?" Cromwell asked.

"Well I hope we are," Trotter said.

Cromwell drew up close enough for the two men to sniff each other's respective aromas. "No, you do not appear to be dead," he said. "What manner of enterprise is the Secret Intelligence Service?" he asked.

"I work for the crown," Trotter said. "I am responsible for collecting intelligence on her majesty's enemies."

"You are a spy?"

"You might call me that."

"Are all of you spies?"

"Only these two," Trotter said, pointing at Bates and Lawrence. "The rest are scientists." He looked down his nose at Smithwick and added, "Well, most of them."

"Are you compatriots of John Camp and Emily Loughty?" Cromwell asked.

"We are. And who are you?" Trotter asked.

Cromwell raised his voice. "I have not finished my questions. Where is the king? What have you done with him?"

Trotter thrust out his chin but it was difficult to act the hard man with both hands engaged in holding up trousers. "We haven't done anything with your king but if he's missing then I expect he's been caught up in all of this. He's probably where we've just come from."

"This would be King Henry the Eighth I presume," Bitterman said.

"And you are?" Cromwell asked.

"One of the scientists, I suppose," Bitterman said, "an old one."

"You have an odd accent, like that of John Camp."

"I'm an American too. Was Camp here?"

"He was but he is no longer."

"And Emily Loughty?"

"She, as well. How do you know of King Henry?"

"When Camp returned a month ago he gave a full report," Bitterman said.

"Tell me, scientist," Cromwell said, "can you return our monarch to us?"

"I'll be completely honest with you," Bitterman said. "I don't know. Most of the experts who would be working on the problem are standing in front of you. I expect our governments will try to work out a way to get us back and return your king. Right now, we're all pretty scared. I'm not ashamed to tell you that. We're at your mercy."

Cromwell nodded and said more gently, "Thomas Cromwell."

"Sorry?" Trotter said.

"I am Thomas Cromwell," counselor to the king.

"How extraordinary," Lawrence said. "When I was at university I fancied myself a bit of a Tudor scholar. I almost feel I know you."

Cromwell permitted himself a thin smile. "What will they do with the king?"

Lawrence said, "I'm quite sure he'll be treated with the utmost respect and care, although I'm sure he'll be as shocked and confused as we are."

Cromwell took his captain aside and the two men discussed how they were going to transport all these people. The soldier dispatched some of his men to commandeer wagons and horses from Dartford and surrounding villages. In the meantime Cromwell bellowed at the curious villagers to bring out benches or chairs for the women and older men and while they were at it, wine and beer.

Duck and Dirk, ran inside their cottage and carried out all their chairs and Dirk reluctantly lugged out his barrel of ale he had brewed for John Camp.

"They'll find it anyway," he groused to Duck. "Don't want to lose my 'ead."

"I'll help you make another cask," Duck said. "Anyways, I feel bad for 'em. Especially the molls. It's a frightening thing to get flung into a new world, believe you me."

Henry Quint had lost a loafer in the mud and he dug it out with his hand. He came over to Trotter who was in whispered conversation with Bitterman, Lawrence, Smithwick, and Bates.

"Can I help you with something?" Trotter said testily.

"Whatever you're planning, I thought I could be of assistance," Quint replied.

"You've done enough," Trotter said, spitting venom. "You're the reason we're in the muck. And by the way, you only have yourself to blame for being here today. I wanted you banished from the lab but Dr. Bitterman insisted we keep you on."

Bitterman fingered his beard and said, "In science, you never know where the next good idea is going to come from. Henry was wrong to exceed the collider's energy parameters but he's an able physicist. He made a mistake."

"It was more than a mistake. It was a goddamn calamity," Bates said.

"I've done my mea culpas," Quint said. "If you want me to go away, just say so."

"Right, sod off," Trotter said. "The grown-ups are talking."

"For Christ's sake, Anthony," Lawrence said. "We don't need any childish tiffs. We're all in this together. Stay, Dr. Quint. We were just talking about our options."

"I think our options are fairly limited," Bitterman said. "We're not fighters. We can't resist. These are armed men."

"We need to remain here," Quint said. "When they power up the MAAC again, this is where the portal will be."

Bates, a tall patrician-like American in his sixties with fine snowy hair and sunken cheeks, was about to say something when an insect buzzed his head. He swatted at it with both hands and his trousers promptly slid down his bony frame, taking his unelastized boxer shorts with them. Some of the soldiers pointed and laughed at his exposed genitals and Karen Smithwick looked away. Bates swore at the indignity and pulled himself together. "How are they going to do that?" he said. "The entire group of operating technicians is here."

"They'll bring in people from Geneva, from the Large Hadron Collider," Quint said. "We were going to merge operations anyway. They know how MAAC works."

"They'd be fools to do it," Trotter said. "My recommendation was to shut the bastard down. They didn't listen and now we're here. They'll listen now."

"You don't imagine they're going to abandon us, do you?" Lawrence asked. Before taking the position as director of MI5 he had been the head of London's Metropolitan Police Service and he still had the clipped speech of a copper giving a report.

"They won't know what to do," Smithwick said. "The prime minister will be cautious. He'll convene a Cobra meeting. He'll weigh all the options."

"If you were there, what would you be advising him?" Bitterman asked.

"I really don't know," she replied stiffly.

"I'd say it depends on factors we're unaware of," Quint said. "Every time the collider's been reactivated, the problem's gotten worse with more point-of-contact nodes popping up. If there are more of them today then maybe Trotter's right. Maybe they'll shut it down for good and we'll be trapped here forever. But if the nodes are stable then they'll try to get us back. At least I hope so. But we'll have no idea of when they'll do it. So we need to stay right here for as long as we can. If that's not possible, we need to escape from wherever we're held and make our way back here."

Smithwick's eyes had gotten moist when she heard the word, forever. "Forever," she repeated numbly, as if she hadn't listened to anything else Quint had said. "I'd kill myself if I thought we were permanently trapped. Look at this place. It's filthy and disgusting. Look at these people, if you can call them people. They're all dead for God's sake."

"I'll not listen to talk about suicide or giving up," Bitterman said. "We'll be fine. It might not be easy but we'll be fine. There's a lot of brainpower among us, especially from our young colleagues. They'll be looking to us for strength and we've got to come through for them."

"I really need to find a way to keep my pants up," Bates said.

The MAAC scientists were huddled together, watching the VIPs confer. Brenda Mitchell, a spectroscopy technician in David Laurent's group sat on one of Dirk and Duck's chairs in the middle of the road and held her head in her hands. Matthew Coppens, the acting head of the Hercules Project who had stepped into Emily's shoes in her absence knelt beside her.

"You all right?" he said.

"No I'm not. I'm not all right. I'm bloody awful."

"I know."

"Do you?" she said, looking up with a glare. "Or rather, did you? Did you know that what we were doing was dangerous? Did you know we were at risk of getting sucked through the portal?"

"I don't think we ever discussed it," he admitted. "I mean we relocated the control room. We just assumed it was far enough away from the nodal activity."

"Assumed. And here we are," she said icily. "And my children have lost their mother, my husband has lost his wife, and I have lost everything. You assumed. Jesus, Matthew."

"We're all in the same boat," he said. "I've got a family too, you know. We'll make it back. You've got to believe that. It looks like Emily made it home. She'll know what to do. We rescued her and she'll rescue us. We'll be okay."

Brenda pointed at a couple of soldiers who were staring at her like starving dogs. "You're not a woman. Maybe you'll be okay, Matthew, but I won't."

Trotter separated himself from the other Earthers and under the watchful eyes of two soldiers found a less muddy patch of road to pace a circle. He had always been a quintessentially self-reliant man. His journey up the ladder of MI6 had been unconventional. The senior ranks of the Service were populated by well-connected public school types with a heavy helping of Oxbridge graduates. He had no such pedigree. His childhood in a council house and his weak second in economics from a middling university were hardly the tickets for a glittering career in the clubby world of MI6. But he was smart, pugnacious, had a facility for languages, and had distinguished himself in a series of postings in the Middle East, including a stint as station chief in Istanbul where he had set up a legendary network of assets in Turkey and Syria. Radical Islam came along just in time to propel his career forward. He was tapped to pull the organization out of its post cold-war doldrums and refocus it on non-state threats. By dint of his outsider's chip-on-shoulder zeal, he rode roughshod over anyone standing in his way and rose to become acting chief of the service. He did it alone, his way. A confirmed bachelor, he didn't even want or need the baggage of a spouse to accompany him on his journey through life.

Now he found himself in a stinking village in a hideous world in desperate straits. He suspected they were well and truly buggered. There would be no rescue. He saw a version of the future play out with icy clarity. The others were weak and they would perish at the hands of brutish men or by their own. He was strong and he was clever. He would survive. But he would have to act quickly.

A soldier drove an empty dray with a tandem of horses down the muddy road. Cromwell inspected it and approached Trotter to tell him that it would hold half of them. Another wagon would be along soon enough.

"Where are you taking us?" Trotter asked.

"Whitehall Palace in London."

"You keep the same place names, I see," Trotter said.

"It is a way for us to remember our happier past," Cromwell said. "Do not expect it to look like the original palace. We suffer from a dearth of craftsmen and artisans. It is a pale imitation."

"May I speak freely?" Trotter said, leading Cromwell away from the others.

"You may."

"We were told by Camp and Loughty that you have a need for expertise in science and technology."

"True enough. Every realm covets new arrivals who possess useful skills. We live in fear of subjugation by foreign powers with superior weaponry."

"Those people over there are some of the finest scientists in the world."

"Are they?"

"Yes they are. Camp brought books with him on his last crossing. Did he give them to you?"

"To the king, yes. Henry greatly valued them."

"I think I can be useful to you, Mr. Cromwell."

"Can you?"

"As you can see, I'm in charge of these people. I can get them to help you. I can get them to apply the knowledge in those books and help you build powerful new weapons."

"I rather think we are capable of compelling their assistance," Cromwell said dismissively.

"Persuasion will work better than threats with this lot."

"And you can persuade them?"

"I'm sure I can. I can also discourage any attempts to defy you or to escape from your hospitality. I know the potential troublemakers."

"And why would you do this?"

"I want special treatment. I want the best quarters, the best food. If we have the chance to go home, I'll gladly go. But if we have to stay here permanently, which I see as a possibility, then I want rank, position, and authority."

"You wish to feather your nest."

Trotter smiled. "Exactly."

"I will consider your offer."

"Is this your decision to make?" Trotter asked. "Who's going to be the decision maker in your king's absence?"

"You may consider me to be his majesty's regent until he returns."

"I don't know how things work around here," Trotter said, lowering his voice to little more than a whisper, "but if Henry doesn't come back, then perhaps you could do better than regent."

Cromwell looked at the compact, mustachioed man holding onto his trousers and nodded curtly. "Please use your considerable influence to get half the people to climb upon that wagon, if you please."

When Trotter returned to the knot of VIPs Bitterman asked him, "What were you saying to Cromwell?"

"I warned him that I am holding him personally accountable for all our treatment."

Quint snorted, "Warning? It looked like you were begging."

Trotter ignored him and told the others, "They want us on the wagon. We're going to London."

4

Malcolm Gough nervously crossed and uncrossed his long legs. He had been kept waiting for over an hour, the only one inside a patient lounge on a cleared-out floor of the Royal London Hospital. A month earlier he had been summoned by MI5 from his academic perch at Cambridge to come to this very hospital where he'd had the oddest meeting of his life. John Camp, recovering from surgery, had asked him questions about Henry the Eighth as if he were a living, breathing person. Gough had left that meeting, baffled and bemused, but having signed the Official Secrets Act he had not been able to share the experience with anyone, even his wife.

Earlier in the day he had received a call from Ben Wellington, asking him to come down to London that evening for an urgent consultation.

"It's not really convenient," Gough had said.

"I'm afraid it's not optional," Ben had answered. "It's a matter of national security."

"I'm a history professor," Gough had reminded him.

"Yes you are."

"Does this have anything to do with the problems in London we're seeing on the news?"

"It does."

"You don't intend to further pick my brain on Tudor monarchs?" he had asked half in jest.

"We do. A car and driver will be outside your house at five. Please pack an overnight bag and bring a good suit. You'll be meeting the queen."

The lounge door swung open and Gough saw John Camp, clean-shaven for the first time in a month, striding in wearing a smart blue blazer, gray trousers and a striped red tie. Though his clothes were fresh his face was weary.

"I thought I might be seeing you again," Gough said.

"How've you been, Professor?"

"I was perplexed the day I left you and I'm still perplexed."

"We're going to try to help you with that."

"Are you?"

"I assume you've been watching the news."

"Who hasn't? It's alarming. The complete and utter babble from the authorities hasn't helped."

John sat across from him. "With fairness, it's not an easy situation to explain."

"This chap, Giles Farmer, has been on the tele making wild claims about the MAAC collider, extra dimensions, portals, and what not."

John leaned forward and said, "He's pretty much got it right."

A visibly shocked Gough exclaimed, "What?"

"I mean he's got no idea what that dimension is. Are you ready for the truth? Once I tell you your life's never going to be the same."

"I presume you're going to tell me regardless."

John nodded and smiled. "Are you a religious man, Professor?"

"I'm not a church-goer but I believe in a higher power, yes."

"How do Heaven and Hell fit into your belief system?"

"Well, I think they're useful abstractions to motivate behaviors."

"I don't know about Heaven but I'm here to tell you that Hell exists. It's not an abstraction."

Several minutes into his monologue, John paused to ask the blanched professor if he was all right. Gough asked whether he might have some water and John left him and returned with a bottle from the nursing station fridge.

"I suppose you're next going to tell me that you met Henry over there,"

Gough rasped.

"I did. And not just him."

John rattled off more. Cromwell. Queen Matilda. Robespierre. Barbarossa. King Pedro. Himmler. Stalin. With each name, Gough's mouth opened a bit more until it was agape.

"This is all quite unbelievable," Gough said, shaking his head like it was on a swivel. "Whether or not I'm prepared to believe you, all of it begs this question: why am I here?"

"Because you know as much about Henry as any living person."

"And why is that a useful skill for a government which seems to have so many pressing interests at hand?"

"Because he's in a room down the hall."

"Who is?"

A unit of the Royal Marines 3 Commando Brigade occupied a defensive position on the Leatherhead Town Bridge over the River Mole. They had been deployed only an hour earlier, taking over from a beleaguered Surrey police unit. Jack Venables, a 2nd Lieutenant, peered through his night-vision binoculars toward the town centre and put them down to rub his tired eyes. He thought that one of his corporals might be dozing but the upbraided soldier demonstrated that his head was lowered to study a map with a penlight.

"Sorry," Venables said. "Carry on."

The squad's sergeant, Callum Ferguson, was still glued to his binoculars and alerted Venables to signs of activity.

"Four individuals coming toward us. Three hundred meters. They're running."

Venables got the eight-man squad to the ready and reminded them of their rules of engagement.

"And tell us again how we're supposed to tell a citizen from an alien?" one of the privates asked. As an afterthought he added, "Sir."

Venables seemed irritated by the insubordinate tone but he patiently acknowledged the difficulty and bizarre nature of their assignment. "Look here," he said. "All of us, me included, are rather far down on the feeding chain on this thing. I haven't been told much more than what's on the tele. But the distinct impression the Lieutenant-Colonel gave at the briefing this afternoon was that the town's been overrun by unidentified aliens who can be identified by their distinctively unpleasant odor."

"So we're supposed to sniff their armpits before we shoot them?" the private said.

"Shut the fuck up, Saunders," the sergeant said.

Another private lifted his head from his riflescope. "Didn't they tell you where they were from, Lieutenant?"

"I'd say the Lieutenant-Colonel was evasive but I got the distinct impression that we weren't talking about little green men from Alpha Centauri or refugees from the Middle East. Sergeant, their position?"

"Two hundred meters. Still coming our way."

"My girlfriend texted me," the corporal said. "She said they were saying they're from another dimension."

"Your girlfriend must be from another dimension to be stepping out with you," Saunders said.

"Button it up right now," Venables ordered. "At fifty meters, hit them with floodlights."

When the klieg lights were trained on the four approaching figures they stopped and shielded their eyes.

"Royal Marines," the sergeant shouted over the sounds of the coursing river. "Approach slowly with your hands on your heads."

The two men and two women complied and walked toward them down Bridge Street. Just before they got to the bridge, the soldiers saw them look to their left, apparently alerted to something coming from Minchin Close, an unlit dead-end street. Suddenly one of the women screamed as a dark figure sprang out and grabbed her and began dragging her away from the light.

"What the fuck!" Saunders yelled.

The three other civilians dropped their arms and began running toward the bridge.

"What are our orders?" the sergeant shouted to Venables.

"Hold your positions!" the lieutenant said. "We are not authorized to enter the town centre."

"But a woman's been snatched!" Saunders said.

"I may have a shot," the corporal said, tracking a glowing, green figure through his riflescope.

"You do not have permission to engage," Venables said. "We have our orders."

Two men and a woman were on the bridge now and the sergeant ordered them to sit on their hands in the middle of the road. They were all young adults and they appeared to be in a state of shock and distress. The woman was crying uncontrollably. The men kept looking behind them to see if they were really safe.

"Check them for weapons," the sergeant ordered his Marines.

"They got Sarah," one of the men moaned. "And you lot did nothing."

Saunders did the frisking and when he was done he loudly sniffed at the bearded young man.

"What are you, a fucking dog?" the man said to him angrily. "People are dying out there, begging for the police and the army. And you're safe and sound on this bridge sniffing at me like a retard."

Saunders ignored him. "The smell's all right," he reported.

Venables came forward and had the other two searched. "It's all right, you can stand up." He looked them in the eyes and said, "We have orders to keep clear until the authorities know what they're dealing with. As I understand it, thousands of civilians responded to our messages throughout the day and made their way out. You'll be transported to an evacuation center in Dorking."

The other woman spit at him and swore.

He wiped the spittle from his cheek with his hand. "I'm sorry your friend was assaulted. There was nothing we could do. Tell me what's been going on inside the town centre."

The second young man spoke evenly. "We hid most of the day in

Sarah's flat not far from the shopping centre. People were running past but we were too scared to move. We saw some horrible things from the windows. Horrible. We heard the loudspeakers but we didn't dare budge. A half an hour ago we heard them crashing through the back door and we ran out the front."

"What did you see?" the lieutenant asked.

"People being butchered," the man said. "They're animals, nothing but wild animals. We saw people being eaten alive."

John led Gough down the hall toward a knot of MI5 officers guarding a doorway. They stood aside when John approached.

"Ready?" John asked the professor.

"I don't know I am," Gough said.

John knocked on the door and opened it. It was an ordinary hospital room, identical to the one he had himself occupied a month earlier. A large man with stubble for a beard and long gray hair laced with ginger lay on top of the made-up bed in a terry cloth robe, his scarred and purplish legs in full view. He was intently reading a book, Gough's book, *The Life and Times of Henry VIII,* but he put it down and exclaimed, "There you are! John Camp, my captor. I am most displeased."

"Aren't they treating you well, Your Majesty?"

"I have been served no wine, I have been served no ale. They have given me water and something vile which tickles my nose and tastes revolting."

John looked at the soda can and smiled.

"And what is this?" Henry pointed at uneaten food on a nearby tray.

"It's called a sandwich."

"It too is revolting. And where are my clothes?"

"They're having them cleaned, I think."

"Damn you man. They were not soiled."

"I think they wanted them fumigated before you met the queen."

"What is fumigated?"

"Um, kill any bugs or lice."

"How dare you. I have no lice!" the king shouted.

"Just a precaution. I'd like you to meet the man who wrote the book you're reading. Your Majesty, this is the scholar, Malcolm Gough. He probably knows more about you than any living man."

Gough looked wobbly on his stilt-like legs and John thought he might go down in a faint. "I-I hardly know what to say," Gough stammered. "Can this be true? Can this be happening?"

"Do you wish to pinch my flesh, sir?" Henry said. "Will that satisfy you?"

"No, no. It's just that …" His knees buckled. John caught him and held him upright while he reached for a chair.

"Do you mind if the professor sits?" John asked the king.

"He had better. If you had done me the courtesy of a flagon of ale I would offer him some."

"Have some water," John said, pouring Gough a glass.

He drank it thirstily and signaled with his hand that he would be all right. "I apologize," he croaked. "I wish I could tell you how powerful this moment is for me. I wish I could tell you how many times I imagined what it would be like possessing a time machine and going back in history to your court. To meet you. To talk to you."

"You are not alone in your bafflement and amazement, scholar," Henry said. "After so many centuries I have grown accustomed to the strange environs of Hell but the collision of our two worlds has left me reeling, this I freely admit."

"Mr. Camp has requested that I ask you some questions," Gough said.

"Questions of what nature?" Henry asked.

"Questions about your life and time."

"Toward what end?"

Gough looked to John to answer.

"Here's the way it is," John said. "I know that you are who you say you are. I was in Brittania with you. I don't need any convincing. But in about two hours we're scheduled to take you to see the queen and the people in charge of the government want to be certain you are, in fact, Henry the

Eighth, not some impostor. After all, you don't look much like the picture of you on the cover of the professor's book."

"Holbein," Henry said. "It was a dread experience to sit for him. His flatulence would foul my chamber imbuing it with an aroma akin to a rotting room. In any event, it is not an easy thing to maintain corpulence in Hell. My present physique is that of my younger self."

Gough cleared his throat and asked his first question. "You mentioned Hans Holbein. He was commissioned by Anne Boleyn to design a drinking cup for her. Could you please tell me what he engraved on that cup?"

Henry swung his legs over the bed, briefly exposing his prodigious private parts before fixing his robe. He scrunched his forehead in thought and said that it was difficult to recall such a detail after five hundred years.

"I can move on," Gough volunteered.

"It was a falcon," Henry suddenly declared. "A falcon perched on a bed of roses."

Gough turned to John and nodded.

"You had some significant involvement with my university, Cambridge," Gough said. "Can you tell me what that was?"

"Yes, I read in your book that you are a scholar at Trinity. Do you wish me to tell you how Trinity came to be?"

Gough nodded again.

"The colleges of Cambridge were awash in riches and land and I might add, papist sentiments. As I was seizing church properties the university feared it would be next and the masters prevailed upon my queen, Catherine Parr, to persuade me not to close them. For the sake of economy I merged two colleges, Michaelhouse and King's Hall, and a number of hostels to form Trinity. I am pleased it still stands."

"Right again," Gough told John.

"In 1513 you led the English army in an invasion of France and there you seized some French towns. Could you name them?"

"Now that I can recall as if yesterday. Thérouanne and Tournai. They were small victories but they were glorious to the young man I was."

"Thank you," Gough said. "I wonder if I might pose one of the questions I had always dreamed of asking? In your petition to annul your marriage to Queen Catherine of Aragon, much was made of her prior marriage to your brother. The issue of her marital status was paramount to your petition to Rome. I mean no offense but could I inquire whether Catherine was indeed a virgin when you married her?"

Henry glowered at the professor. John thought Gough was going to bolt from the room in terror—until the king began to laugh uproariously and slap his bare thigh.

A Royal Airforce Merlin Mk4 helicopter equipped with high-resolution night-vision cameras approached Leatherhead from the south, crewed by three flight officers and two telecommunications techs.

The pilot hailed Lieutenant Venables who had heard the approaching craft just before the pilot came through on his headset.

They exchanged perfunctory greetings and the pilot said, "We'll be sending you real-time images. Any particular sectors of interest?"

"The Swan Shopping Centre, for one, and Bridge Street, on the approach to our position on the Town Bridge."

"Affirmative. Stand by."

The helicopter swooped low over the Marines' checkpoint and Venables opened his laptop and logged into the RAF comms portal. The screen came alive with stabilized images of the flyover.

The chopper flew in a spiraling pattern over the town at an altitude of three hundred feet closing in on the shopping centre. And Venables could see the occasional person emerging from a building and frantically waving for help. Then, on North Street, he saw a group of at least thirty congregating men looking up at the sky but doing no waving or gesturing of any sort.

He did a screen grab and called his sergeant over. "I think these are the scum who've been running amok in there," Venables said.

"I wish they'd let us in to deal with them," the sergeant replied.

"Me too but we're on a short leash. If command knows who they are or what they want they're keeping it to themselves."

"If my wife and kids were in there they wouldn't be able to keep me out," the sergeant said.

The helicopter's spiral tightened until it was almost over the shopping complex and large multi-story car park.

Venables studied the camera feed and looked up in alarm when the image began to rotate wildly. In the distance he and the rest of his squad saw the helicopter rapidly corkscrewing toward the ground until it exploded in a yellow fireball onto the roof deck of the car park.

The Merlin pilot blinked in disbelief.

He was in blackness. The helicopter was gone. His helmet and flight suit was gone. He heard his crewmen screaming and then he heard his own screams as he plummeted three hundred feet to his death.

Five broken bodies lay in an alleyway running behind a row of low cottages in another Leatherhead, this one a small town in the Brittania of Hell.

Prime Minister Lester finished his call with President Jackson and turned up the volume on the TV screen in the backrest of his ministerial Jaguar. A BBC reporter was on the floor of the New York Stock Exchange where circuit-breakers had halted trading following historic market crashes in New York and Europe. He turned to his principal private secretary beside him and said, "We're going to have to issue some kind of statement tonight to calm things down or today's market plunge is going to look like a picnic."

"Shall I get the chancellor for you?"

"Not until we know what we're going to say. We'll have to go farther than we've gone so far today but how far? That's the question."

"Up to but not including the word Hell, I should think," the secretary said.

"I think that's right." He turned down the volume of the TV and the sirens of the motorcycle outriders penetrated the padded interior of the car.

The secretary's phone rang. "Call from Paris. President Rembert."

"How long till Windsor?" the PM asked his driver.

"Ten minutes, sir."

"All right, give me the president."

The prime minister's personal mobile rang. He looked at the caller ID and answered. After a short conversation he ended the call and said, "We've just lost an RAF helicopter over Leatherhead."

The prime minister was escorted to the Garter Throne Room of Windsor Palace. The queen was seated in one of the padded chairs drawn up to face her ornate red throne chair which sat alone on its elevated, carpeted platform. She was fidgeting with her gloves and said, "Ah, there you are," when Lester entered.

"Your Majesty, how are you?" the prime minister said, extending his hand.

"I am most distressed by the day's events, as you can imagine. Also, I felt it was a cowardly thing to flee London for Windsor."

"Until we have a better handle on the situation, it really is for the best," Lester said, taking a seat beside her. "Windsor is probably fine for now. If the situation deteriorates I will be recommending you relocate to Balmoral."

"We'll cross that bridge later, Peter. For the moment I'm quite focused on the gentleman who will arrive shortly. Are you certain, absolutely certain he is who he claims to be?"

"As fantastic as it is, it seems he is. We have several lines of evidence. The first is a thorough interview conducted by Professor Malcolm Gough of Cambridge, a leading Tudor scholar. He reports that no one other than Henry or a major Henry scholar would know the answers to the questions he posed. Combine that with the testimony of Mr. Camp and Dr. Loughty and we have a powerful circumstantial case. The second is more scientific.

Doctors did a DNA swab test this afternoon on the gentleman. Although there are no known living descendants of Henry the Eighth, there is a possible bloodline through Henry's sister, Margaret Tudor, to several living individuals. The DNA analysis suggests a likelihood of a match."

"You might test me, as well," the queen said. "I believe he is my great grand uncle, twelve times removed."

"We can certainly do that, yes," the prime minister said.

"Well, I hardly know what to think," she said. "I've had a word with the Archbishop of Canterbury about the spiritual side of all of this. He is rather less incredulous than most about the existence of a domain called Hell, but he is nonetheless flabbergasted."

"I'm sure he is."

"Before he arrives, what is the security situation?" the queen asked.

"We've sealed off Leatherhead, Sevenoaks, Dartford, and Upminster, as well as two of the sites previously compromised, Iver and South Ockendon. We believe there have been significant casualties, particularly in Leatherhead, but we had not yet authorized police or military entry into the affected zones. However, an RAF Merlin helicopter has just crash-landed in Leatherhead and the MOD is mulling the advisability of deploying a search and rescue operation."

"Good gracious," the queen said, sighing heavily. "I understand that Jeremy Slaine's son is one of the affected boys from that school."

"Unfortunately, yes."

There was a knock on the heavy doors of the throne room and a royal official announced their guests were on the palace grounds. Just then, a large contingent of crown protection officers filed in and lined the walls.

"Is this necessary?" the queen asked.

"It is a prudent precaution in my estimation," the prime minister said.

A videographer entered via a side door, splayed his tripod and affixed the camera.

The queen said, "I was advised we would be remiss not to have this event captured for posterity."

"I agree," Lester said, "although I am not so sure it will ever be seen by the public."

"That is a matter for another day," she said. She rose, took her seat on her monogrammed chair, and donned her white gloves.

Everyone waited expectantly. When the doors opened yet again three men slowly walked inside.

No one paid any attention to Malcolm Gough or John Camp. All eyes were on the equally tall man in the middle.

Henry was dressed in the clothes he had been wearing in Dartford village when John took him hostage. During his spell at the Royal Hospital, his garments had been photographed, inspected, and expertly cleaned by a company in London that specialized in laundering film costumes.

His outfit was one of his hunting ones, not his ornamental finest but still eye-catching. His below-the-knee tunic, worn over a scoop-necked white blouse, was finely brocaded purple and gold. It was parted below the waist revealing a provocatively large yellow codpiece, which caught the queen's gaze for a second. He had a pair of supple, long riding boots, tight crimson breeches, a loose, fur-trimmed brown mantle that flowed over his tunic, and a flat broad-brimmed hat trimmed with feathers. He had been given a choice of half a dozen colognes and had chosen one he had applied so liberally that his foul aroma was obliterated by a jasmine and rosemary spiciness.

He permitted himself a few glances at the magnificence of the paneled Garter Throne Room, its high, ornate and gilded ceiling, the paintings of the queen and predecessor monarchs from George I onwards, but he deferentially paid most of his attention to the queen.

He seemed to sense just how close to approach before he should stop. John and the professor took a few steps back to allow his precedence.

He doffed his hat and without a bow said, "Your Majesty."

John noticed that the queen's gloved hands were trembling on her lap.

She gained her composure and said, "Your Royal Highness, I scarcely know what to say, so I shall simply welcome you back to Windsor Palace."

"Though it is nightfall, your marvelous illuminations revealed to my person that the palace is much changed from my time," Henry said. "It is splendid, indeed."

"Will you sit?" the queen said.

"I will." He pointed with his hat toward the video camera. "Is this a weapon of some sort?"

John and the professor were sitting beside him. John told him it was a machine to record his words and his image. Henry shrugged indifferently.

The queen said, "I would like to present the prime minister of Great Britain, Peter Lester."

Lester made a short welcoming speech but Henry only had eyes for the queen.

When Lester sat, Henry said, "This fine scholar, Master Gough, has been my tutor for the past hours. He has educated me on the state of her majesty's government. In truth, I know well of your reign and of many of the monarchs portrayed on your wall. I diligently study the chronicles of new arrivals to my domain and I have done so for some five hundred years."

"I admit to utter amazement at the existence of your domain, my good King," the queen said. "It is hard to grasp the theological implications, the scientific implications. And to be able to sit here and converse with one of the greatest personages in British history, well, I am overwhelmed."

"You can thank this man, John Camp, for my presence," Henry said, "for it was he who took me prisoner and spirited me to your side. I can thank him too because today, in your royal hospital, I looked from my window and saw something I never thought to see again: the sun."

The queen looked squarely at John. "I thank you for your service and your bravery," she said. "More will be made of this at the appropriate time."

John deeply nodded.

She turned her attention back to Henry and said, "I must admit that I was shocked to learn that upon your death you were remanded to your present realm."

"Hell," Henry said. "You may call it what it is. And I can assure you that no one was more surprised than I, for I never once killed or maimed a man by my own hand, and everything I did, I did for the greatness and glory of England."

"I know you have had a confusing and tiring day," the queen said, "but I have so many questions I would like to ask you about—yes, I'll say it—about Hell."

Henry beamed and relaxed in his chair, casually opening his legs and exposing his codpiece. "Nothing would give me more pleasure," he said. "I have learned that you are not of my direct bloodline, but you are a queen of England, and I feel a kinship and love which warms my ancient heart and lifts my accursed soul. Ask of me what you wish and I will sing my replies like a happy bird released from its cage and returned to its verdant forest."

5

Heath was too tired and drunk to carry on. He dropped to his haunches, leaned against a baked goods rack at the Leatherhead Sainsbury's inside the Swan Shopping Centre, and closed his eyes.

"What's your problem, then?" his mate Monk asked, ripping open a box of cake. Monk was a brutish thick-limbed man who was missing all but two fingers of his right hand. He used them like a claw to extract a wad of chocolate cake and made sure Heath was awake enough to hear how delicious it was.

"What?" Heath asked, blinking.

"This cake. It's fucking amazing."

"My gut's full up," Heath said, closing his eyes again.

Heath's coarse shirt was stained with food and blood, reflecting two of his three main activities of the day—eating and killing. The raping hadn't soiled his clothes. It had been a long day and a strange day, the strangest he'd had since the one in 1899 when he landed in Hell, a moment after getting coshed in the head in a brawl near Tower Bridge.

Though Heath wasn't a large man, he was quick, with lightning reflexes and a pitiless lack of remorse, both qualities which gave him an edge in a fight. When he got a man onto the ground, he finished him off with ruthless efficiency. Since his youth he'd been a hair-trigger brawler who'd usually gotten the better of others but his luck ran out that cold, London night. In Hell, he'd been fortunate, and though he was scarred from head to toe and had lost half his teeth in hundreds of skirmishes, no one had done too much damage.

On his arrival it hadn't taken him long to fall in with a rover gang. Nothing about the conventional, fearful existence of village or town dwellers appealed to him. He was a predator in life and he'd be an uber predator in death. Within a year of roving the dank streets of London he crashed the band's leader and slit his throat. He'd been a leader ever since, the most feared in London. In recent times he'd taken the strategy of subjugating and absorbing other rover bands in and around the city to create a fighting force able to take on fortified towns and even small garrisons of crown soldiers. An eight to ten-membered band of rovers tearing through a settlement was intimidating. A gang of nearer one hundred was terrifying beyond imagination, a horde of human locusts leaving nothing but husks in its wake.

Heath's gang had spent the previous night swarming through the village of Leatherhead. They had been sleeping off an orgy of destruction when they suddenly found themselves in the city centre of a very different Leatherhead. Squinting into the glaring sun, they had stumbled around in disbelief as men, women, and children scattered before them.

Heath had no idea what was happening but one of his men, a thug who'd died of a heroin overdose in 1994, instantly recognized the modernity of the place.

"Know where we are, Heath?" he had called out.

"No fucking idea."

"I swear we're back on Earth. We're back among the living."

"How? Why?" Heath had asked, spinning around to take in the sights and sounds of the twenty-first century.

"No clue, mate, but I see girls. Lots of pretty girls."

Throughout the day, Heath had struggled to satisfy his personal urges for food and sex and his instincts to keep his men together. This land had, he was told, police and soldiers, but armed men had not materialized. Noisy flying machines were soon soaring overhead and voices from the sky were warning people to stay inside and lock their doors and windows and await further instructions. Later in the day, the voices were telling people to make their way out of the city centre if they could safely do so.

In the early hours the rovers had followed their instincts to butcher and cannibalize the victims they ran down, but as the day wore on, they found an unimaginable bounty of food inside houses and shops.

"No need to cannie," Heath had said to Monk, ripping through a ham in an old man's flat. "Tastes better too."

"I like it here," Monk had said, stepping over the body of the old man and finding bottles of lager in his fridge. "Fucking amazing, it is."

By nightfall, Heath had managed to find a good number of his rovers and herd them inside the mall at the Swan Centre. Their reward was discovering the beer, wine, and liquor section in the deserted Sainsbury's. The old heroin addict had taken it upon himself to teach the ancients how to work a screw-top bottle and how to pop a tab on a can of beer, and before long, the few dozen bloodied and stinking men were well toward drunken incoherence. Heath tried to keep his brain functioning but fatigue and brandy took their toll. He was contemplating the blurred image of Monk's chocolate-smeared fingers when he was jolted by a mighty thud and the sound of an explosion overhead.

"What the hell was that?" he said, shaking the cobwebs out and pushing himself to his feet.

"Sounds like cannon fire," Monk said.

"Get some of the lads. Now," Heath said.

In their passage, the men had lost their favored weapons, long curved rover knives, but most had rearmed themselves in the houses and shops in the town centre. Those who hadn't were able to find knives in the Indian restaurant inside the mall and the kitchenware department at Sainsbury's. When a group of the drunken louts assembled one of the men told Heath he'd found a way to the roof and led them up the stairs to the top of the multi-story car park.

The wrecked Merlin helicopter was burning with intensity. The rovers were forced to shield their eyes and keep their distance.

"What is it?" one of them asked Heath.

"I've no idea," he answered before adding, "This is a strange land for which I have little comprehension."

"It's called a helicopter," the addict said. He was almost too drunk to form words. "It's a buggered, flaming, helicopter."

"I like it here," one of the men said, wobbling on boozy legs. "Good drink, beautiful victuals, plenty of molls. Doesn't bother me that flaming machines are falling from the skies. As long as they don't land upon me head."

Heath lost interest in the blazing wreckage and used the vantage point to survey the town below. Encircling the town at key junctions were the flashing red and blue lights of emergency vehicles.

"I don't know why they haven't tried to crash us," Heath told Monk. "No coppers. No soldiers. Doesn't make sense."

"They're probably scared of us," Monk said.

"Maybe, but in time they'll come." He surveyed his gang members and asked, "Who's the least drunk of you lot?"

Amidst sniggers, no one answered. Heath picked three of the least glazed-over and told them to stay on the roof and let him know if they saw any men advancing. He was going back downstairs to have a kip.

Heath had been asleep in one of the supermarket aisles for less than an hour when one of the rovers on the roof came running for him.

"They're coming," the man said.

Heath sat up and massaged his face. "On foot? On horseback?"

"No. Inside machines."

"Motorcars," Heath said to his sixteenth-century gang member. "They're called motorcars. How many?"

"One big 'un what was on the bridge. Heading straight toward us."

Heath was already on his feet, kicking his men awake. There were about fifty of them. Thirty or so were unaccounted for, off somewhere in the town.

"Come with me," Heath shouted. "They're coming to crash us. It's time to fight."

As they made their way out to the street Heath drew two of his new butcher knives from the new belt he'd gotten off his first victim. The kid was pale and pimply and was at the wrong place at the wrong time, rounding a corner shortly after the rovers arrived. He'd looked askance at Heath who, lacking a belt buckle, had been dealing with his loose trousers, turning his head this way and that in utter confusion. The kid hadn't even said anything. It was his look of contempt at Heath's filth and stench that had prompted Heath to bend over, pick up an ornamental stone from someone's front garden, and bash the kid's head in. Before stealing his belt, Heath had stood over him, marveling at this kid's immobility. He'd kicked him a few times to be sure before coming to the conclusion that unlike victims in Hell who were incapable of dying, this one was dead. It had dawned on him at that moment that the incredible had happened: he was back on Earth.

The pedestrian zone beside the shopping centre was deserted. Heath and his men were bunched, waiting for their attackers to arrive. They had fought many soldiers in the past, usually in accidental skirmishes. The king's men didn't like coming out at night to challenge rovers, but these soldiers were different.

There was a buzzing sound overhead. Heath saw the small flying machine with four rotor blades. It swooped low but not low enough for him to swat it with one of his knives.

He looked to his east toward the High Street and told the men to retreat in that direction but the flying machine followed, hovering at no more than twenty feet above the ground.

Inside the armored personnel carrier Sergeant Ferguson alerted Lieutenant Venables to what he was seeing on his laptop. The drone operator back on the bridge was tracking activity in the shopping district and uploading the feed.

"Have a look at this," the sergeant said.

Venables glanced down and as a sign of his interest, snatched the computer away for a better look. Illuminated in the floodlit pedestrian promenade was a group of men fleeing from the drone. They were dressed in shabby, archaic garb and they were brandishing knives.

"Command," Venables said into his headset, "are you seeing this?"

His commanding officer at the MOD in Whitehall replied, "We have it. Stand by while we analyze. How close are you?"

"Two hundred yards."

"Right. Hold your position and stand by."

"What is it, Sarge?" Private Saunders asked.

"An assembly of hostiles, by the look of them," Ferguson said.

"We going to engage?"

"Not for me to say, is it?" the sergeant replied.

Ben Wellington was beside John Camp in the back seat of his Jaguar when his phone rang. The two of them were on the way back to MI5 from their meeting with the queen. King Henry was on his way to an MI5 safe house in the Hampshire countryside with a contingent of security staff, doctors, and nurses, one bewildered royal butler, a few trusted palace housekeepers, and one very willing minder, Professor Gough. Ben listened to the caller and retrieved his tablet computer from his briefcase.

He passed the tablet over to John and said, "This is real-time MOD drone footage from Leatherhead. What do you make of this lot?"

John shook his head. "Rovers."

"Are you certain?"

"I'll peg it at ninety-nine percent. All of them have at least one knife, a lot of them two. They hold them pointed down, like rovers do, best for downward thrusts. And see the way they're running. It's like they're gliding. They're confident runners, especially at night."

Ben thanked him and spoke into his phone. "First off, we believe with a very high level of probability that these are Hellers, not members of the local populace. Second, we believe, also with a very high probability that they are the most dangerous sort of Hellers. These men are predatory killers. Yes, I would absolutely endorse that course of action. Of course. I'll maintain visual contact and remain on the line."

Lieutenant Venables announced, "We've been cleared to engage the enemy. Sergeant, we'll be rolling up on them. We'll dismount with a fifty-yard buffer and on my mark we will open fire. Is that understood?"

"Yes, sir."

Saunders whispered to the private next to him, "'Bout fucking time we kicked some alien arse."

The rovers kept running away from the drone and the Marine armored personnel carrier that had come into view. Heath shouted for his men to stop when the vehicle stopped and soldiers spilled out.

Heath was outside the Victorian redbrick Leatherhead Institute on the High Street. "Are you ready to fight them?" he shouted to his men.

The men raised their knives and gave off blood-curdling cries.

"Let 'em come," Monk yelled. "There's not many of them. We'll strip their flesh from their bones."

Lieutenant Venables raised his hand and gave the order to fire.

The video feed on Ben's tablet had no sound.

John watched the drone's-eye-view of 5.56mm NATO ammo thudding into rover torsos and heads. The rover who seemed to be in charge was directing the others with frantic waves of his arms before taking multiple hits to his chest and crumpling.

Monk fell to his knees beside Heath then rose in anger and charged the Marines. He made it only a few strides before he was cut down.

John passed the tablet back to Ben and said, "You don't know how many times I wanted to rake those bastards with automatic fire."

Venables ordered a cease fire and led his commandos toward the immobile bodies littering the pavement. The first rover they stood over was dead from a headshot. The next one was still alive, just barely, with two bullet holes through the lungs. It was Heath who stared up at the soldiers and mouthed a "fuck you."

"What are our orders?" the sergeant asked Venables.

Venables asked the same question into his headset and the reply came from Whitehall: no medics, no prisoners.

The lieutenant answered his sergeant by dipping the barrel of his rifle and firing a round between Heath's eyes. The rest of the squad didn't require further instructions. They went about their grim business delivering coup de grâces until all the bodies were still.

"Doesn't seem sporting," Ben said, looking away from his tablet.

"They're rovers," John said. "They …"

"I know all about them," Ben said. "I had my own dealings."

"Anyway, they're already dead."

In one instant Heath was staring down the barrel of a rifle, and in the next he was lying on his back in the center of a rank town, the Leatherhead of Hell. The rovers who preceded him were already upright, shifting about in stunned silence.

Monk offered a hand and pulled Heath to his feet.

"Seems we're back where we belong," Monk said. "It were good while it lasted."

"Bloody good," Heath said, checking for injury. "Last I saw of you, your head had a large hole in it."

"Did it now?"

"All the lads back?"

Monk looked around. "Not all. Only the ones with us when the soldiers opened fire."

"They had some rum old guns, didn't they?" Heath said admiringly.

"That they did. Now what?"

Heath shook his head. "I don't know why we were sent back to the land of the living and I don't know why we're back in this shithole. I suppose we'll just have to carry on doing what we do," Heath said. "Let's go back to our camp and take it from there."

"Come on, lads," Monk shouted. "Fun's over. Heath wants us back to the woods."

Fifty rovers began walking toward the forest.

Heath thought his eyes were playing a trick on him. Or maybe it was just the blackness of the night. One by one his men seemed to be disappearing. Monk saw it too and he left Heath's side and cackling, plunged forward.

Heath was alone.

Behind him was the town.

Ahead of him, darkness.

Without hesitation he stepped forward.

"What are we to do with all these bodies?" Sergeant Ferguson asked.

"Not our problem," the lieutenant answered. "We're to proceed to the helo crash site and check for survivors."

John noticed it out of the corner of his eye on Ben's tablet lying on the armrest between the two men. The drone was hovering overhead showing the soldiers milling over the scattered corpses.

"Jesus."

The rovers were back, running toward the unaware soldiers.

"Do you have comms with the Marines?" John said.

In alarm, Ben said he didn't and started to ring Whitehall.

Private Saunders heard something and looked up just in time to see a rush of rovers upon him, punching, kicking and gouging. He smelled their vile odor as he tried to raise his weapon. He saw his knife getting snatched from its sheath and felt the cold steel getting thrust into his chest.

The last thing Lieutenant Venables heard was the sharp warning from Whitehall command in his headset before Heath took him down from behind, ripped his helmet off, and sank his teeth into his neck.

6

The two of them were running on coffee and adrenaline but their fatigue was palpable.

"Look, let's try to keep this short so you can get some sleep," Ben said.

They were in a briefing room at Thames House, MI5 headquarters in London. Through the windows they could see a passing barge motor down the Thames and traffic backed up on the Embankment. From their perch everything seemed normal enough.

John and Emily assured Ben that they were fine but Ben repeated that he would get them back to Dartford as soon as possible.

As other MI5 operatives filed into the room John whispered to Emily, "You do look like shit, you know. You've got to rest."

She replied with a weak smile. "You look worse. We'll sleep soon."

"Right. Let's begin," Ben said. "The situation on the ground has clearly shifted in the past few hours and we need to make some hard decisions. The prime minister and the Cobra group will be meeting within the hour and I'll have to provide our recommendations. So with that, Eva, could you catch us all up?"

Eva Mendel was the MI5 analyst responsible for Ministry of Defense liaison. An efficient, emotionless woman, she was crisp and to the point.

"I'll start with Leatherhead," she said. "Has anyone not seen the drone footage of the attack on the Marines? Fine, in that case, no need to show it again. The Hellers, rovers, whatever we choose to call them, were eliminated by the lads from 3 Commando only to reappear very much, quote-unquote alive, a short distance away with tragic consequences. The MOD has not sent in any further troops but all remote footage confirms without any doubt that there were no survivors on our side. In Dartford, Sevenoaks, and Upminster we haven't had occasion to witness the phenomenon of terminated Hellers reappearing but within the past hour we have witnessed this. Again, what you'll see is drone footage with thermal imaging, starting with Sevenoaks in the vicinity of the Belmeade School."

The large monitor at the front of the room showed a dark empty playing field from a height of approximately one hundred feet. Initially the field was empty. Then a bright image of a person appeared. The person stood still for several seconds then began running in one direction before stopping and reversing course. Then two more people appeared and the first person joined them. A minute passed and five more individuals popped into view. The group of eight then proceeded to the evacuated school building and seemed to force entry.

"This is not good," John mumbled.

"As far as we can tell," Mendel said, "these individuals are still inside the school and no more have appeared. Now for Dartford. You'll recognize the grounds of the MAAC facility, also fully evacuated as of early this afternoon. I'd draw your attention to the tennis court."

The security lights were blazing all around the laboratory complex so the thermal imaging on the drone camera was disabled. The tennis court was fully lit. Three people spontaneously appeared near the net then ran toward the chain-link fence and tried to get out. After a while, one of them found the door and the three of them ran off into the darkness.

"We've seen no more activity at Dartford. And finally, this is Upminster, at a housing estate off Litchfield Terrace. The area was completely evacuated and sealed off but we have detected this group of six individuals going in and out of vacant dwellings."

"Are you sure these aren't returning residents or vandals from outlying areas?" Ben asked.

"We can't be certain," Mendel said.

"Rewind to the place you can see them walking under the street lamp," John said. "Can you zoom in on them there?"

Mendel found the spot, froze the footage and magnified and enhanced the image.

"You see their clothes?" John said. "They didn't buy them at Marks and Spencer. They're rough. They're Heller clothes."

"That was our working assumption," Mendel said. "I think that's all I have. Any questions?"

Emily asked, "Have you detected anything similar at the previous hot spots in South Ockendon and Iver?"

"No, nothing there," Mendel said.

Ben thanked her and said, "Dr. Loughty, I think we need to have your view on what's happening."

Emily started by shaking her head mournfully. "I see this as a very worrying development, very worrying indeed. As you know, previously it took a restart of the collider to generate nodal activity." She saw the blank looks around the table and added, "We're calling the areas of contact between our dimension and theirs, nodes. So far, including today's activity, there have been six known nodes—Dartford, South Ockendon, Iver, Leatherhead, Sevenoaks, and Upminster. Tonight the collider is quite dormant and we've seen bi-directional transfers at three of the nodes."

"Bi-directional?" Ben asked. "I don't believe we've seen any of *our* people disappear."

"Your downed helicopter," John said. "I know you haven't been able to put boots on the ground but I'll venture to say you're not going to find bodies in the wreckage."

"You think the crew wound up over there?" Ben asked.

"I do. And if I'm right, they found themselves up in the air with no place to go but down."

"Christ," Ben said.

"I agree with John," Emily said. "The helicopter probably flew into a node, lost its crew and crashed. It's not appropriate to call them nodes any longer. They're hyper-nodes or hot zones, perhaps. They're no longer transitory and associated with collider activity. That means we can't simply block the channels between our dimensions by mothballing the MAAC. We have to find a different way to plug them permanently."

Ben said, "My understanding is that the panel of experts we convened had no answer."

"I haven't had a chance to speak with any of them personally and all my key people were caught up in the Dartford transfer this morning. I'll take your statement at face value and just say this: the most important expert on strangelets, Paul Loomis, told me he knows how to put an end to this."

One of the officials at the end of the table said, "Well, let's hear him out. Where is he?"

"He's in Hell," Emily said. "And that's why I need to go back and find him."

"Do you know where he is?" Ben asked.

"Roughly," John said. "It won't be easy to extract him, but with the right manpower and a little luck it's doable. The longer we wait, the more chance he'll have moved or worse, gotten hurt in a war that's on full boil."

"In the meanwhile we're going to need a strategy to contain Hellers coming through these hot zones," Mendel said.

"It's going to be difficult," Emily said. "It's possible that the instability of the hot zones is going to increase."

"Meaning what?" Ben asked.

"The affected zones will get larger," she said. "If you cordon off Leatherhead, for example, it's possible that those manning the cordon will wind up within the zone, transported to the other side."

"We can't just let the Hellers out to run amok in London," Mendel said.

"No, of course not," Ben said. "We'll have to set a protective cordon somewhere and monitor closely for signs of a widening problem."

"It's going to be harder than you think," John said. "The word is going to get out over there. Hellers are going to want to escape and make their way back to the land of milk and honey. The hot zones are going to get flooded and over-run. If the army shoots at them, fires off missiles, whatever, we're going to see the same thing we saw on the drone footage. The Hellers are going to reappear. And if we repeat the exercise, all we're going to have is a pile of Heller bodies—maybe multiple copies of the same bodies—and they're going to keep coming. Eventually, they're going to over-run your defenses."

"Then what," Ben said, throwing his hands up as he said, "do we just throw up our hands and surrender?"

"Not what I'm suggesting," John said. "We've got to stop them on the other side. We've got to stop them in Hell."

Ben arched his eyebrows. "How do you propose to do that?"

"With some brave men and the help of someone I haven't talked to in a long time."

Emily ran a finger over John's dinette table and showed him the dust.

"The guy who does the cleaning's been out of town." John said. He cracked two cans of cold beer, gave her one, and the two of them collapsed on the sofa where she sipped and he gulped.

Emily said, "This is a nightmare."

"Yeah, it's bad. Do you really think Paul Loomis has the answer?"

"I take him at his word. Why would he have lied?"

"I wish we had more than that to go on. I don't ..."

She put her finger to his lips to quiet him. "I know. I know you don't want me to go," she said. "But you know that this has gone from bad to worse. Paul and I speak the same language. Whatever his idea is, I'll be able to understand it and translate it into action."

John gently pulled her finger away. "That was your dust finger," he said. "Want me to run you a bath?"

"I'm too exhausted to want one and too dirty to say no."

While she soaked in the tub, John stared at his telephone. He couldn't remember the last time he rang the number but he didn't need to look it up. It was the first phone number he'd ever learned; up until he went to college it was his own.

It was eight hours earlier in Oregon. He was so far removed from the rhythms of Kyle's life that he had no idea whether he'd be home. He expected to get voice mail but a husky voice answered.

"Yeah?"

"Kyle?"

"Yeah, who's this?"

"It's John."

"Fuck." It wasn't a friendly curse. The last time they had spoken was six years earlier at their father's funeral. It had been a visit wholly devoid of brotherly love.

"Yeah, fuck."

"Why are you calling?" Kyle asked brusquely.

"Checking in. It's been a while, bro."

"Yeah. You sick or something?"

"No, why?"

"You sound funny."

"I'm all right. Worn out is all."

"Where are you these days?"

"England. Near London."

"Still doing embassy security?"

"I quit. You?"

"Same old same old, you know, the shop."

"Never got married?"

"No way. I've got a girlfriend, sort of. You?"

"Same, but mine is more than sort of."

"If you quit your job why'd you stay over there?"

"I got a new job a few years back. In charge of security at a government physics lab."

"Aren't they having some kind of situation over there? I don't pay a lot of attention to the news but people are talking about some kind of a cluster fuck."

"Yeah. That's why I'm calling."

"You involved in it?"

"Big time."

"What's it to me?"

"I'm putting a team together. I need a guy who can do what you do."

"Sit around and drink beer?"

"The other thing you do."

"Oh yeah? Why would I want to fly half way around the world to help you?"

"It's not about helping me. It's about a once in a lifetime opportunity to do something important. Dangerous as shit but highly kickass."

"I'm listening."

"You always said you wanted to do some of the things I used to do."

"I couldn't pass a physical then and sure as shit can't pass one now."

"No one's going to give you a physical. If you want in, you'll be in. Come over to the UK to talk about it."

"When?"

"Tonight."

"You're out of your mind. I can't afford a ticket and even if I could I don't have a passport."

"A chopper can pick you up in Bend in a couple of hours. You'll rendezvous with an air force jet to bring you here. No passport needed, everything will be handled by the state department."

There was a pregnant pause and Kyle finally said, "We're not exactly on the best of terms, remember? I'm not real sure I want to hang out with you."

"I need you to come over and hear me out. This is going to sound over the top but believe me, it's not: for the sake of the human race you and I need to bury the hatchet."

Emily was soon slumbering in his bed. John was at the point where exhaustion had given way to a restless agitation. It took a few more beers to mellow him out enough to turn in. The bed was soft. Her body had warmed and scented the sheets. He wanted to touch her but he didn't dare wake her. Before frustration set in he was asleep too.

John was yelling, "Mike, don't!"

Mike Entwistle was stooped over the bearded prisoner, his knife against the man's plastic wrist ties. They were inside the ruined mud-brick farmhouse in Afghanistan amidst a pile of Taliban bodies.

The prisoner was the only one to survive the mortar fire. His squad of Green Berets had been tasked with extracting a high-value target, a Taliban commander named Fazal Toofan, but the mission had gone to shit. John had lost too many men so he lit up the farmhouse. If they couldn't take Toofan alive, he wanted to make sure he was dead.

The prisoner had shouted in good English, "Please help me. Guys, I am interpreter for American soldiers. Taliban took me. I am injured. I can't feel my legs."

Before Mike could react to John's plea, he had sliced through the plastic tie with an upward flick of the serrated blade.

The prisoner reacted with astonishing speed.

He had been hiding a cocked pistol between his legs and in an instant it was in his hand.

He fired at point-blank range into Mike's head. John felt his friend's blood splattering his face. As the Afghani twisted his waist to fire the next round at him, John sprang forward and smashed his face with the butt stock of his rifle. He crumpled, motionless.

The rest of his squad gathered around Mike but there was nothing to be done.

"He said he was a terp," one of John's men said. "He's no terp, he's Tali. Let me smoke the fucker."

"Don't," John said, staring at Mike's bloody head. "Cuff him, hands and feet. Double-check the bodies to make sure they're all dead. We're taking this motherfucker with us. When our bird lands, get a body bag for Mike."

He sank to his haunches and allowed himself to lose it. He didn't give a damn if his men saw him cry.

7

Cromwell had been correct. This Whitehall Palace bore no resemblance to the vast stone palace that Cardinal Wolsey had lavishly expanded for his own use in the 16th century. That Whitehall Palace was said to be the finest house in London and the earthly King Henry had jealously seized it for his own use after deposing his loyal cardinal. Henry had expanded it even further, adding a bowling green, indoor tennis court, and a tiltyard for jousting. Although it had been destroyed by fire in 1691 it had been memorialized in countless paintings and lithographs. It was these images of Whitehall Palace that triggered dissonance when the Earthers first laid eyes upon their destination.

This palace was a substantial timber-frame building with a Tudor exoskeleton and walls of sooty plaster. It was smaller than Henry's Hampton Court Palace, but large enough to accommodate the entirety of his court, albeit in cramped quarters. It was situated north of the Thames on flat, indefensible land. A ring of soldiers guarded it from the intrusions of hungry Londoners who eked out an existence in the densely packed city of low buildings, shabby cottages, vegetable patches, and livestock butchers. It was not a siege palace. The few times that Brittania had been under serious threat of invasion during Henry's tenure in Hell, he had moved his court north to an impregnable hilltop stone castle near York.

Cromwell had the Earthers taken to a large banqueting hall. This would be their collective dormitory for the foreseeable future. Startled servants who had not been expecting a royal visit, much less a gaggle of highly exotic guests, brought in narrow beds and coarse blankets. The eight women segregated themselves to one end of the hall. The privies were down a long corridor but to use them, guards stationed outside the hall had to escort the prisoners one at a time. Dried, leathery meat and loaves of day-old bread were brought in with several jugs of sweet ale. Iron needles, sewing twine, and hook and eye fasteners were provided to fix their clothing.

Beyond a gender segregation, the prisoners, true to their largely British roots, further grouped themselves by station. The scientists occupied one cluster of beds and the politicians and security officials, another smaller one. Henry Quint had to make a choice. He had been the director of MAAC before his ignominious fall but he was also a physicist. But after being largely ignored by the VIPs, he chose a cot on the periphery of the scientists and glumly straddled the divide.

Likewise, Karen Smithwick had a choice to make and she aligned herself with the VIPs rather than the female scientists. As one of the few women on the front benches of government, she was adept at playing her part alongside powerful men.

Sitting on her cot, she watched Campbell Bates fumbling miserably with his sewing and took pity on the courtly American.

"Here, let me do that for you," she said.

"I'd appreciate the help," he said, handing his trousers over.

"This rather feels like *I'm a Celebrity... Get Me Out of Here*," she said.

"I'm not familiar with that."

"It's one of those dreadful reality shows," George Lawrence said. "Minor celebrities sent off to the jungle. One gets voted off every week."

Bitterman grunted. "You can go ahead and vote me off first. I won't be offended."

"If it were only that easy," Smithwick said.

"So what's our play?" Lawrence asked.

Trotter had finished his wardrobe repairs and was lying on his back on a lumpy, hay-filled mattress, staring at the high ceiling darkened by centuries of candle soot.

"Our play is survival," Trotter said. "Mustn't sugar coat it. We've got to offer something of value to these people. Otherwise we won't be worth feeding."

Bates shook his head. "I say we have a duty to escape, just like a prisoner of war. You heard what Quint said. We've got to get back to Dartford in case they mount a rescue attempt."

"The odds of escape are too long," Trotter said. "We're hardly a fighting force. We're a bunch of old farts and pencil-necks." Cromwell had separated them from the three young and fit MI5 agents, squirreling them away elsewhere in the palace. "We need to convince them we're indispensible."

"Are we?" Smithwick asked.

"Maybe not us," Trotter said, gesturing toward the scientists, "but perhaps they are."

The large double-doors to the hall swung open and Cromwell entered with another man and several soldiers. Cromwell was a foot taller than Henry Cameron, the Duke of Suffolk. Cromwell was smoothly shaven, dark, and lean while Suffolk was short and stocky with an unruly white beard flecked with his last meal. Cromwell was given to austere robes. Suffolk, a seventeenth-century naval commander, still wore a showy version of his royal blue military tunic, complete with brass buttons.

Trotter got to his feet, convinced they had come to parley with him and he was not disappointed. They went straight for his bed. Cromwell ignored the other Earthers but Suffolk sniffed the air and rubbernecked the women.

Standing before Trotter, Cromwell said, "This is the Duke of Suffolk. He commands the king's organs of war."

Trotter extended a hand. Suffolk stared at it as if it were a rotting fish until Trotter withdrew it.

"I am told you are a spy," Suffolk said. "I do not, as a rule, trust spies, not even my own."

Trotter thrust out his chin. "I serve my monarch and my country. You are not my monarch and this is not my country so you are right to be suspicious of me. However, I do understand the nature of our circumstances. You can trust me to do what is required to assure the safety and well-being of my people."

"Well said," George Lawrence harrumphed.

"Please come with us," Cromwell said to Trotter.

"Why?"

"I want to show you something."

As the men left the hall, Brenda Mitchell saw that Suffolk was staring straight at her. She turned away until they were gone.

Most of the female scientists were between twenty and thirty years old. Chris Cowles, the deputy head of the magnets department, was only in her early fifties but that qualified her as the grand dame of the group. She was unmarried, shunned makeup and jewelry, and wore her hair in a sensible bob. She rose from her cot and sat beside Brenda as she seemed the worst off.

"You haven't eaten," Chris said. "The meat's tough, a bit like a tasteless jerky, but the bread's passable."

"I'm not hungry."

"You need to keep up your strength."

"Did you see the way that man looked at me?" Brenda asked.

"Yes. He was awful."

Kelly Jenkins, another young woman said, "Like the villain in a really bad panto."

Brenda smiled for the first time.

"Come on," Chris said, "just a bit of bread."

Brenda relented and Chris went to the food table to break off a crust. She delivered it with a cup of beer.

"Look after her," Chris whispered to Kelly.

Kelly nodded but said, "Who's going to look after me?"

Matthew came over and pulled Chris off to a corner.

"How's she getting on?" he asked.

"She's scared. All the ladies are."

"The men too," Matthew said.

"Brenda's got more cause to be scared than the rest of us," Chris said.

"She's young and she's very attractive. God knows what the ratio of men to women is here? We're all at risk but she's especially vulnerable."

"I'll try our best to protect her."

"I know you will, Matthew but you're an excellent scientist. You're not an action hero."

"You haven't seen me in a cape and Spandex," he said.

"And I hope I never do. Can I ask you something?"

He nodded.

"I know we were told to say nothing, but did you tell your wife anything about what we were doing the past two months?"

"Honestly, no," he said. "I took the secrecy seriously, but mainly I didn't want her to worry. You?"

"I told my fish everything."

"I'm quite sure they won't spill the beans but the authorities won't be able to keep this quiet," Matthew said. "Not with all of us missing, and not just us MAAC types. All the muckety-mucks over there. My wife's made of strong stuff—you know about our son, right?"

She did. He was severely autistic.

"Well, she'll be sick with worry about me, whether they tell her the truth or some cock and bull story. And she'll be fretting that in the future she'll have to take care of him on her own."

"We'll get home," Chris said.

His sigh sounded more like a groan. "Emily will try to make it happen but I think what everyone's been saying is right. MAAC's made things too unstable. They'll be shutting it down for good and we'll be trapped."

It meant nothing to Trotter but Suffolk understood the symbolism perfectly well and showed his displeasure with a fearsome scowl. Cromwell had led them to the king's own apartment which he had appropriated for his own use. With Trotter deposited in a chair by the hearth, Suffolk joined Cromwell at the sideboard to fill his goblet with wine.

"I trust his majesty will not be best pleased to return and find you in his bed," Suffolk whispered.

"On the off chance he does return, better to find his most loyal servant there than any other man," Cromwell said.

"This country needs a king," Suffolk said. "You are a talker, Cromwell. If the Russians and Germans invade, talk will not defeat them. I am a military man and thus a worthy king."

"Remember well that you were only one among many military men before Norfolk met his demise and Henry chose to elevate you," Cromwell said in an acid tone. "He could have just as easily elevated Oxford who I am sure is nipping at your heels. He has only had one chancellor for five hundred years. Did you hear me? Five hundred years. Now, this talker has some talking to do. Observe and enjoy my wine."

Cromwell retrieved a cloth bundle, set it on the table before Trotter and parted the cloth to reveal a stack of books.

"I had these brought here from Hampton Court," Cromwell said. "Do you know what they are?"

Trotter recognized them as three of the books John Camp had carried on his last journey to Hell.

"I did not bother with the Bible or the tales of that playwright, Shakespeare," Cromwell said. "These are the volumes of interest."

Trotter thumbed through them. They were books written during the heyday of the industrial revolution: *Blast Furnace Construction in America*, *Steam Boilers, Engines and Turbines*, and *Bessemer Steel, Ores and Methods*. King Henry had understood their importance and so had Cromwell, but there had scarcely been time to exploit the knowledge they held.

"Why are you showing me these?" Trotter asked.

"I have tried to read them," Cromwell said, "and though the words are of my native tongue, I cannot comprehend their meaning. I have showed them to men who are from more recent times but most of these men are dullards or men of good intellect who nevertheless cannot begin to fathom how to turn the words on a page into furnaces or boilers or good steel. We have many enemies. We need superior armaments and we need them quickly."

"I too have had a look," Suffolk said, dismissively. "Balderdash, if you ask me."

"Well, I won't be of any help," Trotter said. "Not in my wheelhouse."

Cromwell offered Trotter a cup of wine. He sipped at it, admiring its quality.

"I do understand these scientists from your realm are not makers of weapons," Cromwell said. "Emily Loughty did explain this to us. Yet, the king maintained, and I do agree, that a latter-day scientist is better suited to make use of these books than any Heller to whom I have spoken."

"What would you like from me?" Trotter asked.

"I require your cooperation. You must persuade your scientists to undertake the construction of these great furnaces. I do not mean them to partake in the physical work. I have laborers aplenty. Bricklayers, carpenters, forgers, men with strong backs who may be directed to implement their instructions. Persuade them, Master Trotter. It is far better for a man to render his service by his own accord than under threat of torture."

"I usually prefer torture," Suffolk said with a sick laugh.

Trotter had more wine while he mulled his response. "I believe I could make this happen," he said, "but what would I receive in return?"

Cromwell smiled broadly, as if to acknowledge, I can work with this man. What he said was, "What do you want?"

"Well, let's see. I'm not one for dormitory life. I'd like private rooms with decent furnishings. I'd like as much of this good wine as I can drink and food as good as you gentlemen eat. I'd like a servant or two to look after me and as much hot water for bathing as I want. And I'm not much of a lady's man but I do like a woman every so often, usually a prostitute. I'm afraid there would be negative consequences if I forced myself upon one of mine. So I'd like a pick of your crème de la crème even if I have to plug my nose while I'm doing it."

"Is that all?" Cromwell said.

"I might have other requests but that's my list for now."

"There is nothing in your demands I cannot provide," Cromwell said.

"Then do we have a deal?" Trotter asked.

Suffolk interrupted. "Since this is the time to lay cards upon the table, there is something that I require."

"And what might that be?" Cromwell asked with a withering glance.

"I want the pretty fair-haired woman for my own."

"You mean Brenda?" Trotter asked.

Suffolk shrugged.

"Well, you've got a good eye, I'll say that," Trotter said, "but I'd be concerned that the other scientists would revolt."

Cromwell commented that the duke's carnal interests were not of paramount importance but Suffolk insisted he would have to be accommodated.

Trotter thought for a while and said, "I've got an idea how we might get her into your bed without losing the others. If I can make it happen do we have a deal?"

Suffolk nodded and Cromwell said, "I believe we do."

When Trotter returned to the hall with the books under his arm he was swarmed by the others.

"What did he want?" Bates asked.

"Have a look at these," Trotter said, laying the books on the serving table. "John Camp carried these with him as a bargaining chip a month ago. They're impressed with the contents but don't really know how to exploit them. I realize this is far afield to your expertise but with all the IQ points on tap, perhaps you can figure out how to at least give them the impression you can build these furnaces."

"Tell me why we should help them?" Southwick demanded.

"It's simple," Trotter said. "They threatened to torture us into submission if we didn't voluntarily cooperate."

Matthew picked up the book on steel production and passed the other two to waiting hands. After most of the scientists had a gander Matthew gave the verdict. "Look, I doubt we can do much with these. I think we can understand the concepts well enough and the books do include illustrations and plans but none of us are industrial engineers."

Campbell Bates slowly raised his hand. When no one noticed him he cleared his throat and added a polite, "Excuse me."

"What is it?" Trotter asked.

"Actually, I have a degree in engineering."

"Do you?" Lawrence asked.

"From MIT. I decided to go to law school instead of getting an engineering job and I wound up at the FBI after that. To call me a rusty engineer would be too kind, but maybe I could have a look."

"Hurry up," Trotter said, excitedly. "Let the man see the books."

Cromwell was alone in his quarters preparing for bed. He had been a rather austere man in life and he was even more so now. His rooms were unadorned, his food plain, his wine watered. He had opted to reside in the king's rooms for appearance sake, but had instructed the servants to remove Henry's personal and decorative items. He slept alone, having lost interest in sex a very long time ago. He existed to work. If he could have ended his eternity in Hell by suicide he would have gladly done so but this was not an option for him or any of his brethren. So he worked. Henry had always been a demanding master and Cromwell was glad of that because there were always tasks to keep him occupied. But Henry was gone and he had hard choices to make. He had no desire to be king but if he did not secure the position, if Suffolk did, surely he would be a threat and would find himself in a rotting room, festering forever. No, he would have to act soon to seize the crown, and if Henry did return, he would have to convince him he was merely keeping the throne away from disloyal scoundrels.

He responded to a soft rap upon his door. His manservant informed him that the Earl of Surrey had arrived at Whitehall and needed to see him urgently. Cromwell stoked his weak fire with a small log and sat beside the hearth waiting.

Surrey was not a regular at court, preferring a countryside life of hunting and whoring, and Cromwell did not know him nearly as well as most of Henry's noblemen. Yet he could immediately sense the man's agitation; he was sweating profusely, his leggings mud-splattered from a hard gallop.

"Where is the king?" the earl said. "I must see the king."

"Unfortunately, he is gone."

"What do you mean gone?"

"It is a long and difficult tale. I will try my best to explain but first you must tell me why you have come to London."

"Has he disappeared to another realm beyond our senses?"

"How do you know of such things?" Cromwell said in astonishment.

"Because I have seen things. I scarcely believed my eyes at first but I know what I saw."

"Come now, man, speak your mind."

"I was summoned to the town of Leatherhead by some of my soldiers. I thought they had been drinking too much ale but I humored them with my presence. Near the town I did myself observe many men, drawn there by the same word of mouth and in the town centre I watched as these men did purposely step forward and disappear into thin air. When I asked a hag what was happening she said that hours earlier a band of rovers materialized from nothingness and announced to a startled populace that they had been back in the land of the living. Soon these rovers did surge forward and disappear once again and many others have since followed them into nothingness. I felt the king must be informed. Tell me Master Cromwell, what manner of miracles and magic are upon us?"

Cromwell peered into the glowing fire. "You have no idea, my good earl, you have no idea."

8

The Belmeade boys stumbled blindly through the black forest. Even the most outwardly macho of the bunch were reduced to raw and clawing despair. But by the time the forest gave way to a meadow and the meadow gave way to a flat plain with a rutted road, Angus had fought his emotions to reclaim the appearance of self-confidence.

"We'll follow this road," he declared.

"Why?" Andrew Pender asked, pleadingly.

"Because roads lead to places," Angus said.

"That's stupid," Nigel Mountjoy said.

"Excuse me, dimwit, *you're* stupid," Glynn said, standing up for his best mate.

"But which way should we go?" Craig Rotenberg asked.

Angus pointed ahead.

"Why that way?" Craig said.

"Why not?" Glynn replied.

"We don't even know which direction it is," Craig said.

Harry Shipley hadn't said a word since they entered the forest. During their trek he'd cried so much he had no more tears. "It's north," he said.

"How do you know that?" Angus asked.

"I've been keeping track," the slight boy answered. "Assuming we didn't get spun around inside the wormhole we were pointing east inside our dorm, and like I said, I've been keeping track since we got here."

"North it is," Angus said.

"Why not south?" Craig asked.

Glynn punched Craig in the meat of his shoulder. "You know, I never realized how bloody annoying you were."

Angus said, "If Harry's right, then London is north."

"We don't even know if there is a London," Andrew said.

"The man who was stabbed in the belly said the place we were in was Sevenoaks," Nigel said. "If there's a Sevenoaks, it stands to reason there's a London."

"I still think we should've stayed by the spot where we landed," Stuart Cobham said. "If they're going to rescue us, isn't that where they'll come? And at least there were fish in the pond. Now what are we going to eat?"

Kevin Pickles said, "Excuse me, unless one of you has a box of matches we couldn't make a fire. And I hate sushi."

"You heard what he said about rovers," Angus said. "I wasn't going to have us hang around there waiting for a gang of murderers and cannibals to return."

"Your father's bound to rescue us, isn't he, Angus?" Boris asked. They all knew Angus's father was the defense secretary.

"If he doesn't, my dad will," Danny Leung said.

"Yeah, Red Danny's dad'll lead the whole Red Army to find us in Hell and bring us great steaming platters of General Tso's chicken," Kevin said.

"Fuck off. You're a racist," Danny complained.

"Yeah, shut it, gherkin," Glynn said. "Just because that guy back in the woods said we were in Hell, doesn't mean we are. It's all bullcrap till proved otherwise."

Most of them had acquired walking staffs and as they traveled, Danny Leung demonstrated a few moves of Yin Shao Gun, Chinese stick fighting.

"I can't do the twirly stuff," Boris Magnusson complained.

"You don't have to do that rubbish," Danny said. "It's mostly for show. It's the whacking and poking moves that are important."

Soon they were just boys again, laughing and shouting and smacking one another, forgetting their predicament for a while.

Kevin had been blowing his nose into the handkerchief that he'd found in his pocket, where he'd stuffed it before maths class. He looked up and said, "Guys."

No one paid any attention.

"Guys," he said louder, dropping the handkerchief, "someone's coming."

From the north a wagon had come into view, and not just one, a train of them with outriders.

Two others saw the wagons coming too. An old man and an old woman had been spying on the boys from behind a hedgerow beside the road. They had been hunting for rabbits when they heard the strange sound of children's voices and when they spotted the lads they had been too amazed to say a single word to one another. Now they crouched down even lower at the approaching danger.

Angus was about to yell for them to run but he saw it was pointless. Riders were approaching at a gallop.

Rough, filthy men perched on thin leather saddles quickly encircled them. Harry burst into tears and Andrew, unnerved by the sound of his crying, lost it too.

"Angus, what should we do?" Boris asked, choking back his own fear.

"Don't do anything," Angus said. "Let me talk to them." Angus looked up into the rider's staring eyes and said, "You'd better leave us alone."

The man who seemed to be in charge circled them twice on his black horse, a pistol in his hand.

"What are you?" the man asked.

"What are we?" Angus said. "Don't you mean, who are we?"

A diminutive man on a small horse, not much larger than a pony, pointed at the boys with a sword and said, "Look, Ardmore, they got sticks. What ya gonna do with them sticks?"

Another man laughed. "They're about your size, Fergie. I reckon they're midget men."

Ardmore stopped circling and dismounted. He had a wide-brimmed hat, a greasy ponytail tied with a long piece of leather, and more gaps in his mouth than teeth. "They're not men at all. Fuck me but these are boys."

"That's not possible," Fergie said.

"Are you taking an opposing view to mine?" Ardmore asked, pointing his pistol at the young man's head.

Fergie quickly backtracked. He apologized and promised to keep his trap shut.

"Well are you?" Ardmore said, addressing Angus.

"Of course we're boys," Angus said, his voice cracking.

Ardmore inched closer to Angus and sucked in air through his nostrils. "It's even stranger than that," he said. "There's something all together peculiar about the whole lot of you."

The lead wagon rolled up. The driver, a grizzled old man, pulled back on the reins of a pair of draft horses. Someone dressed head-to-toe in black, from a hat like Ardmore's to long black boots, pulled open the canvas flaps and climbed out the rear. It was only when she spoke that the boys knew this was a woman.

"What's going on here, Ardmore?" she asked.

"We have ourselves a bit of a situation," he replied.

She was heavily armed with a pistol and a knife tucked in her wide belt. A sword in a scabbard slapped against her leg as she walked toward the boys.

She audibly gasped and let out a "Bloody hell."

"Yeah," Ardmore said, "bloody hell's right."

Even though she was only a few feet away, Angus couldn't tell if she was young or old. Her skin was dirty and leathery, her eyes a dull, muddy color. She wore her dark hair in a ponytail tied with leather, just like Ardmore's.

"Who speaks for you?" she asked the boys.

Angus meekly raised his hand.

"How old are you?" she demanded.

"Fourteen," he said very softly.

"Speak up. What did you say?"

"Fourteen."

"That's impossible."

"I'm not lying. We're all the same age except for Harry who's thirteen."

"How did you die?" she asked.

"What?" Angus asked.

A small voice said, "She thinks we're dead."

Angus looked around. It was Harry, his lower lip trembling.

"We're not dead," Angus said. "At least I don't think so."

"Come closer," she said.

Angus took half a step forward, his head bowed in submissive fear. The woman roughly grabbed him by the wrist and lifted his hand to her nose.

"They don't smell right, Bess," Ardmore said.

Bess tenderly let Angus's wrist go. Ardmore and the others had never before seen her eyes go moist. "You're wrong," she said. "It's us that don't smell right. They smell perfect."

Some of the horsemen began to shout and point toward the north.

"Soldiers!" Ardmore said. "Coming up on us like the clappers."

"Get them in the wagons," Bess shouted to Ardmore.

"No! Leave us alone!" Angus cried. "Run!"

Danny and Glynn took off first and Angus was hot on their heels. Ardmore swore and kicked his horse's flanks and leaned in his saddle to pluck little Kevin Pickles off the ground. Kevin squealed like a rodent as Ardmore deposited him on the pommel of his saddle.

"Stop your running or I'll put a lead ball through this runt's brain," Ardmore bellowed.

Angus turned around and ordered his classmates to stop. Danny protested but Angus shouted that they didn't have a choice.

"Hurry up!" Bess yelled. "Half in that wagon, half in the next. We're not going to outrun 'em. Get ready to fight."

Ardmore delivered Kevin directly into the back of one of the wagons. Harry, Craig, Stuart, and Andrew hastily joined him. Even in crisis, the boys segregated themselves by an unwritten pecking order. The more popular boys, Angus, Glynn, Danny, Boris, and Nigel jumped into the other wagon where they found a few bales of raw wool.

"Are we with the good guys or bad guys?" Nigel asked.

Glynn protectively pulled his knees to his chest and said, "If we're really in Hell then they're all bad."

In the other wagon Craig closed his eyes as tightly as he could and whimpered, "This can't be happening, this can't be happening. When I open my eyes we'll be back at school."

Harry wrapped his arms around his middle and dipped his chin to his chest. "It is happening," he said. "I think we somehow went through an inter-dimensional wormhole."

"Can we get back?" Craig asked.

"Theoretically."

Kevin was shaking so hard he could hardly get the words out. "This is so bad. I'm in the back of a smelly wagon in Hell with Stephen Hawking."

One of the outriders dismounted and gave his horse to Bess. She rode to the rear of the wagon train with Ardmore, barking orders to the men.

The soldiers were coming closer, their horses kicking up a dusty cloud.

"I see about two dozen," Ardmore said.

"They're probably the lot we saw at the inn last night," Bess said. "They was giving us the eye."

Ardmore spat upon the ground. "We're having quite the day, ain't we?"

"That we are."

The soldiers were indeed the squad of King Henry's men who had happened upon Bess and her gang at a crowded London inn near the docklands. Soldiers habitually feathered their own nests by plundering traders. Yet to do so in the city risked the ire of the crown. Cromwell insisted that some wheels of commerce needed to turn to maintain order among the populace. So their thieving was usually done outside city limits, away from the prying eyes of Cromwell's agents.

The soldiers had muskets. Their first volley arrived before Bess was in range to return fire. Her men ducked for cover but she and Ardmore sat tall in their saddles, seemingly unafraid. Inside the wagons, the boys cried and cowered.

"Anyone hit?" Bess shouted.

"We're good," Ardmore said, raising his pistol. "Wait …wait …wait …"

When the soldiers were close enough that the ground shook with hoof beats, Bess screamed, "Fire!"

Two soldiers fell from their horses but the rest charged on, yelling and brandishing their swords. Bess and Ardmore stuffed their pistols in their belts and drew their swords in time for the first clash.

None of the soldiers would have known that the fierce fighter dressed in black was a woman. Bess launched herself at the nearest attacker and delivered a blow to his shoulder that almost took his arm off. Her next victim was the captain of the party whose horse galloped off a ways before its headless rider slipped from the saddle.

Ardmore slashed and stabbed his way through a tangle of horses and soldiers and wheeled around at the sound of Bess crying out. Two of the king's men had pulled her off her horse and were trying to finish her off. She was lying on the ground on her back, flailing at them with her knife.

One of the soldier's was shouting, "She's a …" when he looked down at Ardmore's sword coming through his belly.

The other soldier was distracted for a moment by the bloody sight, enough time for Bess to stab him through the eye.

"Yeah, I'm a woman, all right," she said, picking herself up.

The few remaining soldiers saw the tide had turned and rode off, heading back toward London, the taunts of Bess's men in their ears.

"Lose any of ours?" she asked Ardmore.

"Don't think so."

That was when it grew quiet enough to hear the screaming coming from inside a wagon.

"The boys," she said.

Unsure which wagon it had come from she ran to one, Ardmore to the other. Ardmore opened the flap and saw that Angus and the others were huddled together but fine. Bess saw four terrified, weeping faces and one white, immobile one. There was blood on the wagon floor.

Craig Rotenberg was slumped over with a gaping hole in his chest.

"He's dead!" Kevin shrieked. "He's dead!"

Bess climbed in and inspected his body.

"You're the first live souls I've seen in two hundred years and he's the first dead one," she said. "Day of miracles."

Despite the frantic protests of the boys Bess refused to bury Craig's body. They didn't have a shovel, she explained. They needed to make haste to shelter in Southampton by nightfall. The roads at night were filthy with rovers. And besides, what did it matter?

"Because it's the decent thing to do!" Angus insisted.

"I've no time for such nonsense as decency," Bess said. "If you want to cover him up with branches, I'll give you small time. Then we're off."

"What if we don't want to go with you?" Angus asked.

"You've no choice. You'll all be like your friend by this time tomorrow if you don't."

"Where are you going?"

"We're Devon folk," she said.

All the boys but Harry participated in the hasty ritual of dragging Craig into the bushes and covering him with foliage. Harry had more of Craig's blood on him than any of the rest. He sat beside the wagon, mute and shaking.

"Should we say something?" Boris asked, adding the last few branches.

"You mean a prayer?" Glynn said.

"Yeah, a prayer," Boris said.

"He's Jewish," Nigel said.

"They pray too," Stuart said.

"He was always quiet in chapel," Nigel said.

"What else could he do?" Boris said. "Babble in Jewish?"

"You're so ignorant," Stuart said. "It's called Hebrew."

"We'll have to make do in English," Angus said. Bess was calling for them to hurry along so Angus lowered his head and said, "Here goes: I've got no idea how it is we wound up in the soup but here we are. Craig was a pretty good kid who didn't deserve to get killed. Let's hope he's with his Jewish God now and that he's at peace and that's basically all I've got to say."

"You know what? You suck at praying," Glynn said.

The boys would not get back into the blood-filled wagon and also refused to be split into two groups so Bess allowed them to climb into her wagon, the largest in the train. Bess took her place on a bale of wool and the boys sat cross-legged on the planks. Angus felt something sharp poking him in the back. He was pressed against a wooden box secured with an iron lock and when he shoved it to give him more room he heard clinking.

"Mind my strong box," Bess said.

"Is there money in there?" Angus asked.

"Aye, it's the coin we earned in London," she said.

"Earned doing what?" Glynn asked.

"Trading wool. We're sheepherders. They pay the best in London so that's where we take our wares though the journey's treacherous."

"Back in the woods," Angus said, "we found a man who was badly hurt. He said we were in Hell."

"He told you the truth," Bess said, removing the hat that had been robbing them of a good look at her face. She was middle-aged, not so different in age than most of their mothers, and perhaps she would have passed for attractive if her skin weren't so weathered and dirty.

"I don't believe in Hell," Kevin said. "My parents are atheists."

"I didn't know that," Boris said.

"I never said," Kevin said. "I didn't want any stick."

"What's an atheist?" Bess asked.

"They don't believe in God," Kevin answered.

She chuckled. "In my day, someone who made that opinion known would've been burned at the stake."

"When was that?" Angus asked. "Your day, I mean."

"I died as the seventeen hundreds were coming to a close," she said.

"That's impossible. I don't believe you," Danny said, fiercely.

"Well you'd better believe me, Chinaman," she said.

"That's politically incorrect," Andrew said. "He's Chinese."

Bess shook her head. "I have no idea what you just said. But the lot of you need a lesson in what's what, quick-like. Listen up because I'll only be explaining it one time."

They did listen in rapt silence as she told them about her life. She had been a Devon woman, married to a sheep farmer. They had thirteen children. A pestilence wiped out their flock, her children went hungry, and her husband killed himself in shame. In desperation she set out one night to steal sheep from the property of a local nobleman to repopulate her flock. Unfortunately a young shepherd nabbed her in the act and began to shout for help. She had her husband's pistol in her belt and fearful of what would happen to her children without her, she shot the lad and fled. She was caught and she was hanged. The next instant she was in Hell. She never saw her children again.

Bess talked without a trace of sadness or sentimentality. She was too much of an old Heller. She followed her own tale with a similarly cold, bare-bones description of Hell's grim reality and natural laws. It didn't seem her intent was to scare the boys but that was the effect. When she was done not one of them spoke. She let them be. The wagon bumped along and lacking a suspension their bones were jostled.

After a long while she asked, "After all I've told you, not one of you has a single question?"

Kevin raised his hand as if he were still in a classroom. "Why do you smell bad?"

Angus barked at him to shut up but Bess said it was a fair enough question. "I'd long forgotten 'bout the smell. Pig farmers can't smell the pigs, you know. I reckon it's because we're like dead meat whereas you lads are nice and fresh. Any other questions? No? Well, let me ask you one. How do you suppose a bunch of live 'uns made the crossing to these parts?"

The boys all looked toward Harry. He sniffed his nose dry and by the upward tilt of his chin, showed he was proud to be the nominated spokesman. "Do you know what the universe is?" he asked her.

"Not a clue."

"It's everything we know," Harry said. "It's the Earth, the moon, the stars."

"I see," she said, though it didn't seem she did.

"Well, a lot of really clever people, physicists, they're called, think there's more than one universe, a lot more. Maybe there's an infinite number of them. Some of them may be only a tiny bit different from the universe we know, like everything's exactly the same except that in another one, I'm a brilliant football player."

"Fat chance," Boris snorted.

"Yeah, not likely," Harry said. "Anyway, here's what I think. I think that this place you're calling Hell is one of those different universes, one where you go to if you've done something really bad in your life. Maybe there's one called Heaven where good people go. Ordinarily, there's no way someone live can pass between these universes. For some reason I can't explain we passed through something called a wormhole which is a passageway between our universe and yours."

"That so?" Bess said.

Harry shrugged. "It's what I think anyway."

"You're a clever one, ain't you?" she said.

Harry smiled and without a touch of modesty nodded his agreement.

"Can you go back to your land or are you stuck here?" she asked.

The question made Harry tear up again. "I don't know," he said. "I'm not that clever."

9

Group Captain Mark Twyford, the station commander of RAF Northolt in Ruislip was unable to contain his displeasure. An urgent call from the Joint Forces Command at Northwood Headquarters had pulled him from a twice-delayed holiday with his family. He returned to find an American drinking coffee in his office.

"Captain," John said, rising from a sofa, "I'm John Camp. Your secretary was nice enough to show me in and take care of me."

Twyford was in civilian clothes. "I was up in Norfolk with my wife and children," he said.

"They're canceling leave up and down the line," John said.

"I was told we had a VIP arriving but I wasn't told there'd be someone in my office. Who are you?"

"I'm the head of security at the Dartford supercollider. Ex-US diplomatic security, ex-Green Beret."

"Is this about the incidents in and around London?"

"Yes it is."

Twyford lit a cigarette and sat at his desk. "There's been some wild speculation in the media. What's the real story?"

"I'm not authorized to speak on the matter. My understanding is that you'll be getting some kind of official communication from the MOD. It hasn't been announced yet but the prime minister's going to be making an address later today. Northolt's the closest RAF base to London so I'm sure you'll be busy soon."

"I'm not best pleased to be getting my intel from an American civilian."

"No one's going to be best pleased for a while, captain. Now if you'd be good enough to check on the arrival time of the C-21A Learjet I'm expecting, I'd appreciate it."

John was on the tarmac when the small USAF jet pulled off the taxiway. The RAF ground crew placed wheel chocks and the door opened. The co-pilot climbed down and headed straight for John.

"Are you John Camp?"

"Yeah. Where's my brother?"

"You're going to have to help him down."

"Why's that?"

"He's shit-faced, sir."

John shook his head. Some things never changed. "I didn't know you offered a full beverage service."

"Seems he brought his own. Bourbon, I believe."

Kyle was slumped in his seat, half-awake and mumbling.

"Hey," John said. "Welcome to London. Let's get out of here."

Kyle was five years younger than John but looked older. He had the kind of crinkled, patchy complexion you got from decades of smoking and drinking. He pointed at John as if surprised he was there and tried to rise but he was still belted in. John unbuckled him and helped him to his feet. Kyle was also a big man, a couple of inches taller than him with a mountain-man beard, but while John was in top shape, Kyle was not. His gut filled his flannel shirt and protruded over his belt and moving down the aisle, John saw his limp was more pronounced than he remembered.

He put his arm around Kyle's waist. "Watch the stairs. I got you."

"I don't need any help," Kyle said. Sticking his head out he inhaled the warm morning air. "This London?"

"It is."

"Long flight."

"Let's get you to a coffee pot, all right?"

"You sure I don't need a passport? I thought everybody needed a passport."

"They've made an exception."

Kyle clumsily managed the steps.

"Jack Daniels?" John asked.

"Wild Turkey. Hundred and one proof. The extra one makes all the difference. Why?"

"Why what?"

"Why'd they make an exception?"

"I've got a hotel lined up. You'll have a shower, a quart of coffee, some bacon and eggs, and then I'll tell you why."

Mrs. Jones had held nothing back from her breakfast fare. Trevor could hardly get up from the table after gorging himself on salt cod, johnnycakes, fried plantains, and pepper sauce.

"There's more," she said, poking her head in from the kitchen.

"I'm stuffed, mum," he said.

"But look how thin you've got," she complained.

"Leave him alone," his father said. "He's fine." The man had baggy eyelids and a face lined with worry. He'd barely touched his own food.

They'd come to Brixton Hill in the Jamaican diaspora in the nineteen forties. This had been Trevor's grandfather's house before it was his father's. As an only child it would be his one day if he chose to keep it. The absolute familiarity of the place was a balm to Trevor's troubled soul. He had his own flat in Dartford, close to the MAAC, but as soon as he delivered Arabel and the kids to Edinburgh, he returned to London on an MI5 jet and drove to Brixton instead. He owed his parents a visit.

He was used to worrying them and they were used to being worried. There were the tours of duty in Afghanistan and the nights on street patrol as a police officer. He'd always had some way of reassuring and calming them down and he'd been good at keeping them in the loop by phone and email. But this past month had been different. He'd only said he was going away and wouldn't be able to communicate. He had told them it was classified and they had no choice but to accept that stoically. When he appeared at the door the previous afternoon, gaunt and grimy, his mother cried in happiness and in alarm, drew him a bath and started cooking.

The TV was on in the corner, the volume turned low. The BBC was reporting on the ongoing security situation at Leatherhead. A reporter on the outskirts of the town was saying that a no-fly zone had been imposed overnight there and at Sevenoaks, Upminster, and Dartford. Police and government sources were still not providing substantive information but Downing Street had just put out a statement that the prime minister would address the nation at noon and then proceed to the House of Commons to appear before Parliament.

"They're saying it's something to do with your MAAC," his father finally said.

"Are they?" Trevor replied.

"You probably can't say," his father said.

"I wish I could. Can I use your phone?" Trevor asked. "My mobile's at my flat."

"You don't have to ask," his father said.

"It's a number in Scotland."

"You can call the moon if you like," his mother said. "Who's in Scotland?"

"A woman."

"Does the woman have a name?" she asked.

"Arabel."

"Where'd you meet her?"

"Her sister works at the lab."

"No more questions, mother," his father said. "Let the boy call his lady."

Arabel's father answered the phone at his Edinburgh house and passed it to his daughter. Trevor could hear Sam and Bess playing in the background.

"They sound like they're doing all right," he told her.

"They're children. They bounce back."

"You bouncing?"

"Not exactly." She sounded tired.

"Know what you mean," he said.

"How about you?" she asked. "Did you sleep?"

"Like a log. My mum's spoiling me like she always does. It helps. How's Emily? I haven't talked to her today. You?"

"She rang earlier. She's back at it already, Skyping with scientists in Europe and the States. I don't know how she does it."

"Force of nature. I'm missing you, you know."

"I know," she said. "I wish you weren't going back."

"Did Emily tell you?"

"Yeah."

"I was calling to tell you myself."

"Do you have to go?"

"Don't have to. Need to. We've got a shitstorm in London. John and Emily are going to try and sort it out so I'm going too."

"Is there nothing I can say to change your mind?"

"You can say you love me. I'd like to hear that but it won't change my mind."

"I love you."

Ben unlocked the door of his mews house in Kensington and paused in the hall. He had the sense he was a stranger. In the past two months he had slept there no more than half the time and those nights had been fraught with marital extremes of temperature—coolness at best, hot anger at worst. At first his wife had suspected an affair but when he'd convinced her it was only the pressure of a very big case, somehow that made it more hurtful. Surely, his wife had argued, if his job was threatening to destroy their family then it was incumbent on him to seek reassignment or to walk away. With his family and political connections she argued he could land a good job in the city, but Ben would not engage in a discussion. The one thing she had not done was ask about the case. As an intelligence officer's wife, she was too well-programmed to ask. And what would he have told her if he'd decided to be truthful? That I have become the nation's Heller catcher? That I find them and send them back to Hell? That would have gone down well.

He heard the triplets playing upstairs. The TV was on in the den and that's where he found her having her morning coffee.

"Hello," he said.

She hardly looked up. "Here for a change of clothes?"

"Something like that. I want you to take the girls to my parent's house in the country."

"Why?"

"You're watching the news. I don't think it's safe in London."

She came to a quick boil. "Yes I'm watching the news and they're not saying anything! Is this your bloody huge case, Ben? Well is it?"

He put his bag down. "Yes."

"Why aren't they saying what it is? Is it terrorism? Is it the zombie apocalypse? Why aren't they saying anything?"

"The PM will be speaking at noon."

"So my husband, my knight in shining armor, can't tell me what's happening a few hours in advance."

"You know I can't. After his speech the traffic will be awful. I'd like you to get a head start out of town."

"You know what, Ben, you want to treat me like every other Londoner, then I'll just have to sit in traffic like every other Londoner. Go away. If this mess has gotten so bloody awful then you're obviously as bad an agent as you are a father."

John checked Kyle into his hotel in central London and sat outside the bathroom while his brother showered, feeding pods into the coffee machine. It was clear it was going to take more than a shower and coffee. Kyle needed sleep so John took a taxi over to the Royal London Hospital to satisfy a promise to Emily to have his old stab wound checked. While he waited for his surgeon to come out of the OR he rang Ben.

John heard children in the background and asked, "Where are you?"

"Home for a bit. Returning to the office shortly. Where are you?"

"At the hospital getting checked out."

"Did your brother arrive?"

"Picked him up at the airport. He's having a rest."

"Have you told him what you want him to do?"

"Not yet. What's happening at the hot zones?"

"Drones are detecting a steadily increasing ingress of Hellers. It's not a flood yet but it's worrisome."

"It'll get to flood stage but it's going to take a while," John said. "Word of mouth over there is literally word of mouth. They can't do flash mobs."

"At least that gives us time to get your plan into effect. Can you get to Thames House by two?"

"I'll be there."

His surgeon arrived. He poked around and checked John's wound, declaring that at one month post-op he was healing well and was free of infection. The surgeon clucked like a hen when John told him he'd had a doctor friend remove the stitches. He scolded, "Why didn't you come here for your appointment?"

"I was out of town."

John returned to the hotel just before noon and Kyle was still snoring away. He ordered a couple of hamburger platters from room service and turned on the TV.

"Kyle. Wake up."

He received a foggy reply and some choice curses.

"Come on. You need to see this. You're going to hear why I sent for you."

"From who?"

"The prime minister."

"Of England?"

"Wake up, bro. Yes! You're in England. His name's Peter Lester. You're going to meet him today or tomorrow."

Kyle's eyes blinked open. He propped himself up on an elbow. "I'm going to meet the prime minister?"

"Yeah."

"Fuck. You got any aspirin?"

"I put a bottle in the bathroom."

Kyle returned and sat on the edge of the bed in his boxers, his beer belly on full display.

Peter Lester appeared from the iconic black door of 10 Downing Street, stood at a lectern and looked solemnly into the camera. Behind him, off to one side, stood the Archbishop of Canterbury, his hands tightly clasped at his waist.

"I speak to you today about an unprecedented crisis," Lester began. "While it is an international crisis, it is affecting Great Britain most directly and London and the Home Counties most specifically. The Massive Anglo-American Collider in Dartford, a source of great national pride, has become an instrument of worry. For the past two months the supercollider has been operating at very high collision energies, levels that were not explicitly authorized. There will be ample time in the future to assign blame and as prime minister I am prepared to accept oversight failures on behalf of the government. But this is not a time for politics. It is a time for concern and a time for action. As a result of a confluence of events the collider has opened up a channel into what has been described to me by scientific experts, as another dimensional state, another universe, perhaps. That universe includes a place much like our Earth but with important and disturbing differences. It seems that it is populated by people from our dimension, our world, who are deceased, people who have done great evil during their lives. These people see it as a place of eternal punishment. They see it as Hell. We have knowledge of this dimension because, I can now confirm, we have had several people, including security and scientific personnel from the collider site in Dartford, who have been there and have returned."

"Is this for real?" Kyle asked.

"Afraid so," John said.

"He's talking about you, isn't he?"

"Yep."

Lester had always been a cool customer in front of an audience but his throat sounded dry and he was blinking excessively. He took a sip of water before continuing. "Clearly this development will alter the way all of us look at our place in the cosmos. It will cause some of us to alter the way we think about religion, divine intervention, the consequences of evil. The Archbishop of Canterbury will say a few words on this when I'm done. We will have ample time in the future to debate all the implications. However, for the present we must focus on the safety and security of people living and working in the greater London area. There are presently four geographic areas of concern. They are the towns of Dartford, Leatherhead, Sevenoaks, and Upminster. All these towns lie near the M25 and the collider's tunnels that ring London in a giant oval. We have established a security cordon of police and military around these towns and have been evacuating members of the public. Unfortunately, there has been an influx of residents from this other dimension and some of them appear to be violent criminals who regrettably have caused casualties. We are continuing to evaluate how best to evacuate trapped citizens. For the moment, for those people who are in Dartford, Leatherhead, Sevenoaks or Dartford, we urge you to shelter in place and affix a piece of white paper or cloth to your front door or place of work so security personnel can find you. If you feel it is not safe to shelter in place and you choose to make your way to a security cordon, carry a white cloth when you approach so that you may be recognized as a citizen. Appearing below me on your screens is a special hotline number to call to advise the authorities of your present situation. Presently there is no reason to evacuate other areas of greater London but we will be closely monitoring the situation. Rest assured that the best scientists in Britain and elsewhere are working on finding a way to permanently close the points of connection between our two dimensions."

John switched off the TV.

"He was still talking," Kyle said.

"That's the meat of it. I'll tell you what he isn't going to say."

Kyle found his jeans and pulled a clean shirt out of his bag. "Go on," he said. "You've got my attention."

"This is a grade-one cluster-fuck," John said. "I've been over there twice and it makes the worse shitholes in the world seem like the lap of luxury. It's got all the world's evildoers and major assholes from the beginning of history to the present, all glommed together in medieval kinds of villages, towns, and cities. Geographically it's pretty much identical to the Earth but that's the beginning and the ending of the similarities. Once you die and go there, you're there forever. You can suffer but you can't die. There's way more men than women which isn't surprising since we all know that testosterone is the root of all evil. The only good thing about it is there aren't any children. They've got plants and animals so there's some agriculture and a lot of hunting. The worst of them are called rovers which are basically gangs of rapists and cannibals and there's evidence that some of them have crossed to Earth. There's no way out which is why the Hellers are going to be flocking to the hot zone connections that've formed between the two worlds. Each country is ruled by a feudal kind of ruler and a bunch of nobles who treat their people like slaves. They're constantly at war with each other, launching attacks and land grabs."

Kyle interrupted him. "You're saying all of this with a completely straight face."

"Because it's true. This afternoon you'll be meeting other people who went over with me. They'll tell you the same thing."

"And Satan's cruising around, zapping people with fireballs?"

"No Satan, sorry."

"And who decides whether someone's going to be taking the down elevator to Hell?"

"Wish I knew. When the dust settles maybe I'll pick up a Bible and have a read."

"Okay, I'll make the assumption you haven't gone completely fucking crazy and play along."

He made a move to the mini-bar but John wouldn't let him touch anything harder than a soda.

Kyle cracked a can of Coke and said, "So I assume, since you used the word medieval, that these dudes don't have jet planes and nukes to lob at each other."

"We're talking swords and cannon, flintlock pistols and rifles. They've got bits and pieces of turn-of-nineteenth century stuff like the telegraph and a few steam cars but the people who wind up there aren't exactly the engineers and designers and creative types of the world. So they're mired in old tech."

Kyle pulled the curtains to let the light in. He squinted at the heavy traffic clogging the streets and listened to the sirens of emergency vehicles, some near, others far.

"So what's this have to do with me?"

"I'm going back there real soon with some badasses to try and stop Hellers from crossing over while the scientists figure out how to fix this. I want you to come along."

"Why?"

"Because I don't know anyone else who can do what you can do."

"You don't know anyone who can get drunk and make women hate them?"

John laughed. "I know lots of guys who can do that, me included. I mean the other stuff you do."

"Oh, that stuff. Well shit."

10

"Ben Wellington, Trevor Jones, meet my brother, Kyle."

"It's good of you to come so quickly, Kyle," Ben said, showing them to his seating area.

They were on a high floor in Thames House with a river view. They could see the traffic jammed up on Southwark and London Bridges.

"It's gridlock," John said. "We ditched our taxi and walked."

"I had to walk too, from Brixton," Trevor said.

Ben shook his head. "It appears people didn't take the PM's keep calm and carry on message to heart. They're getting out of Dodge with some urgency."

"Can't blame them," John said.

"My parents won't budge," Trevor said. "I gave up trying."

"Did you hurt your leg, Kyle?" Ben asked.

"The limp's old as the hills," Kyle said. "Car crash from my wild and crazy days."

Ben poured coffees all around. "I see. Is Emily going to be joining us?"

"She begged off," John said. "She's tied up on conference calls with the CERN people and with her experts. She'll meet Kyle tonight at my place in Dartford."

"Isn't that a bit too close for comfort to the hot zone?" Trevor asked.

"It's four miles from the lab," John said. "We'll be okay for now. How we're going to get there's another matter. The M25's going to be a parking lot."

"I'll arrange for the helicopter to drop you off on the way back from Herefordshire," Ben said.

"Before we start," John said, "Kyle needs to hear from Trevor. I spent so much time punking him when we were growing up he doesn't trust a thing I say."

"It's a fact. He's always been a lying son-of-a-bitch," Kyle said, without humor, "but I'm kind of thinking that this is too weird not to be true."

"I can guarantee you it's true," Trevor said. "I've only been there the one time but I'll tell what I saw and what I know."

When Trevor was done, Kyle shrugged and said he was satisfied.

"Does that mean you're in?" Trevor asked.

"I still need to think on it."

"Understandable," Ben said. "What do you say we make our way to the helipad? Don't want to keep the lads waiting."

The Officer Commander, Major Gus Parker-Burns, greeted the occupants of the MI5 helicopter on its touchdown at Credenhill, Herefordshire.

"Gentlemen, welcome to 22 SAS Regiment," he said. "Come with me."

Inside a low, drab operational center, Parker-Burns showed them to a conference room and offered a pot of over-stewed coffee. He was about John's age although smaller, clean-shaven and fit, turned out in a camo uniform and a sand-colored beret with the regimental badge, the downward-pointed Excalibur wreathed in flames. He had a folder and when everyone was seated he opened it and referred to some briefing documents.

"Major Camp," he started.

"Retired," John said.

A thin smile crossed his face. "Duly noted. Happy to host a former Green Beret officer at Credenhill. I've reviewed your particulars and I'm impressed with your capabilities."

"Thank you, Major," John said.

"And Sergeant Jones. Royal Dragoon Guards. Excellent service record. Good innings with the Metropolitan Police. Welcome to you too. Our commander was briefed by the prime minister this morning and he has, in turn, briefed me as to the nature of our, shall we say, unusual operation. I take it that Mr. Wellington has not been tipped for the raiding party?"

"No, I'll be dealing with the London situation," Ben said. "I probably wouldn't be much good over there anyway."

"And this gentleman?" Parker-Burns said, looking at Kyle.

"He's my brother," John said. "We're still working on him. I'm hoping he'll go."

"Do you have a military background?" the major asked.

"None whatsoever," Kyle said, avoiding eye contact.

"He's got some skills which I consider mission critical," John said.

"I see," the major said with a forced politeness. "All will be revealed, I suppose. Now let me be frank. I'm a soldier and I will follow the orders that have been given me by my superior officer. But I'll tell you what I told my commander. A Squadron is a national treasure, sixty of the finest men who ever wore her majesty's uniform. I urged him to deploy A Squadron to the London hot spots where we may engage and neutralize these aliens using the full tactical resources at our disposal. To send these men into terra incognita with no weapons or materials strikes me as ridiculously foolhardy. Furthermore, placing them under the operational control of Major Camp—sorry, former Major Camp—is not acceptable."

"You're welcome to come along and command them," John said with a smile.

"But I was told that I would have to report to you," Parker-Burns said.

"I've been there twice," John said. "I know the lay of the land."

"Still …" the major said.

John jumped in. "Seems to me the bigger issue is where to engage the enemy: here or over there. The Hellers are going to keep on coming if they're not stopped. They'll flood the zones. You'd think that might be something we could control with superior fire power if it weren't for the fact that our experts think the zones are going to be unstable. They're going to expand, and that expansion is likely to be unpredictable, eventually swallowing up a containment force. With all the uncertainties, we're still going to be better off dealing with the threat over there."

"And who better to deal with unconventional threats than the SAS?" Ben said.

"That's right," John said. "And who better to improvise behind enemy lines?"

Parker-Burns raised his hands in mock surrender. "You don't have to convince me of our capabilities. If we get a final order to go, we will go, and we will perform our duties superbly."

John smiled broadly. "Imagine how pissed off you would've been if I got my first choice for the mission, the Navy Seals."

The room got so quiet a pin drop would have sounded like a cymbal clash. The major's head looked like it was going to explode.

"Just kidding," John said, breaking into a laugh.

Parker-Burns exhaled and cracked up. "Thank God for that," he said. "Come on, let me introduce you to A Squadron."

The sixty men of A Squadron mustered for inspection inside a cavernous helicopter hangar. There were four troops of fifteen soldiers designated A through D, each commanded by a captain. John liked their special-ops looks. Most chose to wear their hair on the long side and many had full beards. But most importantly they had swagger. For this mission to succeed they'd need to be tough, cocky sons-of-bitches.

Parker-Burns put the men at ease and said, "Gentlemen, you have had a preliminary briefing on the unfolding security threat in London and you were told to be on stand-by in case her majesty's government called on you to be part of the response. Tonight I can confirm that A Squadron will indeed be called upon to render your unique and efficacious services. Your mission will be quite unlike any you have ever undertaken, one that will present singular challenges and will be fraught with unexpected dangers. I am assured that there was only one group within the military the government considered for this mission and that was this squadron. Captains Marsh, Yates, Greene, and Gatti will be meeting with these gentlemen by my side who are knowledgeable about the mission. The captains will, in turn, brief you tonight at twenty hundred hours. That is all."

Each of the four troop captains was in his thirties. They flopped into their chairs in the officer's room and stared suspiciously at their visitors. Unlike their men, they were clean-shaven with traditional military cuts except for Marsh who was bald as a cue ball. Their body language spoke volumes of their unhappiness about being briefed by civilians and when John opened his mouth, they seemed especially put off getting marching orders from an American.

"Seriously," Marsh said, running his hand over his scalp. "A civilian and a Yank? What kind of bollocks is this?"

John was about to reply when Ben said, "I don't wish to speak for Mr. Camp but I think you'll find you speak the same language. He was fairly recently a major in the Green Berets."

Marsh sneered at that. "Well I'm glad to hear your cap was green not pink, sunshine."

Kyle bristled and said, "Hey, watch it, buddy."

"Another American," Marsh said, "and a limping one at that. Were you the pink beret, then?"

Captain Yates, a broad-shouldered black man said, "Put a cork in it Alex. Let me apologize for my colleague. Once you get to know him you'll realize he really is an ass-wipe."

Captain Gatti was dark and swarthy with a thin moustache. "Yeah, go on," he said. "Don't mind Alex. He gets that way with blokes with hair on their heads."

"Not to worry," John said with a knowing smile. "I would've been rip-shit if some limey bastard showed up in my house to tell me how a mission was going to go down. I'm sorry about that but after you hear what I've got to say, you'll understand that there aren't any active-duty British soldiers who could do this briefing. Trevor Jones and I are it. Trevor's also ex-military. He was a sergeant with the Royal Dragoon Guards with multiple tours in Afghanistan."

Captain Greene, the youngest looking of the officers with golden-boy good looks, fine, closely cropped blonde hair and a cleft chin said, "And you?"

Kyle shook his head. "Never enlisted. Baldy here with his eagle eye spotted my limp. I'm John's brother and I'm still not a hundred percent sure why I'm here."

"He's here because he's got specialized skills," John said.

"Fair enough," Greene said, looking at Ben. "What's your story?"

Ben had answered for John and now John returned the favor. "This fellow's the only one in the room whose ass you ought to be kissing. One of these days, if you survive this mission, you may be knocking on his door for a job. Mr. Wellington's right near the top of the heap at MI5."

"All right, duly impressed by the lot of you," Marsh said sarcastically. "Suppose you go ahead and tell us about these singular challenges and unexpected dangers our CO alluded to."

"I presume this has everything to do with the badness in London," Yates said.

"It does," Ben said. "Mr. Camp will do the honors."

"Okay, guys," John said. "Listen up and prepare to be amazed."

"Nice place," Kyle said, dropping his bag onto the floor in John's hall. The helicopter had put down a half mile away on a dark school football pitch and they had walked through the largely deserted streets of Dartford to get to the flat.

"I haven't been here much lately," John said. "Your bedroom's down that way. It's en suite."

"What's that mean?"

"It means you've got your own shitter."

John went to the fridge, got a couple of cold beers, and gave Kyle one. He watched as his brother finished it in several mighty gulps.

"Want another?" he asked him.

"For starts. Got anything stronger for later?"

"Depends."

"On what?"

"I need to know if you're in or out. If you're in I'll want you to wean off the hard stuff."

"Fuck you." Kyle got up from the sofa and helped himself to another can of beer.

"That's not an answer," John said.

"I think you and I've got some unfinished business to deal with first," Kyle said angrily.

"Oh yeah, what's that?"

"Fucking me over on the store, that's what."

John wasn't surprised. It was the elephant in the room and it had been a wedge between them from the day their father died. The old man's house and gun store, the only thing he possessed of any value. The two brothers grew up in that house. Their father had put them to work in the store as soon as they were tall enough to see over the counter. John had been a student athlete. He got into West Point and never looked back on Bend, Oregon. When Kyle hit high school a few years later he wanted to be a football star like his big brother, date cheerleaders, join the army too, maybe special forces, but a drunken car wreck ruined his leg and his life. He got stuck in Bend, stuck in the shop, and stuck in the house.

"Exactly how'd I fuck you over?" John asked. "It was dad's decision to leave me half of everything. Mom's dead. He had two sons. Splitting the pizza down the middle's the way he wanted it."

When the two of them argued the f-bombs always flew and Kyle unleashed a cluster bomb. "It's not a fucking pizza. It's my fucking house. It's my fucking job. It's my fucking life. You fuck off to Afghanistan and God knows where, you get medals and citations, you live the high life in England. You want to know what my life is? I'm still in Bend in and out of debt with a gimpy leg. And you own half that goddamn life. How do you think that makes me feel?"

John's response jammed up his mind. He wanted to tell Kyle it wasn't his fault he was a pathetic fuck-up, an excuse-ridden, alcoholic loser. He wanted to tell him that thank God at least one son made their mom and dad proud. He wanted to haul off and punch him in the mouth. But he made himself bottle it up. For the first time in his life he needed Kyle for something.

He got up, went over to his desk, and pulled out writing paper. Bent over he wrote out a paragraph, dated and signed it.

"Here," he said, handing it to Kyle. "When Emily gets here she can witness it. If dad's lawyer says it's crap I'll sign his version. You're right. It should be your house and business a hundred percent."

Kyle read it. His Adam's apple moved up and down each time he swallowed. He sniffed back some secretions and looked up to say, "I ..."

There was a key in the door and Emily came in. John was relieved to avoid whatever awkward version of gratitude he was about to hear.

"Emily, this is my brother Kyle. Kyle, Emily Loughty."

Kyle turned the paper upside down and stood up to greet her. After a friendly exchange she disappeared into John's bedroom to change clothes.

"She's amazing," Kyle said.

"Yes she is."

"She's a scientist?"

"A good one."

"If you'd said she was a model I'd have believed you."

"She's got it all," John agreed. "I'm pretty fucking lucky."

"You always were."

Kyle polished off his second beer and started on his third. Emily came out in jeans and a t-shirt, barefooted.

"Have you eaten?" she asked.

"We should do take out," John said.

"Little chance of that," she said. "Dartford's a ghost town."

"How'd you get here?" John asked.

"A helicopter materialized in a courtyard at the Ministry of Defense. How'd you do it? All I saw were red tail lights for miles on the motorway."

"Same as you, thanks to Ben."

She found some frozen entrees and put them up.

"So Kyle, I understand the US Air Force flew you in?" Emily said.

"It was pretty sweet. I had the whole plane to myself."

"What do you think about this mess we're in?"

Kyle put his beer down, using John's attestation as a place mat. "I think we're being tested," he said. "It's our hour of trial. 'Since you have kept my command to endure patiently, I will also keep you from the hour of trial that is going to come on the whole world to test those who live on the Earth.' Revelations 3:10."

"Since when are you a Bible quoter?" John asked.

"You don't know me anymore," Kyle said, shaking his head. "An ex-girlfriend got me into it. She's gone, the Bible stayed."

Emily said, "Well, biblical or not, I agree we are being tested. How we respond in the next hours, days, and weeks will affect our future profoundly."

"Anything new on your end?" John asked.

"I've talked to every expert who was on Leroy Bitterman's panel and a handful of others. No one's got a solution because there really aren't any strangelet experts out there. Paul Loomis was the only one; *is* the only one. My colleagues at the LHC in Geneva are working on ways to get control of the computer systems at MAAC remotely to fire up the collider if and when a fix materializes. We can't risk putting people into the Dartford hot zone."

Kyle said, "I'm not the smartest guy but I'm not a dimwit either. But I've got to tell you I didn't understand any of that."

She apologized and gave him a laymen's version. With John's nod, she also told him about their encounters with Paul Loomis.

"That's why you're going again?" Kyle asked Emily.

John answered. "She's going even though I don't want her to."

"We've got to move fast," she said.

The microwave beeped and John fetched the food. "I've got a chicken curry, a mac and cheese, and a beef lasagna."

"Mac and cheese, please," Emily said.

"I never had curry," Kyle said.

John put the lasagna in front of him. Without asking, Kyle said grace.

They listened in awkward silence.

Emily peeled off the film of her entrée and sunk her fork into the yellow goo. Before her ordeal she wouldn't touch this kind of processed food but now she savored it as if it had come from a Michelin-starred restaurant.

"On the flight from London I got briefed by the government's chief scientific advisor that the hot zones have expanded in Upminster and Leatherhead," she said. "We've lost several more security personnel at both locations and God knows how many residents who were advised to shelter in place."

"Can I ask a stupid question?" Kyle said. "John told me that before, these passageways or whatever opened then closed each time the collider ran."

"That's right," Emily said. "The points of connectivity were transitory. They were wholly dependent on new energy production from the sub-atomic particle collisions."

"But now you're saying that the connections are permanent."

"Well, hopefully not permanent," she said, "but they're persistent and expanding. We're calling the affected areas hot zones."

"Well, okay, here's my question. If you've got someone from either side caught up in this hot zone and they zip on through from one world to another, how come they don't zip right back?"

"It's not a stupid question. It's an important one. I don't have a good answer but there seems to be some polarity at play. What I mean is, there may be some quantum effects caused by the interaction of strangelets and gravitons that …"

John interrupted. "Emily, I'm crazy about you but you've got two dumb shits from Bend, Oregon here."

"I'm sorry. I've been talking to physicists all day. Think of the points of connection as one-way tubes. You go through but you can't travel back on the same tube. It's as if there's a one-way valve that lets you travel in only one direction. That must explain why people aren't shuttling back the moment they arrive in the other dimension."

John put his fork down. "But in Leatherhead we saw Hellers reappear after they were shot by the commandos," John said. "How do you account for that?"

"All this is guesswork based on limited observation. It may be that you reset your polarity by leaving the hot zone. If you then re-enter you can cross back. I wish I knew more. How was your meeting with the SAS?"

"They're pros," John said. "Of course they're apoplectic they'll be reporting to me but they'll be effective, especially if I can get Kyle on board."

"Are you on board?" Emily asked him.

Kyle pushed his chair back and went to the coffee table. He picked up John's handwritten statement and ripped it into several pieces.

"It's the thought that counts, bro," he said. "I'm in. To be honest, I've been spending the last few hours thinking about what you want done and how I could pull it off. I'll need a workshop in the morning."

"Already have one lined up," John said, standing up. He spread his arms. "Come over here."

While the two big men hugged, Emily's cheeks streaked with tears.

Later, holding her close to him in bed, John asked her what she thought of Kyle.

"If it weren't for the family resemblance I wouldn't have known you were brothers. He's very different."

"How?"

"Stating the obvious, he's rough around the edges where you, my dear, are a polished stone. He lacks self-confidence, you are brimming with it to the point of arrogance—and I say that with love. He's suffered from living in the shadow of his accomplished big brother. It's rather sad."

He pulled his arm from around her shoulder and laced both hands around his neck. Staring at the ceiling he said, "Yeah, it makes me sad too. I could've done more to help him along."

She put a hand on his chest and rubbed it. "You're giving him a chance to do something really important. It has the potential to meaningfully change his life for the better."

John turned his head to kiss her. "If it doesn't get him killed."

11

It had been five days. Five excruciatingly slow days.

John and Emily had been pushing to go in three days, four maximum, but Kyle's work was the rate-limiting step. He had been methodical and at first wouldn't accept help, arguing that training someone would just slow him down. He had holed up in a workshop set up for him at Holland & Holland gunsmiths in London where he toiled in isolation until, bowing to reality, he had begun delegating to eager Holland & Holland craftsmen. Due to the sheer volume of work Kyle had put in eighteen-hour days. He gave up bourbon but downed a few beers before collapsing on his workroom cot every night.

After the first day John stopped by to check his progress and had found him hunched over a workbench.

"How's it going?" John had asked.

"It's going."

"Is it doable?"

"My part's doable. We've got to figure out the primers."

"What about them?" John had asked.

"The chemicals, bro. Can't make boom-boom without the primers."

"Shit," John had said. "I didn't think about that."

"Neither did I until today."

"What do we need?" John had asked.

"They got any quicksilver over there?"

On the way to Credenhill John had called Malcolm Gough who was on permanent babysitting duty in Hampshire.

"How's Henry getting on?"

"I think he's rather enjoying himself," Gough had said. "He likes the food and the wine a great deal and thinks the bathtubs and toilets are smashing. Bit of a problem last night when he demanded a wench to be delivered to his bed. Suffice it to say, the MI5 minders were not helpful. Had to dip into my well as a father of young children. I distracted him with television."

"I need you to ask him a question for me. Ask him if he has any quicksilver in Hampton Court or any other London palace."

"Quicksilver? As in mercury?"

"As in mercury."

When Gough rang him back he had told John, "Alas, no. He seemed dimly aware of the substance but has never possessed it. He suggested that one might perhaps find some in Iberia."

John's next call had been to Kyle.

"No joy," he had said.

"Next best thing's something called lead styphnate."

"How do we get it?"

"They got lead over there?"

"Plenty."

"We'd still need a chemist."

"Why?"

"I looked it up. You've got to make it with nitric acid which I assume means you'd need to make nitric acid too. Plus maybe some other stuff."

"That's fucked up," John had said. "On top of everything we need to find a chemist with a death wish?"

John had gotten MI5 involved with the chemist problem while he and Trevor concentrated on training the SAS teams. There was no way to do special-ops-grade preparation for this kind of mission. John knew that but Major Parker-Burns was decidedly uneasy that A Squadron had no objectives to drill against, no mock-ups of compounds, no aerial photos or drone footage to study, no psychological profiles of the enemy to learn. As far as John was concerned, the key was going to be orienteering, finding the hot zones in a world that lacked the landmarks of modern Earth. They had found a good topographical map of Greater London with accurate elevations, positions of rivers, tributaries, ponds, and lakes. Although there were bound to be some differences owing to modern man-made alterations in terrain, John had thought it would be as good a tool as they could get. But how to get the maps over to the other side? John knew from his experience carrying books that untreated paper printed with natural vegetable inks successfully made it across. Ben had been prepared to get the same printing company to do the job but Parker-Burns had come up with a better idea. Silk. During the Second World War the allies produced millions of silk maps of Europe and Asia for pilots to carry and use to find escape routes if shot down. Paper burned and ripped and got soggy and useless. Silk was far better and it was a natural fiber bound to make the transfer. A textile manufacturer in Leeds was identified and MI5 made it happen quickly.

The training John and Trevor introduced to the SAS was in the use of unconventional weapons. The commandos were already expert in hand-to-hand combat and knife-work but none of them had used a sword and only a few had done archery. None of them knew how to load and shoot a black-powder gun or a medieval cannon. Half of them had ridden horses before but fewer than one in ten were accomplished horsemen.

As they trained the men at Credenhill, they had wished Brian Kilmeade were there. Nobody was better at handling medieval weapons but Brian was far away in the Europa of Hell, hopefully enduring the harsh existence he had chosen. There hadn't been time to line up a Brian substitute so John and Trevor had conducted weapons drills in the squadron's gymnasium with sixty trash-talking commandos, irreverently skeptical of the exercises. An afternoon at an equestrian centre had at a minimum gotten the inexperienced men more comfortable around horses.

Then the blow-up. The commander of the SAS had informed Major Parker-Burns that he would not be accompanying A Squadron on the mission.

"This is intolerable," the major had fumed at John. "I was told that because of the inability to effect a centralized command and control it would be better for me to stay behind and reconstitute the squadron should my men not return."

"I can see their point," John had said. "Your captains will have autonomous control of their groups. As soon as we get supplied we're dispersing. It's not as if they'll be reporting to me. There won't be any way of communicating with them. They'll be operating on their own. If you went you'd have to pick which of the groups to accompany which, I imagine, would undercut one of your captains."

"I suppose so, but up until the point of dispersal, they'll have to report to someone. Otherwise it would be chaotic."

John had suppressed a smile at the smallness of his thinking. "Well, I guess it will have to be me. I'm sure your men will let us know what they think of that."

"They're excellent soldiers," Parker-Burns had said. "They will complain vocally amongst themselves but they will follow their orders to the letter."

Three days prior to departure John had found himself on an army helicopter for a flight to Oxford. There he had met with Professor Ted Nightingale at his home near the university campus. Nightingale had appeared frail and had a sickly color to his skin that John later learned was jaundice from his liver cancer. Photos on the professor's piano had revealed a recently vigorous sixty-year-old, hiking in the Yorkshire Dales and scuba diving in the Caribbean. After the first minute of watching the infirm man slowly making him tea, John had wanted to get back in the chopper and head back to London. But the man had quickly won him over with the strength of his spirit.

"Look, Mr. Camp," he had said, pouring the tea in his sitting room. "I, like all of my fellow countrymen, am appalled and horrified by the invasion of London by this unspeakable enemy. I am, or I was, an atheist, but the notion of a real Hell does open up the possibility of a real Heaven, or at least the intervention of an overarching moral power who punishes and rewards. My doctors have given me perhaps six more months to live. That is my fate and I accept it. I have no wife and no children to dissuade me. When I was approached about your needs I thought, 'Ted, you are the perfect person for this job. You are a professor of inorganic chemistry. You have a joint appointment in the faculty of history. You are steeped in the history of chemistry. If your body can bear the rigors, you must do this.'"

"Can it?" John had asked. "Do you have the stamina for it?"

"How challenging will it be?"

John pointed to the photos. "Picture the hardest day of hiking you ever did, then string a bunch of those days together. We'd have you surrounded and supported by the fittest men on the planet but it'll be medieval."

Nightingale's smile had brightened the room and had made him seem younger and healthier. "Medieval. I have pored over so many alchemical and chemical texts from the past that I've often wished I could be a fly on the wall, watching the history of the chemical sciences unfold. It would be a capstone to my career to join your expedition and to help my fellow man defeat this horrible assault. I believe I can withstand the challenges."

"I believe you can too," John had said. "By the way, you don't have any prosthetic devices implanted in your body, do you?"

"None whatsoever."

"How about dental fillings, caps, crowns, et cetera?"

"Plenty of those."

"We'll need to get you to a dentist tomorrow."

Two days prior to departure John and Trevor had been summoned to a meeting with Jeremy Slaine at the secretary of state for defense's Whitehall office. Slaine had pushed his mop of white hair from his eyes and had slumped dog-tired on a sofa.

"Thank you for coming to see me," he had said. "I know how busy you are."

"I'm sure you are too, sir," John had replied. "How are your containment efforts going?"

"Not well, I'm afraid," he said, removing his glasses and rubbing his blood-shot eyes. "We've lost troops to expanding hot zones and before perimeters could be re-established Hellers have certainly made it out of the containment areas. We've been able to track some of them by drone but, I have to say, I've been hesitant to give kill orders. A drone can't distinguish between a Heller and a fleeing civilian. There are still large numbers of civilians who remain inside the containment areas. They call our emergency numbers pleading for help. It's heartbreaking. You've no doubt seen them, but we've been making dynamic maps of where the calls are coming from. It's clear that even inside a hot zone there are shifting islands of territory where transfer between the dimensions is not occurring."

"We've seen the maps," John had said.

"How close are you to expanding the evacuation orders?" Trevor had asked.

"Bloody close. It's a matter of logistics and frankly of pride. Even during the London blitz in the Second World War we only evacuated children. We'll be discussing it again at the Cobra meeting this afternoon. But that's not why I asked you to stop by. It's about my son."

"I'm sure it's an awful situation for you," John had said.

"It is, of course. Especially for my wife who has required medical care for her anxiety. I've been rung by the parents of the other boys from the school, all of them distraught and looking for help. Look, I'm well aware that other children residing in the hot zones have been caught up in this too but I'm asking on behalf of all the Belmeade parents whether you think you'll be able to help these boys."

When neither John or Trevor answered right away, Slaine had said, "I want to make it clear that this is not an official government request. I know full well that the primary mission is to shut off the spigot of Hellers from the other side and to extract information from that Loomis fellow. But if there's a way …"

John had spoken for both of them when he said, "Those boys could still be close to the Sevenoaks hot zone. Alternatively they could have gone off on their own or been taken away from there. There's no way of knowing."

"I understand that some of you will be operating near the Sevenoaks zone," Slaine said.

"We will and we'll be sure to look for them and try to send them back through if we find them. You're right, it's not our primary mission but we're going to do whatever we can to repatriate these boys and any children we find."

Slaine put his glasses back on, rose, and extended a hand. "As a father, that's all I could ask for."

One day prior to departure John had visited the secluded country house in Hampshire to ask a favor of King Henry. When he arrived, Henry had been in the bath for over an hour and from the hall John had heard the monarch loudly singing madrigals.

"He's in fine form," John had said.

"You've no idea," Gough had replied.

"How're you holding up?"

"Me? Despite being away from my family, I'm fine, more than fine. Being able to question him systematically is a boon to historical research. It's fundamentally altering our view of the Tudor period. For a man of over five hundred years, his memory is quite keen."

"Should we expect a new edition of your biography sometime in the future?"

"Only if the pope is Catholic," Gough had replied.

"How long's he likely to be? I'm on a tight schedule."

"No telling, really. Announcing you won't help. He famously kept people waiting at court and he's no different now. But I've got a trick up my sleeve. Hang on a minute."

When Gough had returned to say that the king was emerging from his bath John asked him how he'd done it.

"I'm afraid I've created a bit of a monster. The other day I casually mentioned that there were many TV shows and movies about his life and he demanded to see one. The MI5 research department was very helpful and they had the 1970 mini-series sent over, *The Six Wives of Henry VIII*. Well, he devoured that, binge-watched it, as they say and now he's started the HBO series, the one with Jonathan Rhys Meyers. He thinks he's a splendid Henry. I told him the next episode was ready. He'll be out shortly."

Henry had emerged in a rather fluffy robe, his purplish, scarred legs poking out, to find John waiting in his bedroom.

"Why it is John Camp!" he had said. "Have you come to watch this actor portray my person? It is quite marvelous though I have told Scholar Gough that the lack of verisimilitude is legion. As example of this, I can assure you that Anne Boleyn was not near so fetching."

John had explained what he needed and had to goad a reluctant Henry into cooperating. He had brought supplies with him: special paper, ink, and a quill pen and when Henry had written the letter and signed it he asked John a burning question.

"Tell me, Master Camp. How long do you intend to keep me within this gilded cage?"

"I don't know the answer. Do you want to go back?"

"Back to Hell," Henry had said, his voice trailing off in thought. "What man who possesses his faculties would want that? Yet, I know it was my fate to be sent there and it is my fate to return. When I am ready I will surely demand my release but I am not of this mind as of yet. I have work to do with Scholar Gough to correct errors of record regarding my reign and while I do so I would partake of your excellent food and drink and gaze upon your—what is it called again?"

"Television," Gough had said helpfully.

"Yes, that." The king had then summoned John closer with a crooked finger. "I did something to benefit you," he had whispered. "Now do something for me. Have them bring me women who resemble the actor who played Anne Boleyn, or even better, the actress herself."

John had laughed. "No promises but I'll see what I can do."

"In all seriousness, I must return to my realm before long. You have a monarch, as gracious a queen as any country might possess. There can only be one ruler at a time. And I have tossed about in this wonderful and soft bed at the thought of my throne being usurped in my absence. Cromwell would have it. Suffolk would have it. The snakes will be a slithering, that you can be sure. You travel on the morrow?"

"In the morning," John had said.

"Tell them, one and all, that their king is well and will be returning. Tell them there will be fearsome wages to pay for the crime of treason and usurpation. Tell them that."

On the evening before the mission John had returned to his flat with a bag of take-away curry from one of the only restaurants in the Dartford area still open for business. Despite the logistical problems he had insisted on one last night of normalcy and he had gotten a ride from Credenhill on what he had come to call his heli-taxi. With the evacuation of Greater London in its early chaotic stages, helicopter travel was the only way to reliably travel provided the pilots didn't get too close to the hot zones. Heathrow and the other London airports had been closed. Rail, underground, and coach service were still on. Trains and government-chartered coaches were packed with evacuees heading to temporary resettlement centers in designated army bases around the country. Trevor had opted to return to Brixton to help his parents pack their belongings. With gawking onlookers shouting in anger he waved goodbye to them as his helicopter lifted off from nearby Brockwell Park to ferry them to Manchester to stay with relatives.

Over the course of the evening, Kyle and then Emily, had also joined John.

"All done?" John had asked Kyle.

"Done and packed. Gimme a shower beer, bro. I haven't washed in days."

"You know that ripe smell you've got going on?" John had said. "That's nothing to what's coming. By the way, you're going to be having curry tonight. I got a mild one for you."

When Emily had arrived she was greeted with a passionate embrace.

"Where's Kyle?" she had asked.

"In the shower. How'd your day go?"

"For what it's worth, CERN now has full, remote operational control of MAAC. They can sit in Geneva and safely run the collider. Hopefully, that will prove useful."

"Hopefully."

"All we need now is to find Paul Loomis and, not to overuse the word, hopefully, he'll really know what to do. Is that curry I smell?"

"It's not from our usual but hopefully it's all right."

She had smiled and said, "A good curry and one more night together in our wonderful bed. What else could a girl hope for?"

The day finally arrived. Early in the morning John, Emily, and Kyle were ferried by helicopter first to collect Trevor in Brixton and then to a rally point just south of the River Mole, a large park in Fetcham, a town adjacent to Leatherhead. The SAS helicopters had already landed and A Squadron was mustering. Ben had also arrived, shepherding a doddering Professor Nightingale who seemed to be the only one in the park sporting a smile.

All the travelers were wearing an approved wardrobe of one hundred percent natural fabrics, including wooden buttons. Army quartermasters and tailors had done the work for soldiers and civilians alike. Everyone had his dental work attended to in the preceding days. Their backpacks were canvas with leather straps, their boots leather with cotton stitching and natural rubber soles. The five critical backpacks, large, heavy, over-stuffed affairs, were allocated to John and the four group captains. Kyle had lobbied for one because, after all, they bore the fruits of his labor, but John had gently persuaded him that his bum knee made mobility hard enough without the extra weight. There had been considerable debate about weapons for the SAS troops. Everyone was aware their guns and knives wouldn't make it across but there was concern among SAS brass about adequately dealing with hostiles within the hot zone prior to transfer. John had argued that the men would have to make do without guns when they crossed so he wasn't too worried about getting to the transfer point but the army didn't want any unnecessary risks. There had been some discussion about carrying assault weapons into the hot zone but the notion of leaving a pile of rifles behind for Hellers to find inside Leatherhead hadn't been palatable. The final decision was to procure sixty biometric smart handguns keyed to the palm prints of the SAS men which, when left behind, would be useless to foraging Hellers or civilians.

As small drones circled overhead Emily introduced herself to Professor Nightingale.

"Ah, yes, I was told there'd be another scientist on the journey," he said.

"It was very brave of you to volunteer," she said.

"My days on this side of the grass are limited," he said. "A young person such as yourself, you're the brave one. Tell me, how awful is it over there?"

"I won't lie. It's pretty bad. There are some noble souls among the Hellers, men and women who did evil but, in my judgment, aren't truly evil, but most of the people you'll encounter are vile."

"I'm told a different set of natural laws is operative," he said.

"If you're able to keep your revulsion in check I think you might find some of it fascinating."

"Not many scientists there, eh?"

"Not many at all, I'm happy to say. There's one I need to find."

"Your Dr. Loomis."

"Yes," she said, "Paul."

John mingled with the troops. Captain Marsh, good to his reputation, objected to John inspecting his A Troop.

"My men are properly kitted out and ready and don't need you having a butchers, mate," he said.

"I'm sure they are," John said, moving to B Troop where he had a decidedly friendlier reception from Captain Yates. Yates had his men stand at ease while John chatted with them, admired their SAS shoulder patches with the Who Dares Wins mottos stitched onto their jackets with cotton thread, and had a look at one of the biometric pistols.

"They're in fine form," John told Yates. "If you'd like to let them lob in a question or two, I'm open to it."

"Yeah, why not?" Yates said. "Can't see the harm."

One of the men, a lance corporal named Jarvis, asked in a Geordie accent, "Will I really have to ride a horse? I hate the bloody creatures."

One of his mates answered, "We'll ride. You can muck out the stables for the rest of us."

John smiled, and clapped the soldier on the shoulder. "You never know, but if you have to, a fine specimen like you should do fine. Trevor Jones over there never rode a day in his life and wound up covering some serious territory on horseback when he went over."

Captain Gatti's C Troop and Captain Greene's D Troop got the same treatment and while John was talking to a knot of D troopers, Major Parker-Burns climbed onto the bonnet of his Husky and called A Squadron to formation.

"Men," he shouted when they were lined up, "you are embarking on a mission unlike any the SAS or indeed, any regiment within the British Army, has ever undertaken. I can hardly imagine the circumstances you will shortly encounter, the perils you will face, the challenges you will endure. While training for this mission has been bare-bones, A Squadron is the finest, best-trained, most nimble, and fearsome group of men in her majesty's service. And what is your mission? It is nothing short of saving this great nation from an existential threat as great as any which has faced Britain. When you return, not if, but when, you will have entered into the annals of the SAS and your accomplishments will be celebrated until the end of time. I only wish I had been given permission to join you but rest assured, you are under the command of your superb officers and will have the able assistance of some fine men and one brave lady who will accompany you as mission specialists. Now that the appointed hour is upon us, I wish you Godspeed and safe return."

Gatti's C Troop had the point with A and B Troops just behind and flanking, and D Troop at the rear, the fourth element in a diamond formation. A corporal in D Troop, a ginger-bearded giant whom the lads called Moose, had been tasked with carrying the chemist on his back.

"How much do you weigh?" the soldier asked Nightingale.

"Just over nine stone," the professor replied, waiting for his piggyback. "Will you be able to carry me, do you think?"

"Nine stone? I've had shits bigger than you."

The one thing they had neglected to game out was where the civilians would march in the formation so John hastily made the call. He tucked Emily, Trevor, Kyle, and the professor just in front of D Troop for maximal protection.

"Where are you going to be?" Emily asked.

"Right by your side," he said. "I'm not letting you out of my sight."

Ben came over and wished them well. "Make sure you return, all right?" he said.

"We'll try to come back with all our bits," Trevor said, giving him a hug. "Don't envy you your job. You've got a damn sight more Hellers to deal with this time around. Don't let them get the upper hand. We're counting on you."

"We'll prevail," Ben said. "We have no choice."

As they began marching toward the bridge over the River Mole, Trevor said with a sigh, "Once more into the breach."

"Ah, you know Shakespeare," the professor said from high on Moose's back.

"Do I?" Trevor asked.

"Why yes," Nightingale said. "Henry the Fifth, Act Three, I believe. 'Once more unto the breach, dear friends, once more; Or close the wall up with our English dead!'"

Moose cocked his neck and said, "What's he going on about?"

They marched at double-time until they crossed the bridge when Captain Marsh at the point slowed the formation to a walk. They had come off the bridge too bunched up for his liking and he ordered them to fan out along Bridge Street.

It wasn't long before they encountered the first bodies. It was late spring. The daytime temperatures were not very warm but the corpses had begun to bloat and discolor. The soldiers glanced at them but they had all seen worse in deployments to the Middle East and Africa.

"Jesus," Kyle said when they passed the first victims. "Is that from rovers? Were they murdered?"

"Yeah," John said, "Poor bastards. They didn't have a chance."

Nightingale cried out in alarm as the smells from the victims reached his nostrils. Emily trotted ahead a few paces to hold his hand before falling back to John's side at his insistence.

The Swan Shopping Centre was coming up on their left. The pedestrian way looked desolate. Small drones whirred overhead.

John may not have seen it first but he was among the first to act, grabbing Emily by the forearm and pulling her to his right side.

The attack came from their left with as many as a dozen rovers spilling out of an abandoned restaurant.

"Hostiles left!" John shouted.

Kyle froze but Trevor moved toward the left to further insulate Kyle and Emily from harm.

A D-trooper closest to the restaurant didn't have time to raise his pistol. Two rovers set upon him and slashed at his throat with kitchen knives. His gun clattered to the paving stones. Other members of D Troop began firing, dropping the attackers. A third rover managed to kick the errant pistol toward the restaurant before he was killed by an expert shot to the head.

One of the rovers in the rear of the pack, a man who had arrived in Hell in the 1980s, picked up the gun and shouted to a member of his gang, "I know how to use a semi-auto pistol, asshole! I'll kill you bastards!"

He rushed forward, took aim at the highest target, the professor bobbing on Moose's shoulders, and pulled the biometric trigger. Nothing happened. A second later, the confused rover was dispatched by a hail of bullets.

All but two of the attackers fell to gunfire. The survivors dove back into the restaurant.

Captain Yates fell back from his position at the point of B troop to check on the civilians.

"All right, then?" he shouted to John.

"We're okay," John said. "We've got one friendly down."

Captain Greene who was kneeling over the bloody, fallen soldier, called out, "He's gone!"

"We've got to keep moving," John said.

A nearby soldier said, "We don't leave our men behind."

"Drones," John said. "Your people are watching. They'll come pick him up."

A D Troop sergeant yelled, "Eyes right!"

Two men and a woman were running toward them from a block of offices on Elm Street waving white paper.

"Hold your fire!" John shouted. "They're not Hellers!"

"How do you know?" Yates said.

"They're showing white signals," John said.

"And their clothes are modern," Emily shouted.

"Help us!" one of the men called out. "We've been trapped for days!"

"Back across the bridge," Yates shouted at them. "The army's that way. It's safe."

They didn't need coaxing. They kept running and didn't look back.

"This is exciting, isn't it?" the professor said, leaning sharply over Moose's ear.

"I'm glad you're having a good time," the corporal replied, trying to balance his load.

From ahead they heard Captain Marsh shouting something.

"What's he saying?" Greene asked. "We're half deaf without bloody radios."

"Get used to it," Trevor said.

They saw Marsh running back toward their position.

Yates called out to Marsh, "What's the problem?"

The bald captain pulled up in their midst, red in the face.

"Gatti and most of C Troop are gone!" he said. "I saw it with my own eyes. They were moving forward and then they were gone. All that's left of them are their sidearms on the ground."

"They hit a node within the hot zone," Emily said.

"We need to follow their track," John said. "That's why we're here."

With the captains back in position, orders were given and the column advanced down the promenade.

Ben and Major Parker-Burns were watching the video feed from their position across the river. Neither said a word until every member of the column had vanished.

"May Heaven help them," the major gulped.

"I don't know if Heaven will be of any help," Ben said. "They're going to have to help themselves."

Holed up in the restaurant by the promenade the two remaining rovers discussed their hunger. Their gang had finished every scrap of food days earlier.

"It's time for cannie grub," one of them said, eyeing the closest rover bodies on the road.

"We'll wait for dark," the other said. "Could be more of them soldiers."

The first one looked out the plate-glass window up into the sky and swore at the hovering drones, lamenting, "Where the blazes did Heath go? The bastard left us to fend for ourselves in this infernal place. If I had me druthers I'd be back in Hell where there an't no wingless birds flying about and at least we knew how to shift for ourselves."

12

Heath had not been much interested in Leatherhead. After his murderous attack on the platoon of Marines he led his gang north. London was what he wanted and London was what he got. True to their rover habits he and his fifty-strong group had sheltered during the day and traveled by night. The A24 had not been there in his day but he instinctively followed its course through Epsom and Mitcham and into Wandsworth. On their first night they invaded a large country house where they made fast and bloody work of a family of seven who had not heeded evacuation calls, and were it not for a well-stocked pantry, three generations would have wound up as cannie food. On their second night they took over multiple terraced houses, none large enough to hide them all. On that night human flesh was on the menu. The heroin addict had split from the pack and without him, none of them had a grasp of modernity; Heath, a nineteenth-century man, had been one of the more recent arrivals in Hell. None of them fathomed electronics but they stumbled upon the correct operation of light switches and faucets and the function of refrigerators.

"What's this for?" Monk had asked pressing the flush lever of a toilet.

"Could be some sort of a water closet," Heath had answered.

"What's that?"

"Never mind. Do your shitting in the garden and stop asking me questions."

They slept during the day and moved at night and on the third night they stood on the south bank of the Thames at Battersea.

Heath took in the twenty-first-century vista on the opposite bank and breathed in the brackish smells. He declared, “It’s not as I remembered. It was busy in my day but not like this.”

“I can’t make out any of it,” Monk said, scratching at his scraggly beard and puzzling at the lights of a passenger jet streaking through the night sky.

“Time don’t stand still,” Heath said. “Things change. Why in the devil’s name have we been brought back?”

“We’ve been given a second chance at life, that’s what I think,” one of the rovers said.

Recalling the carnage they had wrought since their return Heath said, “I don’t reckon we’ll be Heaven-bound next time ’round.”

“Where are we off to, then?” Monk asked him.

“There.” Heath was pointing across the river toward the heart of the city. “That’s where we’re headed.”

For almost a week, Dirk and Duck hardly left their cottage in Dartford. For the most part, they were fearful that Cromwell would reappear, looking for news on the return of King Henry. Cromwell had left a small party of soldiers behind in case Henry might suddenly reappear. The soldiers hadn’t given the brothers any problem, especially since Dirk let them have every drop of ale he had and promised them first crack at the new barrel he was brewing. But Cromwell was another matter. His dark visage and sharp tongue scared them witless and they wanted to be well hidden if he were to ride into the village. They subsisted on their store of dried meat and consumed the last of their root vegetables. One of their neighbors, an old man who kept a few chickens, came by their back door to see if they had any beer to trade. Dirk was the best brewer about and his beer was as valuable as copper coins.

“Another few days and we’ll be well sorted,” Dirk told him. “I’ve put up two barrels. One for the king’s men, one for me and my brother. How go your birds?”

"Alive and pecking," the man said.

"None lost to thieving?"

"Not with soldiers about. Keeps the scum away."

Rovers didn't come to Dartford often. There were richer pickings elsewhere. The problem was the scavengers, men like their old nemesis, Brandon Woodbourne, not depraved enough to join a rover gang but too uncivilized to live in a village or town.

"Any sign of Woodbourne?" Duck asked, his brow furrowed with worry. Woodbourne had a soft spot for Dirk but not for him, and Duck lived in fear that he'd make good on his perennial threats to crash him for denying him a chicken some time back.

"I didn't see him but he was spotted nearby yesterday," the old man said.

"Got any eggs?" Duck asked. "Wouldn't half like a fry-up."

"Might have a few stashed aside."

"Tell you what," Dirk said. "You advance us four nice eggs and we'll give you a flagon of ale from our new barrel in straight trade."

The old man was thinking about the transaction when they heard some shouts from the road. From the front door they saw a bunch of villagers pointing and talking loudly.

"What's the fuss about?" Dirk shouted.

"The soldiers," one of the men replied. "I saw them walking up by Alfred's house and they vanished. They were there and then they weren't!"

The old man was standing behind the brothers and shouted directly in their ears, "You haven't been drinking, have you?"

Duck rubbed his right ear. "You'll make me deaf, old man!"

"How could we be drinking?" the man in the road replied. "We're all waiting for Dirk to brew a new barrel, same as you."

Thoughts of eggs vanished as quickly as the soldiers and the brothers shooed the chicken man away.

"I reckon I know what 'appened to the king's men," Duck said.

"You think they're off to where you were?" Dirk asked.

"I do indeed."

"If that's the case, then where are the ones who were swapped in trade?" Dirk asked.

"It's true enough," Duck said. "Every time some of us got sent there, some of them got sent 'ere. Yet gone they are and no one's taken their place."

The brothers spent the rest of the day and well into the evening arguing about what to do. Duck forcefully made his case and Dirk just as forcefully made his.

"We're half-starving 'ere," Duck said. "You can't imagine the glorious victuals they got. I told you 'bout pizza, didn't I?"

Dirk said he was sick of hearing about these flat pies.

"Yeah, but you won't be sick of tasting them. And ice cream and cakes and juicy fruits and such. And vids about mermaids and snow dwellers. And …"

"And did you forget that they kept you locked up and sent you back when they was done with you?"

"I didn't mind being locked up. It were better than the day I roamed free. I'm going to try and cross," Duck insisted. "My Delia will look after me. And I'll tell you this, Dirk; I'll do it whether or not you come with me. But we are brothers and I dearly want you by my side."

Nightfall came. While Dirk went through the motions of checking on his barrels, Duck paced back and forth inside their small cottage, every so often opening the shutters to peer onto the dark street. Finally, he couldn't contain himself any longer.

"Brother, I love you more than anything in this dark world of ours but I must go. If you 'ad been there, if you 'ad seen the things I seen, you would be walking beside me."

With that, Duck wrapped his arms around Dirk, kissed him on the cheek, and was out the door.

He slowly trekked up the road toward Albert's house. As he approached the point where the soldiers had last been seen he heard the squishy sounds of another pair of feet slogging through the mud behind him.

"Yeah, I'm coming with you," Dirk said. "You know that they'll be stealing all my beer when we're gone, don't you?"

An overjoyed Duck said, "They've got all manner of beer where we're going. In bottles, in metal tins, any way you please. Come, take my 'and so we won't be separated on our journey."

Hand in hand they walked forward.

Suddenly they were standing on the service line of a tennis court. To their right were the low-slung buildings of the MAAC labs illuminated by security lights.

Dirk began to tremble but Duck exuberantly reassured him everything was all right, better than all right. It was perfect. He knew exactly where they were, ever so close to all the marvels he'd been crowing about.

"But we're in a giant cage," Dirk cried, reaching out to touch the chain-link fence. "I seen a bear in a cage like this once and it didn't end pretty for the beast."

"It's called a tennis court. It's a game they play in modern times."

"In a cage?"

"Come with me. See those buildings yonder? That's where they keep the fine grub. We'll knock upon the door and once they see that old Duck is back, they'll surely let us in. But we must tread carefully in case we run into the king's men who crossed before us."

The grounds were dark but the night sky was full of light. Dirk pointed in awe at the crescent moon and the big dipper.

"Look, Duck! The 'eavens. We 'aven't seen them even one time in 'ell."

"And wait till the morning!" Duck said. "You'll see the sunshine too. 'Tis a stirring sight."

Duck was leading his brother toward the lab when they heard the tennis court gate creaking open.

A hulking figure began running toward them.

Duck froze in terror and in seconds the man was upon them.

Duck was too scared to speak his name but Dirk managed.

"Woodbourne. It's you."

"Fancy meeting Duck and Dirk here," Woodbourne said, wildly looking about.

"Please don't hurt me," Duck said, falling to his knees. "Next time I'll give you all the chickens I got. I swear I will."

"I can't believe I'm back again," Woodbourne said, his black eyes reflecting the moonlight. "Don't worry, you miserable sod, I've got more pressing things to do than crash your miserable arse. Seen any guards about?"

Duck got to his feet but kept his distance. "None. Not the modern kind, not the king's men neither."

"King's men here?"

"A whole platoon crossed earlier, or so we was told," Dirk said.

"Strange times," Woodbourne said, "but I'll be making the best of it. I'll be off. Don't say you saw me or next time we cross paths you'll be headless, the both of you."

"We won't say nothing," Duck said. "Where are you headed?"

Woodbourne didn't say. He hurtled across the lawn and disappeared into the darkness.

"I thought I was done for," Duck said. "Nearly peed my trousers. I'm glad he didn't want to cast in with us. Don't trust 'im as far as I could toss 'im."

The door Duck tried to open was the one Delia and his minders had used for his walks on the laboratory grounds. It was locked.

"What now?" Dirk asked.

Duck told him to stay put while he found a rock in the flowerbeds that he threw through the plate glass.

Dirk cackled and wondered out loud what kind of a fool would fashion a door of glass.

Stepping inside Duck called for the two people he knew best, Delia and Barry, one of the security guards. "Delia, it's Duck back among you. Barry, are you there?"

He led his brother through the empty and dark corridors, illuminated only by yellow security lights and red, glowing exit signs.

"It's like a castle in 'ere," Dirk said. "But not the ancient and smelly sort."

"It's massive, all right. This way. I'll show you where they was keeping me."

The door to the jail built to house Hellers was wide open and the doors to the individual cells were unlocked. Duck almost ran to his old quarters and when Dirk caught up with him he excitedly showed off all the amenities: the bed, the TV, the shower, and the toilet which he flushed over and over, explaining its miraculous now-you-see-it-now-you-don't features.

"Now for the best part," he exclaimed. "I'll show you where they keep the grub."

The kitchen was around the corner. As an inmate, food had been delivered on a tray but Delia would sometimes take him into the pantry to pick out snacks. There were still a good number of provisions in store: biscuits and crackers, canned soups with pull-tabs which Duck had learned how to open, cans of soda, bottles of beer, peanut butter, jelly, loaves of sliced bread, and the *piece de resistance* in the freezer—tubs of ice cream.

Duck grabbed a spoon and dug out a scoop of chocolate ice cream and presented it to his brother.

"What do I do with it?" Dirk asked, sniffing at it.

"You lick it and then you chew on it."

Dirk gave it a lick. His face became all grins and he licked the spoon until there was nothing left.

"What did I tell you?" Duck asked.

"It's a marvel," Dirk said. "Can I have more?"

"You can 'ave the entire boxful. Come on, you 'ave that one and I'll 'ave this one, the white one with chunks. We'll take it back to my quarters and I'll show you my favorite vids on the tele machine."

Delia was trying her best to relax, aided by a nighttime cup of cocoa. Following her return to Earth, she had left London for her elderly mother's place in the Cotswolds. The old woman was mentally sharp and could have fully grasped her daughter's ordeal but Delia elected to stay mum. With a daughter in the employ of MI5, she was used to hearing little about her work. What Delia told her was that her last assignment had left her drained and it was left at that. But as her mother pottered about the cottage, she cast frequent sidelong glances of concern at Delia who couldn't seem to find a comfortable rhythm, spending much too much of her time staring out the window at the greenery and chewing her nails.

"Frightful things happening down in London," her mother had clucked at the morning TV.

"Yes, quite. Frightful."

"I expect your colleagues are involved."

"I expect they are."

The phone rang. Her mother took the call and gave Delia the handset. "It's a Mr. Wellington calling from London."

Delia put down her mug of chocolate.

"Delia, how are you doing?" Ben asked.

"As well as can be expected," she replied in little better than a monotone.

"Well, take it slow. Look, sorry to bother you. Tried ringing your mobile with no reply. The duty officer had your secondary number. Do you have your computer with you?"

She dutifully fetched it from her bedroom and listened to what Ben had to say. Her mother didn't have Wi-Fi so she tethered it to her mobile to retrieve and view the file Ben sent through.

"Christ. When is this from?" she asked.

"About an hour ago. Silent alarms were triggered. We weren't actively monitoring the feeds from inside the lab but we had a look-see and there they were."

"Bad pennies turning up," she said.

"Right. So the question for you is who's the other one?"

"His brother, Dirk."

The video was from inside of Duck's old cell. The two lads were lying side-by-side on the narrow bed, spooning ice cream and watching *The Little Mermaid.*

"We have a good profile of Duck," Ben said, "and we can be quite certain he's not much of a threat but we wanted to get a sense whether the same was true for the other one."

"Dirk's equally harmless. I hope you're not going to ask me to come down and mind them. I really couldn't, not in my state."

"Heavens no," Ben said. "You've done more than enough. Wouldn't be on. Even if you were chafing at the bit. The entire MAAC complex is a no-go zone. We couldn't roll them up if we wanted to. We'll just keep eyes on them and see what they do once they've cleaned the place out of food."

"Duck's like a locust," Delia said. "He'll eat everything he can lay his hands on. How are John, Emily, and Trevor getting on?"

"They went back on a mission with a squadron of SAS to find Paul Loomis and stop Hellers from coming over."

"Oh my ..." She began to cry and had to hang up the phone without saying good-bye.

All night a steady stream of Hellers materialized on the grounds of the MAAC compound. They were men mostly, but a smattering of women too, from Bexley and Gravesend mainly, Heller towns in the vicinity of Dartford village. All of them made their way to the muddy road near Dirk and Duck's cottage, propelled by tales of a miraculous passageway back to the world they had late departed.

And when they arrived on Earth, painlessly and instantly transported, they stumbled about in and around the tennis courts, trying to process the weird sights of manicured grounds, electric lights, modern buildings, security fences, and parked automobiles. None approached the shattered glass door leading inside the lab. Instead, they made their way across the car parks toward the town, breaking into houses along the way to scavenge food and drink. There weren't many residents left within a mile or two of the lab but there were some who had refused evacuation orders. Those who encountered Hellers didn't fare well. None of these invaders were rovers, at least not that night, but they weren't gentle souls either. Although human flesh was not devoured, murder was in the air.

While these Hellers were flying about in a state of euphoric confusion, Brandon Woodbourne's activities were measured and purposeful. As soon as he cleared the MAAC perimeter he began breaking into those vacant houses with cars in the driveways or lock-up garages, looking for keys. Inside one house he found a set of Volvo keys and a meat cleaver in the kitchen. Soon he was driving west on familiar but largely empty roads. Compared to his last visit to Earth, the lack of traffic was startling. He began pushing buttons on the dash trying to make the radio come to life. When one of the buttons made the radio glow he heard the explanation. An announcer was warning residents of London and the Home Counties, those who had not yet attempted evacuation, to stay indoors with doors and windows locked. The BBC was aware of an increasing number of emergency calls regarding invaders but emergency services were unable to respond to the vast majority of incidents.

He drove on, wondering if she'd still be there and if she were, what he would say to her.

Like a dog returning for a long-buried bone, Heath pushed his gang through the strange, dark, and largely empty streets of London, east toward Shoreditch. Along the way they invaded shuttered public houses, murdering landlords who had stayed behind and raping their wives and daughters. Fueled by beer and gin they grew ever bolder, kicking in the doors and windows of flats and shops, helping themselves to silver, jewelry, and coins, leaving paper money behind unaware it had value. Not that they knew what to do with their booty. Many of them had been thieves on Earth and larceny was in their bones. Monk emerged from one closet wearing a tuxedo jacket and a strand of pearls, sending Heath into drunken hysterics.

During the nineteenth century, the East End of London and Shoreditch in particular had been the center of the furniture and textile industries. Young Heath had grown up as a shepherd boy but one day he'd had enough of the beatings his father delivered for even minor transgressions. He ran away to London and found a menial job around stinking vats of dyes. As he grew into a hard-edged man who preferred crime to labor, Shoreditch declined in tandem with his own diminishing morals on its way to becoming the epicenter of London's crime and prostitution scene. A man like Heath fared well in a place like Shoreditch and with fond memories churning inside his fevered brain, he tried to make sense of the geography of the modern borough of Hackney.

"I don't remember none of this," Heath said, spinning in place on the sidewalk at the head of his pack of drunken men. "It's all jumbled up."

"If you don't, I don't," Monk said, choosing to urinate on the spot. "In my day which was much before your day I hardly ventured into London. What is it you're seeking?"

"My old diggings. Me and my mateys used to hole up in a cellar in a building near the railway line. I wish to see it again if it has not been torn down. I have memories of the place, you see, good memories."

"Well, let's find it then," Monk said, weaving away. "Look there!" he exclaimed. "A tavern."

The rovers needed no coaxing. Soon they had smashed through into another shuttered pub, stealing bottles from the bar. Heath waited outside, looking for a landmark which might help him. His eye settled on a street sign embedded into the side of a building.

"Fuck me! Shoreditch High Street. I know where we are. Monk! Come out of there. We're going this way."

Benona Siminski was frantic. It had been a bad couple of months, a terrible time, and just when she thought things could get no worse, they did. Polly, her little girl, was ill with a high fever. Two months earlier, she and Polly had been hostages, held by the Heller, Brandon Woodbourne, until he shot and killed two policemen and a visiting welfare worker from the council. In the aftermath, she had been debriefed by MI5 agents and threatened with deportation if she breathed a word of what they called, "the ravings of a lunatic."

"If Woodbourne was lunatic, why you care what he say?" she had asked.

They would not provide an answer. It was a security matter.

"If he was lunatic, why did I see a death certificate for him online from 1949?"

These kinds of online documents were unreliable, she was told.

"Okay. I don't care," she had said. "I keep my mouth shut. Just leave me and my daughter alone."

Yet being left alone was not enough. There were scars, emotional scars. Polly became withdrawn. She refused to go back to school. She had nightmares. Benona knew because she had to quit her cleaning job and stay at home at night. She heard her calling out in her sleep. For Benona, sleep was elusive. Her insomnia made her nerves raw. She took it out on the social workers and psychologists the school foisted on Polly. She was labeled a difficult parent. She had to sign on for benefits. Money was tight.

Then the troubles came to London. She, more than anyone, knew what Hellers were and she was frightened. Her neighbors on Glebe Road in Hackney heeded the evacuation orders. She thought about returning to Poland but she didn't have the money for the flight so she hunkered down in her modest walk-up flat by the railway tracks. Then, the catastrophe. Polly got one of her recurrent ear infections. Her local doctor wasn't answering calls. The casualty wards were closed. Polly was howling in pain and spiking a high fever. She needed to get antibiotics.

"Baby, you stay here. Don't answer the door for nobody. I'm going to get you some medicine."

"But mama, don't leave me alone!"

"I'll come back before you know it. Lie on sofa and watch your video, okay?"

She kissed her and was soon alone on Kingsland Road at two in the morning.

The road was always deserted this time of the morning. She was used to being out late alone because she finished cleaning offices in the city late. But there was something in the still air that filled her with dread. Kingsland

Pharmacy was dark as were all the shops. She didn't know why she bothered but she tried the door. It was locked, of course. A metal sign stand had been left outside the Chinese takeaway next door. She lifted it over her head and, closing her eyes, rammed it into the plate-glass window of the chemist. An alarm went off. She stepped back to see if any lights went on in the flat above but the windows stayed black. After using the metal stand to clear away the shards, she climbed into the store. With the alarm sounding in her ears she found a light switch and went to the back.

She knew which antibiotic had cured Polly in the past and she started searching for them among the racks of plastic bottles. Amoxicillin. She found a huge bottle, a five-hundred count, and briefly thought about taking only as many as she needed but the thought of Polly alone persuaded her to take all of them and beat a hasty retreat.

She climbed out of the broken window backwards, trying to avoid the sharp glass on the ledge but before her second foot touched the sidewalk she smelled the odor she thought she would never smell again.

She slowly turned around and found herself staring into the coarse, leering face of Heath and fifty drunken rovers.

13

The men of A Squadron had been in peril so many times they had lost count. From Afghanistan to Iraq to Tajikistan to Sierra Leone to Libya they had been asked to do the impossible time after time. They had seen it all; tempered by the crucible of firefights, nothing fazed them. Until now.

They were in a clearing on high enough ground to see they were only a short distance from a meandering river. In the opposite direction but equally close was a row of low cottages and one substantial house. It had a square stone tower rising into the dull, overcast sky.

While the SAS soldiers, Kyle, and Professor Nightingale tried to get a grip on their abrupt change of venue, John, Trevor, and Emily instantly alerted to the danger.

"Trev, stay with them," John said, sprinting to the head of the column where he snapped Captain Gatti out of his trance.

"Is this according to plan?" Gatti asked him.

"We're here," John said. "We've got to move fast. That tower's a bit of bad luck. There'll be some kind of feudal lord in there, possibly with his own militia. I don't see how they'll miss us."

"Any of you have your weapons?" Gatti said to the men in D group.

They were all unarmed.

"If that's The River Mole," John said, "that's north. It's twelve miles to Richmond that way. We should push west around the village and hope we're not seen."

"Pick up any good-sized rocks, heavy sticks, anything you can weaponize," Gatti told his people.

"I'll pass it along to the trailing groups," John said, falling back.

From his vantage point on Moose's shoulders, Nightingale exclaimed, "All that was modern has disappeared. Marvelous, absolutely marvelous. Emily, as one scientist to another, I am literally gobsmacked."

"That's the right word for it," she said.

"Is it?" the burly corporal said, giving the chemist a tour as he swiveled on his feet. "I'd say the right word is fucking hell."

"Two words that," Nightingale said, "but they're two precise ones."

John rejoined his people and told everyone the plan.

"This is seriously messed up," Kyle said looking around in bewilderment.

"You got that right," John said, checking Kyle's backpack. Like the other four it was still full of vital materials. "Stay low and follow the pack."

Emily touched John's arm. "We're back," she said ruefully.

"Third time lucky?" he asked. "Stay by me. Every step."

"You know I will."

As the column swung around the village, John saw a distant figure atop the tower, then two more, gesticulating wildly.

He called out to the squadron. "We've been spotted!"

Gatti ordered a double-time march and the column picked up speed. John kept eyes on the tower. He thought he saw one of the men with something in his hand. They were out of range of a long bow and in the best of hands a musketeer would have to get amazingly lucky so he wasn't too worried. But then he heard the air rippling.

"Crossbow!" he shouted, pulling Emily around so that he was shielding her.

The bolt fell short but not by much.

He called out to Moose, "Get Nightingale down. He'll be their aiming point."

Moose scooped the chemist off his shoulders with one arm and began carrying him like a baby as everyone broke into a full run. Another bolt whistled overhead, then another fell in the midst of A Group, narrowly missing a soldier who paused to dig it out of the ground.

"Come on," Captain Marsh shouted at him. "Don't muck about."

"Who's mucking about?" the trooper shouted back. "I'm the only one who's got a weapon now."

They covered enough ground to the northwest that John had to keep looking over his shoulder to keep tabs on the threat and what he saw was not good. A dozen or more horses and riders appeared from behind the tower and began to gallop toward them.

Captain Yates saw them too and barked orders. The squadron had done some limited training on tactical options to repel an attack unarmed but there hadn't been time to drill on all scenarios. An attack from horseback was one of those.

The squadron halted their march and spontaneously formed into dispersed groups of four to five. John led the civilians to their rear, he and Trevor ready to deal with any rider who broke through. Each of the captains shed heavy backpacks and tossed them to John and Trevor for safekeeping.

The Leatherhead militiamen, led by the lord of the manor, swooped down on them, brandishing swords and a few pistols.

Twenty yards away, a shot rang out and one of the troopers in B Group clutched his chest and fell. Another flintlock fired and a corporal in C Group was hobbled.

"Single shots only!" John shouted. "They won't be reloading on horseback. Watch the swords!"

Ever resourceful, the SAS troopers improvised. While one man waved his arms to attract a swordsman like a matador coaxing a bull, three or four others did a pincer maneuver, launching themselves at the horse's flanks and the rider's legs, trying to dismount him before he could deliver a cutting blow. The Geordie Lance-Corporal who had professed his hatred of horses, had two of his mates bodily launch him into one of the riders, taking him down. For a moment or two he rode the beast, belly to saddle, before slipping off and spewing curses at the horse as it galloped away, riderless. As soon as a militiaman went down, he was swarmed by a knot of SAS, kicked, punched, and gouged into oblivion and then his sword was theirs.

John watched the battle play out, itching to get his licks in but unwilling to leave Emily and the others unprotected. Soon, there were as many weapons in the hands of the SAS as their attackers.

"The tide's turning," Trevor said.

"Man, these guys know how to fight," Kyle said.

Suddenly the lord of the manor, a longhaired brute with a flowing beard, pierced the SAS curtain and charged the civilian group.

Trevor ran out to distract him and John ordered Emily, Kyle, and Nightingale to lie flat on their stomachs. The lord swung his heavy sword, missing Trevor's shoulder by inches. John was next. The swordsman was right-handed and just as the horse was upon him John sidestepped it to the left ducking the cross-saddle lunge. The lord had to turn his horse to re-engage John and as he did, John saw that Kyle had disobeyed and was grabbing at his left foot in the stirrup.

The lord raised his sword to bring it down on Kyle's head but as he did John reached his opposite leg and got a fistful of trousers. With a sharp yank, the man was off his saddle and Trevor was there to deliver a deadly kick to his head and retrieve his sword.

"I told you to lie down, goddamn it," John shouted at Kyle.

"You're welcome," Kyle replied. "God, you're an asshole, you know that?"

"Disobey an order and you bet I am."

"I don't take orders from you," Kyle said. "Never did, never will."

They heard Nightingale say excitedly, "Look! We've won!"

All of the militiamen were down and a few horses had been commandeered.

"We've got casualties," John said.

Emily was already running to help. She knelt over a fallen trooper, bleeding from a scalp wound. She took a roll of cotton bandages from her backpack and began dressing the man's wound. Each group had a medic, equipped only with bandage rolls, and they fanned out, doing the best they could.

Marsh had lost his cap. Breathing heavily, he rubbed the sweat off his bald head, and pointed at one of the militiamen writhing in the grass, his neck grotesquely crooked and broken.

"This man should be dead," Marsh told John. "Is that what you were going on about?"

"That's as good a demonstration as you'll get short of seeing him headless," John said.

"So there's no point putting the sod out of his misery?"

"None whatsoever. He's permanently screwed."

Marsh shook his head and said, "Fuck me, what a place. We've taken casualties but at least we've got a few horses and some proper weapons."

A medic from A Group called Marsh and John over. Kneeling by the trooper who'd taken the bullet to his chest, the medic declared the man killed in action.

"Our lot seem to die just as surely as they do back home," Marsh said. "This was a good man. Wife and two children."

"We should bury him and keep moving," John said. "If we don't rovers might take his flesh tonight."

Marsh spit on the ground as a sign of his disgust. "Petersen," Marsh shouted over to his group sergeant. "Use swords and hands to bury Jonesy. Get it done and let's get cracking."

The march north took them about six hours. Although they checked their progress against the silk maps, the navigation wasn't difficult. The River Thames ran a northerly course between Leatherhead and Richmond and they had only to keep it within sight to their left. Moose was spared carrying Nightingale. He lifted the professor onto the saddle of a horse and led it by its reins. Emily, Kyle, and the wounded men also rode. One horse was used as a pack animal for their five heavy backpacks.

Along the way, most of the unarmed SAS men picked up ersatz weapons, makeshift clubs mostly, though one trooper found a shovel leaning against a tree. Any time they saw distant smoke coming from a chimney or open fire they gave the area a wide berth. They didn't go completely unnoticed. Sailors on a few passing river barges spotted their column and pointed though John doubted they looked any different from a troop of King Henry's army from a distance.

Five hours into their trek, the river made an eastward loop. In the distance they saw it make a switch-back, westward loop.

"We're getting close," John told Emily.

He left her in Trevor's care and sprinted through the ranks to let the captains know what he thought.

They all concurred but Marsh ladled up some sarcasm. "Thank God the Yank's here to help us poor bastards read a map."

Gatti, at the point, asked, "You're sure there's no bridges across anywhere close?"

"Pretty sure," John said. "Can all of you manage the current?"

"All the lads are strong swimmers. We'll have to find a way to get the civilians across. A boat would be handier than driftwood."

The last mile of their journey across a large, grassy plain corresponded to the earthly location of the Old Deer Park in Richmond. Ahead, John identified their crossing point by the thin column of black smoke rising into a parchment-colored afternoon sky. On reaching the south riverbank, the civilians and the wounded dismounted. Greene led his group east and Yates led his men west. The rest of the soldiers stayed put on guard duty. It took an hour but both groups returned, one empty-handed, Yates' group with something better than gold—two medium-sized rowboats which they portaged.

They tethered the watered horses to trees and left them mounds of pulled-up grass. Moose was assigned the precious cargo of Nightingale, two of the wounded, the backpacks, and their assorted weapons. He began rowing, surrounded by half of A Squadron swimming alongside. The rest of the squadron swam with the other boat. John took its oars and rowed Emily, Kyle, Trevor, and one wounded man. The current was swift but they chose the narrowest section and all made it across safely.

From there it was a short walk uphill toward the brick chimney belching out smoke.

There was no one outside the low brick forge. Using hand signals, the SAS men split into two groups and ducking below the windows glowing orange from the hot furnace, they encircled the building.

When they were in position, John strode up to the main entrance and called out, "Is William the forger here?"

A small man, naked from the waist up, emerged, squinting into the daylight. At the sight of the strangers he yelped like a dog whose tail had been trampled and ran back inside.

Gatti's C Group who were closest to the entrance prepared themselves for a fight but John reassured them with a calming hand gesture.

A giant of a man emerged at the entrance wielding an iron rod. He too was bare-chested, his skin black with soot and shiny with sweat. "Who's looking for him?" he bellowed before spotting John. "Well, would you look at this?" he cried. "It's John who is not from here. Were you not able to return to your own land?"

"I made it back, all right. Twice. This is my third visit to your fair country."

"Fair? This shit hole? Always good for a laugh, you are. Come here."

The two men embraced and much of William's soot wound up on John's shirt. The last time John saw him, William was atop the chalky cliffs on Brittania's southeastern coast, manning a battery of John's La Hitte cannon and John was setting sail for Francia aboard the *Hellfire*.

"So, you make it to the Norselands," John said.

"I did but how did you come to know that?"

"A certain king told me."

"Well, we had a winning campaign against old King Christian and seized his mines. As you said, the Norse iron is, indeed, superior stuff. We did bring back a goodly amount. Who are all these men deployed around my forge? They do not look like Henry's men."

"They're not from here either."

"Live men? All of them?"

"They are. Most of them are British soldiers, the best of the best.

They're called the SAS. And there's one live woman. Emily, come and meet an old friend of mine."

William wiped his hands against his leather apron, took her hand in his huge paw and kissed it.

"So he found you, did he?"

"He did," she said. "He brought me home. He was very brave."

"If you've come back here then you are the brave one," William said. "And fair. And comely. And …"

John put an end to the compliments with a laugh. "You're going to step on your tongue if you don't shut your mouth, my friend. So the ore. Is there any left?"

"Some. Why?"

"I need it."

"I'd love to help you but it's not mine to give. It belongs to the king."

John was ready for that. He reached into his trouser pocket for the folded piece of paper he had carried from Earth and presented it to William.

William read it out loud, "I Henry, King of Brittania, do command that my master forger, William, give unto John Camp the iron ore he may need for the making of steel, the brass he may need, and all the good labor required of the forgers of Richmond." He looked up, nodding. "It is signed by the hand of my monarch and I will certainly obey. Tell me John who is not from here, what is it you wish to forge?"

John called Kyle over. "William, meet my brother, Kyle, who is also not from here. Kyle is a gunsmith, one of the best I've ever met. There isn't a pistol or long gun he can't fix or fabricate. Kyle, show him what you've got in your pack."

Kyle opened one of the backpacks and began laying out its contents, about a hundred cotton-wrapped parcels ranging in size from a square inch to a square foot. He unwrapped one of the larger ones revealing a deeply imprinted rubber mold.

William examined it carefully. "A mold, yes, I see."

Kyle unwrapped a smaller one and handed it over.

"Tell me, gunsmith Kyle, are all of these molds for one weapon?"

"They are," Kyle answered.

"And what is this gun called?"

"It's an AK-47."

William repeated the name slowly with a lilt, as if it were a magical incantation, and asked about its attributes.

Kyle spoke almost lovingly about the rifle. "The AK-47 is the single most successful weapon of modern times. It's a rifle with two modes. In semi-automatic it fires one round with each trigger pull. In automatic it fires a burst as long as you hold the trigger down. It holds thirty rounds in a detachable magazine. It rarely jams, even when it's wet or muddy. It's been called the freedom-fighter's rifle because it's cheap to make, reliable, and cheap to manufacture. I've got molds for all the parts including the magazine parts and assorted screws. I've also got molds for the bullets and a press to make them. What we'll need from you is your best quality steel to do lost-wax casting."

"You know what that is?" John asked William.

"I do know the method and I have used it before. How many of the AK-47s do you wish to manufacture?"

"About thirty-two," Kyle said, "eight for each of four groups of the SAS. We've brought five sets of molds to speed up production. We'll also need about a hundred magazines and several thousand rounds of ammo."

"Ammo?" William asked.

"Sorry, ammunition, bullets," John said. "But here's the thing. These bullets contain the lead bullet and the gunpowder all in a single cylinder. To set them off a firing pin strikes a primer at the bullet's base. The primer needs to hold an explosive chemical. We've brought a scientist with us, a chemist who knows how to make it, but we'll need to find the starting materials. That's Professor Nightingale over there."

The chemist was sitting under a tree looking pale and worn out but he gave a chipper wave.

William removed a rag from his apron and blew his nose into it. "These AK-47s sound like mighty weapons. I've heard modern men speak of guns that can fire rapid-like but no one I know's been able to tell an old forger such as myself how to construct one. And here you are, molds in hand. Tell me, John, what is it you intend to do with these guns?"

"We're going to try to stop an invasion."

William took up the challenge of feeding his hungry guests. After wondering how to stretch his forge worker's meager rations to meet the needs of so many, he had a brainstorm. It was common knowledge down in the nearby village that King Henry had ordered William to use the village as target practice to test the accuracy and range of his new singing cannon. It had been John who had slipped extra powder into the charge, sending the cannon ball sailing over the village and splashing harmlessly into the river. William personally went down to the village to let them know that their savior, John Camp, required sustenance for his party and, though poor, the villagers emptied their larders and casks to honor their hero.

A cart from the village, pulled by a pitifully thin horse, lumbered up the hill to the forge. A handful of rough-looking men and one thin woman in a threadbare dress unloaded the provisions. The woman was perhaps sixty, though she was so weather-beaten it was hard to tell. Initially she was frightened of the strapping young soldiers and refused to make eye contact. Emily seemed to scare her less and the woman managed a timid hello. But for some reason, she immediately seemed comfortable around Professor Nightingale. She asked him his name, made him a plate of food, and poured him a cup of ale. For his part, he politely eschewed wrinkling his nose at her rancid body odors and asked her name.

"Mrs. Smith," she said. "Eugenia Smith."

"I am pleased to meet you, Eugenia," he said, extending a hand. "Ted Nightingale."

"How can live men come Down?" she asked in a whisper so only he could hear the question.

"It's amazing, isn't it?" he replied. "I'm a scientist and I'm not sure I even fully understand it."

"Then why have you come?"

"It seems our world is under attack from your world. Something needs to be done about it."

"You're sick, are you not?" she asked.

"As a matter of fact, I am. How did you know?"

"The color of your skin, the yellowing of your eyes. My own mother had the yellowing before she died."

"I'm afraid I am dying," he said with as much insouciance as he could manage. "Final adventure of a thoroughly interesting life."

"Well, I hope you don't find yourself here when you pass," she said. "There isn't a day that passes that I don't wish I could have taken back my wickedness."

The visitors and the forge workers spread out on the grass and ate bread, cheese, and dried meat. The soldiers kept to themselves. John sat in a circle with Trevor, Emily, Kyle, Nightingale, and William talking about the logistics of getting their castings started.

"We can begin tonight if you're up to the task," William said.

"Sooner the better," John said.

William had the iron ore ready, plenty of wax, and a supply of casting plaster.

"Might we talk about the primers?" Nightingale asked, energetically, revived by the meal. "I'll need a supply of lead as a precursor for lead styphnate."

"No shortage of lead," William grunted. "We make our musket shot with lead."

"Excellent, excellent," the chemist said. "Now I'll need a supply of nitric acid. Best if you have it on the shelf but if not, I'll have to synthesize it."

"What is this nitric acid?" William asked.

"The old name for it is aqua fortis. Or perhaps you know it as spirit of niter?"

"Sorry, I've no idea what you speak of."

"Do you know of any chemists or even alchemists in the environs?" Nightingale asked.

William could only stare at him blankly.

"Oh well, we'll have to make it then. If you have gunpowder, presumably you have potassium nitrate, also known as saltpeter."

William brightened. "Saltpeter. That we do have. Comes from bat droppings in caves."

"Yes, that's right, good. And I presume laying hands on some good-quality clay is not problematic."

"Clay? Ha. Plenty of that."

"White clay, actually."

"We've got white, red, brown, whatever sort of clay contents your heart."

"Then all I'll need is a bench to work on, some glass vessels, lead, white clay, saltpeter, clean water and a source of heat."

"Have a look in there," William said, pointing to the orange glow coming from his forge. "There's all the heat a man could ever want for."

John leaned over and said to Emily, "Today's gone about as well as expected."

"Not for Trooper Jones," she said.

"Every time these men go on a mission they accept they might not return."

"I'm not hardened to it like you are," she said.

"Thank God you're not."

"I expect we'll have some pretty awful days too," she said, "but the sooner we cross the channel to find Paul, the better."

"Amen to that." He got up and pulled Kyle to his feet. "Ready to get to work, baby brother?"

Kyle took a few crooked steps, getting his stiff knee loosened up. "That's why I'm in here in this ridiculously weird place."

14

Heath was giddy. Benona was the prettiest woman he'd encountered since arriving on Earth and he licked his cracked lips like a salivating wolf.

"Stay back," he warned the other rovers. "This one's mine."

Monk was nearly legless with drink but he put a hand on Heath's shoulders to make a plea. "Come on, Heath, after all we've been through you and me, the least you could do is give me a little taste of nectar."

"Fuck off," Heath bellowed. "All of you. I'm having her all to myself. Right here on the pavement. Right now. What's your name, blondie?"

Benona could hardly get the words out. "I know who you are."

"Who am I then?" Heath asked, coming within inches of her face, his hands almost twitching at the prospect of squeezing her fair flesh.

She took a step backwards and felt the building wall blocking any hope of escape. "You're from Hell."

"Pretty and clever, but that's not the full story, dearie. I'm from Hell and I'm going to spend the rest of the night raping you and once I get my appetite back I'm going to eat your pretty lady parts."

She closed her eyes and thought about Polly. Her ears filled with the noise of her own pounding blood. Then the sound seemed to morph into a high-pitched squeal.

The car was speeding down Kingsland Street when the brakes locked and the tires lost a layer of rubber. It jumped the curb and slammed into rovers, tossing bodies like ten-pins.

Heath wheeled around to be splashed in the face by the blood of one of his men. Some of the rovers who stayed on their feet began running. The car came to a halt on top of a pile of bodies and a man got out. He began slashing his way through the confused and drunken sods who hadn't yet fled, making his way toward Heath.

Before the man got there, Monk grabbed Heath by his shirt and pulled him away.

"Let's be gone!"

Heath wasn't a man to flee danger but he was too drunk and stunned to stand and fight. At least ten of his men were dead or wounded; the rest were disappearing down the dark road. He let Monk pull him away and soon he was running too.

Benona's eyes were still closed. The sounds she was hearing were horrific, the peril paralyzing. Finally she willed her eyelids open, prepared for her last earthly sight.

What she saw was Woodbourne, a bloody cleaver falling from his hand.

She collapsed into his arms. "Brandon, it's you. Thank God."

"Where's Polly?" he asked. "Is she safe?"

"She's at home."

"Then let's go home."

Peter Lester was at his desk at 10 Downing Street piling papers into his ministerial red box. He tested its closure and fretted about it being overstuffed to the breaking point.

His principal private secretary entered and took over the task.

"Leafing through the papers the secretary said, "Many of these documents are on the secure cloud, you know."

"I like to have hard copies," Lester said, inspecting his desk drawers and pulling out a few personal items.

"There will be printers in Manchester," the secretary said, leaning on the briefcase and snapping it shut. "There. We have it."

"What work space will we have?" Lester asked.

"The Lord Mayor of Manchester has graciously offered you his rooms at Town Hall. Other city councilors are expected to follow his lead for the benefit of the cabinet. If not, we shall insist. Her Majesty's government will be in cramped quarters but we shall make do. The speaker of the commons is already complaining but …"

"That man complains for the sake of complaining," Lester said.

"I don't disagree. The opposition—well, they will no doubt be particularly unhappy with their accommodations. Vacant commercial space, as I understand."

"Can you imagine if Churchill had to put up with all these spineless wingers during the war?"

"I shudder at the thought."

"And what of the royal family?"

"The queen *et al* are finally on route to Balmoral. Quite reluctantly. Her parents refused to move from the palace during the Blitz."

"This enemy is a damned sight worse than the Nazis, if you ask me," the prime minister said, red box in hand. "All right, let's turn off the lights and lock the doors."

The decision to relocate the government functions to Manchester had been taken at the morning Cobra meeting. London was no longer safe; all public transport had been suspended. The evacuation had slowed to a trickle. The best estimates placed the number of evacuees at five to six million of the eight million who called Greater London home. Around the hot zones, the proportion of leavers was highest. Those who stayed were mainly the poor, disabled, and elderly who couldn't or wouldn't get to evacuation points, skeptics and conspiracy theorists who doubted the narrative, and the childless who, with only themselves to protect, bet they could weather the storm. TV coverage of evacuation camps on military bases that showed wild overcrowding, minimal services, and embittered evacuees dissuaded many from leaving their homes. Yet reporters who ventured into affected parts of London were describing scenes of barbarism and carnage. The net result was a population caught between a rock and a hard place. For those who elected to shelter in place, London was far from hospitable. To be sure, there was electricity, water, and gas but the only stores remaining open were a few mom and pop businesses that eventually sold out and could not get re-supplied. Hospitals were closed, having sent patients and staff elsewhere and emergency services were not responding. Army units patrolled key installations, museums, and landmarks but the Metropolitan Police and other Home County forces, other than elite armed units, were assigned to keep the peace at evacuation centers. On occasion, a squad of soldiers or a unit of armed police happened upon an assault in progress and when that occurred they sometimes struggled in the heat of battle to tell citizens from Hellers. Shooting at anyone who ran away could have disastrous consequences and the rules of engagement kept shifting. But by and large, Londoners who elected to stay behind were on their own to deal with the invaders.

What had begun as a trickle was now a torrent of Hellers pouring into the city. As word spread throughout Brittania, the dead flocked to the hot zones for one more chance at life. On arrival, some were meek and awestruck at the sight of the sun and the trappings of modernity. They wandered about London, searching dustbins for food and timidly entering houses, retreating if they were occupied. But others were determined to satisfy all their lustful desires and they proceeded to terrorize whomever they encountered in homes and on the streets. The worst were the gangs of rovers who took what they wanted and when they were ready to move on, left behind empty cupboards and pools of blood. In the more rural areas where farmers kept shotguns, Earthers sometimes fought back. But for the most part, a party of Hellers was as effective as a swarm of locusts in consuming everything in sight.

Many Hellers realized their coarse peasant garb or military uniforms identified them too easily so they stole clothes from victims' houses. A few heard from victims about their rancid smell and disguised themselves with perfumes and colognes. But when one Heller encountered another, they knew instantly by the look in the other's eyes, who they were and where they were from. A small smile, a few choice words, and they were on their way in search of the next house to invade, the next desire to be sated.

"How you getting on, then?"

"It's changed so much but it's bloody marvelous."

"I'm never going back."

"Me neither, at least not by choice."

"How do you mean?"

"I saw two of our lot dead under the wheels of a motor car."

"Dead for real?"

"Dead for real."

"Where do you think they've gone to?"

"Back Down I reckon."

"Then we'd best not wind up dead again."

One of the government buildings protected by a cordon of soldiers was MI5 headquarters at Millbank. Ben was inside in the basement ops centre. He and his people were trying to get a handle on the movement of Hellers into the hot zones and their dispersal patterns once they arrived. The video feed on a tile-work of screens arrayed on the walls was sourced from drones that crisscrossed the London skies.

An aide told him the PM was on the line.

"Yes, Prime Minister," Ben said. "How may I help you?"

"I'm on the way to Manchester and when I arrive I will address the nation. I need the latest data. Is there any sign the flow of Hellers has abated?"

"None whatsoever. If anything there are more of them."

"So might we assume that the SAS has not yet been able to take up their positions?"

Ben's mobile went off and he fumbled for the mute switch. "I think that is the correct assumption."

"God help us."

Ben hung up and saw the missed call was from his wife. He quickly rang her back at his parents' house in Kent.

"Everything all right? Are the girls okay?" he asked in a burst of concern.

"We're all fine. The girls are doing coloring with your mum. Here's the thing. Marjorie's just rung. She's deeply regretting not obeying the evacuation orders."

"Well she should. Stupid woman," Ben said.

"She didn't want to leave her dog. Can't you understand that? Why didn't they let people take their pets to evacuation centers?"

"Wasn't my call."

"She tried calling 999 but there was no reply so she called me."

"What's the problem?"

"She heard the sounds of someone breaking in below her. She's panicked out of her mind. She thinks she's next."

"What would you like me to do, divert critical resources and respond to her unsubstantiated anxieties?"

"That's exactly what I want. You owe me, Ben. You've been a real shit to me and the girls and it's time for you to make it up."

His first instinct was to let his rising anger boil over into something along the line of, I've been a shit? For working nonstop for two months? For not being there for bedtime baths and stories? For doing my bloody job to try to save the country from an existential threat? Instead he bottled it up and said, "All right, I'll do what I can."

He took off from the underground car park with a driver and two of his agents. Marjorie was one of his wife's schoolmates from Roedean, a rather morose woman who worked in publishing. When the two of them talked by phone Ben had to leave the room because he was irritated by even the faint sound of her husky voice leaking from the ear set in a torrent of complaints. The route along the river past the Tate was surreal as they were the only vehicle on the Millbank in what should have been, in the normal course of the affairs, the evening rush hour.

On arrival outside Marjorie's terraced house in Pimlico, the street was empty. Ben had been at a party there once and knew which of the street-facing windows were hers. There were one or two lights on at her flat but the lights in the first floor dwelling were blazing. Ben rang Marjorie's bell and waited. There was no response so he tried again and when that failed he tried ringing the flats below and above. Coming up empty, he rang her mobile and got voicemail.

"How do you want to play it?" one of his men asked.

"There's a small back garden," Ben replied. "Let's see if we can get in through the ground floor."

They had to go down the street to the end of the row of houses to get into the rear-facing gardens, and then, they had to scale several dividing fences until they got to Marjorie's house. The top half of the ground-flat garden door was glass. One of the agents broke the pane with the butt of his pistol.

"Here, take this," the agent said, offering his gun. "I've got another."

Ben didn't much like guns but he took it and checked the safety.

"There's a round in the chamber," the agent said.

"I doubt I'll need it," Ben said.

They cautiously made their way through the flat to the front entrance and climbed the first flight of stairs. The door to the flat was open, the door bashed in, the jam shattered.

"We need to check this one first," Ben said, his heart rate soaring.

Ben followed the other men in, guns at the ready. The hall and sitting room were a shambles with furniture upended and belongings tossed aside. The bedrooms were likewise ransacked. In the kitchen, the refrigerator door was left open showing empty shelves. The cupboards were all open and tins of tuna and soup were on the floor, dented, as if someone had tried to open them without using the tin opener still in a drawer.

"It's clear," one of the agents said. "No one here."

"Upstairs, then," Ben said.

On the next landing they saw that Marjorie's door was also bashed in. A small dog barked at them from the landing.

Ben clicked his pistol off safe mode and took a steadying breath.

"Is the layout the same?" an agent whispered.

"I think so. Pretty much. It's been a while."

The hall was dark. No one was in the sitting room. From there they could see the kitchen, also empty. The master bedroom door was closed.

Ben and one agent stood there while the other checked the guest bedroom. He came back and whispered that it was clear.

"On three," the other agent whispered, putting his hand on the doorknob.

They heard a woman scream.

"Three!" the agent said swinging the door open.

One man was standing by the bed watching while the other was on it, or more precisely, on Marjorie who was thrashing under his weight. There was a stench in the room. Heller stench.

The agent fired twice at the standing man, felling him efficiently. The rapist rolled off the bed, his filthy trousers around his ankles. He came to rest on the floor between the bed and the closet. Ben stood over him. His gun felt heavy and important in his hands. The man, a scowling giant, had blood on his genitals. He began to swear at Ben. Marjorie was too traumatized to cover herself. Ben glanced at her and saw blood running down her thigh.

He fired once into the man's forehead and he stopped swearing.

After several seconds, Ben lowered his weapon, clicked the safety back on, and pulled at the corner of the bedspread until it covered a sobbing Marjorie.

"It's Ben, Marjorie, Ben Wellington. We're going to take you away from here now to some place safe."

The first thing she said was, "Can I take my dog?"

He didn't dare touch her, though he wanted to give her a reassuring pat on the shoulder, a sign to her that in the midst of all this evil there was still some goodness.

"Yes, of course, you can take your dog."

15

First they poured melted wax into the openings in each rubber mold. The wax was allowed to harden and when it was solid, the wax casts were removed. Plaster was mixed and poured into an investment mold surrounding the wax cast. Those molds were kiln fired, melting away the wax and leaving a formed chamber within the plaster. They melted steel in the forge crucible and when it was orange and molten they poured it into the plaster casts. When the steel hardened they hammered the plaster away, leaving perfect steel pieces.

The AK-47s materialized piece by piece. Each of the ninety steel components was quenched in water, emitting puffs of steam. Some were large and hefty like the receiver, some small and light like the firing pin and some of the delicate springs. Kyle inspected each part with a practiced eye and when they were cool to the touch he smoothed off any burrs and rough spots using William's assorted files. The barrels went straight to William's foot-pedal lathe for rifling. Kyle rejected the first attempts and made some modifications in the drilling bit until the barrels had the desired twist.

A full assemblage of parts for each of the thirty-two rifles were laid out on planks on the grass outside the forge where Kyle and the others could work in the cooler air. Trevor and John took part in the assembly along with a dozen SAS men who self-identified as being especially proficient at the disassembly and assembly of firearms. One of the troopers from C Group was a keen woodworker so he and a bunch of SAS volunteers were tasked with carving rifle stocks, upper hand guards, and fore-end grips from a pile of cured wood stacked outside the forge.

The casting had taken a full day. Kyle hadn't slept more than an hour but when he was satisfied he had cast all the rifle parts he turned his attention to the bullets.

"You look like a zombie," John said. "Sure you don't want a couple of hours of shut-eye?"

"No bullets, no boom-boom," Kyle said, plunging back into the hot forge.

Marsh came over to inspect one of the pallets of parts.

"You really think these things are going to fire?" he asked, full of attitude.

"If the chemist can make the primers then they'll spit lead. My brother knows what he's doing," John said, pointing at the delicate pieces of the trigger assembly. "Look at the quality of this work under these primitive conditions. It's amazing."

"We'll see, won't we?" Marsh said. "But it wouldn't shock me if we wind up having to use flintlocks and crossbows. Building AKs in a medieval forge. Daft idea, if you ask me."

Inside the forge Kyle began mobilizing William and his workers on ammunition production. Lead brass casings and primer caps had to be cast from molds. Bullet presses had to be cast as well, to enable them to make thousands of rounds in a timely fashion. Before long, the forge was spitting out flames and molten lead, brass, and steel were flowing.

In a corner of the forge, far enough from the furnace to be tolerable but close enough to get ingots of hot steel as a heat source, Nightingale and his assistant worked into the night.

The chemist had tramped down to the village with Emily and a few bodyguards and to bargain for glassware. Mrs. Smith was his negotiator, and in exchange for a few copper coins that William provided from the forge coffers, the villagers parted with some cups and glasses.

"Not ideal," Nightingale had told Emily, "but we'll make do. Wish I knew how to blow glass. Not many regrets in life but that's one of them."

Emily had taken a grand total of one chemistry course at university but that was enough to qualify her to be Nightingale's assistant. They set up a makeshift bench and prepared for the first step, the production of nitric acid.

The years fell away and the toll of illness all but vanished as Nightingale sat on his wooden stool and worked at his primitive bench.

He seemed happy and light as he guided Emily along. "We are going to make *spiritus nitri* as the ancients called it. Now, without scales we're going to have to rely on instinct but here goes: about fifty grams of saltpeter, nicely ground fine in a mortar and pestle. Yes, add it to that crucible pot and let's mix in one hundred and fifty grams of this nice white clay, kaolin it's also called. Mix it up as thoroughly as you can. Good, very good. Then to the furnace we'll go."

He told her they were aiming for a temperature of about one thousand degrees centigrade, and in the absence of a thermometer, instinct was required.

"The ancients didn't have a thermometer and they did just fine," he said, pulling the crucible in and out of the fiery furnace with long tongs, watching the color change. "That's it! Look at that lovely blue-green color. I believe we've made nitric acid of the appropriate purity."

"That's brilliant," Emily said. "You'll make a chemist of me yet."

"Not so fast, young lady. We're only in the alchemy stage. Now for the next step. We'll use hot ingots to heat our water bath and we'll need to cover our faces from the fumes. Are you ready?"

"Lead styphnate, coming up," she said cheerfully.

Nightingale called over to William, "We're ready for the lead, if you will, my good man."

The next morning came as all mornings came in Down, a creeping lightening of the black sky until it turned a flat, whitish gray. The SAS men who were used to sleeping rough, made fires and reheated the carcass of the deer they had bagged the previous day. John and Emily had found a private spot behind the forge, a soft, grassy patch where they had laid out a blanket donated by one of William's workers. They awoke in unison. John kissed her; they wanted each other but love was not on the schedule. Nightingale slept closer to the forge entrance wrapped in bedclothes which Mrs. Smith had pulled from her own bed. He was too exhausted and ill to rise. As the camp stirred, people walked around him, careful not to disturb. The four captains found John and Emily by the water trough.

"How'd you get on last night?" Yates asked.

John splashed his face and said, "I packed it in a few hours ago. They were still working."

Marsh headed for the forge door. "Time's a wasting. We've got to start deploying today with or without the AKs. Personally I think it'll be without."

"Ye of little faith," John said.

Inside, Trevor was sitting at a workbench, his head buried in his arms. Beside him, Kyle was running the hand-lever on the press, pumping out finished bullets that he tossed into a bucket. About ten SAS troopers were asleep on the floor.

Kyle saw the delegation entering and elbowed Trevor awake. "Showtime, Mr. Jones."

"Kyle, you're a fucking machine," John said. "Two days without sleep."

"That's nothing," Kyle replied. "Two days without booze. That's the impressive statistic."

"We're here to see guns and ammo," Marsh said, "not an alcoholic with a limp."

John reacted with fury and bumped his chest into Marsh's. "I think it's about time I kicked your sorry ass, you know that?"

The sleeping SAS troopers were on their feet now, looking on.

"Let's do it then," Marsh shot back. "Right here, right now."

The other captains jumped in, separating the two men before fists began to fly.

"For Christ's sake, Alan, put a sock in it," Yates said, shoving Marsh back. "We're all on the same team."

"Same team?" Marsh spat. "Not even close."

Trevor held an object in his hands wrapped in a cloth. He winked at

John but spoke directly to Marsh. "You want to see guns and ammo, mate? You've come to the right place."

With that, he removed the cloth and held up a fully assembled rifle, the pale wood of the stock and handgrips set off against the matte-black steel of the receiver, barrel, and iron sights.

Kyle handed Trevor a steel magazine, heavy with bullets and said, "This alcoholic with a gimpy leg is proud to present you boys with the official AK-47 hellcat model, capable of semi-auto or full-auto firing modes, complete with thirty-round banana clips and 7.62X39mm cartridges."

"Let's have a look," John said.

Trevor seated the magazine and passed it to John who tested its balance in his hands and looked down the sights.

"It looks and feels right," John said, passing it on to Yates for inspection.

It passed through other hands before winding up with Marsh who gave it a once-over and said, "All I care about it whether it goes bang when I pull the trigger."

"Then let's go outside," Kyle said, taking it back.

William and all his forge workers joined the line of men exiting the forge. Outside, John found a tree about fifty yards away and using one of the forge knives, pinned a piece of scrap leather to it.

All the soldiers assembled for the show.

Kyle lined up the shot and said, "The gunsmith's the guy who ought to take the first shots in case the receiver blows up in his face."

"Jesus, John, is it safe?" Emily said.

"Have faith," he replied. "It'll work if the primers work."

"The professor was quite confident."

"In that case you'd better stick your fingers in your ears."

Kyle pulled back the bolt and let it snap forward. He put the butt stock against his cheek and peered through the front sight. His finger curled against the trigger.

Birds took flight from the surrounding wood when the huge boom cracked the air. The piece of leather moved slightly. Kyle smiled and pulled the trigger five more times in rapid succession, the leather rippling with each impact.

Nightingale was awake at the first shot. He got to his feet and came over to Emily and said giddily, "The primers work, Emily! They work!"

"I never doubted you, not for an instant," she said, delighting him by planting a kiss on his cheek.

"Now for full auto," Kyle shouted above the ringing in his own ears. "I don't recommend it, 'cause there's only so much ammo, but here goes."

He flipped the selector switch and held the trigger back. The rifle spit out the remainder of the magazine in a hail of deafening fire. When he was done, he removed the magazine, made sure the gun was empty and shouted, "This hearing thing is over-rated! This baby sure makes some noise!"

William ran to the tree and returned waving the shredded piece of leather.

"What a marvel!" he said. "My forge did that! My forge!"

The soldiers began whooping and yelling. John squeezed Emily's arm and went over to his brother.

"You are a fucking all-star," he said.

"What did you say?"

He shouted this time. "I said you're a fucking all-star. A deaf all-star."

"I do three things well," Kyle said with tears welling. "Build guns, drink, and fuck up relationships."

"Come here," John said, enveloping him in a bear hug.

Marsh and the other captains came over to check out the blistering-hot rifle that reeked of gunpowder.

"I guess I owe you and your brother an apology," Marsh told Kyle. "Bloody well done. Provided all of them work as well."

"Apology accepted," Kyle said. "They'll all work. Will they jam more than a usual build? Probably. But we've got ourselves a Turtledove situation."

"What's that?" Captain Gatti asked.

"Harry Turtledove. One of my favorite writers," Kyle said. "He wrote a book called *Guns of the South*, where some racists use a time machine to bring a bunch of AK-47s back to Civil War times. That's all the Confederates needed to turn the tide against the Union army. Lee won and Grant lost. Alternative history."

"We're writing the history this time," John said. "What do you say we pack up and move out?"

"One more little trinket to help us move in the right direction," Kyle said, reaching into his pocket. He pulled out five brass compasses and gave one to John and one to each of the captains. "In the middle of the night while we were making primer caps and bullets I had William make these."

"How'd you magnetize the pins?" Captain Greene asked.

"Easy. Rubbed them against the silk maps. Old camping trick."

Marsh stuck out his hand. "We're going to make you an honorary member of A Squadron," he said. "If any of us make it out of here."

The captains organized a trial firing of each rifle. All of them but three worked perfectly, and with some filing and fussing, Kyle made these work too. All the magazines were loaded with a double-stack and the rest of the ammo was divided into four sacks. Each group was issued eight rifles and one sack.

Kyle went back inside the forge and returned with a surprise: three more rifles under his arm. He gave one to John, one to Trevor, and kept one for himself.

"Had a little extra time," he said. "Made a few extras."

John shook his hand and Trevor said, "Thanks, mate. Outstanding."

"Sorry I didn't make one for you, Emily," Kyle said. "I'm probably coming off as a sexist pig."

"That's quite all right," Emily said with a smile. "I really don't want one."

As they rolled up their blanket Emily told John, "We can't take Ted with us, you know. He'll never make it."

"The plan was to bring him back to Leatherhead and try to send him through."

"I doubt he'll survive even that. He can hardly hold his head up. The trip will kill him."

John watched the chemist for a while. He was sitting against a log looking frail and dazed. "What do you suggest?"

"That."

She was pointing at Mrs. Smith ambling up the path from the village with a small basket of food for Nightingale. She came up to him, engaged in conversation, sat beside him, and got him to munch on a crust.

"Think he'll go for it?" John asked.

"His job's done. He's sick and worn out. I'm guessing he will."

Emily was right. Nightingale admitted that he had awoken with considerable trepidation at the thought of doing hard traveling, on a horse, or astride Moose's shoulders. But always the gentleman, he announced in Mrs. Smith's presence that he wouldn't presume to force himself upon her hospitality.

As it happened, the old woman beamed at the idea and said, "Well, I'd be delighted to take in Mr. Nightingale as a lodger. I've been alone for a very long while and a bit of company would do nicely. He'll be safe and sound with me."

Emily gave the chemist a kiss on the cheek. "You're a hero, Ted," she said. "I've never met a braver man in my life."

"You really think so?" His cheeks, the only part of his face not yellowed by jaundice, turned pink.

"Take it from me," John said. "Soldiers put themselves into harm's way after training and indoctrination. "You were cold-called for this assignment and you didn't hesitate. You're the real deal."

"The real deal," he said, rolling the Americanism over his lips. "How marvelous."

Moose was summoned for the trip down the hill. The huge soldier cradled the chemist in his arms.

"Hang tight," John said. "We'll be back for you. I can't say when exactly but we'll be back." John looked at Mrs. Smith and wagged his finger at the professor. "And don't do anything I wouldn't do."

A Squadron was ready to pull out.

John thanked William for his help but the forger said, "Don't thank me, John who is not from here. Thank King Henry. Will you be seeing his majesty?"

John smiled. "Not right away. But I'll be sure to tell him how great you were. If I don't see you again, keep using that good Swedish iron."

The plan was simple. They marched to the river as one. Once there Gatti's C Group would peel off right away, using the stashed rowboats to move rifles and ammo across. The men would then march back the way they came to Leatherhead.

The rest would head east on foot until they found boats to commandeer. They would sail downstream as far as Dartford where Greene's group would march north to Upminster and Marsh's men and Trevor would head south to Sevenoaks where Trevor would seek out the lost schoolboys of Belmeade. Yates's men together with John, Emily, and Kyle would approach Dartford to look for the MAAC scientists and VIPs. Then John and Emily would head east, seeking a way across the channel.

Tramping through the meadow, John said to Emily, "This has been a good start."

"Better than we might have expected."

"We need to be honest with ourselves. The mission's too aggressive. We always knew that. There's no way we can save everyone: the MAAC people, the kids, the civilians in all the hot zones."

"I know," she said. "As harsh as it sounds, we've got to keep our eyes on the prize."

"I know," he said. "Paul."

"Even if one or both of us has to be sacrificed trying."

The river came into view and he took her hand. "Day by day you're becoming a warrior, did you know that?"

16

The others were angrily glaring at him but Trotter was standing his ground.

"Tell me what you would have done differently?" he asked.

Every one of the Earthers assembled in the banqueting hall turned dormitory was angry and scared. The women were weeping.

George Lawrence had lost considerable weight and had taken to wrapping himself in his blanket throughout the day for warmth. "I certainly wouldn't have been Suffolk's pimp."

"How dare you!" Trotter fumed. "As your representative I have had to make hard decisions to save lives."

"Self-appointed representative who lives apart from us as their fair-haired boy," one of the scientists called out.

"And what about Brenda's life?" Chris Cowles asked. She was sitting on her cot holding a trembling Kelly Jenkins.

"Her suicide is a tragedy," Trotter said. "She went into this clear-headed. None of us had much of a choice. We are prisoners and our captors, at least some of them, are animals."

Trotter had sown the seeds of Brenda Mitchell's death. She had placed the drapery cord around her neck but he might as well have been the one to do it and kick away the stool. He might not have been proud of it but he was proud of his prowess in playing human chess. He had sacrificed Brenda as one might sacrifice a knight to set up a checkmate. He had done black work at MI6 as recently as the fatally botched assassination of Giles Farmer and he had always slept soundly.

"Here's the way to go about it," he had suggested to Suffolk. "Threaten to kill our security men if this Brenda woman won't agree to sleep with you. Make it her decision. Play on her altruism."

"What if she refuses?" Suffolk had asked.

"Then hang them and threaten one of her friends. I'd suggest Chris, the older woman."

"Are they not your men?" Suffolk had asked with a knowing smile.

"They're MI5. Different agency altogether. Hardly know them."

Trotter had used Smithwick for the gambit, pulling her to one of the corners of the dormitory.

"You can't be serious?" she had said.

"I'm just the messenger, Karen," he had replied gravely. "This Suffolk chap approached me and told me he wanted Brenda delivered to his quarters. When I told him to stuff it, he delivered the threat. I don't know what to do. You've got to talk to her."

"I hardly know her. Chris is the one who's bonded with her."

"Then talk to Chris first. He said he'd hang our MI5 minders if she doesn't play ball."

The discussion with Brenda had not gone down well. She reacted by entering a near-catatonic state, refusing to leave her cot and hardly eating. After two days the Earthers were told to look out the windows onto the earthen courtyard. Everyone but Brenda watched in horror as the agents were hung from three gallows.

That evening Trotter had informed Smithwick that Suffolk had upped the ante. Chris would be hung in the morning.

Trotter had watched from afar as Smithwick sat beside Brenda whispering bad tidings. The young woman hadn't said anything but an hour later, when Chris was using the privy, she had picked herself off her bed and had shuffled to the door to announce to the guards that she should be taken to the Duke of Suffolk. When Chris returned and had learned what she had done she became hysterical.

All had been quiet for a day until Cromwell appeared at Trotter's rooms, interrupting his supper of roast game.

"Cromwell," Trotter had said, slightly drunk. "Come and join me. I think it's rabbit or at least I hope it is."

"Your young woman who was Suffolk's wench has hanged herself."

"What? Really?"

"Indeed. Suffolk is angry. He has lost a concubine. I am angry. I have lost a scientist. I have seen too little progress in the deciphering of your texts."

Trotter had more wine. "Best thing that could have happened."

"Why is that?"

"They've been slow-playing me too. I think they're all in on it. Campbell Bates and the rest of them. They'd rather talk about escaping than getting down to work. They've got this mentality that one doesn't aid and abet the enemy and you most certainly are the enemy."

Cromwell had arched his brows as high as they would go. "It was you who orchestrated the threats and measures we have undertaken against your people."

"I did. It's too bad she killed herself but in a way it's helpful. They're already scared out of their minds. This will only heighten their anxiety. Now's the time to come down really hard. Threaten them directly. Tell them it's time to start building a blast furnace. Apparently that's the thing that enables all the rest—at least they've told me that much. Tell them if they don't get on with it or if any more of them take the easy way out like Brenda, then you'll kill the whole lot."

Cromwell had shaken his head in amazement at Trotter's brazen tactics. "No, I'll leave it to you to speak to them. After your supper, of course. We wouldn't wish to interrupt. Perhaps you can tell them that the next to die will be you."

"Ha! Good one. That would have the opposite effect. They'd cheer the move."

Before he left Cromwell said, "Methinks you will arrive here permanently one day, Master Trotter."

"That may be. If so, maybe I'll find a position working for you."

Now, facing his people, Trotter continued to act the part of a victim.

"I live apart from the rest of you simply because Cromwell and his ilk do not understand or respect egalitarian principles. In order for me to best represent our collective interests it is necessary for me to be seen as our leader. And that means certain trappings of privilege which I would gladly give up if another strategy were more beneficial."

Leroy Bitterman shook his head vehemently. "You know, Tony, you really know how to sling the shit."

"I quite agree," Smithwick said. "If and when we return to London—the real London—I shall condemn you publicly for being our Quisling."

"Listen to all of you," Trotter said, his voice swelling. "You don't seem to understand the survival game. Perhaps Brenda's suicide is the wake-up call you needed. The other side is holding all the cards. They are killers. They are ruthless. The only thing that's keeping us sheltered and fed is our potential usefulness to them. They don't understand how brilliant scientists who can make supercolliders can't make blast furnaces. They want action."

Campbell Bates said, "I've tried to explain the difficulties but …"

"But Cromwell won't listen," Trotter said, finishing the thought. "He doesn't trust us. He thinks we're stalling. I need to tell you what he told me when he informed me of Brenda's suicide. He's lost patience. He wants a tangible show of progress. He is organizing a trip to one of the royal forges where he expects us to lay out plans for enacting the designs in the blast-furnace book. If we do not fully and productively cooperate he will execute one of us."

A quiet fell over the room. Trotter chose not to break the silence but to let it linger like an exquisite pain.

"Who? Did he say who?" The question came from Stuart Binford. For someone who made his living being voluble, the public relations man had become one of the more reticent presences among the group. He wasn't one of the VIPs; he wasn't one of the scientists. He seemed to try to make himself as small and innocuous a presence as possible, fearing his irrelevance.

"Not you," Trotter said. "I'm afraid it's you, Chris."

"Why me?" she cried. "Why kill me?"

"He's a canny one, that Cromwell," Trotter said. "I think he's observed you're popular. And you're a woman so he probably thinks, quite rightly, that we'll be fiercely protective."

"Then there's only one thing we can do," Bates said, slipping his shoes on. "We'll have to try and build him his goddamn furnace."

"Will you go talk to her?" Boris asked.

They were inside what the Hellers were calling the boy's cottage. It wasn't much of a cottage really. There were four walls and a hearth, but there were no windows. The door was a sturdy affair that latched from the outside to keep the boys in at night. A leaky roof spared no one when it rained. Their beds were no more than hay, and old hay at that, stuffed into burlap. Their utensils and bowls were crudely made of wood. The blankets were the only well-made things at hand. There was no shortage of wool on a sheep farm.

"And tell her what?" Angus said, tossing his porridge bowl aside.

"Tell her we don't want to be her slaves any more," Boris said. "Look at my hands. They look like raw meat."

"Tell her we're sick of her sheep," Glynn added.

Angus gave Glynn one of his *e tu, Brute* looks, reserved for when even his best friend seemed to turn on him.

"As if she listens to me," Angus said.

"Well she definitely doesn't listen to me," Danny said. "All I get is, Chinaman, go and shovel the shit over there."

"She's nice to me," Harry said, sucking on his wooden spoon.

"That's because she can't understand a thing you say," Stuart said. "Wormhole, parallel universe bollocks."

"It's not bollocks," Harry said.

"Look, Harry," Kevin said pointing an accusatory finger, "while we're working like bloody slaves, you're in her cottage sitting by a nice fire telling her tales."

"She likes to hear about modern times," Harry said. "I think she's quite intelligent."

"Then maybe Harry ought to speak to her instead of Angus. Maybe Harry's the one to persuade her."

"Harry the head boy, Harry the head boy," Nigel said in singsong, mocking Angus's authority.

Angus wasn't going to let that stand. He flung himself toward Nigel and began pummeling him until Danny and Boris moved to break it up.

Nigel spit out some blood and Angus began to stalk out when Andrew began crying, "If we start fighting amongst ourselves then we're no better than they are. We should be better than them. They're evil. They've all done horrible things. We haven't. At least not yet."

Angus stared at the floor as if the right thing to say would be found scrawled upon the rough planks. "I'm sorry for bashing you, Nigel."

"No you're not."

"Shut up, Nigel," Glynn said. "He's trying to apologize and you're just being a shit like usual."

That earned Glynn a look of thanks from Angus who said, "I'll go talk to her about letting up on us, all right?"

"I just want to go home," Andrew said, blowing his nose into a dirty rag.

"I do too," Angus said, pushing through the door.

Ardmore was drinking ale on a patch of grass in front of the cottage he shared with Bess.

"I didn't ring the work bell yet," he said to Angus. "What do you want?"

"To talk with Bess."

"Why?"

"I'm carrying a message from the others."

"Are you now?" Ardmore grinned, exposing some yellow teeth. He called out, "Bess, Angus is bearing a message from the tykes."

Bess came out, all in black as usual. She never smiled in front of Angus, or any of the boys. Except for Harry. If she still had a tender spot in the reaches of her soul occupied by unsullied memories of childhood, she didn't show it. She had told Ardmore recently that the boys were nothing more to her than laborers. They didn't produce as much as her usual workers but they didn't eat as much either.

"That runt, Harry, doesn't hardly do a lick of work," Ardmore had said.

"I'll make an exception of him," Bess had said. "He's my storytelling boy."

Bess frowned at Angus and asked him why he'd disturbed her rest.

Angus cleared his throat. "We think you're working us too hard," he said. "We think ..."

Ardmore quieted him and backed him up, coming at him with his arm cocked for a backhanded slap. "You little shit!"

"Leave him be," Bess said. "I'll hear his complaint. What is it you think, Angus?"

"It's not just me, it's all of us. We're schoolboys. We're not used to wrestling sheep to the ground and shearing them. We're not used to cleaning out their pens. We want to go back to Sevenoaks and try to find our way home."

"You do, do you?" Bess said. "And how do you propose getting there? Will you be riding in one of these motorcars that Harry's told me about? Or maybe one of these winged machines what carries people up in the skies? If not these then I expect you'll be walking all the way, dodging brigands and rovers along the way. Or not dodging them. Maybe winding up as cannie food instead. You want to wind up as cannie food, is that what you desire, Angus?"

"No, of course not. We were hoping you might take us back with you the next time you're bringing wool to London."

"That won't be for quite a while, boy," she said angrily, "and you won't be coming when we do. You need to face the truth. Plain and simple. You're not going home through your precious wormholes. You're staying here, maybe not forever like us, but as long as you have life within your bodies. You work for me. How I want. When I want. Ardmore, ring the work bell and go ahead, you've my permission to strike him across his miserable little face."

The delegation arrived at Richmond by royal barge. One of William's forge workers had spotted the flag before it docked and had run to notify his master. William had time to wash the grime from his face before his monarch arrived.

But it was not King Henry at his door but Thomas Cromwell, the Duke of Suffolk, a contingent of guards, and a handful of bewildered Earthers eyeing the tall chimneystack, belching smoke.

"Master Cromwell," William said, deeply bowing. "When I heard the barge was sighted I thought his majesty was coming to inspect our recent handiwork."

"What handiwork is that?" Cromwell asked.

"The modern rifles he tasked John Camp with fabricating."

"Did that man say, John Camp?" Campbell Bates asked Trotter.

"Christ, I think he did," Trotter said.

"What are you speaking of, man?" Cromwell demanded. "John Camp was here?"

"He was," William said, puzzling at the confusion.

"When?"

"He departed not two days past, having arrived earlier bearing a letter by the hand of the king. Were you not aware?"

"No, forger, I was not!" Cromwell shouted. "Who was with him?"

"Earthers, all. Miss Loughty was present, Master Kyle, Master Jones, Master Nightingale, and many, many soldiers."

"What manner of soldiers? How many?" Cromwell said, unable to keep his voice from rising.

"What manner?" William said, rubbing his chin. "Englishmen, I'd say, but modern men and like the others, very much alive. As to number, well there were three score of them."

Trotter edged his way to Cromwell's side and addressed William. "Did these soldiers give you more information? Did they say if they were from the British Army?"

"They did say something which I did not understand," William said. "What was it? SAS? Yes, that was what they said."

Bates whispered it to David Laurent who passed it along to Henry Quint who passed it along to Leroy Bitterman. "The SAS are here. We're going to be rescued."

"Tell me of these modern rifles you spoke of," Cromwell said.

"They are frightful weapons to behold. Each one holds some thirty lead and powder ammos, as they are called, and spits them out with great rapidity without the need for any manner of reloading. Mr. Kyle called them AK something or another."

"AK-47s?" Trotter asked.

"Yes, that's it."

"My God," Trotter muttered, "Brilliant move."

"Where did Camp go with these soldiers?" Suffolk demanded.

"I presume they left to deliver the weapons to the king. Where is the king? Is he waiting on his barge?"

"He is not here," Cromwell said, curtly. "Think man, did they not make any mention of where they might have gone?"

William thought hard and said, "I did overhear one of the soldiers, the captain with a moustache, say the name, Leatherhead."

"Leatherhead," Cromwell said excitedly. "This is one of the towns where men are making a crossing to Earth. Suffolk, you must assemble a troop with field cannon to make to Leatherhead. Find John Camp, kill him if you must, but if he is seized, bring him to me at Whitehall."

Suffolk seemed to bristle at receiving orders from Cromwell but agreed to the action.

Cromwell turned to William. "These new and frightful weapons. Can you make these weapons for me?"

"I cannot, Master Cromwell. Master Kyle threw the rubber molds into the fire and John Camp smashed the plaster molds."

Cromwell flew into a rage and grabbed his captain of the guard by the sleeve and pulled him away.

That left an opening for Trotter to approach William and say, "My name is Anthony Trotter. I'm in charge of these people. We're being held against our will."

"Are you now?" William replied.

"Indeed we are. John Camp and the SAS soldiers—they were undoubtedly sent to find us and take us home. Did they mention my name?"

"Trotter, you say?"

"Yes, Anthony Trotter."

"I can't recollect anyone doing so."

"Well, did they mention any other names? Smithwick? Lawrence? Bates? Bitterman?"

William shook his head.

"Did they ask where prisoners might be held? Was there any talk of rescue plans?"

"Not to me."

Red in the face, Trotter was going to keep firing questions but Cromwell returned. His captain ran down the hill in the direction of the barge.

"We will endeavor to find John Camp and his perfidious minions before they can harm the crown," Cromwell growled. "My barge is being prepared for my departure. I will take my leave but I will leave these prisoners and a party of my men with you. They are men of science for the most part. Well not this one," he said, referring to Trotter, "but he pleaded his case for being in attendance and I acquiesced. The scientists have brought a text with them together with plans to create a great furnace, far larger and more powerful than your present forge. I would have you begin work on this furnace immediately. Once built, we will make excellent steel from the iron we have within Brittania with no need to send our ships to the Norselands. Then we will build machines of war that harness the power of steam. We will repel all invaders. We will conquer all of Europa. Work quickly, William. If you perceive any diminution of effort, any slackness or sloth, I command you throw this one, Master Trotter, into your hottest fire."

17

Finding a boat had not been a problem. A fast-moving scouting party from D Group had located a large, unballasted sailing barge several miles downstream from Richmond moored on a floating dock. The sprawl of London extended to the area and there were too many people about to snatch the vessel without an attention-grabbing fight. So they had laid low in tall grasses until nightfall when Captain Greene led his men into the river for a silent assault. A lit lamp announced the all clear and when the rest of them boarded down the gangplank, John had expected to see a pile of broken bodies. Instead, the fishermen had been neatly tied to barrels of fish and gagged, not a drop of blood spilled.

"Fancy a bit of sushi?" Greene had asked, chomping on a slice of raw bream.

Arriving in the vicinity of Dartford, Greene's group disembarked on the north shore of the Thames, and with no more than a simple "good luck and good hunting" began a fast-march toward Upminster. The rest of them beached the boat on the south shore, gave the terrified fishermen some water and left them to be found by passersby.

"This is goodbye for now," Trevor said, getting ready to move out with A Group for Sevenoaks. He shouldered his AK-47 on a rope sling.

"Try to find the boys," John said, pulling him aside, "but don't do anything crazy. I'm going to need a best man at my wedding."

"Don't suppose Emily knows anything about this, guv?" Trevor said.

"I'm saving it for when we get back. Don't want to jinx it."

"You're assuming she's going to accept."

"Isn't that what shallow narcissists do? Seriously, Trev, don't get killed. Hang with Marsh who's an asshole but the good-soldier kind of asshole. When it's time to go home someone will be sent through to let you know. And if it gets too hairy, if you think you're going down, then bail. Get your butt inside the hot zone and get home."

With Trevor and A Group peeled off, John and Emily got ready for their farewells to Kyle and D Group.

"Here's the thing, John, I'm not going with them," Kyle announced.

"Fuck that, Kyle, that was the plan you agreed on," John said. "You can't change it up now."

"I can and I did," Kyle said. "Anyway, I talked to Emily about it last night and she said she was cool with it."

"Thanks a lot," John told her with a dose of sarcasm.

"It's for you boys to work out," she said. "Leave me out of it but if Kyle wants to come, yes, I am cool with it."

"Tell me why you don't want me along?" Kyle asked.

"It's going to be unpredictable," John said. "It's going to be tough sledding. We're going to have to move fast."

"That's basically code for you don't think an out-of-shape guy with a fucked up knee can keep up with you."

"Come off it, Kyle. I didn't want Emily to come either but she convinced me she might be the only one to persuade Loomis to cooperate."

Kyle sniffed back tears. He looked away for a few seconds before laying into him. "All my life I've lived in your goddamn shadow. I've been so scared of that shadow I'm almost scared of my own. The last few days—the last few days I've picked up a whole lot of self-respect and you know what? It feels pretty damn good. I'm hungry for more, John, and you're not going to stop me from getting it. I'm coming. Besides if your AK jams, I'm probably the only one you know around here who can fix it."

John shook his head a few times and smiled. "Yeah, I suppose you are. Good gunsmiths are hard to find in Hell or so I'm told."

Behind him John heard Emily calling his name.

"I know, I know, I'm a good guy," he said.

"You certainly are but that's not it. Look."

She was pointing downriver where the top of a mast was poking over a thicket of bushes and trees.

Yates saw it too. Using hand signs he split his group into three and signaled for John, Kyle, and Emily to join him in the middle platoon while the two others flanked them, rifles ready. They cautiously plunged into the thicket and moved through it as silently as they could, climbing a modest, heavily wooded hill until they were at its crest.

Yates was the first in the middle group to get a clear view of the river below. "Christ," he said.

The others came up beside him.

John exhaled deeply. "This is bad, way worse than I expected."

What they saw was a sea of humanity, hundreds of people making their way toward Dartford village, the meager cluster of cottages John and Emily knew so well. From their vantage point the village itself appeared empty. None of the chimneys were producing smoke. Yet streams of people were approaching from all directions. Those coming from the north had to ford the river. A bevy of small rowing boats was providing some kind of ferry service. From the landward directions most were walking but some rode on horseback or horse cart. Amidst the peasantry were some king's soldiers, identifiable by their uniforms and standards. The march seemed slow, deliberate, cautious, not a headlong rush by any means, the effect of which was the formation of a perimeter of Hellers around the village. As the Earthers watched from their vantage point, a few Hellers took tentative steps forward until they vanished.

"We're seeing a hot zone in action," Emily said. "I shudder to think what's happening on the other side."

Yates let out a low whistle. "I don't think we have nearly enough ammo."

"The SAS has a reputation for improvising," John said.

"Then improvise we will," Yates said.

"I don't think we're going to find the MAAC people among that lot," Emily said.

"We're going to have to leave that to the captain while we move on," John said.

"What do you think the story is on that ship?" Kyle said.

It was a large four-master with a tall quarterdeck sitting at anchor in the deepest part of the river channel. A longboat was being lowered over its side.

"It's a warship," John said. "A galleon, but I don't think it's English. Look at the flag."

"My God, John," Emily said. "I think it's flying French colors."

"An invasion?" Yates asked.

"It's on its own so I doubt it," John said. "I think it may be a sign of something more serious. Word of the hot zones may have spread to the continent. That's the bad news."

"What's the good news?" Kyle asked.

"We may have found our ride to Francia," Emily said.

The operation required the cover of darkness and had to be conducted in absolute silence. While it was hard to spend another day waiting, the prospect of commandeering the French galleon was too tempting. John gamed it out with Yates and his staff sergeant, O'Malley, a fellow with a heavy Belfast accent. If the entire crew had abandoned ship to join the migration to Earth then the galleon would be essentially useless and the wait would have been a waste. If the crew were still on board they would have to be subdued and pressed into service for the channel crossing. The safest way of achieving this was to use all of A Group for boarding and capture. But keeping a dozen or more crewmen in check during a crossing to Francia would take more than John, Kyle, and Emily, even with a couple of AK-47s. There was simply too much ship to cover to avoid an insurrection.

"But the French are allied with Garibaldi now," Emily said. "Maybe they'll cooperate freely once we tell them who we are and what we've done."

"Any crew that decided to take passengers to Dartford has gone rogue," John said. "We couldn't trust them."

"There's no way around it," Yates said. "You'll need to take some of my men with you. You'd know better than I the minimum number needed to keep a ship like that under control."

"Two of your people ought to do it," John said.

"How many AKs will you need?" Yates asked.

"None. You'll need all of yours. One of your men can take mine. I'll find a musket on board."

"I can reload a blackpowder rifle pretty damn fast," Kyle said. "The other guy can use mine."

"All right," Yates said. "I'll be looking for one volunteer."

"I thought you said two men," John said.

O'Malley grimaced. "I think the captain just gave me an order. He's a sneaky bastard that way. I'll go and canvas the others for the volunteer. Hearing none, it'll be Culpepper."

When fully dark, A Group left the thicket and made its way to the riverbank upstream of the galleon and a good distance from the Hellers still coming toward the promised-land of Dartford. John, Emily, and Kyle waited among the bulrushes with all the rifles and ammo while the SAS men slipped into the water and began swimming toward the warship armed only with knives procured from William's forge.

And then they waited.

Half an hour passed, then an hour.

In the distance they heard some shouting coming from the direction of Dartford but nothing from the river. The night was impenetrable; it was an act of faith that the ship was even still there. Finally, they heard something that sounded like oars slapping the water and a longboat appeared at the river's edge carrying Yates and six of his troopers.

"Hop in," Yates whispered.

"Was the crew there?" Emily asked.

"Yeah, about a dozen men and their captain."

"What took so long?" John asked.

"Taking them down didn't take much time at all. It was searching for the ones we might've missed that took some doing. That plus rounding up all the guns, knives, and swords. Do you have any idea the nooks and crannies in one of these things?"

"Actually, I do," John said, recalling his all-too-recent channel crossings.

"What's the captain like?" John asked when they were on their way, rowing back toward the galleon.

"He's pissed off," Yates replied. "Speaks English, swears in French."

"Does he know what we want him to do?" John asked.

"Thought I'd leave that to you. Hungry?" Yates opened a basket stuffed with bread and cheese. "Found this in the captain's cabin."

"Famished," Emily said, reaching in.

The captain, a man named La Rue, was indeed pissed off. Sergeant O'Malley had done him the courtesy of not sticking a gag in his mouth but he was confined to his cabin, his hands and feet bound.

"I hear you speak English," John told him.

"Who are you?" La Rue asked.

"John Camp. I don't suppose you've heard of me."

"Why should I know you?" he asked contemptuously, sniffing at him.

"Didn't know if you were informed about recent events inside Francia."

"If you mean the demise of King Maximilien and our alliances with Italia and Iberia, yes, I am well-informed. What has this to do with an outsider such as yourself?"

"My associates and I are, how can I put it, in the service of your new king, Garibaldi."

"None of this has anything to do with me. I owe my allegiance to the Duke of Bretagne. He cares little about these alliances. We attend to our own affairs."

"You're a long way from Brittany. Why are you here?"

"Why are *you* here?" La Rue challenged back. "And why have you seized my vessel?"

"I like you, Captain," John said. "Sergeant, would you untie him?"

O'Malley began to undo the knots.

"I'll go first," John said. "I think you know about the channel that's opened between our two worlds. I think you've just dropped off a load of passengers who want to cross over. My associates and myself are here to try and cut the connection between Earth and Hell. It's supposed to be a one-way journey and we need to keep it that way."

"Thank you," La Rue said, rubbing his wrists. "Yes, that is why I am here. Word of the miracle of this English village has reached Britagne and many people want a second taste of life and are willing to pay someone like me for the chance."

"I'll bet your duke doesn't know you're moonlighting."

"What is this word?"

"It means you're on your own. He doesn't know anything about it. That way all the payments go to you."

"I would rather not speak of such matters."

"Of course not. Tell me this. Why didn't you cross over too?"

La Rue asked if he could have some of his own wine and poured a glass. "I admit I gave it some thought," he said, "but then I asked myself, why? I have heard from recent men how wondrous your world has become. Would I like to see the sun again, watch children at play, read a book, listen to a chamber orchestra, walk among men who are not all cutthroats and despicable scoundrels such as myself? Yes, of course. But I am a sea captain. I command a galleon. I am told there are no galleons in your world. What would I do? I get along well enough, I have the patronage of the duke, a good house in Brest, better than the one I had in life, and so far I have avoided the salles decomposition. I will stay in Hell. I am reconciled."

"Well I hope you'll be reconciled to taking us to Francia. Tonight."

La Rue delivered a mighty Gallic shrug. "How much will you pay?"

"Here's my best offer," John said. "If you cooperate I won't put a bullet in your head."

The captain puckered his lips in contempt. "Your generosity staggers me, monsieur."

18

From his perch on well-concealed high ground, Captain Yates kept saying he wished he had a pair of binoculars. He and his men had bided their time until daylight and now, an hour past dawn, they were still debating their strategy. With Sergeant O'Malley off to Francia, second-in-command duties fell to Lance Corporal Scarlet, a fast-talking Londoner.

"It's not going to do us a bit of good to go in with guns blazing," Yates said. "My guess is that most of them are either unarmed or too lightly armed to do us much damage. We'll burn up too much ammo and we won't necessarily get what we want."

"I don't disagree with you," Scarlet said. "This is more like riot control than an assault, isn't it? We've got to teach 'em who's boss then get control of the inner perimeter. See the clear zone around the village? It's almost a perfect circle. From where that bloke just disappeared to the opposite side, I reckon is a quarter of a mile. We can't cover every inch of it with the men we've got."

"More than controlling it, we've got to hold it for an extended time."

"How long?"

"Anybody's guess but I can't see it being less than a fortnight," Yates said.

"That means we've got to treat each round of ammo like it was a bloody pearl."

"It also means we've got to work out our supply lines. We can't box ourselves out of access to the river for drinking water and this wooded area for game. Seems to be rabbit and deer about."

Grabbing a stick Yates cleared out a patch of ground with his boot and drew a circle in the dirt, then four X's. "We position two men at each of these four compass points," he said. "That'll leave me plus four other men outside the perimeter to respond flexibly to threats as they arise and to fetch water and hunt. We'll rotate, do shifts and whatnot to keep it as fresh as we can. Right?"

"Too bad we had to give up O'Malley and Culpepper."

"Yeah, well, had to rob Peter to pay Paul, didn't we?"

"The plan sounds plausible," Scarlet said. "But how are we going to part the Red Sea?"

"Assemble the men," Yates said. "I'll tell everyone how it's going to go down."

Before long the men of B Group marched from the woods onto the flat flood plain of the river. Yates had chosen a protectable flying V formation with ten paces separating each man. He took the point. Rifles were on semi-auto, facial expressions on full badass. A few Hellers just arriving in the area saw the marching formation coming but the vast majority of the crowd of several hundred had their backs to them, engrossed by what was happening at the border of the hot zone where the intrepid souls who stepped forward into the void were disappearing.

Most of them turned to the sound of Yates's firing his rifle once into the air and following up with his booming voice.

"Now hear this all you dead motherfuckers! We are from Earth. We are alive. We are British soldiers. More specifically, we are the SAS, the biggest, baddest fighting force you have ever seen. You will stand aside. You will disperse. You will not approach the disappearing point. You will go back to your homes. You will get the fuck out of here immediately. You will not try to pass to Earth. We will not let you. We know we can't kill you but we can seriously fuck you up."

A few Hellers on the periphery ran away but most remained rooted, talking and arguing about what to do. The crowd was large enough that not everyone heard what Yates was shouting and his message had to pass from person-to-person.

Scarlet was to the right and rear of Yates. “They’re not responding, Captain.”

Yates replied, “Lance Corporal, pass the word to hold steady. Let’s see if we can avoid bloodshed. I see some belted knives and swords but no firearms but that doesn’t mean there aren’t any.”

Yates shouted his instructions again at the top of his voice.

From the other side of the crowd a small number of King Henry’s soldiers, a unit of sweepers tasked with roaming the countryside looking for new arrivals to Hell, talked among themselves.

“Let’s circle around and get the better of them,” their captain said.

“I don’t wish to get crashed just as we’re on the brink of passage to Earth,” one of his men said.

“You’ll do as I say,” the captain said, sticking his flintlock into the man’s ribs. “Follow me.”

Yates fired another round into the sky and the sound reverberated like a clap of thunder. A few more Hellers ran off toward the river. The six sweepers pushed their way through the crowd and got clear of their fellow Hellers some fifty paces to the left of where Yates was standing.

A trooper on the left-hand side of the V formation spotted the captain and screamed, “Gun! Left! Gun! Left!”

The trooper closest to him took aim and fired a single shot, shredding the sweeper captain’s head. The five other sweepers charged. Three had swords. Only one had a pistol. He got off one shot that flew high before he and his companions were dropped by a volley of SAS fire. The Hellers nearest the felled and bleeding sweepers began to scatter.

“Cease fire!” Yates shouted. Then he bellowed, “Who’s next? If you haven’t raised your hand then move away from here while you can still walk. Now!”

That final “now” had the desired effect. Hundreds of Hellers took off like runners hearing a starter pistol. As the crowd thinned, those closest to the hot zone bucking up their courage for the final steps into the unknown had to make a decision. Yates saw two men and a woman leap forward and disappear but the rest of the Hellers opted to retreat.

Seeing only the backs of fleeing men, Yates ordered a few of his troopers to check the bodies of the men they had shot.

"They're all still moving," a trooper called back. "Even this one missing most of his fucking head."

Yates swore under his breath. "Leave them as a warning. Teams one through four, take up your positions. Don't get too close to the hot zone. The boffins told us it might be expanding. If you pass through I'll take it as a desertion, not an accident. Team five, do some hunting. I fancy a nice joint of venison for supper."

Thanks to their compass and silk maps, Marsh's A Group quickly located the Sevenoaks hot zone. They discovered a similar situation to the one Yates had found in Dartford. Hundreds of Hellers ringed the zone, daring one another to take the plunge into the unknown. A nobleman from Maidstone had come to inspect the scene, accompanied by his well-armed militia, and this was the group that Marsh focused on.

Taking cover behind a shabby stables about a hundred yards from the crowd, Marsh conferred with his sergeant and with Trevor.

"We dominate that lot, we dominate all of them," Marsh said.

"I can work two men up along that line of bushes and set up a sniper nest by that big tree," the sergeant said. "I reckon the bloke with the helmet on the tan horse is the big cheese. We'll take him out first then anyone with a long gun. Wouldn't be surprised if that starts a stampede."

"I like it," Marsh said. "Once they clear out we can set up a defensive perimeter around the hot zone and dig in for the duration." Then he sniffed a few times and said, "What the fuck smells so bad?"

Trevor said he thought he knew and told them to wait. His rifle at the ready he crept around the wooden building. A latch held the door shut and when he slowly swung it open he recoiled at the concentrated stench.

"What was it?" Marsh asked him when he returned.

"Come and have a look," Trevor said. "John told you about them before we left but seeing's believing."

There was just enough light coming through the door to let them see what was inside. The sounds of groaning, moaning, and pathetic pleas filled in the rest of the picture. Marsh and the group sergeant only penetrated a few paces before turning in disgust.

Gasping at the fresher air Marsh said, "Is this a rotting room?"

Trevor nodded.

"Bring each trooper in here," Marsh ordered his sergeant. "I want the men to see what it is we're up against. I swear, we are going to keep every goddamn Heller from coming to where we live or we're going to die trying."

Trevor had set out on his own, trying to figure out where the Belmeade schoolboys had entered Hell. He had left Marsh and his men to their plan and it had gone off without a hitch. After sniper fire cut down the Baron of Maidstone and his men Marsh established his perimeter. The baron had taken a bullet to the mouth so he couldn't be questioned but those militiamen who could still talk were interrogated about the boys. None confessed to knowing anything about them or any Earthers. Trevor didn't fancy being back in the British army so he had left A Group as soon as he could, telling Marsh he would rejoin them at some point, with or without the schoolboys. He began wandering the surrounding meadows looking for clues.

In the near distance was a heavy forest. He wondered if it would have attracted or repelled the boys. He had to admit he didn't much fancy being in the woods come nightfall so he decided to see what he could find in that direction while there was still daylight. After a while he noticed a well-trodden path through some low bushes leading into the forest. Almost immediately his eye fell upon a small piece of bright blue and gold wool stuck to a bush. He plucked it off the thorns and inspected it. Blue and gold. Weren't those the Belmeade colors?

He plunged into the woods and tentatively called out, "Angus Slaine? Are you here?"

Trevor kept moving, calling Angus's name every minute or so.

"Help me."

He wasn't sure what he was hearing until he heard the faint call again.

"Hello?" Trevor called out in response. "Angus?"

"Help me."

"Where are you?"

"Over here."

The voice was coming from behind a naturally fallen tree. Trevor swung the stock of his rifle against his shoulder and came up over the tree.

He recoiled at the sight. "Christ!"

A man was laying there, his abdomen split open, intestines visible and covered in insects.

"Help me."

Regaining his composure, Trevor asked, "How can I help you?"

"Water."

Before departing William's forge, everyone had been given a waterskin, gifts from one of William's workers, the bellows man. Trevor knelt down, trying not to breathe in the smells of putrefaction, and gave the man a few sips, watching the liquid soon drain out the holes in his gut.

"Thank you kind sir," the man rasped. "Unless I am dragged away by the fox I've been battling with all these days, this shall be my final place of repose."

"Yeah, you're in a fix all right," Trevor said, standing.

"You are a living man," the man said.

"How did you know that?"

"You're not the first I seen."

"Who did you see?"

"Young 'uns. Boys they were. Live boys."

"When?"

"I have lost all sense of time. It was not yesterday. It was not today. I am unable to say."

"Which way did they go?"

"I am too weak to raise my hand but I am looking in the direction they ran."

"What were they running from?" Trevor asked.

"To be truthful, I believe it was me."

Trevor began to run through the forest too, calling for Angus every so often, pausing only to catch his breath and take compass bearings so he could find his way back to Sevenoaks. After an hour he broke through into another featureless meadow and without any sign of which direction the boys might have taken, he kept going straight until he came upon a road cut by cart tracks.

"If I were them, which direction would I go?" he asked himself. "If they came this way at all." He checked his compass and picked south but after only a few yards he reversed himself and went north instead. He had gone less than a mile when he saw something ahead, something white amidst a palette of brown and green.

He stooped to pluck it from a deep rut. It was a cotton handkerchief with two monogrammed letters: KP. What were the boys' names? Wasn't there a Kevin?

It came to him because he remembered smirking when he read his name off a list. Pickles. A lad named Pickles would be in for some stick, wouldn't he? Kevin Pickles.

He looked around. There was still some light before evening descended but he didn't have all the time in the world. He'd keep heading north. Toward London. He began jogging but stopped almost immediately when he glimpsed a cottage mostly concealed by a hedgerow. He found a passable gap and shouldered through the hedges and saw a row of six rundown cottages but no people. A skinny horse was tethered in front of one of them.

Cautiously, he went to the closest cottage and rapped on the door, rifle ready. There was no response. The door wasn't latched from the inside and it opened with a gentle push. It was empty, the hearth cold, the cupboards bare. He entered the next four cottages one after another and found the same thing. That only left the last house in the row, the one with the horse. Again he put his knuckles to the door but this time he heard a muffled, "Hallo?"

"I'm looking for a little help," Trevor called back.

"Go away."

"Not before I talk to you."

"Go away. We've got a gun."

Trevor moved away from the door and shouted, "Believe me, I've got a bigger one. Open up or I'm coming in. I just want to talk. I won't hurt you."

The door opened. The elderly man with a scraggly beard and one yellow tooth was armed only with a piece of firewood, no more than a thin branch. He stared at Trevor and his large AK-47.

"You're from the other side, ain't you?"

"How did you know?"

"We've seen things. We've heard things."

"Can I come in?"

"I reckon I can't stop you."

Inside, an old woman sat on the floor at a rickety vertical loom weaving a brown cloth. She had white hair the consistency of straw and a deeply folded and lumpy face that looked like a decaying gourd.

"I'm sorry for barging in," Trevor said. "I'm looking for some people."

The woman sniffed the air. "You're one of them."

"Yes I am."

"We seen plenty of live ones a short while back," she said. "They come from near the Sevenoaks village. Most didn't last long."

"What happened to them?" Trevor asked.

The old man tossed his piece of wood into the hearth and lit the kindling with a candle. "They got taken by sweepers mostly. There were women too. They got passed around I reckon. Some poor souls met rovers. That happens when nights come around. I seen a few bodies. Dead they were. Imagine that."

"I'm looking for a group of boys. To get them out of here. They would have been the first to come through."

The man didn't reply. He hung an iron pot over the fire and began to stir its contents then tasted something gelatinous on the tip of his spoon. Only then did he say, "Are you hungry?"

"I asked about boys."

"Well I'm hungry and I'm going to eat some."

It was the woman who said, "What will you pay?"

"For information about the boys? Just tell me if you know anything."

"We know things," the woman said.

"I don't have any coins but I have this." He reached into his satchel and pulled out a knife from William's forge.

The man rose slowly from his crouch by the fire and inspected the blade.

"It's a good one. What we know for your knife."

"It has to be good information. And I'll want the use of that horse. Is it yours?"

"It is now," the man said. "The fellow who lived in the cottage at the end left for the other side. All of them did."

"How come you didn't?"

"Too old and tired for such adventures," he said.

"I wanted to go," the woman said, casting an irritated look at her mate. "He wouldn't have nothing to do with it."

Trevor said, "Like I was saying, the use of your horse. I'll try to bring him back."

"We have a deal," the man said. "Give me the knife."

"Give me the information."

The woman spoke and while she did, the man spooned the thick, brown contents of the pot into a wooden bowl and began slurping it down.

"Some days ago, as you said, when the first live 'uns began to appear, we was by the road when we spied these boys of yours walking down the road. Well some was walking, others was playing with sticks, pretend fighting it was."

"Which direction were they heading?"

The man pointed toward the north.

"Go on," Trevor said.

"They came upon a train of wagons coming from London. They was taken."

"Taken by force?"

"They had little choice but to get into the wagons once the king's men attacked."

"I don't understand."

The woman explained that a party of soldiers rode into their midst intent on robbing the wagon train. The wool traders fought them off but a musket ball hit one of the boys. The other boys wanted to bury him but Bess, the woman in charge, insisted they only cover him and leave him near the road.

"I seen the body," the man said. "He was well and truly dead, something I've not seen here."

"Where's the body?" Trevor asked.

"In between the road and the nearest house to us," the man said. "Can't hardly miss it."

Trevor shed his heavy shoulder bag but kept his rifle with him, telling them he'd be back. As soon as he was out the door, the couple sprang into action with surprising spryness. The man opened Trevor's satchel. Inside were provisions for his journey and a heavy cloth sack. He opened the sack and whistled at its contents: a few hundred rounds of AK-47 ammo and a fully loaded magazine. He scooped the bullets up with his hand and hid them inside a wooden bucket while the woman raced out the back door with one of her woolen cloths and returned with a makeshift bag filled with stones that the man transferred to the empty sack.

Trevor smelled the body before he found it. Craig Rotenberg was decomposing under some loose brush and what flesh hadn't been lost to decay was lost to insects and vermin. It was only the diminutive size of the corpse that convinced him it was one of the Belmeade boys.

He said a quick prayer and returned to the cottage. The man was at the table with his bowl of brown stuff and the woman was beside her loom.

"Do you know who took them?" Trevor asked.

"We do. We know them well enough," the woman said. "Wool traders they are. They come from the shire of Devon. Bess is their leader. Her man's called Ardmore. They come through here every so often selling their wool to London. We trade for a bit sometimes. For my weaving."

"Were they going to London?" Trevor asked.

"Opposite," the man said. "To Devonshire."

"With the boys."

"Aye."

"Where in Devon?" Trevor asked. "Do you know?"

"Bess said once," the man said. "I can't remember what she said."

"Hawk something," the woman said.

"Hawkchurch," the man said. "That was it."

Trevor tossed his knife on the table. The man picked it up and showed his only tooth.

"Sure you won't eat?" he asked.

Trevor picked up his heavy satchel and shouldered it.

"No, I'll be going now. I'll be back this way." He pointed at the saddle by the door. "Show me how to saddle it. I'll return it too."

When Trevor was on his way, riding south, the old man retrieved the bucket to inspect his loot.

He held up a bullet and said, "What do you think this is?"

"I wouldn't know, would I?" the woman replied.

"This here part is brass. A beautiful bit of brass. I reckon if I melt all of it down we'll have a nice brass bar, worth a fortune."

He had a small iron fry pan that he placed on top of the burning logs. He put the bullet in the center and stooped over to watch the melting.

The explosion came soon enough.

The woman let out a piercing scream.

The lead bullet tore off into the brickwork of the hearth and ricocheted into the man's chest, sending him onto his back, his heart blood leaking onto the floorboards.

19

The videoconference screen at the MI5 Ops Centre came to life with the split image of two tired and irritable middle-aged men. Ben imagined how his own face appeared on their screens. Pale and puffy at best. On the left was the prime minister from the mayor's office at Manchester Town Hall, to the right, Jeremy Slaine, back in London from Manchester, installed somewhere in the bowels of the MOD in Whitehall.

A bit of small talk kicked things off with the prime minister asking after Jeremy's wife.

"She's in Oxford with her brother's family doing as well as can be expected. It's hard to know what to tell her about Angus. One doesn't want to extinguish hope but one must be realistic. It's like walking a tightrope."

"I understand perfectly. Tell her Marjorie sends her love."

"I will, thank you," Slaine said.

"Right then," Lester said, turning business-like. "Has anything changed on the ground within the past twelve hours?"

Ben and Slaine began speaking at once then both stopped in deference to the other. Lester's irritation spilled out into the open.

"All right, all right, go on, Ben, you first," he snapped.

"Thank you, prime minister," Ben said. "Amidst the deteriorating security situation we discussed last night, we do have some positive news to report this morning."

"Yes? What?"

"Surveillance and drone footage from all four hot zones indicate that the entry of Hellers has virtually ceased."

"Really?"

"Yes, it was first seen at Leatherhead, then Upminster, Dartford, and lastly at Sevenoaks."

"Your interpretation?"

"Not only the most optimistic scenario but also the most plausible one is that the SAS has deployed on the other side and is effecting a deterrence."

"Jeremy, do you concur?"

"I do."

"Are there any other explanations?"

Ben was ready with an answer. "I've had a word with Professor von Strobe from Geneva, the director general of the Large Hadron Collider at CERN. He says it's conceivable the connectivity between the two dimensions has spontaneously been eradicated."

"Well that would be good news, wouldn't it?" Lester said.

"Not for my son and the hundreds if not thousands of Britons trapped there," Slaine said.

"Yes, quite right, Jeremy, quite right," Lester said, retreating.

"Time will tell," Ben said. "In the interim, turning off the spigot is helpful."

"And what of London and the surrounding areas?" the PM asked.

"That's the bad-news part," Ben said. "And it's getting worse. It's impossible to get our arms around the numbers but there are certainly thousands of Hellers who have already crossed. In an attempt to characterize their behaviors we've been tracking with drones and documenting the activities of a random selection of men, and I'd say at least ninety-five percent of Hellers appear to be men. Most of them will spend some time out in the open, on streets and parks, but almost all of them will enter shops, offices, or private dwellings staying put for hours to a day or more."

"How do you know they're Hellers?"

"It's not perfect but mostly on the basis of their clothing. Of course, if they obtain modern clothes, we wouldn't be able to differentiate them from the air. I spoke of deterioration. While we have been unable to respond to the vast majority of 999 emergency calls, our analysts have been actively monitoring social media postings from the many citizens who ignored evacuation orders. There has been a dramatic uptick in reports, photos, and videos of violence and mayhem perpetrated by aggressive Hellers. I'm sorry to report a deluge of murders, rapes, and even cannibalism, the latter undoubtedly at the hands of these rover gangs."

Ben saw Lester turn away from the camera for several seconds. When his face was once again visible, his jaw seemed set, his eyes fiery.

"I've thought of little else since our last call," Lester said. "I believe it's time to reverse course. I didn't wish to put our security forces in the impossibly difficult and dangerous position of policing urban areas where they couldn't reliably distinguish between civilians and aliens."

"Not to mention the possibility of getting caught up in expanding hot zones," Ben added.

"Yes, that too. But I cannot in good conscience let the slaughter in our capital city continue. Enough is enough. It's wholly my decision to make but I did consult with President Jackson to get the American view on this as they are our partners in the funding and operation of MAAC. The president concurs with my way of thinking and says he'd do the same if this were happening on American soil. Jeremy, I want you to deploy the army far more aggressively. I want a dramatic ramping up of boots on the ground, I want armed drones deployed over London, and I want the Drone Warfare Centre at RAF Waddington to develop rules of engagement."

Ben saw Slaine vigorously nodding. Slaine had been arguing for these measures for the past several days.

"With respect, Prime Minister," Ben said. "The deterioration we're seeing was predicted. I don't wish to be hard-hearted but we did ask for complete evacuation. Most of the two million or so people who did not heed the call did so voluntarily. Our warnings were explicit. Nevertheless, the vast majority of these people are safe, sheltering in place. If we deploy vastly more troops and armed drones, there will be terrible errors. We will kill our own citizens. Of that, there can be no doubt."

Slaine answered. "I understand we now have some two hundred sniffer dogs trained to Heller smell."

"That will be of limited help," Ben said. "But we are dealing with six hundred square miles of territory. There will be many collateral deaths, and life or death drone decisions will be in the hands of remote operators in Lincolnshire with limited ability to identify friend versus foe."

"I wasn't planning on having the kill decision in their hands," the prime minister said. "I'll want MI5 to authorize each missile fire. It will be in your hands, Ben."

They crept into Polly's dark room trying not to wake her too suddenly.

Benona clicked on a table lamp. The low-wattage bulb revealed a shape under a comforter.

"Polly? It's mama."

From under the bedclothes came, "Is Brandon here?" Her head appeared. "Brandon, it is you!"

"How'd you know?" Woodbourne asked.

"I smelled you, silly. Where have you been?"

She held out her arms for a cuddle but seemed too weak to lift her head off her pillow. He bent down low and let her envelope his big head.

"I missed you," she said.

"I missed you too."

Benona touched her forehead. "You're burning up," she said. "I have medicine for you."

"Is it icky medicine?"

"It's pills. You're a big girl. You can swallow."

Benona went to the kitchen and returned with water. She sat the girl up and put two capsules in her mouth.

"I did it," Polly said, showing her empty mouth.

"Good girl. Go back to sleep."

"Brandon, will you be here when I wake up?"

"I'll be here."

In the living room Benona and Woodbourne looked at each other until he said, "I know. I smell."

"Bath and cologne," she said with a weak smile.

"Are you all right?" he asked.

"I was almost killed by these men, my daughter is sick, this man comes back to me from Hell, and you ask me if I'm all right?"

"I don't know how to talk to people proper anymore."

"Is okay, Brandon. You hungry?"

"Yes."

"You go, I make some food."

Later, he emerged from the bath wrapped in a towel, holding a bundle of his dirty clothes. She told him she'd wash them after dinner and sat him down on the sofa with a plate of meat pie and potatoes. She watched as he devoured it.

"You're not eating?" he asked.

"Not hungry. I'm too worried about Polly. I want her to see a doctor."

"Let's take her."

"The surgery is closed. They evacuated."

"Because of us?"

"Yes. Many Hellers. Everyone ran away."

"Not everyone. You're here."

"I didn't want to go to fucking army camp in the north. Someone would come here and take few things I got. I would have gone back to Poland if I had money for travel. Looks like I made a mistake not going. I always make mistake in my life."

"We can take her to the hospital."

"I think they're closed too. No one answers phone anywhere. It's not safe on the streets."

"I can protect you."

Her eyes softened. "I know you can."

"The pie was good. You got enough food?"

"Only thing I did right. I got plenty before the shops all closed." She took his plate and put it in the sink. Without looking up she said, "I'm glad you came back."

"I thought about you every minute I was back there."

She kept her eyes on the suds she was making with the washing-up liquid. "You want to go to bed with me, Brandon?"

The answer came quickly. "Yes."

Willie Oakley looked through the peephole into the hallway. He didn't see anyone but that was little comfort. Someone could be lurking just out of view. He put his ear to the door. Once his hearing had been so acute he could hear a wristwatch ticking from his night table. Now his hearing was diminished. All his senses were diminished. Age did that.

As he gently pushed the door open he second-guessed himself. Did he really need to take out the trash? He was always a tidy man, a clean man. He didn't like his flat smelling. His garbage disposal unit under his sink had packed up weeks ago and the management company had given him some poppycock about a back-ordered part. Those were the days when a back-ordered part was the problem. The managers, the maintenance people, the caregivers, even his fellow residents had evacuated the Battersea retirement complex, leaving him alone with his smelly trash. It was time to be bold, time to take the trash bags out to the wheelie bins, or at least the stairwell.

Clutching the bags in one hand and a claw hammer in the other he started down the hall. The stairwell was empty too and Willie thought about dropping the bags and retreating, but a bit of his old courage and pride surged through his eighty-year-old body. He had early-childhood memories of surviving the blitz. He had fifteen years of army service in the Southern Command Ammunition Inspectorate, clearing unexploded German bombs from London and the Thames Valley. He could make it to the wheelie bins.

The bins were neatly lined up behind his building. There was no one about. He could have used any of the bins but he was a creature of habit and protocol and chose his assigned one. There was trash in it. Checking others, they were empty. He looked around suspiciously. He had imagined he was the only resident who had stayed behind but maybe there were others. Perhaps his imagination was getting the better of him but he had the sensation of eyes on him. He scanned the windows overlooking the alley but saw nothing. It was time to declare victory and beat a hasty withdrawal.

Back on his floor he moved as quickly as his bandy legs allowed but as he was retrieving his keys from his pocket he heard a door opening behind him. His mouth got very dry very fast. He could either keep going until he got to his door or turn to face the danger.

"Willie Oakley! For fuck's sake."

He wheeled around. Del Ruddles was poking his big, mostly bald head out his door.

"I didn't know you was still here," Willie said.

"I didn't know you was here neither. What do you think you're going to do with that hammer?"

"Build a garden shed, I expect. You want a cup of tea?"

"Yeah, could do."

Willie saw that Del had a pistol. "You're asking me about a bloody hammer. What are *you* going to do with that?" he asked.

"Murder a Heller or two," Del said, clomping his big frame down the hall.

Willie poured the tea. "So how come you stayed?" he asked.

"I never ran away from nothing in my life," Del said, his south London accent in full bloom. "I'm seventy-eight years young. I'm not starting now. How 'bout you?"

"I wasn't going to go to no army base. Had my fill of those when I was young. Is it just us two?"

"I've no bloody idea but you're the first one I've spotted since this mess started."

"Where'd you get the pea shooter?" Willie asked.

"This?" Del said, pointing at the revolver on the kitchen counter. "Tools of the trade. Never got rid of it."

Willie knew about Del via retirement-home gossip. He'd been a gangster, one of the old-timers who'd had his fingers in lots of pies. A real survivor who'd done long stretches in the nick. Neither man had been much interested in collecting new friends so they'd never done more than nod and grunt in passing.

"Well, we got electricity, water, and the tele," Willie said. "As long as the food holds up we'll be all right."

"The food'll hold up," Del said. "I had a look in the cafeteria in the nursing building. There's loads in the pantries and fridges."

"Good to know. You think there're any of them Hellers in Battersea?"

"Expect so. The tele says they're everywhere."

"Can you imagine?" Willie said. "There's really a Hell."

"Did you ever doubt it?" Del said.

"Sure I doubted it. I was never much for church. Should have paid more attention."

"I always assumed there was a Heaven and a Hell. In my line of work you tended to think about what was waiting for you on the other side."

"And what did you conclude?" Willie asked.

"I figured I was probably fucked. Now I know I am. No pearly gates for Del Ruddles. I've got a mind to collar one of these Hellers and ask him what's in store for me. You play cards?"

"'Course I do."

"Want a game of gin rummy?"

They were tired from miles of walking but most of all they were hungry. Their numbers had dwindled to about thirty yet they were still a cutthroat gang to be reckoned with. They'd kept to their practice of going to ground during the daylight but the last place Heath had chosen to stop had virtually nothing to eat, not even cannie food. His first choice had been a very grand looking building on the Millbank, a palace by the look of it, but even their iron bars couldn't get them inside the locked Tate Britain galleries. They settled for the Chelsea College of Arts next door but exhausted themselves looking for food in the cavernous building and went to sleep hungry inside a classroom.

Even though the night was young, hunger drove them to break down the doors of a one-story brick building with the sign that read, Food Deliveries to the Rear.

Within minutes, the grumbling among the ranks turned to praise for their leader as Heath led them through an empty cafeteria to a massive kitchen stuffed to the gills with provisions.

"Eat up," Heath said, reaching into a bag of oats.

"There's dressed chickens in the cold box!" Monk said.

Although a mouthful of dried oats wasn't bad, Heath liked the notion of chicken better and he elbowed Monk aside.

"Someone's even cooked the birds up for us," Heath marveled, taking a whole chicken in both hands and lowering his face to it.

"Did you hear that?" Del said, getting up to look out the window.

He and Willie had spent the entire day in each other's company and only minutes ago had gone to Del's flat to drink some of his whiskey.

"I heard it too," Willie said. "Was it glass breaking? Where do you think it came from?"

"The nursing building. I'm sure of it."

"Your hearing's better than mine," Willie said.

"Why don't you get hearing aids?"

"Can't stand the things. I can hear the tele fine when it's turned up. Why do I need them?"

"Well come on then," Del said, sticking his pistol in his waistband.

"Come on where?"

"To see what's going on."

"Why do we need to know?"

"Because we live here, that's why."

"If it's them Hellers, what can we do about it?" Willie protested. "It's not like the police are responding to citizen's calls."

"Don't be so lily-livered. I thought you were ex-army and all."

"I am. But I'm also an old man if you hadn't noticed."

"Then I'll go on my onesies. You stay here hiding in the wardrobe."

Del took his keys and a plastic torch from a drawer and started to leave. Willie swore and followed along.

"Good man," Del said, leading the way.

They crept along the alley past the wheelie bins and around to the assisted care building. All the windows were dark. They stopped by the front entrance to look for broken glass but everything was intact.

Del cupped his ear. "Hear that?"

"Didn't hear nothing."

"I thought I heard voices."

"Maybe they're in your bloody head."

"I'm serious. Let's go around."

Closer to the rear, by the cafeteria, Willie heard the voices too, punctuated by fits of laughter.

"We should go back," he said.

"Nonsense. We'll just peek in and see what we're dealing with."

They got to the floor-to-ceiling cafeteria windows. The room was dark but there was a soft glow coming from the kitchen area. Del was relentless. He followed the flowerbeds around the corner until they got to the smaller kitchen windows. Del was almost a head taller than Willie and he got a view inside first. Willie had to stretch for a glimpse.

Illuminated by the lights of a bank of open refrigerator doors they saw Heath and his men ripping through food.

The two old men ducked down and retreated, not stopping before they arrived back at Del's flat.

Only then did they talk.

"You think it was them?" Willie asked, out of breath.

"You saw the way they looked. Like bloody animals. They weren't from these parts, I'll tell you that."

"You think they'll come to our building?" Willie said.

"I should think they might."

"What should we do?"

Del removed the revolver from his trousers and put it on the kitchen table. “Do? These bastards came to our world, to our city, to our very house,” he said, his neck veins pulsating. “We should do what you should always do when someone tries to muscle in on your territory. You do violence.”

20

John pointed into the mist at the ghostly outlines of a dark, jagged coastline.

"Francia," he said.

"How do you know?" Kyle asked.

"It's not our first rodeo."

"Indeed not," Emily said grimly. "No shortage of unpleasant memories on these shores."

Sergeant O'Malley and Trooper Culpepper were roaming the deck of the galleon, safeties off their rifles, guarding against any last-minute hostilities. Captain La Rue was giving out orders and his crew was turning the ship into the wind and dropping sheets until they were dead in the water. Only then did the captain call for both port and starboard anchors to be dropped.

La Rue climbed down from the quarterdeck to the railings. "Well, monsieur, it seems our transaction is complete. In exchange for not receiving a bullet in my head, I have delivered you to Calais. My men will row you to the beach and then I will depart for Brest where I will do my best to forget your face."

John held out his hand and La Rue, after casting his eyes to the sky and shaking his head in disbelief at the gesture, took it then quickly released it.

"Captain, I'd like to make you an offer. This voyage was on you. How'd you like the next one to be on me?"

"On me, on you? Whatever are you saying?" La Rue said.

"What I'm saying is that if you wait here for our return, I'll fill your pockets with gold to return us to Brittania."

"Where is this gold? Is it buried in a chest? Is it inside the hollow of a tree? Will you find it up your posterior parts?" La Rue asked.

Kyle snarled at the Frenchman but John cooled him off.

"Why don't you tell me how much gold it'll take?" John asked.

La Rue pointed to a slop bucket. "That much."

"All right. We'll return with that much gold. If we don't have it, you don't sail to Brittania."

"Monsieur Camp, you will come with your big guns and La Rue will be threatened with a bullet again."

"You have my word I won't do that."

"I do not trust your word. However, I will trust the word of mademoiselle who I have come to know as an honorable woman. And she is very beautiful."

"Thank you, captain," Emily said. "I will promise you."

"Very well, when will you return?" La Rue asked.

"As soon as we can," Emily said. "We are in a great hurry but I'm afraid it will be at least a fortnight. Please wait for as long as it takes."

"For a bucket of gold I shall wait one month. A day beyond that, I will assume you have met a bad end and La Rue will set sail and be gone."

The longboat approached the same beach where John had battled French forces on his first arrival in Francia. Gazing up on the high cliffs where soldiers had peppered him with arrows and cannon fire, he thought about that harrowing journey to find Emily. Less than three months had passed but it seemed a lifetime. He ached for his simple life at the lab, a life devoid of adrenaline rushes but filled with the tranquility of ordinary pleasures. He had his work, Emily had hers, and when they weren't working they retreated to a magical space of togetherness where time seemed slower and sweeter. Would he ever have this life again?

Emily, seated beside, must have seen his wistful look.

Over the sound of oars stroking the chop she asked, "Are you all right?"

"I was just thinking."

"Always a dangerous thing."

"Tell me about it."

"Thinking about what?"

"You. You and me."

She put her mouth closer to his ear and said softly, "Do you still love me?"

"More than ever."

Kyle was behind them, O'Malley and Culpepper in front of them, French sailors manning the oars. It was hardly a place for intimacy. The best she could do was press her shoulder into his.

"When we get home," she said, "when we fix this, we're going to have the most beautiful life together."

"You're a scientist," he said. "What's the probability of that happening?"

"Close to one hundred percent."

"Close to. That worries me."

"Ninety-nine point nine nine nine. Complete certainty is a difficult concept."

"Yeah, I suppose it is."

The five of them splashed through the low tide and waved off the French oarsmen. The SAS men took the point and Kyle took the rear, all of them weighed down by their provisions and ammunition. The beach sands were soft and yielding, making walking especially tough for Kyle but John let him soldier on in silence. They weren't going to reach Paris on foot. They needed horses and he knew where to find them.

John had raided the nearest coastal village for horses before. The village was on the prosperous side owing to its smuggling trade, and he had found a stable there with horses and tack. He wasn't inclined to waste a day waiting for the cover of night so they barged into the barn with guns raised.

The stablemen tending a dozen horses were the same men John had ambushed before. They cursed their fate when they saw him.

"Hi boys, I'm back," John said. "Miss me?"

They answered in rapid-fire French, pointing to some rope and crossing their wrists.

"I don't think they speak English," O'Malley said.

"They're speaking the universal language of surrender," John said. "Tie them up and pick your horses."

They rode due south on the Paris road until darkness fell, encountering only a few travelers on foot and some men driving carts. All showed fear and averted their gaze as they passed. They found a lightly wooded spot by a pond to camp for the night and water the horses. They took sentry duty by shifts and in the morning they were well enough rested to talk about a hard push to make Paris by nightfall.

At midday the road bent sharply, limiting their line of sight. O'Malley, a better horseman than Culpepper, told John he intended to ride ahead to make sure they weren't heading into any problems.

"Good idea," John said.

O'Malley was about to head off when he hesitated and said, "Can I ask you something?"

"Sure, go ahead."

"When this is done will we be able to talk about what we've seen and what we've done?"

"Not for me to say. You allowed to talk about your other missions?"

"No way."

"It was the same when I was a Green Beret. Why do you think the army will treat this mission differently?"

"I dunno. Maybe they won't but I hope they do. There's been nothing like this before. It's like Star Trek and we're on another planet."

"Why're you thinking about it?"

"Just trying to picture who'd play me in the movie version, that's all."

"Any ideas?"

"Thought about Colin Farrell, him being Irish and all."

"Shit, O'Malley, you're prettier than him."

O'Malley rode off with a smile. The others dismounted and had some water.

"Hey Jack," Kyle said to Culpepper, "how long have you guys served together?"

"Four years, give or take."

"Good man in a fight?"

"None better. Always has your back."

"Good to hear."

In a few minutes O'Malley came into view, approaching at a blistering gallop, shouting something.

John didn't need to understand what he was saying. He got the message and cocked his musket.

"Emily, grab the reins and take the horses. Get off the road behind those trees. Jack, you and the sarge have the AKs. Don't shoot unless I give the order but if I do, make every shot count. Kyle, you got your musket ready?"

"It's all primed. What do you think's happening?"

"We'll find out in a few seconds."

A shot rang out and then another. O'Malley was the target of the unseen shooters but he wasn't hit. He rode up and did a swift dismount.

"Some kind of soldiers, lots of them," he shouted just as the first of them came around the bend.

"Scatter," John shouted. "Stay low. Sarge, toss your ejected mags to me and Kyle. We'll reload for you."

O'Malley grunted and assumed a firing position on his belly. A musket ball whizzed close to his cheek.

A multitude of horsemen appeared, bunched together.

"Fire!" John said.

O'Malley and Culpepper began squeezing off rounds. Their heavy bullets tore into the attackers, tumbling inside their bodies, causing devastating injuries. The soldiers seemed to be in confusion and disarray at the quantity of accurate fire coming from so few men. The riders in the lead would have pulled up and turned if it hadn't been for the crush of riders coming around the bend to their rear.

Both SAS men emptied their thirty-round mags and mounted their loaded spares while John and Kyle fed loose bullets into the empties.

John had his head down, concentrating on smoothly seating the double-stack of ammo, when Kyle looked up and saw a soldier creeping through the woods, trying to get into sniper position. He was twenty yards away when he stopped to cock and sight his rifle.

Kyle dropped the magazine he was loading, grabbed his musket and in one fluid move, raised it and fired.

At the sharp percussion, John looked up in time to see the man in the woods clutching his chest and falling backwards.

"Jesus, Kyle, good shot," he said.

The bodies piled up on the road but the soldiers kept coming. Some of them began to ride off the road into the woods, making them harder to hit.

"Watch those guys!" John yelled. "They're trying to outflank us."

"There're too many of them!" Culpepper shouted. "They're going to break through."

John made sure he had eyes on Emily. If they were going to be overwhelmed he'd go to her side and make a stand there.

"Here's a fresh mag," he shouted to O'Malley. "Maybe a full-auto burst will give them a little shock and awe."

"At the risk of wasting ammo," the sergeant yelled back.

There was another volley of gunfire, more distant. Soldiers fell at the back of the attacking pack. Others turned to address an unseen threat. Still others turned their horses into the woods and began to flee.

"What's happening?" Kyle shouted.

John kept loading an empty mag and replied, "I'm not sure but it doesn't suck."

In under a minute the attackers who weren't cut down evaporated into the forest and the threat was over as quickly as it had begun. Then, from around the bend in the road, a new threat emerged, another fighting force, led by a man with a smart blue jacket and long yellow hair. He halted his horse amidst a pile of writhing bodies and pointed toward John's group.

"Hold your fire!" John shouted to his people. "Let's figure this out."

"Who are you?" yellow hair shouted in French.

John put his hands in the air and took a few tentative steps forward.

"Do you speak English?" John shouted back.

"Yes, a little," yellow hair replied. "Who are you?"

"We are traveling to Paris on an important mission."

"What mission?"

"It's a long story."

"How you destroy so many dogs with few men?"

"We have powerful weapons."

"Make low these weapons and approach me."

"I'll meet you halfway," John said.

Kyle told him to watch himself and Emily called out to John from the woods to be careful.

Walking past O'Malley and Culpepper, John told them to keep their weapons down, but to be ready in case.

Yellow hair, clearly an officer, gave his men some orders and guided his horse slowly through the bodies, calmly firing his pistol into one of the wounded men on the ground who had made some threatening move.

As the two men got closer to one another, John saw he had a second pistol in his belt and a sword.

Then the officer pulled on his reins and stopped some thirty paces away from John.

"It *is* you," the officer exclaimed. "John Camp!"

"How do you know me?"

"We fought the Germans at Drancy. I see you from afar with Garibaldi. Everyone talks about the live general with his new cannon."

"I'm not a general."

"But you are alive, no?"

"I am."

"You found your lady. Did you not return to your land?"

"I did but we had to come back."

"This mission you speak of."

"That's right."

The officer dismounted and led his horse by the reins to shake John's hand.

"I am Marcel Rougier, captain in the army of Francia, or should I say, the combined army of Francia, Italia, and Iberia. Such change."

Rougier explained that his men had been in pursuit of a rogue group of French soldiers who had stolen weapons and horses and had defected from their posts. "Garibaldi says stop them so I stop them, with your help. I would like to see these powerful weapons."

John called O'Malley over to show him one of the AKs and at John's coaxing, unloaded it and handed it over for inspection while Emily came out of hiding.

"I never have seen such a musket," the captain said, admiring its heft. "A marvel from your world, I expect. So, you are going to Paris?"

"To see Garibaldi," John said. "Is he there?"

"Yes, he is there but the road is dangerous, Monsieur Camp. You will have my protection if you wish."

Joseph Stalin was cold and miserable. Following his defeat at Boulogne-Sur-Mer where his attempt to capture the fleeing John Camp, Emily Loughty, and the Earther children he so coveted had been thwarted by the surprise arrival of Iberian ships, he had withdrawn to one of Barbarossa's more gloomy castles in Cologne. Built on a chalky promontory over the Rhine, the castle had been built from limestone blocks with a loose chalk and flint infill between stone faces, a rather ineffective insulation. The wind whipping down the river valley seemed to penetrate the castle walls and from there, penetrated the tsar's bones. When he discovered that the rooms of his secret police chief, Vladimir Bushenkov's, though smaller than his, were warmer and less damp, he evicted the man and took possession, sitting by the fire all day wrapped in a blanket.

"Nikita!" he called out. "Come and put more wood on the fire. Nikita! Where the devil are you?"

His young, freckle-faced secretary came running in, apologizing profusely. "I am sorry, Tsar Joseph. I was just speaking with General Kutuzov. What do you need?"

"I need more wood on this fire!"

Nikita sprung into action and stoked the hearth.

"What did Kutuzov want?" Stalin growled.

"He asked if you would be willing to entertain the Slavic ambassador tonight."

"Am I?"

"Are you what, my tsar?"

"Willing."

"That is for you to say."

"I am willing if the Slavs will send me men."

Nikita adjusted Stalin's lap blanket and said, "I do not know of these matters."

"Well, send me those who do. Get me Bushenkov and Kutuzov. And have you seen Pasha?"

"I will find out if he has returned."

Kutuzov and Bushenkov made an unlikely pair. Kutuzov, Stalin's field marshal, responsible for planning all military campaigns, looked like a fat and jovial uncle, his tunic spread by his big belly, his rubbery face, more mirthful than threatening. Bushenkov was a one-eyed, patch-wearing, sliver of a man, tough and sinewy, an expressionless cipher.

"So, gentlemen," Stalin said. "I am getting tired of this damned castle. I wish to return to Moscow full of victory. I despise Germania. When do we attack this pig, Garibaldi? Are we sure the Iberians are firmly with him? Who will join our campaign? Answer me."

"Allow me to respond," Kutuzov said, rocking back and forth on his heels, a habit which Stalin despised.

"Stop your rocking. You make me dizzy."

"I apologize," the field marshal said. "Here is what we know. Our spies tell us the Iberians are now led by Queen Mécia. King Pedro was shot through the eye by one of the living men."

Bushenkov reflexively touched his leather eye patch at the mention. "Not *our* spies, Comrade General, *my* spies."

"We have also heard," an annoyed Kutuzov continued, "from *your* spies that the queen has taken as a consort, another of the living men who did not return to Brittania with John Camp and Emily Loughty."

"What became of them?" Stalin asked.

"We do not know," Bushenkov said. "Their intention was to return to Earth but we do not know if they succeeded."

"So," Stalin said, "we are forced to deal with a troika of powers. Italia, Francia, Iberia, all aligned against us."

Kutuzov said, "Our might, combined with the might of Germania is not to be underestimated."

Stalin threw off his blanket and stood, sending his general into a nervous fit of heel rocking.

"A word such as underestimated means nothing to me!" Stalin bellowed. "I require victory. Guaranteed victory. They have more men than we do. An opponent with more men does not guarantee my victory. I want more men. What of the Slavs?"

Kutuzov sought out Nikita with his eyes. "I told Nikita just a short while ago that I thought a banquet honoring the Slavic ambassador would be a good thing."

"If we fill his stomach with food and get him drunk on wine will we get an ironclad agreement tonight?" Stalin asked.

"I believe we are close."

"What are the terms?"

"Old King Theodore wants gold of course."

"Of course he does," Stalin said contemptuously. "Can we afford it?"

"I believe we can."

"What else?"

"He wants women."

Stalin snorted at that. "He can have all the German women he wants. I don't want them. But not a single Russian lass. What else?"

"He wants a pact of assurance that we will not invade the Slavic kingdom for two hundred years."

"Fine. Pacts are meant to be broken."

"That is all."

"And what do we get? How many men?"

"Five thousand."

He clapped once, making a sound like an auctioneer announcing a sale. "Okay, make a banquet."

Bushenkov had been listening quietly, his tense lips stretched into a pale thin line.

"Fifteen thousand men would be better," he said.

"The Slavs don't have that many," the general said with a dismissive backhanded gesture.

"I am not speaking of the Slavs."

"Who then?" Stalin demanded.

"Alexander," Bushenkov said. "Alexander the Great."

"You can make an alliance with the Macedonian?" Stalin asked.

"I can and I did. My operative, Baburin, has returned from Rome where Alexander has been contemplating his next campaign. With Garibaldi away and Italia vulnerable, he was of the mind to continue toward Florence and Milan. However, with the right inducements, he has been persuaded to forgo these smaller conquests and help us to take all of Europa."

Kutuzov unleashed a furious barrage of criticism, saying it was outrageous that the secret policeman had kept the negotiation secret from him and the Tsar.

Stalin listened and answered on Bushenkov's behalf. "Yes, yes, but what are the terms? Fifteen thousand men!"

"Assuming we achieve victory and you are able to proclaim yourself Tsar of Europa, he will first, accept you as his Tsar, second, continue to rule Macedonia and his lands to the east as king, third, add Italia and Iberia to his kingdom, and fourth, claim the Slavic kingdom as well."

"And you agreed to these terms?" Stalin asked.

"I did."

Stalin smiled broadly and told Nikita to bring a bottle of good wine. "I agree too. Deal is done."

Kutuzov sputtered, "But we're already double-crossing the Slavs."

"Vasily, Vasily," Stalin clucked, "We did this kind of treachery on Earth all the time in full fear of what could happen to our immortal souls. In

Hell, we do what we want without these fears. We are already here. We have worst- case scenario. This is our existence. Let Alexander eat King Theodore's liver with onions for all I care. If Alexander gets too powerful we give his liver to someone else. Deal is done.

21

Giuseppe Garibaldi hastened to get out of his bed but his stiff joints always got the better of him in the mornings and this morning was no different. As king of a huge and far-flung empire he could have had all the servants and attendants he wanted but at heart he was just an old soldier who needed and wanted few creature comforts. What he burned for was something to lift his spirits and the spirits of his new subjects. He wanted something that had never before been achievable in the heartless domain of Hell: he wanted humanity.

"Are we not still human?" he had asked his acolytes who hung on every utterance. "We have done wrong. We have done evil. We have been rightly punished and we cannot be redeemed. We are in this most unhappy place for all of eternity and we will surely suffer greatly at every turn. But must we condemn ourselves further by stripping ourselves and our fellow man of dignity? Is there not a better way, a way with less fear, less degradation, less war, more, dare I say, hope?"

He had been in Hell for such a short time compared to many others, fewer than one hundred fifty years. At the time of his death he was already acclaimed as father of the fatherland, a unifier of a fractured Italy. Only he remembered his shameful act of violence as a young soldier that condemned him to Hell. Since his arrival he had been privately contemplating a humane unification of the warring fiefdoms of Hell. Looking back on the lightning-fast events of the past few months he was astonished at how fast his plan had come together. First, Italia came under his control, then Francia, and now Iberia. He was under no illusion as to the role one man had played in realizing these gains, one living man. And now he had been awakened with the incredible news that John Camp was back. Here in Paris, at his very palace.

Garibaldi threw on his ever-present red shirt and black trousers and fought his sore wrists to pull up high black boots. As king of this large empire he might be expected to wear clothes befitting a monarch but his egalitarian sensibility prevented it. Likewise, he refused to sleep in King Maximilien's bedchamber that had stayed empty ever since he was toppled. Instead he slept in a modest room down the hall from the royal apartments, a room that Robespierre had used as one of several dressing rooms, this one for his hunting clothes.

Walking down the wide hall Garibaldi heard someone running behind him. He turned to see his friend and compatriot, Michelangelo Amerighi da Caravaggio, flashing a joyful smile.

"Is it true?" Caravaggio said.

"I haven't seen them yet but I'm sure it's true," Garibaldi said.

"Them? I only heard about John Camp."

"The lady Emily is here also, and others."

Caravaggio caught up and put an arm around his master's waist. "Emily too! I don't know if I should be happy to see them or sad they did not reach home."

"Well, we shall see. They're in one of our ridiculously opulent state rooms."

"Don't let the French nobles hear you, Giuseppe. They don't understand your philosophy yet."

Down another corridor, they ran into Guy Forneau, Robespierre's principal minister and now Garibaldi's.

Without being asked Forneau said, "Yes, I've heard too. I am overwhelmed, positively overwhelmed."

"Have you notified Simon?" Caravaggio asked.

"I sent someone to his room," Forneau said. "He will be along."

"You mean they will be along," Caravaggio said with a wink.

Forneau smiled. "Yes, the lady Alice as well, I am quite sure."

Alice Hart, one of the Earthers caught up in the South Ockendon incident had astonished her companions by refusing to return home with them, electing to stay in Hell with the man she had fallen for, Simon Wright, the English boilermaker. Since then the two of them had never been seen apart, not once, and the Italians and French ribbed Simon mercilessly, dubbing him Signore or Monsieur Hart.

On cue, Simon and Alice came running down the hall until they caught up with them.

"I don't know if this is the worst news or the best news I've heard," Alice said. "Didn't they make it home?"

"Do we know why they're here?" Simon asked.

Garibaldi pushed open the large double-doors. "Let's ask them, shall we?"

The greeting was chaotic. John and Emily were mobbed like rock stars, bouncing from embrace to embrace, all the while pelted with questions.

"Let them breathe!" Garibaldi said, grinning from ear to ear. "Give them a chance to talk."

"Giuseppe," John said, clapping Garibaldi's shoulders. "It's good to see you."

"I don't know if I am supposed to be happy or sad," Garibaldi said. "But in any event, simply allow me to be pleased to lay these old eyes upon you and Emily."

Emily kissed his cheeks. "You look well," she said.

"You are a liar," he said. "A charming liar. I am an old, tired man."

"Nonsense," she said. "You put us all to shame."

Caravaggio came up behind Emily and whispered, "So, have you finally decided to leave John for me?"

"Not exactly," she laughed, "but it is splendid seeing you again."

"I have something to show you later," he promised.

When Emily hugged her, Alice broke down in tears.

"I've thought of you every day," Emily said.

"And I, you. Did you and the others not get home?"

"We did but we had to come back. We'll explain. Have you had second thoughts?" Emily asked.

"Of course, how could I not? But I do love Simon and I'm needed here. I wasn't loved or needed back home. So I'm good. I'm really good."

"Everyone," John announced. "I'd like you all to meet my brother, Kyle, and these two fine British soldiers who've risked their lives to get us here, Sergeant Tom O'Malley and Trooper Jack Culpepper."

"Gentlemen," Garibaldi said, "I could not be more pleased to meet you."

"John's told me all about you, sir," Kyle said.

"If you are John's brother, then you are also my brother," Garibaldi said. "I noticed you are limping. Were you injured?"

"A long time ago," Kyle said.

"And these fine young soldiers," Garibaldi said, addressing the SAS men. "I couldn't help notice your rifles. What are they?"

"AK-47s, sir," O'Malley said. "Thirty-round magazines, capable of firing in full-auto or semi-auto modes."

"Wherever did you get them? I've seen nothing like them in Hell."

"Kyle Camp's responsible for them, sir. He's a gunsmith. He made them here in a forge in England—sorry, Brittania I guess it's called."

"Well, I will wish to see what they are capable of," Garibaldi said.

Forneau ordered wine and food brought in and everyone took to chairs and sofas to listen to John talk.

"I suppose I'd better start with what happened when we got to Bulogne-sur-Mer," he said.

"We know all about it," Simon said. "Brian Kilmeade came to Paris and gave us a full accounting."

"Where is he?" John asked.

"He returned to Iberia with Queen Mécia," Forneau said. "The queen has committed to raising a large army to assist our alliance. We do expect them in Paris any day now."

"Brian saved the day," John said. "If it hadn't been for him we'd all be learning Russian in one of Stalin's prisons. But getting out of Francia wasn't the end of it. We had more fun and games when we got back to Brittania."

He told them about returning to Dartford only to be ambushed by King Henry and Thomas Cromwell, about taking Henry hostage moments before they were transported back to Earth, about learning that the MAAC technical staff, a class of schoolboys, and untold numbers of Londoners had been lost to Hell, and about the spontaneous opening of passages between the two worlds that had unleashed a veritable floodgate of Hellers to Earth, rovers included.

"There have been whispers about a passageway back to Earth," Simon said. "I didn't believe it but it's really true?"

"It's true," Emily said.

Caravaggio said, "Can you imagine? Who wouldn't wish to return to the living, if only for one day, one hour?"

"Put it out of your mind," Garibaldi said. "This is our home now and we have much work to do."

Caravaggio bowed. "Of course, maestro."

"What happened to Trevor, Arabel and the children, and all my friends from South Ockendon?" Alice asked.

"They all got back safely," John said. "Trevor returned with us and a squadron of British special forces soldiers, colleagues of Tom O'Malley and Jack Culpepper. He's trying to find the schoolboys. The soldiers have deployed to the four known passageways with Kyle's rifles to block more Hellers coming through."

The wine and food arrived. Kyle lifted his full glass and caught John's eye. His brother gave him a nod and a smile, brotherly permission to hit the bottle.

"And what is your mission?" Garibaldi asked John.

"It's Emily's mission. The rest of us are here to support her."

"We need to find my former colleague, Paul Loomis," Emily said. "He's with Stalin who's latched on to him as a science advisor. When we saw Paul in Germania he told me he knew how to plug the passages. No one else on

Earth has an idea how to do it. We've got to find him, learn the method, and return home to put it into place."

Simon swallowed a mouthful of pheasant and asked, "What will happen if you can't, as you say, plug the holes?"

"The passageways could widen on their own," Emily said. "There's no way of predicting where it could lead. A connection as large as all of London? All of England? All of Europe? It would lead to complete and utter chaos and destruction."

"A tide of bad souls polluting your shores," Caravaggio said.

"We need to know where Stalin is," John said. "We find Stalin, we find Loomis."

Forneau said, "We know precisely where he is. He went to Cologne to prepare for a coordinated assault upon us. Our spies tell us he is seeking allegiances to surpass our own forces."

"He is likely to get the Slavic kingdom to join with him," Garibaldi said.

"How significant would that be?" John asked.

"It would not be good for us," Garibaldi said. "But I am more troubled by reports suggesting he is having negotiations with Alexander, the Macedonian. Here I am in Francia. If I were to turn south to meet him in Italia, then the Russians and Germans would take Francia. If I stay here, then he will continue to lay waste to my kingdom."

"Then maybe it's for the best if he joins Stalin so you can whip both their asses," John said.

Garibaldi almost fell off his chair laughing. "Whip their asses! You Americans are priceless."

Forneau frowned. "I do not know what would be gained by whipping enemy donkeys but if I understand the point John is making, one decisive victory over all our foes would be sweet indeed."

"And to that end," Garibaldi said, "Simon has assembled a team of French and Italians, some of them modern men. They have been working tirelessly at the principal forge in Paris to use the knowledge from your books to build better weapons."

"How's it going?" John asked.

Simon began talking with a full mouth only to be gently rebuked by Alice.

"She's trying to teach me manners which is like teaching a pig to fly," he said. "To be honest with you, John, it will be some time, a good year I should think, to modify the forge's chimney stack and build a steam engine to achieve the kinds of heat the blast furnaces are meant to put out. Only then can we make this marvelous Bessemer steel and really get somewhere."

"Not a short-term solution," John said.

"That is so."

"Stalin has the books too," John said. "So we have to believe he's no further ahead."

"I don't see how he could be going any faster than us," Simon said. "And he doesn't have what we have: Simon the boilermaker."

Alice patted his curly head. "If this melon gets any larger he won't be able to pull on his undershirt."

"If Stalin has Paul Loomis working on the same project, I'm sure you're in the lead," Emily said. "I'd put my money on a boilermaker over a particle physicist every day of the week."

"So how do we get to Loomis in Cologne?" John asked.

"Let's finish our meal," Garibaldi said. "Then I'd like to see these new rifles of yours in action. My old brain is slowly forming a plan."

After they had eaten, Garibaldi led them toward a courtyard but Caravaggio asked Emily if she would come with him instead. She agreed, saying she had no interest in watching men shoot.

"Where are we going?" she asked.

"Come, it's not far."

The destination was a room toward the rear of the palace, not far from the bustling kitchen. He asked her to wait in the hall while he went inside and when, moments later, he returned to bring her in, she saw it was a painter's studio. There were pots of brightly colored paints and artist's palettes on the tables. A cloth he had thrown over the easel was concealing a large canvas.

"This is what I wanted you to see," he said, pulling the cloth away.

She gasped at the nearly completed painting.

It was Emily, standing at the window of a castle turret, her blonde hair caught in a breeze, gazing at a green, sun-splashed countryside. He had imagined her in a sumptuous red and green Renaissance frock with a low-cut bodice and heaving breasts, her cheeks flushed with excitement, her lively eyes searching below.

"Is this how you see me?" she asked softly.

"Yes, in Earth, not in Hell, with the sun shining and birds singing and love in the air."

"It's the most beautiful thing I've ever seen," she said. "Thank you."

"It is I who must thank you. You have given me this inspiration. It led me to remember what it felt like to be alive and in the presence of beautiful women."

They heard loud gunshots.

"Soldiers at play," she said.

He touched her wrist. "Do not forget my offer, Emily."

"I remember it and I'm flattered but John Camp is the love of my life."

Caravaggio sighed and re-draped the painting. "And he doesn't have the aroma of a dead artist. Let us go and watch the soldiers at play."

They arrived at the courtyard to the aftermath of the shooting exhibition. Splintered wood from the small round table set on its side as a target littered the grass.

"Michelangelo," Garibaldi called out to Caravaggio. "You must see these incredible repeating rifles. Go ahead and show him."

Trooper Culpepper seated a new magazine and destroyed what was left of the table in a series of deafening booms.

"Bravo!" Caravaggio shouted. "May I hold it?"

Culpepper got a nod from John and put the rifle on safe mode.

Caravaggio tested its weight and exclaimed, "This merchant of doom is lighter than the archebuser I myself carry. How many of these do you possess, John?"

"Just the two."

Garibaldi couldn't contain his excitement. He waved his hands like a youngster and said, "But we need dozens of these, hundreds, thousands. There is nothing we cannot achieve if we have them."

"Hang on, Giuseppe," John said. "Making new ones isn't going to be as simple as that. First of all we're going to need these two rifles in case we need to shoot our way in to get at Paul Loomis. If and when we make it back, we'll give you one to break down and make castings. But the harder part will be making the bullets and the primers to set them off."

"But surely you left the English forgers with the ability to fashion additional rifles," Forneau said.

"We didn't take any chances of the technology falling into the wrong hands," John said. "When we left the forge we melted the rubber molds and smashed the plaster molds."

Kyle raised his hand like a kid in the back of a classroom. "Excuse me. I've got a confession to make." He removed his backpack and took out a cloth-wrapped bundle. "I probably should have told you this but I kept one set of rubber molds."

John looked furious. "Why'd you do that?" he asked.

Kyle shrugged, "I don't know, just in case we got ourselves in a jam. I probably should have run it by you."

"Let's talk," John said. "Just the two of us."

He pulled Kyle over to one of the arched doorways and slammed him. "Look, if these molds had fallen into the wrong hands then Garibaldi would be crushed like a walnut."

"But they didn't, did they?"

"That's not the point," John fumed.

"Yeah, it is. If these are the good guys then we've just put AKs into the right hands. Are they the good guys?"

"Yeah, I think they are. But will they be forever? You know what they say about absolute power corrupting absolutely."

"Guess that's a chance we're going to have to take."

"Did you save the bullet molds too?"

"Yep."

"Well, without primers it's all going to be moot."

"I saved a jar of the chemicals too."

John threw his hands in the air. "Christ, Kyle. I'm glad we're on the same team. If you were in my unit I'd have you referred for court martial."

Kyle got up and pushed his face inches from John's. "Well, I'm a fucking volunteer, so fuck off."

"Do you also have Professor Nightingale in your backpack? Without him, once your jar's empty, there's no more primers and no more bullets."

"Emily knows how to make them now."

John shook his head and stepped away to walk off his anger. A minute later he returned and said, "Well, you know what we're going to have to do?"

"What?"

John smiled. "We're going to make Giuseppe some rifles and ammo."

Kyle nodded. "Thought you were going to say that."

22

The morning light flooding her windows woke Benona with a start. She wasn't used to sleeping all the way through the night. Ever since the Heller invasion she had risen every few hours to look out the windows, check the radio news, look in on her daughter.

Woodbourne was fast asleep under the covers, still smelling strongly of the cologne he'd splashed all over before slipping into her sofa bed. His Heller odor was slight. She felt protected and loved for the first time in ages. Something close to a smile softened her face but then she remembered.

Polly.

She'd gone the entire night without checking on Polly.

At first she was relieved to see the girl lying so peacefully under her duvet.

Then she was horrified.

She shook her. "Polly? Polly?"

The girl was unresponsive and red-hot to the touch, her breathing heavy.

"Brandon! Come quick! It's Polly!"

The big man was fast to wake. He was in the girl's room in a flash.

"She's sick," Benona wailed, "she's real sick."

"But you gave her the new medicine, didn't you?"

"Yes, but maybe it was wrong medicine. I think she's dying. Polly, please wake up for mama."

"I'll go fetch the doctor," he said.

"The surgeries are all closed."

"Can you ring for an ambulance?"

"Nobody's picking up emergency number. The radio keeps saying this."

"Then let's take her to the hospital. What's the nearest?"

"Homerton. I'll see if they pick up phone."

Her hands were shaking as she paged through the directory assistance book looking for the number. She punched in the number. The phone rang again and again. She hung up and tried numbers for different departments. Finally she put the phone down and began to cry.

"Tell me where the hospital's at. I'll go over there and see if I can find a doctor."

"Is dangerous, Brandon."

"I can take care of myself."

Woodbourne left her in Polly's room, pulled his ragged clothes on and ran out onto the street. Glebe Road was deserted and so was Richmond Road. It was about two miles to the hospital and he flat-out ran. In a weird way he was fitter in death than he was in life. He had been a big smoker in the 1930s and '40s and never walked when he could hop in a motorcar. There were no smokes in Hell and frequently he had to run to save himself from soldiers, rovers, and villagers he had robbed. Now, his legs churned under him and his coat billowed behind as he sped down the middle of the carless road.

Ben was in the loo at MI5 headquarters when his mobile went off. He fished it out of the trousers around his ankles and saw it was the Drone Warfare Centre at RAF Waddington.

"Wellington."

"This is Major Garabedian, sir. We're tracking a target and we're going to require your firing authorization."

"I'm just away from the ops centre. I'll ring you back in two minutes. Is the target imminently threatening known civilians?"

"I think we can wait two minutes, sir."

Ben washed his hands and hurried to the lifts. He'd been chained to the office ever since the prime minister put him in charge of drone-kill authorizations. Every time he had given the nod he had felt diminished, made smaller and cheaper by self-doubt. Had he killed any civilians? Would he ever know for sure? There weren't enough soldiers deployed throughout London to do an after-action evaluation on each missile strike.

"What have they sent us?" Ben asked on arrival.

"Putting it on the big screen now," one of the techs said. "You're on speaker with RAF Waddington."

"This is Wellington," he said. "Just this one man?"

The zoomed-in image showed a solitary figure with a billowing coat running down the middle of an empty street.

"Just the one, yes," the air force major said.

"Hardly worth the fuss," Ben said.

"We were concerned because he may be closing in on a civilian hospital. He appears to be continuing on that course."

"Which hospital is that?"

"The Homerton University Hospital."

"Where did you pick him up?" Ben asked.

"We started tracking him on the Richmond Road in Hackney."

"Kip, do we know if there are any medical staff remaining there?"

The young analyst said he'd check and quickly came back to say that no one was responding at the casualty department.

"The hospital might be fully evacuated," Ben announced.

"It's your call, sir," Major Garabedian said. "From his clothes we're making the call he's a Heller."

"Yes, thanks for that," Ben said curtly. "Which street is he on?"

"It's Fenn," Kip said. "If he makes a right on Homerton Ave the hospital's right there."

"Stand by," Ben said. "You do not yet have my authorization."

Woodbourne ran to the end of Fenn Street. To his right he saw the low, tan-brick hospital buildings and a sign for the casualty entrance. He turned down the empty Homerton Grove, his lungs aching.

From Drone Warfare: "He appears to be about to enter the hospital. Do we have permission to fire?"

Ben studied the image of the speeding man. If he was going to the hospital, why was that? What would possess a Heller to run as fast as he could through Hackney toward a hospital neither pursuing nor being pursued?

"Do we have permission to fire?"

Ben watched the man veer into the casualty forecourt and then he was gone from view, presumably inside.

"Target lost," Garabedian said. There was a crackling sound from over the speaker then Garabedian again with a different, less professional tone saying, "Hope to fuck he doesn't kill any innocents."

The staff at the ops centre looked away from Ben in discomfort.

"What did you say?" Ben demanded.

There was a brief silence as Garabedian realized he hadn't hit the mute button properly. "Sorry, sir. Slip of the tongue."

"Don't second-guess me again, Major. It won't be good for your career. Keep eyes on this area and let's see what develops if anything."

Woodbourne got to the sliding glass doors of the casualty department and tried pushing on them. When that didn't work he tried pulling them apart. Pounding on the doors with his fists didn't raise anyone. In frustration he put his shoulder against the door once, twice, three times and then for the fourth try he stepped back and hurled himself at the safety glass which shattered into thousands of rounded pieces.

He stepped through and was at the reception desk.

"Hello?" he called out. "I need a doctor."

His words echoed.

"Anybody?"

He wandered through casualty, the empty patient cubicles, the trauma room, all neat, tidy, and empty. The sun streaming through the large panes in the corridor leading to the wards stung his sensitive eyes. He had to blink and squint to read the directory. The Starlight Children's Unit was on the first floor.

Exiting the stairwell, at first he thought the unit was as vacant as everywhere else but then he heard a whooshing sound and followed it. It took him to the open doors of the pediatric intensive care unit. In the closest glass-lined room to the doors he saw a small boy, motionless in bed, a tube down his nose, a ventilator bellows rising and falling.

"Excuse me, may I help you?"

The voice was a woman's, urgent, authoritative, challenging.

"Help me? Yes. I need a doctor."

The nurse said, "You're not supposed to be here. The hospital's closed. How did you get in?"

"There's a girl. She's very ill."

The nurse seemed to suddenly focus on the things about him that were wrong: his clothes, his furtive, darting eyes, his body odor.

She started walking backwards, a hesitant step at a time. "Are you …?"

"I need a doctor," he said matching her, step-by-step.

"George!" she screamed. "George, I need you!"

A tall, lanky man with heavy stubble and a stethoscope draped around his neck appeared from another room.

"What's the …"

He didn't finish the sentence because he saw Woodbourne and he too must have recognized the nature of the threat.

"Listen," the doctor said, "we don't want any trouble. We've got three very sick children here who were too ill to be transported. We're the only ones left in the hospital. If it's food you want, we can let you have some of ours. Then we need you to leave."

"Are you a doctor?"

"Yes I am. Dr. Murray."

"There's a sick girl not far from here. Her mother's with her. I need you to come with me to sort her out."

"I'm confused," Murray said. "You don't seem to be from …" He paused, appearing to search his brain for the right way to put it. "You don't seem to be from around here."

"I'm not. But I used to be."

"What's your name?"

"Brandon. Brandon Woodbourne."

The doctor's tone turned soothing but it didn't come across as genuine. "Brandon, may I call you by your first name?"

"I don't care."

"Brandon, our understanding from what we've heard from the authorities is that there are no children from where you're from."

"You can call it by its name. Go ahead, say it."

"Yes, well, Hell, I suppose. Hard to fathom it."

"The girl's from here. So's her mother."

The nurse asked, "We didn't think …"

Woodbourne interrupted, "Didn't think that Hellers did anything good? We're not all animals. The girl and her mother—they mean a lot to me."

"Terrible things are happening in London," the nurse said. "We're all scared."

"You should be scared," Woodbourne said. "You should be scared of me. I was a murderer. I am a murderer. But I need your help and I won't hurt you. I promise."

"What's the matter with this girl?" Murray asked.

"She had a bad earache. Her mother gave her medicine last night but it didn't help. Today she's got fever and won't wake up."

"How old is she?"

"I don't know children's ages. She's about this high."

He held his hand at his waist.

"I see," Murray said. "Do you know what medicine she was given?"

Benona had given him a capsule. He showed it.

"We're seeing a lot of resistance to amoxicillin lately," the doctor said, handing it back. "It may be that the infection has spread to her brain and spinal cord. She may have meningitis."

"Is that bad?"

"It can be very bad," the nurse said. "She probably needs to get a different antibiotic via a drip."

"I agree," Murray said. "You've got to bring her here."

"No. I want you to come with me," Woodbourne said.

"Neither of us can leave," Murray said firmly, though his voice had a quaver. "These three children are far too ill for one person."

He turned menacing. "I can make you come."

"Here's the thing," Murray said. "Even if I went with you, even if both of us went with you, this girl sounds too sick to care for at home. She likely needs more than medicine. She may need to be on a breathing machine and a vital signs monitor like these. She may die at home. She may live if you bring her here."

"If I do, will you promise to treat her?"

"Yes, I promise," Murray said.

"If you don't, you know I'll kill you."

"Yes, I believe you."

Woodbourne rubbed his face as he thought. "All right. I'll bring her here."

"How far is it?" the nurse asked.

"About two miles."

"How did you get here?"

"I ran."

"You won't be able to get an unconscious girl here on foot," the nurse said.

"I'll steal a car."

The nurse fished some keys from her smock. "The red Vauxhall parked in front of casualty in one of the ambulance spaces. That's mine."

Woodbourne seemed surprised at the unfamiliar sensation of a tear running down his face. He wiped it and looked at the moisture on his fingers before taking the keys.

"Thank you."

The camera on the Predator drone picked up the large man exiting the hospital.

"There he is again," Major Garabedian announced over the speaker.

"I see him," Ben replied.

Ben watched the man approach a car.

"He's breaking into a car," Garabedian said.

"Is he?" Ben asked. "It appears he's just used a key."

The red car sped off down Homerton Grove and made a left, the wrong way down one-way Fenn Street, the camera tracking along.

"In any event, it is our opinion that he is a Heller and he has taken command of a vehicle. Do we have your permission to fire?"

Ben remained quiet, intently watching the car work its way westbound through Hackney.

"Do we have permission?"

"Something's off here," he said, too softly for Garabedian to hear.

"Sorry, what was that?"

Ben looked down from the monitor and glowered at the Polycom speaker as if it were animate.

"You do not, repeat, you do *not* have permission to fire. You will continue to track the car. I want to see where he's going."

A testy "Affirmative" came down the line.

Ben returned to the monitor. The car was being maneuvered on a seemingly decisive course through the borough. On the straight stretch of Richmond Road it opened up to a speed that Ben estimated to be at least sixty miles per hour.

"Looks like he's heading over to Kingsland," Kip, the analyst, said.

"Maybe," Ben replied.

The car crossed over the railway bridge and made a left onto Glebe Road but instead of making a quick right to Kingsland carried on straight down Glebe and pulled over to the curb. The man jumped out and entered a building.

"Jesus," Ben said. "Jesus Christ."

"What is it?" Kip asked.

"I know that building. I've been there before. A Polish woman lives there with her daughter. Two months ago a Heller held her hostage there. We captured him and sent him back. This man we've been tracking. I know his name. It's Brandon Woodbourne."

Garabedian's voice came over the speaker, "Then we've missed our chance to kill the scum."

Ben didn't answer him. "He's just been to the hospital and back. I think he's just done something all together decent. Kip, get into my files and find that Polish woman's phone number. I need to ring her straight away."

"So how many bullets you got?" Willie asked Del, arriving back at Willie's flat.

"Just the five in the gun," Del said.

"That's pathetic. I thought you were a gangster and all."

"Who told you I was a gangster?"

"It's what everyone says," Willie said, pouring a fresh pot of tea. "Is it poppycock?"

"Well, maybe I was one. It's just I don't like it when people talk about me behind my back."

"What do you expect? What else do people have to do in an old-age home?"

"Well, it's all I got. Five slugs."

"Can't do much damage with that, can we?"

Del admired the tea and asked what brand it was. "PG Tips? Lovely cuppa. So, Willie, what did you used to do?"

"Different things. When I was a young pup, right after the war I was in a bomb disposal unit in London. Used to get ten, twenty calls a day to defuse unexploded German bombs. Hairy work but I got out with all me fingers and toes. After that I got my master electrician qualifications and went to work for …"

"I don't give a toss about the electricals trade," Del said, suddenly interested. "Tell me more about the bomb trade."

"What's to tell? A bomb got found. We lads removed the fuse. Full stop."

"Yeah, but can you build 'em?"

"Build a bomb? Me?"

"No, not you. The queen of England."

"I never built one but I know how they're built. Why?"

"To blow up the bloody Hellers in our cafeteria, of course. What are you, thick?"

"You want me to build a bomb?"

"Yeah, why not? What would we need to blow them back to Hell?"

Willie looked around his one-bedroom flat. "Oh, let's see. I've got black powder in my wardrobe, lengths of iron pipe in my socks drawer, det-cord in the loo."

"Don't be snarky with me," Del said. "I never liked snarky blokes."

"Look, Del, I don't know what to say. I'm an old man with old-man possessions, none of them deadly save my dirty underwear. Even MacGyver wouldn't have anything to work with."

"No, I'm serious. Yours ain't the only flat in the building. What would you need to build a bomb that ordinary folks might have lying about?"

Willie got up and paced around the sofa.

He began to mumble to himself and Del heard things like "won't find any gunpowder, will we?" and "won't find fertilizer around here" and "might find a propane tank" and "we'd need something bloody efficient in a small package" then, more brightly, "iron oxide's no problem, vinegar, check, got plenty of nuts and bolts, but, there's that, isn't it?"

Del couldn't stand it any longer. "There's what? What have you figured?"

"If we could get at a toy store, I reckon I could build something that would wipe out a roomful of those buggers."

Del picked his gun off the kitchen table and grabbed Willie's sleeve.

"Come back to my place. I've got a whole chest full of toys."

Willie stared into a large wooden chest crammed with puppets, plastic musical instruments, building sets, videos, and board games.

"What the hell are you doing with all this gear?" he asked.

"Grandkids, of course. They leave them off with me on weekends and go off for a curry and a few pints. If I didn't have the magic chest I'd go absolutely bonkers."

"Mind if I rummage?"

"To your heart's content."

"Give me a pillow, then."

"What for? You need a kip?"

"For my bloody knees."

Willie got down on his knees and began poking through the box, pulling things out to see what was beneath. He showed interest in a plastic car with rubber wheels.

"You got the remote control for this?"

"If it's in the chest I've got it. If it ain't I don't."

Willie found it, stuffed inside a hand puppet.

"Could be useful," he mumbled, plunging further into the depths. Then, with the wooden bottom beginning to show he reached down and said, "Jackpot."

He held it up triumphantly. A red Etch-a-Sketch.

"What do you plan to do with that?" Del said. "Draw a picture of a bomb?"

"Ye of little faith," Willie said. "Come on, back to my flat. Chop chop."

They worked into the night, Willie using the kitchen table as his workbench, Del on guard duty making forays with his pistol into the hall and the stairwell, checking the windows for signs of the Hellers.

Willie had a small assortment of tools spread out before him with a smashed Etch-a-Sketch and remote-control bits off to one side and his kitchen fire extinguisher, unscrewed and emptied. With his reading glasses low on his nose and his gnarled hands drilling holes and stripping wires, the years seemed to fall away. He even took to humming as if he didn't have a care in the world. Every so often he added to his running commentary about the qualities of thermite.

"You see, the aluminum powder in the Etch-a-Sketch, that's the key, my son. Now you need to add iron oxide, which is where the steel-wool pads and vinegar comes in, but when it's all nice and mixed together you've got thermite. Generates a hell of a lot of heat and energy when it's ignited, say with a nice little spark of electricity from a battery."

"I really wish you'd put a sock in it, mate," Del said, having a bit more whiskey. "I'm sick of listening to you prattle on. As long as it goes bang, I'll be happy as a clam."

After a while, Willie looked up from his work to rest his eyes. "So you were a gangster then?"

"I said I was, didn't I?" Del said. "What's it to you?"

"I was just wondering."

"Wondering what?"

"If you ever, you know, did someone in."

Del shook his head. "Just because I got a gun don't mean I ever killed no one. It was just a tool of the trade."

"A screwdriver was a tool of my trade and I used one all the time."

"Look, we did a lot of thieving in my day and I used to bring a piece with me just in case but I never used it. You see all this rot on TV and you think all us old-timers used to go around like Dillinger. It wasn't like that. Sometimes we'd rob a jewelry store or a bank and give 'em cigarettes to calm themselves while we went about our business."

"So you were a humanitarian," Willie said with a laugh.

Del sneered back. "Yeah, exactly."

At 4 a.m. Willie declared victory and woke up a napping and disoriented Del to show him the finished product.

The fire extinguisher was screwed back together. Inside was the home-made thermite, packed tight with cotton strips from a pair of undershorts and all the nuts, bolts, screws, and nails that both men had in their flats. An electrical wire plunged through the small hole drilled into the fire extinguisher. The wire was connected to the toy car remote-control receiver and battery pack that were strapped to the extinguisher tube with black electrical tape.

"That's not going to go off in here, is it?" Del asked.

Willie held up the remote-control box. "Not unless I push this button."

"Well don't."

"You ready?" Willie asked.

"Yeah, let's send them cunts back to Hell."

They were afraid to use a torch lest they attract a Heller on walkabout so they gingerly made their way in the dark around the retirement-home buildings until they were back at the cafeteria. Their plan was simple. They'd both sneak inside just far enough for Del to toss the bomb inside. Then Willie would push the button, a large explosion would ensue, splattering the Hellers, and they'd go back to bed.

Del pulled himself up from the flowerbed until he was high enough to look through the cafeteria windows. An open refrigerator door in the kitchen cast some light into the dining area.

He lowered himself.

"Well?" Willie whispered.

"The bastards are lying all over the floor."

"Are they asleep?"

"Well, they're not dead, are they?"

"Ready?" Willie asked.

"I was born ready," Del growled, raising his revolver.

They went around to the side door of the cafeteria and tried the knob. It turned and with a few shuffling steps they were inside.

Monk was sleeping beside Heath.

He was a light sleeper even while drunk, a survival skill honed by two centuries of roving. He heard something and poked Heath.

Heath was lying with his face in the crook of his elbow and produced a muffled something.

"Wake up, Heath. There's someone coming."

Heath groggily lifted his head. "Is there now?" he said. "I'm never too tired to rip someone apart."

23

Trevor's horse was scrawny and incapable of sustaining much of a pace. As he rode along the rutted westbound road toward Devon he remembered that the first time he rode a horse was only two months ago. He busied himself thinking about the training he'd gone through with Brian Kilmeade. Now that Brian was out of the picture, maybe he'd apply to the BBC for Brian's old TV job as a medieval weapons presenter. If he ever made it back.

When those thoughts played out he turned to Arabel, wondering where she was, how she was doing, how the children were coping with the traumatic memories. They were sweet kids. He hoped they weren't scarred for life. If he survived this he'd make a play to be a permanent part of Arabel's life. He'd be a good dad to those kids. Maybe they'd get some new brothers and sisters along the way.

He was so deep in thought and hypnotized by the rhythm of the trot that he didn't see the threat coming as early as he would have liked. But the Cornish soldiers at the head of the pack saw Trevor coming, a speck at first, then a man on horseback. They were riding eastbound, lured by stories of magical channels at Leatherhead and Sevenoaks that could transport a Heller back to Earth.

By the time Trevor saw them the lead soldiers had already quickened to a gallop. Trevor swore and dismounted, tying the horse's reins to a roadside bush. He shouldered his AK-47, crouched into a firing position, and opened his satchel to get access to more ammo if needed. It was hard to tell how many riders were approaching because they were kicking up a cloud of dust. He hoped thirty rounds fired from a long distance would be more than enough to turn the threat. He didn't try to take cover. His effective range was over ten times farther than the blackpowder muskets he might be facing.

He controlled his breathing and looked down the iron sights. The lead rider was about two hundred yards away. Trevor was an expert marksman but the sights were fixed and couldn't be calibrated. He didn't fault Kyle for that. It was a miracle he'd been able to forge the rifles at all. If he took the man out it would be a lucky shot but it was worth a try to convince the others to turn tail.

He held his breath at full exhale and squeezed the trigger. The rider kept coming. He didn't see any dirt kick up to the sides and the horse hadn't been hit so he figured he was high. He lowered his aim point and fired another round.

The rider fell, his foot caught in a stirrup. The horse veered off into the woods. From this distance he couldn't see the startled expressions of the other soldiers who couldn't understand how their captain had been felled from so far away.

They kept coming.

Trevor kept firing, hitting two men or a horse with every three shots.

Despite the rising casualties the other riders weren't deterred.

"How many are there?" Trevor said out loud.

They were a hundred yards away when he emptied his magazine, ejected it, and reached into the satchel for the loaded one. From this distance it didn't look like there was more than six to eight soldiers left so the spare mag was probably going to do it. But he didn't want to take a chance; he wanted to quickly reload some rounds into the spent mag before seating the spare. But as his hand explored the satchel, he didn't feel the spare mag. He didn't feel loose ammo. He felt rocks.

"What the fuck?"

He took his eyes off the threat and looked inside but it was pointless.

He'd been robbed and he was in serious trouble.

One of the soldiers must have thought Trevor was close enough and fired his musket from the saddle. A lead ball splatted into the road short of the mark but uncomfortably close. Trevor briefly considered getting on his horse and trying to ride away but the animal was too pathetic. If he took off on foot into the woods they'd run him down.

He made up his mind. He'd do something irrational. He began running in a zigzag toward them, aiming his rifle and shouting at the top of his lungs.

Fifty yards away another shot rang out. He heard it whistle past. He waited for the next one. And waited. But it didn't come. He saw the rest of the soldiers drawing swords and it dawned on him. None of them had a gun.

He stopped his zigzagging and began running straight for them yelling, "This is your last chance! I will shoot you!"

One of the riders pulled up and turned his horse around. Then three more. The last three looked over their shoulders at their comrades fleeing and that was enough. They too turned tail and galloped off the way they had come.

Trevor dropped to his haunches, suddenly exhausted. He found himself speaking to Arabel. "Keep waiting for me, all right? I'm doing my level best to get back to you."

He led his horse past the shot-up men and dead horses collecting their weapons as he went. Soon he had a sword on his belt, three others strapped to the saddle, a crossbow and a handful of bolts. Instead of rocks, his satchel was now loaded with a pistol, powder, and shot. He hated to part with his AK-47 but it was only dead weight. He used his sword to bury it in a shallow grave along the verge and he continued his journey toward Devon.

It was Danny who pried up one of the coarse floorboards under his hay-filled mattress and discovered the dirt under the boy's cottage was moist and soft. While the boys ate their thin, disgusting gruel, they debated the subject of escape.

They split into opposing camps. The stronger boys, Glynn, Boris, Nigel, and Danny supported escape. The weaker ones, Kevin, Stuart, Andrew, and most vocally, Harry, thought it was a crazy idea. Only Angus stayed silent, perhaps sensing that his vote would be the deciding one.

"If we stay here, we'll die," Nigel said. "We'll get sick or we'll get stamped on by a horse or, or, I don't know what, but we'll die."

"That's stupid," Kevin said.

"Why is that stupid?" Boris asked.

"Because it is, that's why," Kevin insisted. "We'll die if we try to get back to Sevenoaks. We'll get lost and we'll be eaten by rovers."

"We'll get food-poisoned if we stay here," Danny said. "Or Ardmore will beat the crap out of us for working too slow."

"If we stay, we're kissing our homes good bye," Boris said. "You really want to do that?"

Angus held back and listened as the arguments went back and forth but when he couldn't take it any longer he got off his mattress and angrily said, "All right. Shut up everyone. It's four to four and I'm the deciding vote. We're going to go with Danny's idea. We're going to dig our way out of here. We're going to escape. I'd rather die trying than die in this shit hole."

And that was that. It wasn't only the strongest boys, it was a majority and even the opposing boys could understand the fairness.

They began that very night. They dug with wooden spoons, working in shifts throughout the night so that all of them had a go, even Harry. It was the ever practical Stuart who had the idea how to conceal the dirt. He tore a hole in his burlap mattress cover and began stuffing it with soil and within a few days, the boys' mattresses were more dirt than hay.

Finally, the tunnel under the floorboards was four feet in length, long enough to make it under the wall of their cottage and wide enough for even Boris, the largest boy, to squeeze through. On the agreed upon night none of the boys slept. They put their ears to the walls listening until they could no longer hear any laughing or talking from the farm workers. Then they waited another couple of hours to be sure everyone was asleep. They pulled Danny's heavy, dirt-filled mattress away from the tunnel opening and lifted the floorboards.

"I'll go first," Danny said. "Wait here until I come back and give the all clear."

He was gone for too long for anybody's comfort. It fell to Angus to convince the rest of them that nothing had gone wrong but even he seemed relieved when Danny's head poked back up through the floor.

"I didn't see anyone," Danny said. "It's really, really dark. We'll have to feel our way along the sheep fences till we get to the woods behind the horse barn."

"The road's not far from there," Angus said.

Harry hadn't said a word all night. He'd been sitting against a wall with his knees drawn up, staring at the floor. "Then what?" he asked.

"You know what," Nigel said. "I know you're not thick so you're just being difficult. Like we've planned, we'll make it as far down the road as we can and when it's light we'll hide in the woods in case they come looking for us."

"So we'll travel at night, same as rovers," Harry said. "Brilliant."

"You never offered a better plan," Glynn said.

"That's because there isn't one," Harry said. "At least we're safe from rovers here."

Glynn went to the wall and pulled Harry up by his arms. "You know the only one who's safe here, Harry? It's you. We're worked half-to-death like slaves while you hide under Bess's skirt telling her stories and eating better than us." He curled his hand into a fist and cocked it back. "I'm sick of you."

Angus ran over and pulled Glynn away from the small boy. Though Glynn, the wrestler, could have thrashed any two of them he didn't fight Angus. Instead he slipped from

Angus's grasp and sulked off.

"We're all going to stick together," Angus said. "And we're not going to fight among ourselves. Does anyone want to change his vote?"

Each boy shook his head.

"Then it's still five to four," Angus said. "It's majority rules. We've worked hard on the tunnel. Tonight's the night."

Danny went through first again, followed by Kevin. They alternated one strong boy with one weak boy until only Andrew, Angus, Harry, and Boris were left.

"Go on, Andrew," Angus said. "You're next."

Andrew began to whimper. "I don't like small spaces."

"Go on," Angus said. "The faster you're in the faster you're out the other end."

"I don't want to."

Angus had planned to go last but after a quick word with Boris he said, "Tell you what. I'll go in right behind you and give you a gentle push to keep you moving."

"You'll be right next to me?" Andrew sniffed.

"Yeah, you'll feel my hand on your ankles."

Angus talked Andrew into the tunnel and before joining him he told Harry and Boris not to dawdle. Soon Angus was gone too.

"Right then," Boris said to Harry, "In you go."

"No."

"What do you mean, no?"

"I'm not going," Harry said, firmly. "I've thought it through and I'm staying with Bess. She's nice to me and I'm scared so I'm staying."

"Oh no you're not you little shit," Boris said, wrapping the small boy up in his beefy arms and picking him up like a rolled-up rug.

"Leave me be!" Harry shouted.

"Shut up," Boris said. "Do you want them to hear?"

"Yes I do!"

Boris rammed the boy headfirst into the tunnel opening and pushed him in as if he were breech-loading a cannon. The boy's protestations became muffled and Boris kept pushing him through until there was enough room for him to crawl in after him. Harry tried to crawl backwards while Boris plowed forward but Boris' brute strength and superior mass overwhelmed the small boy and both of them inched toward the other side.

Angus heard the commotion and half-crawled back into the tunnel headfirst to see what was going on. He felt Harry's arms pressing against the tunnel walls instead of drawing him forward so he grabbed for a wrist and pulled on it.

"What the hell are you doing?" Angus whispered.

Angus could hear Boris telling him to pull Harry through so he did with all his might. Finally Harry's head was above ground but the boy was still kicking furiously.

Angus felt a rumbling vibration.

The tunnel collapsed behind Harry.

Boris let out one sickening, muffled cry and was silent.

Harry began to scream.

Again and again.

Angus hit him hard in the mouth twice and he stopped screaming.

"Help me pull him through," Angus said to the others.

Danny and Glynn tugged on Harry's limp arms and got him free. Once he was out Angus began digging furiously with his hands through the collapsed dirt.

There were shouts coming across the way from Bess and Ardmore's house.

Glynn roughly pulled Angus away from the tunnel mouth.

"It's too late! We've got to go!" he said.

"We can't leave Boris!"

"He's crushed, Angus. He's gone. Please!"

Angus got to his feet. He heard more indistinct shouting. It sounded like Ardmore.

"Everyone, run!" Angus said.

"What about him?" Glynn said pointing at Harry.

"Leave the bastard."

"We can't do that," Glynn said. "Help me get him on my shoulder."

Angus capitulated and soon Glynn had Harry in a fireman's carry, following the other boys to the fence.

Ardmore's voice was intelligible now, "Stop them! Hurry along!"

"They're going to catch us," Danny shouted.

Stuart was running along the fence when he heard the sheep bleats welling up from the agitated herd. He would later take credit for the brilliant idea, but in truth, after the fact, he could hardly remember opening the gate and running among the herd until two hundred sheep were fleeing their pen.

As the boys fled into the night, Angus could hear Bess's shrill voice rising over the frightened sheep, ordering her men to round up each and every precious beast. Then he heard one last thing that made his blood run cold.

"Angus? Do you hear me?" Bess cried, "You're going to pay for this you little bastard! You'd better hope the rovers get you, not me."

24

Once again they were pulling an all-nighter inside a hot forge, this one within the city walls of Paris on the north shore of the Seine.

The forge master, an eighteenth-century man named Jean, had similar mannerisms and habits to William the forger. Jean had a large belly and fierce eyes and commanded his forge workers like a drill sergeant, bellowing commands, criticizing and slapping laggards with his burn-scarred hands. His English was rudimentary but he and Kyle communicated through the language of iron. Once Jean saw an AK-47 demolish a gourd at fifty paces he grasped the importance of the project and stopped all other work to begin casting the myriad rifle parts. His iron ore was of a lesser quality than the Norse ore Kyle had used at Richmond but it would have to do. The rifles might be more brittle and prone to fracturing under the stress of rapid-fire but they would still be light years ahead of any weapons Stalin's forces possessed.

When Kyle showed Jean the small rubber molds for the rifle's screws, Jean was baffled at first.

"What this is?" Jean asked.

"Screws."

Then Kyle made the universal hand motion of screwing something with a screwdriver and Jean's face lit up.

"Ah, vis!"

"Yeah, screw."

"Ah, screw! Yes."

Emily set up shop in the coolest reaches of the forge searching her memory for every detail of Professor Nightingale's synthesis of lead styphnate. She wished she had kept notes, but in truth, her recollection was nearly perfect and she was soon grinding and mixing and pouring just as she had done as the chemist's apprentice.

Well into their first full day of work John arrived with some Italians carrying heavy chests from the royal palace.

"What you got, bro?" Kyle asked, wiping his hands on his apron.

"Giuseppe had an inventory done and decided to donate this stuff to the Kyle Camp Weapons Factory."

The lids were lifted. The chests were stuffed with ornamental brass pieces, representing centuries of booty from Robespierre's palace.

"Should make enough bullet casings for an entire war," John said. "How's it feel being a merchant of doom?"

Kyle smiled sheepishly. "Back home in Oregon I'd be politically incorrect if I said I was enjoying it but, shit, I am. I always envied what you did. Badass Green Beret. You were a part of something. I never was."

"Until now," John said.

"Yeah, until now."

"You're turning into a heck of a soldier," John said.

"Even with a fucked-up knee?"

"Despite your fucked-up knee. You're also a heck of a man."

Kyle couldn't seem to respond to that compliment. He blinked and gulped and looked away before pointing John to the forge worker who was going to melt down the brass.

John snuck up on Emily and kissed the back of her downturned neck.

She didn't flinch. "Hey."

"How did you know I wasn't some big fat iron worker stealing a kiss?" John said.

"Because unlike a Heller you only smell of BO."

"Charming. How's it going?"

"I'm actually quite pleased with myself. I think the chemistry's turning out all right but we'll have to wait and see if my primer goes bang. Have you talked to Giuseppe again about getting help finding Paul?"

"He says he's working on some kind of plan. If he doesn't come up with something, in a week we'll have enough rifles and ammo to storm Stalin's castle."

"I hate that idea," Emily said. "What if Paul were killed—well, not killed but …"

"I know. I don't love the idea either."

At the forge entrance a voice called out to them, "There you are!"

It was Garibaldi, accompanied by an entourage that included Caravaggio, Simon and Forneau snaking out the door.

"I have a new friend for you to meet," Garibaldi said, approaching Emily's bench, "and an old one."

He theatrically pointed toward the door and in came Brian Kilmeade, bouncing along on his powerful legs. In the orange glow of the forge fire his large shaved head and flashing smile gave him the look of a carved jack o'lantern.

"Did you miss me?" he shouted, opening his arms.

There were hugs, kisses, and tears.

"I don't think a minute's gone by that I haven't wondered how you were doing," John said.

"We've been so worried about you," Emily added.

"Worried enough to come back for a visit?" Brian said. "It's not like popping across town to see a mate for a meal and a chat."

"Didn't they tell you what happened and why we're here?" Emily asked.

"Of course they did. Just teasing. Sounds like bloody chaos. Hellers belong in Hell. Not like I'm prejudiced, mind you. Some of my best friends are Hellers but the two worlds aren't meant to be connected, are they?"

"Queen Mécia hasn't soured on you yet?" John asked.

"Au contraire mon frere," Brian said, evoking a smile from the listening Forneau. "We're getting along swimmingly. Guess what she's made me?"

"A leash?" John asked.

"Fuck off. She's made me a General of the Iberian army. Imagine me, little Brian Kilmeade from the BBC, a bloody general."

Simon leaned in and said, "We're done for."

"So you don't regret staying," Emily said.

"Look, I'll be honest. There's tons that I miss but I'm having a blast." He clapped his scabbard. "I was meant for this. Carrying a sword, drawing up battle plans, drinking ale with sweaty warriors. I was born in the wrong era. I've always said that. So where's my man Trevor?"

"Somewhere in Brittania with the SAS looking for a group of schoolboys who came over," John said. "Let me introduce you to a couple of the guys."

John made a megaphone with his hands and called over to O'Malley and Culpepper who were working on some plaster molds on the other side of the forge.

"I've seen you on the tele," Culpepper said when he was introduced to Brian. "Had to go to bloody Hell to meet a celebrity."

"I know your outfit," Brian said. "22 SAS. You lads are fierce."

"We do what we have to do," O'Malley said.

"I know you do," Brian said, pumping his hand. "Good to have you on the same team. So, you're making AK-47s, I hear. Brainy idea."

"Meet the man who made it happen," John said. "Brian, this is my brother, Kyle Camp, the best gunsmith in the USA."

Kyle and Brian began to chat and soon Brian was off, examining molds and casts and O'Malley's finished product.

Garibaldi nudged a stranger forward, a blue-eyed man with a sober face, greatly elongated by a goatee. A second man with a long scar, poorly hidden by a reddish beard, stood behind him.

"This is the new friend I want you to meet," Garibaldi said to John and Emily. "I introduce Valery Ostrov, who has offered to help you find your man, Loomis. And this gentleman who speaks not a word of English, French or Italian is his compatriot, Pavel Antonov. Ostrov and I have cooked up a plan."

Much of the entourage retreated to the cool air outside and sat on the grassy bank of the Seine while Garibaldi explained his idea to John and

Emily. Ostrov, though simply dressed in rough peasant clothes, had been a high-ranking officer in Stalin's army until he defected a fortnight earlier, making his way to the French lines where he offered to join Garibaldi and betray Stalin's military preparations.

John wanted to know how Garibaldi could trust him but instead of asking the Italian he asked Ostrov directly.

Ostrov, a man with a straight spine and a military bearing, spoke excellent English with a thick, lugubrious Russian accent. "I have long history with Stalin, you see. I was a colonel in the Red Army, very loyal to Stalin, serving in 8th Army under Colonel General Grigori Mihailovich Shtern when he and many officers were arrested in purge. Under Stalin's orders, Beria had us shot. What were our crimes, I ask you? None. When I come to Hell for my own sins, I find myself serving Stalin again. Irony, yes? When I see him again, do I ask him why I was purged? No, I am scared to be in rotting room. Much worse than being purged. So I do what I must do to survive, like my silent friend Antonov here, and I become soldier again. Then I hear men talk about this new king of Italia, King Giuseppe. I know of Garibaldi from school. I hear about how he want to make better world here. I like these ideas. Antonov like too. So when we have chance we defect. Now that we meet this great man and talk to him I want to help his cause with all my might."

Garibaldi patted him on the shoulder in a fatherly way and said, "This plan of ours, it's not a perfect one. None are. There are always risks but with Ostrov's help and one of your AK-47s I think we might just get you safely into Stalin's palace in Cologne."

The essence of the plan was this: Ostrov would reappear at the Cologne castle with the story that while on patrol near the border of Francia he had been captured by Garibaldi's forces. Transported to Paris, he was tortured but gave up nothing. He escaped from prison with the help of a sympathetic jailer and overpowered a guard who was carrying this weapon. He would present the trophy to Stalin as a demonstration that he had not been recruited as Garibaldi's spy. However, his real mission would be to pass a letter from Emily to Paul Loomis and bring him to a place outside the castle where Emily and John could interrogate him.

"You're right," John said when Garibaldi and Ostrov had finished. "It isn't perfect. It's got so many holes in it I almost don't know where to start. I take it back, I do know where to start. You're giving away your biggest strategic asset. Stalin will be able to rip the rifle apart and cast each piece. He'll be mass producing them in no time and then at best, you'll be at a draw."

"We will have the primer chemicals," Garibaldi said. "He will not."

Emily said, "Within all of Germania and Russia, surely he'll find someone with enough knowledge of chemistry to make the lead styphnate or another explosive primer."

Garibaldi said he had considered that. "But we will have the advantage of time. We can begin to mass-produce the rifles, the ammunition, and the primer. If we strike early and strike hard with conventional and singing cannon and an infantry carrying these new rifles then we will surely crush Stalin and crush his coalition. Perhaps we can achieve this dream of unifying Europa. And, armed with the knowledge that Loomis will impart, you might achieve your dream of severing the connections between our unhappy world and yours."

"I think Giuseppe's idea could work," Emily said. "It's better than trying to take the castle by force."

John kept raising objections to the Trojan horse plan but everyone else challenged him to come up with a better alternative.

In the end he admitted he couldn't. He looked into Ostrov's unblinking eyes and asked, "Here's what I don't get. Tell me, what do *you* get out of this?"

Ostrov answered smoothly, "I get satisfaction of helping this noble cause of King Giuseppe's and pleasure in seeing the butcher Stalin sent to rotting room."

"Is that it?" John asked.

"And maybe if all goes well, the king will give me nice palace in Moscow and enough gold to buy many pretty women to fill rooms."

While Emily cringed, John nodded and told Garibaldi, "You know, that's the first believable thing this guy's said. Let's go to Germania."

25

King Henry was not amused and neither was Malcolm Gough. The basic issue was that both men wanted to go home. Henry was no longer enchanted by the mysteries of television and the day before he had flung the remote control across the room, smashing it against the wall.

"I will not gaze upon it any longer," he had shouted. "It makes my head throb and it gives me no more pleasure. Take it away."

He had also grown tired of all the new foods he had, at least, initially sampled and begun to demand the same simple roasted meats and savory pies he ate in his own land.

Then there were his constant demands to be allowed to leave the confines of his room and go riding and hunting in the green countryside he saw through his windows. The cadre of MI5 minders stationed in the country house summarily turned down all requests and he ranted and raved about the outrage of imprisoning the king of England.

"Does the present queen know of my treatment?" he had demanded of Gough.

"She certainly does," Gough had said.

"I am astonished she would permit this injustice." Henry had used his learnings of the queen's royal heritage to assert that it was no wonder she would treat him so, she being the patrilineal product of German royalty, to wit the House of Wettin.

Gough had made some remark about the preference of the present quarters to the Tower of London and Henry had unleashed a tirade.

"Teutonic blood!" he had raged. "The queen of England possesses Teutonic blood. Is it any wonder she treats a pureblooded son of Tudors in such a beastly manner? And you, what of you, Gough?" the king had shouted, a pint mug in his hand.

"My father is English, my mother Italian."

"Another half-blood!" Henry had screamed, throwing the mug and narrowly missing Gough's head.

"I will return when his Majesty has settled down," Gough had said, pulling his sports jacket from the back of a chair. He had stayed away for several hours until the king had settled down.

On this day the issue was once again women. Henry resumed his daily demand to have comely women introduced into his bedchamber and Gough lost his patience. The professor had been under considerable stress over his own confinement and his separation from his family during a period of unprecedented national emergency. Perhaps if he had been allowed to tell his wife that he had been tasked with babysitting Henry VIII and given some sort of documentary evidence of the truth of the outlandish statement, she might have understood. But all he could repeat, when she agreed to take his calls at all, was that he had been given a top-secret assignment by MI5 and couldn't talk about it, alluding to the fact that his calls were undoubtedly monitored. When she asked what in God's green Earth did the security services need from a professor of Tudor history, he could only spout silly non-answers and infuriate her further.

Perhaps the straw that broke the camel's back was the conversation Gough had that morning with Ben Wellington. The professor had been sustained by the treasure trove of interview material he had amassed, all of it carefully recorded on a small digital recorder he had been provided. The insights and sheer volume of detail about Henry's reign he had collected during their time together was staggering. He had begun outlining the structure of the book he would write. It would be the mother of all Henry books, the mother of all Tudor books, the mother of all history books. He would call it something like, *From the King's Mouth to My Ears—The Life and Times of Henry VIII.* It would rise to the top of the bestseller lists, something none of his previous books had come close to achieving, and it would stay there for years. He would be booked solidly for speaking engagements for a decade. His snarkiest academic critics would be sick with envy. It would transform the rather shy professor into a national institution. But when he asked one of the more-senior MI5 people on site to review one of the transcripts concerning Anne Boleyn from a recording made a few days earlier, he was denied access.

"Mr. Wellington," he had said on the call, "are you telling me that you won't reverse this refusal to let me have the transcripts or the primary digital files?"

"I'm afraid that is correct, professor. The decision to limit the distribution to people with the highest level of security clearance in the government has been taken by the prime minister."

"But how am I to write my book without access to these files?"

"Book? What book?"

"Why, my book redefining Henry's reign? Surely you must know I intend to write about the staggering insights I've gleaned from talking to the man."

"Look, I don't know how to say this more plainly,"

Ben had said, "but there can never be any book or articles or interviews or any mention whatsoever about your interactions with Henry as long as the government deems the material to be secret."

"And how long is that likely to be?"

"Until Hell freezes over, I'd imagine, excuse the inappropriate expression."

After the longest pause, Gough had announced that under the circumstances he would be leaving immediately. Ben, realizing he had a situation on his hands, had sought to mollify him by promising a thorough review of the matter once the crisis was over then played the patriotic-duty card. In the end, Gough agreed to stay.

Now, he lost his temper with the pouting king who was flopped on his unmade bed, chewing on a chicken leg.

"For the last time, I am not a procurer of women. I am not a pimp. You and I are both prisoners here, if you must know, and neither of us will be granted conjugal visits!"

Henry threw the covers off and bounded out of the bed toward the professor who pushed his panic button for the first time. Two MI5 men rushed in with Tasers drawn.

Henry stopped dead in his tracks and glowered at the oddly shaped weapons in their hands.

"I will speak to the queen immediately," he said. "Tell her it is not a request, it is a demand."

To Gough's surprise, the word came through an hour later that the queen would, indeed be calling. A telephone was brought into the room and placed on speaker mode.

At first Henry refused to believe the voice coming through was the queen's but she assured him that it was indeed she.

The queen asked how he was getting along and Henry responded with a litany of complaints, up to and including his lack of carnal pleasurement. The queen replied that she had been assured his basic safety and comforts were being well attended to and that the details of his confinement were in the hands of the security services.

Far from satisfying Henry his ire was merely stoked. He unleashed a tirade of abuse, impugning her Germanic heritage and comparing her unfavorably to a host of farm animals.

A male voice suddenly came on the line. "See here, you. How dare you speak to her majesty in this despicable manner. This call is over."

The line went dead.

"And who was that?" Henry said, staring at the quiet telephone.

Gough shook his head and said, "I believe that was the queen's husband."

Woodbourne bounded up the stairs to Benona's flat and knocked on the door. When there was no reply he banged harder.

"It's me," he called through the door. "I've been to the hospital. I found a doctor. I've got a car to take her to him."

He heard the door unlocking and it slowly swung open.

Benona was ashen. She walked away from the door, with small, shuffling steps.

"Did you hear what I said? I've found her a doctor. I've got a car downstairs to bring her to hospital."

"No hospital."

She sat down on the sofa.

"What do you mean, no hospital?"

"She's not going to hospital." She began to sob.

Woodbourne strode past her into Polly's room. The curtain was drawn. The duvet was pulled up to her neck.

"Polly, it's Brandon. Wake up. What's the matter? Wake up."

He sat beside her and felt her head. When he left it had been hot. Now it was cool. He shook her.

"Polly, wake up!"

He stumbled into the other room.

"She's not waking up," Benona said. "My baby is dead."

"She can't be."

She made an animal sound, a cross between a wail and a groan. "She's dead, Brandon. Is all over. My life is over. My baby is dead."

He swallowed hard. "I don't know what to say. I'm sorry. I …"

"You what?"

"I loved her. I love you."

She looked at him. Though her face was wet she made no effort to dry it.

"You love me?" she asked.

"Yes."

"You sure I go to Hell when I die?"

"You told me you had your husband killed," he said. "Was that the truth?"

"Yes, is true."

"Then you'll go."

"I want you to kill me."

He recoiled as if yanked by a cord. "What?"

"Kill me."

"I can't. I won't."

"I thought you were a killer."

"I am but I won't kill you."

She got up and went to the kitchen and got a paring knife from the drawer.

"You said when I got to Hell if you found me you'd take care of me there. If I'm going, I go now. I can't live another minute without Polly. You come too. We can be together and you can take care of me. Here, take it."

With every step she took forward, Woodbourne took one backward until he was pressed against the wall. She kept coming until she was inches away. Looking up into his horrified face she pushed the knife handle into his palm.

"Do it. I don't care if it hurts."

He stared at the knife. "It won't hurt."

"You promise?"

"I promise."

"You promise you come with me?"

"I promise."

He'd always been a blade man. He knew how to kill a victim slow and he knew how to kill one fast. His hand moved so quickly she never saw it coming. The carotid blood hit him in the chest and then the face when bent over to catch her falling body. He felt her go limp and slowly lowered her to the floor.

He hadn't cried since he was five or six but his chest began to shudder. He caught himself. There wasn't time for grief. She'd be there, scared, waiting for him. Who knew what scum might be wandering about London, set to pounce on a new arrival to Hell. He took the knife, red with her blood and smoothly slit his own throat, ear-to-ear.

Ben and his security detail pulled up in front of Benona's flat. The red car Woodbourne had taken from the hospital was still running at the curb. His agents insisted Ben stay downstairs while they made entry. He'd interviewed Benona there two months before after Woodbourne released mother and daughter and fled the scene, after he'd been caught and sent back to Hell. While Ben waited, he wondered why Woodbourne had returned and why he'd rushed to the hospital? He had so many questions. A pair of agents had been dispatched to the Homerton Hospital after calls to the place went unanswered.

An agent came down to get Ben.

"They're all dead," he said.

Ben ran up the stairs and stumbled through the small flat taking it all in.

The agent said, "It looks like he killed the girl, maybe suffocated her. Then he killed the woman and committed suicide."

"I'm not so sure," Ben said.

His mobile rang. It was one of his people calling from the hospital. He listened and rang off.

"No, it didn't go down like that," Ben told the agent. "What happened here was something entirely different."

Del and Willie pushed the cafeteria doors open a few inches at a time and were relieved they didn't creak or squeal. Once inside they closed them just as carefully.

The lobby of the cafeteria housed the administration offices and a lounge where residents congregated before entering the dining area. The only light came from the glowing fire exit signs. The swinging double doors to the dining room were closed.

Del cradled the fire-extinguisher thermite bomb in his arms, his pistol stuck in his waistband. Willie had the remote-control unit.

Willie whispered to him, "I'll push the right door open and you slide it in. Don't roll it. It'll knock the battery off."

"I know, I know," Del whispered back. "I'm not stupid."

Willie tiptoed up to the doors and put his hand on the right one. Del was a pace behind.

He mouthed the words, one, two, three, and pushed hard.

Del took a step forward and blinked into the faintly lit space. There was no sign of the sleeping Hellers he had spied through the window.

"Why aren't you tossing it?" Willie whispered urgently.

"'Cause I can't see no one," Del replied. "Maybe they footed it. I'm going in."

"You sure?"

"Yeah, I think they're gone."

Del went in first and Willie followed. The cafeteria floor was a mess of discarded food containers but it was empty.

"I'll get the lights," Willie said.

"We should check the kitchen first," Del said, but it was too late. Willie hit the switches.

Heath and a large bunch of Hellers barged in from the kitchen. Willie and Del turned to flee but their way out of the swinging doors was blocked by Monk and another rover. Both men had been hiding in the lobby.

"Toss it!" Willie yelled.

In his high anxiety, Del forgot to slide it. Instead he rolled it like a cylindrical bowling ball and it clattered and bumped along stopping a couple of yards short of Heath.

"Set it off!" Del screamed.

"We're too close!" Willie shouted.

"Set it off!" Del repeated.

Willie pushed the detonator button.

Nothing happened.

Willie pushed it again and again. Shouting that the wire must've gotten detached he ran toward the bomb only to be met by Heath who punched him in the gut with a kitchen knife, bringing Willie to his knees.

"You trying to do us harm, old man?" Heath said with a maniacal look on his face.

"Shoot it," Willie croaked as loudly as he could.

"Get him, he's got a gun," Heath shouted to Monk.

Del had his revolver in his hand. He turned and shot Monk in the chest, the other rover in the face.

"Shoot it," Willie groaned one more time before Heath slashed his throat.

Del took a step forward and aimed his pistol with both hands at the red fire extinguisher.

He fired.

The shot missed and slammed into the tiles. All the rovers except for Heath scattered around the cafeteria.

"You're dead, old man," Heath said, calmly walking toward him, "but not before I skin you alive."

"Two left," Del said, his hands shaking.

"What's that, old man?" Heath said.

Del fired again. A spray of tile fragments flew into the air but the bomb didn't budge.

"One left," Del said.

Heath was no longer walking. He began to close the distance between him and Del at a run.

Del held his ground and squeezed the trigger one last time.

The bullet caught the cylinder on its end, piercing the skin.

The thermite exploded in a flash of pure yellow.

The fireball consumed Heath a fraction of a second before it reached Del and the rest of the Hellers, vaporizing everyone and sending the rovers back to Hell.

26

Campbell Bates probably wouldn't admit it but there were times he actually seemed to be enjoying himself. Seated at a makeshift drafting table set up in a grassy area outside the Richmond forge he found himself humming Gilbert and Sullivan while he transferred drawings from the blast furnace book to sheets of parchment. He hadn't done drafting since his days as a mechanical engineering student and though he hadn't thought about it in years, there were certainly times at law school when he wished he'd remained an engineer.

After studying the design of William's forge Bates had decided to attempt to modify its design rather than building a new furnace from scratch. When he showed his first design to the group of Earthers camping out at the forge, Leroy Bitterman had said, "There's not much I have to offer, Campbell. I'm not even sure why I'm here. I should be back in London with the others."

They had split roughly into two groups. The male scientists plus Trotter had been sent to the forge and the female scientists and non-scientists like Karen Smithwick, Stuart Binford, and George Lawrence remained at Whitehall Palace. It was Cromwell's opinion that the women would be too vulnerable staying at the forge, surrounded by lecherous forge workers and soldiers. But the women were just as frightened to be left behind at the place where the lecherous Suffolk had assaulted Brenda Mitchell. It was left to Karen Smithwick to demand an audience with Cromwell to seek his assurances the women would be safe. Cromwell would later tell one of his ministers that this woman had more steel in her spine than Suffolk ever did. He had promised Smithwick upon his honor that the womenfolk would be free from assault.

The men at the forge had shared Bitterman's opinion about their utility. Particle physicists, computational scientists, and electrical engineers were hardly suited, they claimed, to the task of designing and building nineteenth-century blast furnaces. But Cromwell had not been persuaded and all of them had been mustered into service.

Bates had tried to rally them to the cause. "Look," he had said, "Hopefully the cavalry is going to arrive in the form of the SAS and automatic rifles. But until they do, we've got to show some progress or Cromwell and Suffolk might just decide to have one or more of us killed as an example. None of us know what we're doing but we've got this book with schematics and we've got some world-class mathematicians among us. So what I need is for you to work out the temperature, pressure, and thermodynamics of modifying this forge's chimney stack to get as close as possible to the examples in the book."

"We'll do the best we can," Henry Quint had said and Bates had shaken his hand in appreciation.

Bates had not tried to convince Anthony Trotter of that man's usefulness because he didn't think he had any. Trotter resented that he'd been dragged out of London, much preferring his comfortable rooms and decent food at the palace, but now that he had been sent here, he tried to work out the angles of escape versus cooperation. If a rescue attempt were going to be in the cards then he'd have to make sure that none of his fellow captives would bad-mouth him and sabotage his career upon his return to Earth. But was that even possible now? They all hated him for seeking special privileges and some harbored suspicions he'd had a role in Brenda Mitchell's death. If they were stuck here for good, he would need to earn his keep with Cromwell. He would need to become invaluable. While the others worked he napped upon the grass or walked, deep in thought around the perimeter of the forge, watched all the while by Cromwell's soldiers ringing the site.

The time came to start dismantling the brickwork of the now-cooled chimneystack. It pained William to destroy his precious forge even for the sake of building a better one. He complained that his men were iron-makers, not bricklayers, but work began nevertheless. He sent his younger men scrambling up ladders with hammers to remove bricks and toss them down to the grass to be stacked and re-used. Others began shoveling and carting river mud to be mixed with straw and laid into wooden molds to make new bricks. When William saw Trotter sitting idly by, he approached him.

"So, Master Trotter, will you be involved with taking down the chimney or fashioning new bricks?"

Trotter frowned at him. "Neither. Go away."

William spit on the ground. "Do you know that you're a worthless sort of man?"

"William, you're the sort of lout who thinks that only manual labor is useful. I do my work in my head. I'm a thinking man, something you probably never understood during your miserable life and now that you're dead, I'm sure you are quite beyond learning. Off you go. Flex your muscles and go shift something heavy. I've got some serious thinking to do."

Captain Greene's D Group had fallen into a rhythm of patrols in their defense of the Upminster hot zone. They had cleared the initial crowds of Hellers streaming into the zone with minimal bloodshed and expenditure of ammunition. As the days wore on they were aware of a continuing presence of Hellers in the surrounding woods but there were only sporadic challenges to their dominance, mostly from poorly armed men desperate for a second chance at life. Their mission, however, had not been without dramatic turns.

Early on, Greene had ordered a squad of three troopers to go on a game hunt. One of his men had built a rudimentary smokehouse of branches and leaves and Greene decided to build up a stockpile of smoked meat. While stalking a deer, a trooper named Finch had fired at what he thought was a deer obscured by undergrowth.

The pleading voice of a woman had called out, “Stop, don’t shoot!”

The other soldiers had closed on the spot and Finch had yelled, “Show yourself and show your hands.”

Another female voice had said, “You’ve shot her. She can’t raise her arms.”

“Come out slowly, the both of you,” Finch ordered.

“Please don’t hurt us.”

Both women were only partially clad, missing various articles of clothing. One was in her forties, the other, bleeding from the upper arm was twenty years younger. They had both appeared petrified and weak.

“Walk this way,” another trooper had ordered. “Keep your hands where we can see them.”

The older woman had stared at their uniforms.

“Who are you?” she asked.

“We’re SAS,” Finch said.

“Our SAS? From home? From England?”

“Jesus,” a trooper exclaimed to his mates. “They’re not Hellers.”

“Come closer,” Finch had said. “Need to give you the sniff test, luv.”

The two women had worked in a seamstress and alteration shop in Upminster and were among the first wave shuttled across when the hot zone opened up. They had congregated with a few hundred of their fellow travelers, wandering about dazed and utterly confused on the outskirts of a small medieval-looking village until Hellers from the village descended on them. At first the villagers had thought these were the recent dead, worth a pretty penny to the sweepers who’d be along on their regular rounds. When they descended on them, the Earthers had scattered into the nearby woods, screaming in terror. Most of them had been rounded up quickly enough. But very soon the Hellers had realized these people were not dead. And then one village man said he had witnessed another villager who was tramping through the high grass looking for new arrivals, disappearing into thin air. Some of the wiser men connected the events and surmised that a miracle had occurred, a passageway had opened, and soon the braver ones were launching themselves into the hot zone because almost anything was better than their grim existence.

The two seamstresses, the owner and her employee, had made it into the woods where they had been hiding since their arrival, sustaining themselves on brook water, mushrooms, and grubs. They had heard the shouts of other Earthers when they had been captured and worse—cries of pain and anguish one night, when unbeknownst to them, a band of rovers had found some Earthers hiding in the vicinity. They had also heard the gunshots of the SAS when C Group established their perimeter but they had feared it was just more brutes after them.

"Yeah, you're one of us," Finch had declared. "You're safe now. We're the good guys. Let's have a look at your arm, luv. Looks like a flesh wound. We'll patch you up quick enough."

"But where are we?" the older woman had said, trying to protect her modesty with the few pieces of non-synthetic fabric she was wearing. "We don't know what's happening. It's been a nightmare."

"Come with us," Finch had said. "The captain will explain everything and then we'll be sending you home, I expect."

"Home?" the younger woman had said. "Really?"

Greene had given the women a bare-bones explanation of the situation while his medic bandaged the young woman's arm. He hadn't been too sure if the shell-shocked woman had understood what he was saying but it hardly mattered.

He had pointed toward the center of the large field his men were encircling. "Look, I want you ladies to walk that direction. We can't go with you. One instant you'll be here, the next you'll be back where you belong in Upminster. As far as we understand it, you won't be flung back here but I wouldn't take any chances. Run as fast as you can away from town. The army will be surrounding the area. Identify yourself as victims. Tell them you've just spoken to Captain Greene, 22 SAS Regiment. Tell them our mission is progressing well and that we are armed with AK-47s.

Do you think you can remember that?"

And then the soldiers had watched the women walking into the hot zone, helping them along with shouts of encouragement, and cheering when they had disappeared.

Some days later, the group had experienced another incident. A pair of troopers had been patroling the perimeter of the zone in the eastern quadrant when one of them, a trooper named Kendrick, took a step and disappeared, leaving behind his rifle, a spare magazine, and a knife.

Greene had been summoned and came running to the scene shouting orders for everyone at the perimeter to withdraw a hundred yards. Then he had subjected Kendrick's partner to a harsh interrogation.

Had Kendrick gone AWOL? Had he talked about abandoning the mission? Had he given any hint of instability?

But Kendrick was a gung ho squaddie, not a man to bail on his mates and Greene had concluded that an expanding hot zone had snared him. He widened the perimeter further and had ordered Kendrick's rifle be abandoned where it lay.

On this misty morning Greene was awoken by shouts from one of the perimeter guards.

It was Trooper Finch yelling, "Captain, come here. You're not going to believe it."

Greene ran through the mist and pulled up laughing at the sight of Trooper Kendrick coming toward him, waving his retrieved AK-47.

"Did you miss me, Captain?" Kendrick said with a shit-eating grin.

"Jesus, Mary, and Joseph," Greene said. "Tell me what happened."

"I bring you greetings from the bloody prime minister," Kendrick said. "That's right. Hazel Kendrick's son, little Kenny Kendrick, was drinking cups of tea yesterday with Prime Minister Lester, the defense secretary, and a room full of generals, explaining everything what's happened since we got here. They wanted to send me up to Balmoral to see the bloody queen but I said, no way, I wanted to rejoin my unit 'cause I miss eating horrible, stringy venison."

Finch shook his head. "I always thought you were a complete wanker,

Kenny. Turns out I was right."

Greene was about to ask Kendrick for a full debrief when there were distant shouts from the northern quadrant and then a single AK rifle shot, their signal of an attack. The captain ordered Kendrick to follow him in a clockwise route around the perimeter and Finch and the other soldier to travel counterclockwise, sweeping up the other patrols along the way.

When Greene and Kendrick got closer to the north quadrant the mist had lifted enough to see the nature of the threat.

"Fuck me," Kendrick said.

"Glad you came back?" Greene said, snapping back his bolt carrier and sighting his rifle.

Hundreds of men were approaching on foot and on horseback, the closest ones a hundred yards away now. Greene had no way of knowing it, but three rival East Anglian barons from Colchester, Ipswich, and Bury St. Edmunds had buried the hatchet to mount a joint attack on the Upminster crossing point.

"Spread out, every twenty yards!" Greene shouted to his assembling men. "Single shots only! Don't waste ammo! The ones on horseback are likely the big men! Take them out first! Let's try to turn them! On my mark, fire!"

The Duke of Suffolk slithered on his belly and fully extended the brass tubes of his spyglass. He was on a hillock overlooking the village of Leatherhead and the surrounding meadowlands. It was midday and though it was not bright in the conventional sense, it was as bright a morning as it ever got in Hell. The first men he saw through his glass were sitting outside a small teepee-like structure fashioned from long branches. They were cooking something over a campfire. He couldn't be sure but he thought one of the soldiers had a moustache and might be the captain William the forger had spoken of. He shifted his gaze to a pair of men with rifles on slings patroling a featureless patch of meadow and then visually worked his way around a large circular perimeter, spying pairs of soldiers spaced quite far apart from one another.

When he was done he handed his spyglass to the Duke of Oxford and asked for his opinion.

Oxford was subordinate to Suffolk but had made his contempt for his superior apparent. Suffolk had been born to nobility and King Henry inherently trusted a man with a good pedigree. That is why Henry gave him command of all his field and naval assets following the recent demise of the Duke of Norfolk at the hands of John Camp.

In death, the Duke of Oxford had achieved the prominence he had found elusive in life. Absent high birth, he had been a mere major with the 17th Lancers during the Crimean War and had been at the infamous charge of the Light Brigade. In Hell his military skills had caught the attention of Henry who elevated him time and again until he was given the duchy of Oxford and was made Henry's field commander. Suffolk regarded the pugnacious Oxford as a potential rival and distrusted him immensely. But he had to admit he was an able cavalryman. Suffolk was a navy man and here on dry land he all but admitted his insecurity about field tactics by seeking Oxford's opinion.

Oxford's flat, broken nose and thrusting chin gave him a menacing look. He finished his spyglass survey and said with his customary arrogance, "If these guns of theirs are as powerful as we have been given to believe, then it would be foolhardy to mount an attack on foot or horseback. I will bring up my four-pounders and demi-culverins and train them on any group of two or more of the enemy. Once we have thinned the herd we may consider mounting a charge."

"Very well," Suffolk said. "You may proceed."

Captain Gatti was chewing a mouthful of rabbit when he heard the first artillery boom. He stood, spit out the brown meat, and shouted, "Incoming!" before the canister charge loaded with musket balls unleashed a shower of metal at the teepee. The trooper standing next to him fell, his right leg blown away at the knee.

Gatti called for the medic but he realized he was out on perimeter patrol. The captain ordered his men to stay low and ripped off his jacket, using the sleeve as a tourniquet.

"Stay with me," Gatti told the glassy-eyed young man.

"Captain, I ..."

"Don't talk. We're going to get you out of here."

At the sound of another cannon blast, Gatti threw himself over the injured soldier. The canister charge spewed metal over their heads.

Gatti called to the three soldiers nearby who were pressed flat into the tall grass. "We've got to evac Everly. Maxwell, you're going to be the one to do it."

The trooper protested but Gatti repeated the order.

"I'll come back," Maxwell said.

"Don't worry about that now," Gatti shouted, "both of you get him close to the HZ and Maxwell, you bring him home."

Before they were deployed, the squadron had drilled on evacuation plans. "This isn't a suicide mission," their Officer Commander, Major Gus Parker-Burns had said. "I expect that critically injured men will be evacuated if at all possible. The boffins tell me it appears that one will be able to re-enter the hot zone from the other side without immediately boomeranging back. Don't understand it, but I don't need to."

Maxwell and the other two soldiers picked the injured man off the ground and began running toward the hot zone. Gatti fired off a single shot from his rifle, the signal for the group to muster, and his men began circumnavigating the perimeter of the hot zone, running toward the shredded teepee, keeping low.

Oxford's cannon continued to rain metal down on the SAS. Gatti signaled for his assembling troops to keep spread out. The captain found his sergeant and sprawled beside him in the grass.

"Their cannon are up on that hill," Gatti said. "It's about a quarter mile, well out of our range. We can't all stay here or we're done for. Take three men and sweep around from the east. Use the high grass as cover. Have Evans take three men and sweep from the west. I'll stay down here with the rest of them to draw their fire. On your mark, rake them with crossfire. Now go."

Gatti looked toward the hot zone. The two troopers had helped Maxwell get Everly over his shoulder and now Maxwell was making his way past the outermost edge of the hot zone.

"Keep going, keep going," Gatti said out loud.

A cannon shot targeting them landed awfully close. Maxwell fell, dumping Everly.

"Come on, get up," Gatti said, and Maxwell did just that, slowly lifting the wounded man again.

He kept stumbling forward and suddenly, twenty yards into the hot zone, they disappeared.

Gatti looked into the gray sky and mouthed a thank you.

Suffolk was getting irate. He had been leaning against a tree, using his spyglass to track the cannon fire but he was having trouble spotting the enemy soldiers hunkered down in the dense meadow grasses. Every so often he saw a head pop up and exhorted Oxford to change his aiming point.

"The grass cover is making this devilishly difficult," Oxford complained. "Perhaps we are striking home, perhaps not. In any event, we must persist. They will be hoping we …."

A shot rang out and his half of Oxford's head was gone. Then a volley of persistent AK-47 fire drove Suffolk onto the ground. He began crawling but couldn't decide which way to go. The gunfire seemed to be coming from all directions.

"Get me my horse!" he screamed. "My horse!"

Suffolk's soldiers and artillerymen were in disarray, running wildly, trying to escape the withering fire. The SAS slowly and methodically advanced, tightening the pincer vise.

The duke heard a whinny and raised his head, amazed to see that one of his soldiers had indeed fetched his stallion. As the man was about to hand over the reins, he was rewarded for his loyalty by being shot in the stomach.

"Help me," the man cried, but the duke snatched the reins and mounted the horse.

Suffolk kicked the animal hard and took off, veering around trees, trampling wounded men, and not looking back until he was down the hillock, fleeing Leatherhead at a full gallop. When finally safe he began muttering to himself. "Disaster. Unmitigated disaster. Except of course for losing Oxford. Most welcome, that,"

Ben's security convoy was approaching Thames House through the empty streets of London when urgent calls began hitting his phone. He had been deep in thought with images of Polly in his mind, cold and dead under her duvet. But the call from Drone Warfare Centre, followed within seconds by a call from the prime minister, wiped the slate clean.

"Yes, sir, I actually have them on hold," Ben said. "Shall I conference them in?"

When he had both parties on the line he listened to the alarming news. A minute later, his car pulled inside MI5 headquarters and he kept the line open as he hurried down to the ops centre to see with his own eyes what everyone had been talking about.

The aerial view of Upminster showed hundreds of men running and walking down Station Road and St. Marys Lane.

"I'll wind the clock back five minutes and let you see how this unfolded," Major Garabedian said.

Ben watched as one man, then three, then a dozen, then more began materializing in the empty town centre.

"Can you give us some magnification?" the prime minister asked.

Close-up views showed men in non-modern clothes, peering into shop windows and cars, some walking in small, uncertain circles, some shielding their eyes from the sun.

"I'd say they're Hellers," Garabedian said. "No doubt in my mind."

A voice Ben didn't immediately recognize came on the line. "I concur." It was Jeremy Slaine who was at the prime minister's side in Manchester.

"Upminster was rock-solid until now," Ben said. "What's happening in the other hot zones?"

"They've been quiet. Just checking again," Garabedian said. I'm putting up real-time images now."

Dartford and Sevenoaks were deserted. Then Ben spotted something on the feed from Leatherhead.

"Hang on, could you zoom in on Leatherhead near the white van and the red car?" he said. "Yes there."

One man was carrying another man on his shoulder. On further magnification, the men were wearing the SAS camouflage fatigues specially provided for the mission. The man being carried appeared to be missing part of his right leg.

Slaine said, "This looks like a wounded man being evacuated. I'll inform the 3 Commando Brigade outside Leatherhead that they're coming their way."

"Right, keep an eye on this," the prime minister said, "but let's get back to Upminster. I think this must be very bad news for Captain Greene's D Group. I can't help but conclude they've been over-run."

"I'd have to agree," Ben said.

"What are our orders, sirs?" Garabedian said.

"What assets do we have over Upminster?" Lester asked.

"One Predator overhead, a Reaper two minutes out."

"Ben," the prime minister said, "I believe I know my mind on this but I want to hear from you."

Ben thought about Woodbourne, lying in a pool of blood next to the Polish woman. He knew he'd been a murderer and yet, he'd tried to help that little girl. There had to have been some good in him. And these Hellers flooding Upminster. How many of them were thoroughly and unrepentably evil? Did all of them deserve what they were about to receive?

Ben wet his lips with his tongue and swallowed the moisture so his voice wouldn't sound too thin.

"I am concerned about how many will get through our security cordon. I fear there're too many of them to contain. I think we need to act before they disperse."

"I have to agree, and Jeremy Slaine is nodding his approval," the prime minister said. "Major Garabedian, you may fire."

A few seconds later Upminster centre erupted in a fireball that forced

Ben to shut his eyes. When he did he saw the image of Woodbourne lying on the floor, his pool of blood merging with the Polish woman's. Ben couldn't shake the feeling that Woodbourne's dead eyes seemed to be staring directly into hers.

27

Angus and the boys were desperately afraid of the dark woods but equally afraid of the road. One held the danger of rovers and wild animals, the other the danger of Bess and Ardmore. It had been Stuart's idea to prevent getting lost by keeping to the woods with the road never more than twenty yards away. In the pitch dark with all the uneven ground and myriad obstacles achieving that proved difficult. By the time dawn came, the boys were surrounded by woods, the road nowhere to be found.

Fortunately for Glynn, Harry had woken up soon after Angus decked him, and though he moaned all night that his face hurt, at least Glynn didn't have to carry him for long.

In the meager light of early morning, surrounded by towering pine trees, the boys took stock of themselves. All of them were scuffed and bruised from tripping on roots and vines and bashing into branches but Harry complained more than anyone, rubbing at his swollen jaw and split, blood-caked lip.

Angus couldn't take it any longer.

"Shut your mouth before I shut it again," he shouted. Danny shushed him and pointed randomly into the woods as a reminder that Bess might be out there somewhere. Lowering his voice Angus fumed, "Boris is dead because of you and all you can do is winge and cry like a little fairy."

"It wasn't my fault," Harry moaned. "I didn't want to go. If he'd just let me stay none of this would've happened."

"I think you really ought to shut up, Harry," Kevin said. "You're pressing your luck."

"I'm thirsty," Andrew said. "We've got to find some water."

"We need three things," Stuart said. "We need water, food, and we need to find the road."

"Four things," Danny said. "We also need weapons." He picked up a long piece of fallen branch and snapped it in two over his knee. "I'll be in charge of that."

"We stay together," Angus said. "If we split up we'll never find each other again."

Stuart began examining all the trees in the immediate area and said, "Do you think the moss grows on trees like it does back home?"

Harry didn't seem sure if he was allowed to speak so he raised his hand first.

"There's no direct sunlight here because of cloud cover but since the geography seems to be the same as in Earth, my guess is that the solar system in this parallel world has the same configuration. After all there are similar light and dark cycles. Since we're in the northern hemisphere, there still should be some subtle differences in the temperature on one side of trees than the other."

"Does anyone have any idea what Shitley just said?" Nigel asked.

"He said that moss ought to be growing on the north side of the trees," Stuart said, "which means that way is north."

Angus looked around the forest. "The farm was on the north side of the road and we definitely never crossed the road last night. London is northeast of Devon so the road has to be southeast of us."

"That way," Stuart pointed.

"All right," Angus said, "Danny, you're in charge of making everyone a walking and fighting stick, Stuart, you're the outdoorsman, so you need to find edible mushrooms and berries, that type of thing, and all of us need to listen for the sound of running water as we go, and the first one to spot the road gets a gold star. No, I take that back. Stuart gets the gold star for letting the sheep out of the pen last night."

To laughs and whistles, Stuart took a deeply appreciative bow.

They walked for hours without finding water or anything remotely edible, though Danny did make a half-hearted attempt to club something under a bush he thought might be a snake or a rabbit. Each boy except for Harry, who declined, did wind up with a stout stick and a pocket full of rocks. And it was a beaming Andrew who finally claimed the prize for spotting the road.

It was empty.

They were so tired of walking on boggy, uneven ground, weaving through trees and thorny bushes that they allowed themselves the luxury of tramping for a while on the hard, flat road. Their luck seemed to be changing, for shortly afterwards Glynn heard a gentle gurgling noise which they followed back into the woods, throwing themselves on the ground to gulp beautifully cold water from a small creek.

After they could drink no more, Harry sent them into paroxysms of laughter by asking whether they thought the water was safe.

They rested for a few minutes until Angus exhorted them to get moving again.

"We should stick to the woods now," he said.

"Oh, come on," Glynn said. "Just a while longer on the road. I'll keep an eye out to the rear if you watch the front."

"All right," Angus said, "but the last thing we need is to run into Bess."

"Maybe she isn't even following us," Nigel said.

"She'll be coming," Kevin said. "Know how I know?"

"How?" Danny asked.

"Because she'll be missing her little Harry bedtime stories."

"Did you tell her your favorite ones?" Nigel asked. "Goodnight Moon? Ant and Bee?"

"No, that's not it," Glynn said, "It was probably shit about the universe in a Stephen Hawking computer voice."

"Leave me alone," Harry shouted, "just leave me alone!"

He ran off crying toward the road, his face getting whipped by the branches he failed to deflect.

"Come on, Harry, we didn't mean it," Nigel shouted. Then to the others he giggled, "Yes we did."

"Let's go after him," Angus said.

Harry kept running, ignoring Angus's calls to wait up. Angus yelled again for him to stop and as the woods gave way to the road, Harry turned to shout back, "Leave me alone!"

The huge black horse hit the small boy, throwing him into the air and as he landed in the road, the front and rear hooves trampled the life out of him.

Angus and the others emerged from the woods and stopped to stare in mute horror. It was impossible to know which was worse, the sight of Harry's broken and bloody body or Ardmore, swinging his leg off his black horse and drawing a pistol from his belt.

Bess climbed down from her wagon, ran to Harry's side and knelt beside him.

"He's dead," she said. Her tone wasn't sorrowful, it was angry. She pointed a bony finger at Angus. "This is your fault, Angus. Now you're going to pay. Shoot him, Ardmore. Put a bullet into his hateful face."

Angus couldn't seem to move. Ardmore's arm was raised, the pistol at pointblank range. The other boys also were frozen in fear.

There was a high-pitched sound, a crescendo of a whine, as if the air was being parted. Ardmore dropped his pistol. Though cocked it didn't discharge.

"Ardmore!" Bess screamed, running over and half-catching him as he slid onto the road. Her fingers latched onto the short length of bolt protruding from his chest but it was too well seated to pull it out.

Ardmore sputtered and tried to speak but the only thing coming out of his mouth was red froth.

She let out a blood-curdling "No!" and sought out the solitary rider up the road who was loading another bolt into his crossbow and kicking his reluctant horse to a gallop.

Bess shouted at her outriders, "Get him!"

None of her three henchmen had firearms but they had swords and though Trevor was pointing a crossbow at them they charged him full on. Trevor was bouncing in the saddle too heavily to aim another shot carefully. He chose the horse coming at him the fastest and fired at its huge brown mass. The mare pitched forward into an earth-thudding somersault, steamrolling the rider and crushing his pelvis.

Trevor threw the crossbow down and with one hand on the reins he pulled his loaded pistol from his satchel and cocked it. The two other riders were almost on top of him. He pulled the trigger but the powder must have been damp. The gun didn't fire.

One of the swordsmen slashed at his horse's neck. The wounded animal whipped around so forcefully that Trevor was thrown clear. He scrambled to his feet, drawing his own sword just in time to parry a series of blows from the closest rider while the other man dismounted to challenge Trevor on foot.

The sword fight played out some fifty feet from the boys. "Who is he?" Glynn asked the others.

"I don't know but he's trying to help us," Angus said.

Bess had been cradling Ardmore's head in her lap but now she gently lowered it to the ground and reached for his gun.

Angus saw what she was doing and so did the other boys. They all began to scatter but stopped when she didn't pursue them. Instead she slowly walked toward the clashing swordsmen.

Trevor's back was turned; he didn't see Bess coming. Her shooting arm was extended straight and unwavering as if the heavy pistol was weightless.

Glynn was by Angus's side. "We have to stop her," Angus said.

They both still had their heavy walking sticks. Glynn caught up with Bess first and swatted her across the back, cracking the stick in two. She didn't fall, she didn't cry out. She merely turned to Glynn and calmly fired into his forehead.

Angus screamed, an agonized guttural scream, and he began laying into her with his stick. She shielded her face with one arm and reached into her trousers with the other. That's when Angus saw she had cocked her own pistol. All he could do was continue to flail at her but she seemed immune to pain. She was too strong.

Angus heard footsteps coming from behind and then, in a blur, he saw all the other boys—Nigel, Danny, Stuart, Kevin, even frail Andrew—swinging their sticks at Bess, preventing her from raising her gun hand. Then Danny delivered a lunging strike to her breastbone and she fumbled the pistol.

Angus picked it up.

The gunshot tore into her jaw, ripping the mandible clean away.

The man who was fighting Trevor on foot momentarily turned toward the blast giving Trevor a split-second edge. A vicious downward thrust cleaved the man's shoulder. He reeled away and staggered into the woods. The swordsman on horseback saw Bess lying in a pool of blood and decided he was done. He turned toward Devon and soon, all that remained was a trail of dust.

Trevor put his hands on his knees to catch his breath and after several moments, began walking toward the boys.

"Is one of you Angus Slaine?" he called out.

Angus let the smoking pistol fall from his hand. "I am."

Trevor saw two boys motionless in the road. He counted six of them standing. "There were ten of you," Trevor said.

Angus began to cry. He managed to say, "Glynn, dead. Harry, dead. Boris, dead. Craig, dead."

"I'm sorry."

"Who are you?" Angus asked.

"My name's Trevor. Your father sent me to find you. I'm here to bring you home."

28

They covered the distance from Paris to Cologne in one full day, showing their true colors through Francia, but disguising themselves as a caravan of Russian soldiers when they crossed the border into Germania. They were split between two sturdy, covered wagons, each pulled by a team of excellent horses. Traversing the French territories, Brian and John drove one wagon with Emily, Sergeant O'Malley and Trooper Culpepper riding inside. Simon and Caravaggio drove the other team, with the Russian, Ostrov, under wraps. Inside Germania, Ostrov emerged to drive the lead wagon and talk his way through the Russian checkpoints while Simon and Caravaggio hid inside.

They arrived at Cologne in the morning. With the limestone castle looming overhead, perched on a jutting chalk promontory, they found a small glade in the woods on the west side of the Rhine. There, they set up a protected camp, the SAS soldiers doing picket duty with their last remaining AK rifle. Ostrov unhitched a horse and with the other AK-47 slung over his shoulder, he bade the rest of them farewell, vowing to return as quickly as possible with Paul Loomis in tow.

"You really don't like the bloke," Brian told John as they watched him disappear.

"It shows, does it?" John said. "There's something about the guy. He says all the right things but he's too glib for my liking. I hate having to trust a stranger."

"You and me both," Brian said. "Shame to see us lose half our lovely rifles."

"By the time we get back Kyle will have cast plenty of new ones."

"He's a good 'un, that brother of yours," Brian said. "How come you never mentioned him to me?"

"He *is* a good guy, I should have. I guess he and I had our differences but that's behind us. He's covered himself in glory this trip, that's for damn sure. I am so fucking proud of him."

All nights in Paris were dark but this night was particularly black. If there was a moon orbiting the planet, forever cloaked by dense clouds, then it must have been the thinnest of crescents tonight. The royal forge was beastly hot but there was something almost cheerful in the way its glow spilled out the doors, pushing back the blackness. Inside, Kyle and the forge master, the fat-bellied, bellicose Jean, had been working over twenty-four hours straight without so much as a break for a proper meal. The workers had a small baking oven off in a corner and one man knew how to make bread. So it was freshly baked loaves that had sustained them all.

As Kyle quenched part of a trigger assembly in cold water, Jean looked over his shoulder and grunted his approval. The cast piece was uniformly black in color. When it was cool enough to handle Jean took it and inspected it more closely.

"Good iron," Jean said.

"Yeah, doesn't suck," Kyle said.

"What means suck?"

"You know, something that's bad. Like Hell. Hell sucks."

"Ha, oui, Hell, she sucks."

Kyle reached for a half-eaten baguette. "Why are you here, Jean?"

"Me? In Hell?"

"Yeah."

"I kill my brother."

"Really?"

"Oui, c'est vrai."

"Was he an asshole?"

"What means asshole?"

"Someone who sucks."

"Yes, asshole."

"There were times I probably wanted to kill my brother," Kyle said. "Fortunately I never acted on it."

Jean shrugged. He hadn't seemed to understand any of it.

"Speaking of assholes, I think that guy's an asshole."

Kyle was looking across the forge at Pavel Antonov, the mute Russian whom Ostrov had left behind.

"Ostrov asked us to put him to work," Simon had told Kyle before they left for Cologne. "He says he knows a thing or two about making lead balls for shot."

So they had given him a job casting lead bullets alongside a bench full of Frenchmen. But the Russian stuck to himself and creeped everyone out with his hard stares, fixed frown, and thick facial scar.

"Oui, asshole," Jean agreed.

As the night wore on, Kyle found himself dozing at his bench, each time waking with a start, unsure of how long he'd been out.

This last time he figured he had been napping for at least several minutes because the warm iron piece he'd been filing was now cold.

He blinked a few times and saw that Jean too was napping, fully stretched out on some straw in the corner. In fact, half the forge workers also seemed to have petered out. He noticed that Pavel Antonov was by the main door. The Russian turned to look at something and their eyes met for a moment before he was gone. Kyle couldn't be sure but his expression seemed to have changed.

Was there a hint of a smile?

Something about that moment made Kyle get up to see what Antonov had been looking at.

He saw it too late.

A length of cord was on fire; a thin trail of ash led from the bread oven and snaked over the floorboards toward a large barrel standing upright in a corner.

A barrel of black powder used for bullet-making.

The brightly burning cord was only a foot away from the barrel when Kyle launched himself across the room, shouting for everyone to get out. Jean woke and swore at the disturbance.

When the powder keg went off it blew out the ceiling and the walls. The fireball that lit up the skies of Paris was as bright as the midday sun that none of the Hellers had seen since last they walked the Earth.

Joseph Stalin sat in Barbarossa's old throne chair in waiting to receive his visitor. The reception hall was gloomy and archaic, reflecting the old king's love of hunting. The walls were studded with centuries of trophies—boars, deer, stags, and bears. Stalin had ordered the windows to be opened to air out the stuffiness and allow thousands of flies to escape but the direction of the wind was unfavorable. The pungent smells from the rotting room in the castle cellar wafted into the hall so the windows were closed and the flies were buzzing.

"Nikita," Stalin said gruffly, "bring me something to swat them," and the young secretary scrambled off to find some suitable implement.

General Kutuzov, Stalin's field marshal, had just eaten a rich stew and brown gravy soiled his tunic. He noticed the streak and began rubbing at his belly with a moistened finger. Stalin saw his attempt and made a disparaging comment. The secret policeman, Vladimir Bushenkov, sat motionless, staring at the closed doors at the end of the hall with his one good eye.

The doors opened and Ostrov entered accompanied by armed guards, one of whom carried something wrapped in a cloth. At the sight of Ostrov, Stalin's face compressed into a fearsome frown.

"So, the traitor returns. What do you have to say for yourself Valery Aleksándrovich?

Ostrov stopped a dozen feet away from the throne chair and lowered his head.

Then he slowly raised it and smiled broadly. "I say it is good to be back among my comrades."

Stalin rose and approached the man with open arms and enveloped him in a slapping hug, followed by a kiss to each cheek.

"So, has our gambit worked?" Stalin asked, swatting a fly that settled on his leg with the leather strap Nikita had produced.

"It worked brilliantly, my tsar. Garibaldi and his stooges believed everything. They accepted Comrade Antonov and me as the defectors we claimed to be. Garibaldi is like an eager child who wishes to be loved. I showed affection for his ideas and the rest was easy. He readily accepted us into his inner circle."

Bushenkov said, "We want your complete report."

"And that you shall get, comrade," Ostrov said. "I know much of their military capabilities and the state of their alliances. But permit me to begin with the most startling news. John Camp and Emily Loughty have returned."

He told the astonished men that they and the Earther adults and children had succeeded in making their way back to their homes. But the situation on Earth had deteriorated. The portals between the worlds had multiplied and remained wide open. There were four locations in Brittania where Hellers were pouring into Earth. Camp and Loughty had been obliged to re-enter Hell to find the one man they believed had the knowledge to close down the connections.

"They want Paul Loomis," Ostrov said.

"Pasha," Stalin said quietly. "They want my dear Pasha."

"I was sent to bring him to them," Ostrov said, reaching into his jacket. "I carry this letter from the woman."

Stalin unfolded it and read it then handed it to Kutuzov, forgetting he could not read English. Bushenkov took it next and scanned it with his eye.

"You are to bring him to them in Paris?" Bushenkov asked.

"Not Paris," Ostrov said. "Cologne. They are here, not two miles away."

"Camp and Loughty here?" Stalin said, clapping his hands in

celebration.

"Not just them. Two of Garibaldi's top men too, men you met when they came to Marksburg as emissaries, the Englishman Wright and the painter, Caravaggio. Also two modern English soldiers who came over to protect Camp and Loughty. And finally, the Englishman Brian Kilmeade."

"The bastard who conjured up the Iberian fleet out of the mist," Stalin said. "So he returned too."

"He never left," Ostrov said. "He elected to stay as Queen Mécia's consort."

"A true madman," Stalin said stamping his feet in merriment. "Staying in Hell to lie with a corpse. This is too much. All of them, within our grasp. You have done well, Valery Aleksándrovich.

"There is more, my tsar." Ostrov asked for the cloth-wrapped object and offered it to Stalin.

"What is this?" Stalin said, reacting to the weight of the package. As he unbundled it his eyes opened wide and his mouth parted. He ran his fingers back and forth over it as if he didn't trust his own eyes.

Kutuzov didn't know what it was but Bushenkov did. He got up to bend over Stalin's lap to see for himself.

"An AK-47," Stalin said in a hushed, reverential tone. "I remember as if it were yesterday bestowing the Order of the Red Star on young Mikhail Timofeyevich Kalashnikov for inventing this beautiful weapon. But who has made this? We have not seen a weapon so advanced in Hell. I have been demanding something to propel us beyond the primitive state of blackpowder guns but no one could answer my prayers."

"John Camp and his brother, Kyle Camp, a gunmaker, brought it with them from Earth."

"Impossible," Bushenkov said. "Do you think we are fools? Metals do not come through."

"But rubber does," Ostrov said. "Rubber molds. A hundred of them for each part of the weapon, the magazine, and the bullets."

"Genius," Stalin murmured.

"They went to a forge in Brittania, cast the parts, and assembled the weapons. They made them for the English soldiers to defend the portals in Hell and prevent Hellers from crossing. This was to be a temporary solution while they sought Pasha."

"Can we get these molds?" Bushenkov asked.

Ostrov shook his head. "We will have to disassemble this weapon and have our iron workers in Russia or Germania make their own casts. The bigger problem is making the explosives for the primer caps on the bullets. These I could not obtain."

"We will find chemists in Russia," Stalin said. "This problem will be solved."

Ostrov was about to say something when Bushenkov cut him off. "Tell me," he asked, "did you steal this rifle from under their noses? And what of Garibaldi? Is he not interested in producing his own arsenal of AK-47s?"

"Steal it? No! It was much sweeter than that. They handed it to me and wished me luck. I told them I would pretend to have doubts about my defection and tell you I stole the rifle as a display of my true loyalty to the tsar. All this would be a ruse to get the letter to Pasha and spirit him away for a meeting with the Loughty woman."

"You see how clever our Valery Aleksándrovich is?" Stalin said. "You will be rewarded for your heroism, my son.

"There is more to tell," Ostrov said. "John Camp's brother gave Garibaldi a complete set of molds and has set to work at the royal forge of Paris to manufacture large numbers of rifles and ammunition. Loughty knew the recipe for the primer chemicals."

Stalin's mood darkened in an instant. He pushed himself off the throne still holding the rifle. "Then we are finished," he spat. "An army with these weapons will be victorious."

"Yes, I agree," Ostrov said. "And that is why we will be victorious."

"Whatever do you mean?" Kutuzov said. "I am confused."

"I left Pavel Antonov behind to assist John Camp's brother. Pavel is very clever with gunpowder, you know. By now Kyle Camp is dead, the forge and all the workers are destroyed, the molds and gun parts and chemicals are destroyed. We have one of the two AK-47s in Europa. The other is not two miles away."

Stalin told Nikita to bring wine. He wearily sat back on the throne with the rifle propped against his knee.

"You know," he said, "I am too old for all these ups and downs and ups. Is this the end of the fun-fair ride, Valery Aleksándrovich? Do you intend to wrench out my guts with more ups and downs?

"I am sorry, my tsar," Ostrov said. "Perhaps I have too much of a flair for the dramatic. Yes, that is everything."

Stalin took a cup of wine and told Nikita to pour some for the others, Ostrov first. "So, all we need to do is seize Emily Loughty and have her make these primer chemicals for us," Stalin said. "Then, when we have hundreds, maybe thousands of these rifles and wagonloads of ammunition, we will need to construct the largest rotting room in Hell to receive the broken bodies of Giuseppe Garibaldi and all his filthy allies. Nikita, bring Pasha to me."

Loomis' room was at the opposite end of the castle. By the time Nikita brought him to the hall the men had finished one bottle of wine and started another.

"Ah, Pasha, come, come," Stalin said, his speech happily sloppy.

Paul, Pasha—the man hardly cared what he was called anymore. His face was a permanent, heavily lined mask of sorrow. All his puckish good looks that Emily still clung to when she thought about their years together as his junior—they had long-ago faded away during his years in Hell. On his best days he looked old and wilted; on his worst days he was catatonic, refusing to rise from his bed or eat.

"Pasha, you look like shit," Stalin said when the man shuffled in.

Loomis shrugged.

"You just get out of bed?" the tsar asked. "You don't shave. You don't bathe. You smell even worse than me."

"Is that why you asked for me?" Loomis said. "To tell me how bad I smell."

"No, no. Have you ever met this man, Ostrov?"

Loomis looked at him and shook his head.

"Well, now you've met him," Stalin said. "He brings some excellent news. I know how much you have been pining for the company of someone who speaks your language."

"I don't care about speaking English. My Russian is getting good enough."

"Not that language, Pasha. The language of science. Ostrov has brought you someone, someone you know very well, a scientist. Show him the letter."

Ostrov gave him an honorific little bow and handed over the parchment.

> Paul, I've come back to find you. The strangelet-graviton tunnels have gotten worse. There are four of them now, permanently open without MAAC activity. No one knows what to do. You told me you know the answer. This man, Ostrov, is a friend. He will bring you to me, Urgently, Emily.

Loomis' knees buckled and had it not been for Nikita's attentiveness, he would have fallen. The young man helped him to a chair.

"Where is she?" Loomis asked.

"Very close, in the woods just at the start of the Aachen road," Ostrov said. "She is in hiding with her friend, John Camp, and some of Garibaldi's men."

Loomis looked confused. "She says in the letter that you are her friend."

"That's what she thinks," Ostrov said.

"Ostrov is a clever fellow," Stalin said. "Maybe one day he will make a good secret policeman, like Bushenkov here. Maybe he will even replace him one day, what do you say, Vladimir Dmitriyevich?"

A less than amused Bushenkov chose not to answer.

"It was an elaborate scheme," Stalin told Loomis. "But that shouldn't be of any concern to you. Be prepared to leave with Ostrov and a squad of soldiers as soon as it becomes dark. They have a powerful weapon so you will have to be careful." Stalin showed off the AK-47. "It is like this one but unfortunately they have bullets, we do not. We will have you draw out Dr. Loughty. Our men will seize her before they know they are surrounded. They won't shoot if they think she'll be harmed. They are too sentimental."

"What will you do with Emily when you have her?" Loomis asked.

"She will join you in the new institute I will build for you in Moscow. You will make many powerful weapons together. You may take her as your woman if you want. Many men will be jealous, even me a little. This will be my reward to you, my English scientist."

"I won't participate in double-crossing her," Loomis said.

"Don't think of it like that," Stalin said. "You will help keep her safe. We wouldn't want her to be hurt or even killed."

"Why bother with all of this?" Loomis said, shaking his head.

"All of what?"

"These wars, the power grabs. If what Emily says is true why not just sail to Brittania and cross back to Earth? Wouldn't you like another chance at life? I know I would."

"An interesting question, Pasha," Stalin said taking another sip of wine. "Maybe for someone like you it would make some sense. But for me, no. I have spoken with recent arrivals from Europe. I know what they say about Stalin. They call me a mass murderer. They say Stalin killed tens of millions of my own countrymen. They forget what Stalin had to do to stop reactionaries from thwarting the principles of the revolution. They forget what Stalin did to save Russia from the Nazis. They would put Stalin in a cage and show him like a circus animal." His face was getting redder and redder and his voice was rising to a yell. "Do I like Hell? No. Would I like to be back on Earth? No. No. No. I will stay here and so will you, and goddamn it, you will help me become the ruler of every single motherfucker in Hell!"

As the morning turned to mid-day and mid-day turned to late afternoon, John and Emily, and their entourage grew more and more restless. Within the glade, a small depression filled with rainwater kept the horses quiet. The only way to relieve nervous energy was to walk around the wagons but the appeal of pacing in tight circles was wearing thin.

John offered Emily a piece of dried meat.

She made a face and declined. “How long will we wait?” she asked.

“As long as we have to.”

“What if he doesn’t come?”

John chewed off a piece of meat and spit it out. “Good call.”

“What I wouldn’t give for pizza,” she said before repeating her question.

“This was always going to be a high-risk mission. If Loomis doesn’t show we’ll have to go back to Paris and return with a few hundred AKs. Don’t underestimate brute force as a battle tactic.”

“Paul could be killed.”

“That’s why we’re trying this way first.”

“I know. I guess my nerves are frayed.”

“That makes two of us.”

They thought Brian was asleep in the back of one of the wagons but he poked his head out and said, “Three of us.”

“Good thing we weren’t talking about you,” John said. “Want some disgusting dried meat?”

Brian hopped down. “Don’t mind if I do.”

He tried it, swore, and declared it delicious, sending them into fits.

“Glad to be your matinee entertainment,” Brian said. “So, John, I never asked. Did you ever manage to get a message to Ronnie, my agent?”

“I did. I told him what we agreed, that you were recruited for a classified government mission and would be out of the country and out of touch until further notice.”

“How’d he take it?”

“He didn't sound happy. You’ll like this though: he asked whether they were paying you.”

“That fucker! He’s looking for his ten percent. If I got a kidney transplant Ronnie would demand a piece of the organ.”

Caravaggio and Simon had been checking on O’Malley and Culpepper.

They returned to the glade and sat down near the wagon.

"What's happening?" John asked.

"It's quiet," Simon said. "Your two army gents said a few horses and riders passed by an hour ago heading toward the castle but that was it."

Caravaggio pulled his ubiquitous pad from his pocket and resumed working on a pencil sketch he'd begun earlier.

"Still drawing my lady friend?" John asked.

"Of course. Who else would I draw among this group? There is but one rose."

"It's lovely," Emily said, peeking at it. "And don't mind him, he's just being a jealous male."

"Then perhaps I'll paint him as Phthonos, the Greek god of envy and jealousy. John, I'll give you green skin and red ears. You'll be wonderful."

John laughed. "Try it and you'll be doing a self-portrait of an Italian guy with a black eye."

Each of them reacted to the sound of someone running by grabbing a weapon. John cocked his musket while Brian removed an arrow from his quiver. They relaxed only slightly when Culpepper bounded into sight.

"The sergeant's holding a man just by the road. He came on foot from the direction of the castle calling Emily's name."

"Did he say who he was?" Emily asked.

"I didn't hear it if he did. The sergeant told me to hoof it and get you. He didn't want to bring the bloke into the camp."

They all ran through the woods and found O'Malley standing over a kneeling man, his AK-47 trained on him.

Emily rushed forward. "Paul!"

Loomis tried to stand but O'Malley wouldn't let him.

"It's okay," John said. "He's our man."

Loomis got up and accepted Emily's hug. "I couldn't believe it when that man said you'd returned. You're the bravest and craziest woman I know."

"It's so wonderful to see you, Paul."

"Where's Ostrov?" John asked.

"You've been played," Paul said. "He's with Stalin, always has been. He was sent to Paris as a spy."

"Fuck. I knew I didn't like him," John said. "What's their plan?"

"They're coming at nightfall to capture you. They've got your rifle. Stalin wants Emily to make primers for the bullets and then work with me on weapon development. He wants the rest of you buried. I snuck away to warn you."

"We've got to hitch the horses and get out of here," John said. "Emily, get your business done and let's get moving."

Culpepper and O'Malley kept up watch along the road. Everyone else headed back to the glade, Emily holding Loomis's hand.

"He gave you my note?" she asked.

"Yes."

"Then you know the situation. After the last MAAC restart the four channels remained open even after power-down and they've been expanding spontaneously."

"Where are they?"

"Dartford, Upminster, Sevenoaks, and Leatherhead."

"All along the MAAC tunnel," Loomis said. "The strangelets are auto-propagating."

While they talked, John ordered both teams of horses hitched to a single wagon.

"It has to be that," Emily said.

"The phenomenon won't stop spontaneously at this point," Loomis said. "The active sites will keep growing. New sites might form along the tunnel route. Eventually the entire area of land circumscribed by the tunnels could become an open channel."

"All of London," she said.

"For starters. Then that area could expand. Eventually Earth and Hell could merge into one bloody awful dimension."

Emily visibly shuddered. "That's been at the very back of my mind but I haven't let myself go there. Paul, the best people in physics have been consulted. No one has any ideas. You said you know what has to be done."

"I do. I mean I can't be certain of course, but I'd bet my life on it if I had one to bet. The strangelets must be obliterated. It's the only way."

"How? How do we do it?"

"I'll tell you but I won't tell you now."

She lit into him. "For God's sake, Paul, why not?"

"I need to get away from here. Stalin will crush me for this and throw me into a rotting room. Take me with you to Brittania. I'll tell you there."

"Paul, I promise we'll take you with us, but you need to tell me now in case something happens along the way. The fate of the world is on your shoulders."

His countenance shifted. He looked harder, sounded harder. "Understand this. I don't give a damn about the world anymore. I'll only talk once I'm in Brittania."

"How could you not care about the world?" Emily said, her voice rising in indignation. "Your children are in that world. Don't you care about them?"

His shell didn't crack. He seethed at her, "I thought you were an intelligent woman. I'll say it one last time. Take me with you. That's the long and the short of it."

She left him standing there and told John the situation.

"Want me to beat it out of him?" he asked.

"You're joking, right?"

"Only half. Get him in the wagon. We're taking just the one for speed's sake. It'll be cozy in there."

Nikita burst into Stalin's bedchamber after the most perfunctory of knocks. The tsar was on the bed next to his precious AK-47.

"What is it, Nikita? Can't you see I am lying next to my beautiful new rifle? She's not soft like a woman but I find her more attractive than most, don't you think?"

"I'm sorry, my tsar, but Pasha is gone."

Stalin was upright in a second. "Where has he gone?"

"He was not in his room. Ostrov and the soldiers were preparing to leave to seize the Earthers and sent for him."

"Have Kutuzov and Bushenkov been informed?"

Nikita nodded quickly.

"Then bring them to my study."

When they arrived Stalin raged at the two men to report what they knew.

Kutuzov was drunk. When he slurred a non-answer, Stalin called him a useless cow and threw him out of the room. Bushenkov was better prepared.

"I have just been informed the guards at the drawbridge saw Pasha leave on foot one hour ago. They didn't ask his business."

"Good heavens! Didn't you or Ostrov have eyes on him? You just let him walk out?"

"This was not my operation. Ostrov set the timetable and handpicked the soldiers to perform the arrest. I was not even invited."

"You're invited now, you imbecile. Go find them. Bring them back to me tonight. Tell Ostrov what I am telling you. If you fail your severed heads will spend an eternity staring at your roasted bodies inside the worst rotting room in Moscow. Why Moscow? So I can visit you whenever I like to piss on your faces."

With daylight fading they hit the road, a team of eight rested horses pulling the covered wagon at a break-neck speed. Brian and John flanked Simon, all of them squeezed together on the driver's seat, Simon taking the reins, the other two riding shotgun with muskets and longbows. In the rear, the SAS men kept a lookout for followers. Loomis sat mutely, his arms drawn across his chest. Seeing Emily distraught, Caravaggio scowled at Loomis like a protective lion. Because of the rutted road and poor suspension, all of them spent more time bouncing in the air than riding the benches.

It was forty miles from Cologne to the French frontier. Crossing into Francia wasn't a guarantee of safety but the threat of an enemy patrol might deter pursuing Russians. At least that was how John saw it. As darkness fell Simon squinted at the road, trying to see what the horses were seeing but there was no visibility beyond twenty feet. The pelting rain didn't help. Fortunately the horses had better night vision. Even at speed they kept to the road and successfully navigated the bends.

After almost three hours Brian called to John over the clattering of the wagon. "How far do you reckon to Francia?"

"I'm guessing ten miles or so."

"Almost home free."

"Don't jinx us."

Not ten seconds later they heard someone calling out from the rear. It sounded like O'Malley.

Emily parted the front flaps and said, "The sergeant thinks we're being followed."

"Can he see anyone?" John said.

"He says he thought he saw a torch bobbing up and down as if it were carried by a rider. Then it went out."

"Keep low. I'm coming back."

John climbed through and wriggled his way to the back where O'Malley was sighting his rifle into blackness.

"You sure?" John asked.

"I saw it too," Culpepper said.

"We don't have all the ammo in the world," John said, "but if you want to put a few rounds down range I wouldn't object. There's no one friendly in that direction."

O'Malley said he was thinking the same thing. John warned Simon and Brian of the impending action and when the road straightened O'Malley aimed straight down the middle and fired twice.

As soon as the ringing in their ears subsided they heard some shouting, alarmingly close. Then musket blasts pierced the blackness.

"Get down!" John screamed, pushing Loomis to the floor and throwing himself over Emily.

Culpepper grunted once and said, "Sarge, I ..." before slumping over.

Caravaggio climbed over John to pull Culpepper as far away from the rear as possible.

Loomis cowered in terror but Emily, cool under fire, told him they'd be okay.

O'Malley fired off another three rounds. They heard a horse's whinny or maybe it was a human cry.

"Jack!" O'Malley said, looking back. "How bad is it? Jack!"

"What's going on back there?" Brian called out.

John rolled off Emily enough to have a look at Culpepper's chest. It was soaking wet with blood. He felt for his neck pulse and detected one or two faint beats then nothing.

"He's bleeding out," John said quietly. "There's nothing we can do for him."

"What did you say?" O'Malley asked. "How is he?"

"Keep firing," John replied. "Even if you don't hit anyone it'll make them keep their distance."

It was as if the horse and rider appeared from nowhere. The blackness behind the wagon suddenly belched out a charging and snorting white horse ridden by a Russian soldier who was confidently riding with both hands holding a bow and arrow. He released his arrow the instant O'Malley drilled him with a rifle shot. The arrow was equally deadly. Its sharpened steel tip knocked out O'Malley's top teeth on its way through his brainstem. He was dead before he pitched back onto Culpepper's legs.

The rifle was half in and half-out of the wagon and John grabbed it before it fell out.

"Brian, I need you back here!" he shouted. Brian clamored over the living and dead and half-kneeled on O'Malley's body, peering into the blackness.

"What do you need?" Brian shouted.

"Shoot at any sign of movement."

Brian nocked an arrow.

"Michelangelo, you've got three loaded pistols and a musket. Anything Brian doesn't hit, you take them out," John said.

John was squatting beside Brian, looking down at the road, trying to judge the speed of the bouncing wagon. He picked up two of O'Malley's spare mags, stuffed them in his trouser pockets and swung a leg over the half-door.

Emily was watching him and cried out, "John, what are you doing?"

"Trying to save our lives. Just keep going till you get to the border. I love you."

"John, no!" she screamed as he vaulted out the rear, disappearing from sight.

Another arrow whistled past the wagon and one lodged in the half-door. Brian picked up a faint outline and let an arrow fly. There was a sharp cry followed by a thud. Before he could ready another arrow a rider pointing a pistol appeared but Caravaggio was already aiming. He pulled the trigger, striking the man in his gut.

John rolled three or four times, swearing at each hard knock but keeping an iron grip on the rifle he had tucked against his middle. When his body came to a stop he picked himself up and scrambled to the side of the road where he assumed a firing position on one knee. He felt for the selector lever and clicked the rifle into full auto mode.

The approaching Russian troops were bunched fairly tightly and came past him fast. John opened up on the first rider and slowly turned at the waist raking them with fire.

As horses screamed and bucked and bodies flew onto the road, John changed out mags and flicked the selector to single-shot. He rose and took two long strides to position himself in the middle of the road, firing isolated shots at any soldier who was moving rapidly.

He didn't see the pistol rising from behind a felled horse but he heard and felt the blast. It hit the AK-47 squarely in the lower receiver and ripped it from his hands. A head popped up over the horse. Unless the shooter had another loaded gun at hand he was one and done. John charged him and leapt over the horse landing on top of the shooter. He began pummeling the man with his fists and when the man rolled over on his back John saw who it was.

Ostrov.

"You fucker!" John said, smashing his fist into his nose. The cartilage crunched and blood streamed over his mouth.

A fist with a knife in it came toward John's flank and was about to penetrate the area of his surgical scar, when John countered it with a Krav Maga combination—a lateral blocking move with his left arm and a simultaneous upward thrust with the heel of his right hand into Ostrov's broken nose. The force of the blow drove his nasal bones deeply into his brain.

Ostrov stared ahead in seeming surprise but then his mouth curled into something resembling a smile.

"I have last laugh on you because …"

His eyes rolled back and the rest was gibberish.

John shook him. "What do you mean? What do you mean?"

But there was nothing but mouth movements and gurgling.

A horse whinnied and John looked up into the barrel of a pistol. He heard the hammer drop with a loud click. The gun didn't fire. Then he looked up at the rider. The two men recognized each other from their last encounter at Marksburg weeks before.

"John Camp," Bushenkov said.

"First rule, keep your powder dry," John said, standing up and looking around for a weapon.

From his perch Bushenkov saw his entire squad was gunned down and that Ostrov was destroyed.

"Want to come down and fight me? I'll keep one eye closed to make it more even."

"Not tonight, Mr. Camp, but soon perhaps. I think we shall meet again soon."

With that he turned his horse and rode off into the wet night.

John went looking for his rifle and found it in the grass beside the road. There was a large through-and-through hole in the lower receiver just above the trigger. The metal around the hole was buckled. He was lucky his hand hadn't been hit. He threw the rifle deeply into the woods. There'd be plenty more in Paris.

The wagon was a quarter of a mile down the road when Emily shouted at Simon to turn around.

They'd all heard the burst of automatic fire and then a few isolated shots.

Loomis sounded panicky. "But he said to keep going."

"I agree," Caravaggio said, "we must go back."

"Do it, Simon," Brian shouted.

Simon pulled back on the reins until the horses stopped then climbed down to coax the lead horses to turn tightly on the narrow road. Brian climbed onto the buckboard seat and readied an arrow. It didn't take long to find John's handiwork in the road.

When the horses pulled up, Brian and Simon both stood, weapons ready.

"I thought I told you not to stop before the border."

John emerged from the woods with a grim smile.

Emily heard him and was out the back running toward him.

She threw her arms around him and said, "Don't you ever do that again."

He held her tightly. "Believe me, I don't plan to. Dumbest thing I ever did."

29

It was late in the evening. Forneau was out of breath from running through the vast palace. "They have returned."

Garibaldi looked up from his writing desk. "All of them?"

"The two soldiers are dead."

Garibaldi tried to stand but his arthritic hips locked up and sent him back to his chair. Uncharacteristically, he accepted Forneau's help for a second try.

"I don't think you've slept or eaten, have you?" the minister said.

"I don't recall," Garibaldi said, tucking in his shirttail. "Did they find the man Emily sought?"

"He is here."

"That wasn't the plan."

"There were some complications."

"Are you sure no one will mention the news?"

"The court is carefully instructed but it would be best if you could speak with John Camp quickly."

Garibaldi lashed him with his tongue. "Well that's what I'm intending, Forneau."

Forneau dropped his head. "I know, I know. It is hard for me to bear, that is all."

"I'm sorry, my friend," Garibaldi said. "We're all under considerable stress."

Garibaldi came into the hall where John and the others were wolfing down a spread of food and drinking the best wine from old Robespierre's cellars.

"I am so glad to see you all," Garibaldi said, "and so pained to hear of the deaths of the English soldiers."

"They died heroes," John said. "I'd like to bring their bodies back to England but I don't think it's practical."

"We will have them buried with great honor and dignity," Forneau said.

Emily said, "Giuseppe, this is Paul Loomis, my old mentor."

"A great pleasure," Garibaldi said.

"I've heard many good things about you, sir," Loomis replied.

Caravaggio and Simon approached the king for embraces.

"I take it from the casualties that there were complications," Garibaldi said.

John nodded and said, "There were. Big time complications. Ostrov was a traitor all right, but not to Stalin."

Garibaldi's face twisted in rage. "Damn him! And damn me for trusting him!" he cried. "That explains everything."

"Sorry, what does that mean?" John said. He suddenly felt a chill, as if a cold wind had passed through his body. "Where's Kyle? Is he still at the forge?"

He didn't like Garibaldi's answer of, "John, come and sit with me."

Emily lay beside him. He was drunk and inconsolable and was thrashing around so much she didn't know if she could contain him.

"I know, baby, I know," she said over and over.

"My fault, my fault," he babbled. "Shouldn't have. Should've let him be."

"It wasn't your fault," she said. "Kyle made his own choices. He knew the risks."

He rolled onto his stomach and buried his head in his arms. "Glad they're dead."

"Who? Glad who's dead?"

"My parents. Couldn't face them."

Her eyes stung as she conjured up an image of two young boys, playing on a carpet at their parents' feet, a gentle, happy moment long past.

"Go to sleep now," she whispered, stroking his back. "I'll be here. I'll be with you."

The rotor wash from the Black Hawk blotted out the night sky. A few moments earlier, waiting for the bird to land, John had allowed himself a second, maybe two, to seek out the North Star.

It was hard to fathom how, in such a brief snippet of time, the mind could compress a much longer memory. But as he acquired the sight of the heavenly object John remembered lying in his boyhood bedroom on the top bunk while his mother sat on the bottom bunk with his younger brother, Kyle. He remembered her lilting voice saying, "Star light, star bright, first star I see tonight …"

The helicopter touched down hard.

"Get Mike in first," John said, and his men slid Mike Entwistle's body bag into the Black Hawk.

"Now him."

Fazal Toofan was unconscious, his jaw broken and swollen from the blow John had landed. The Taliban commander, trussed with plastic ties, was manhandled and dumped like a sack of garbage on the metal floor beside the body bag.

The remaining members of the Green Beret squad piled in. John did a fast headcount, subtracting out the casualties who'd already been evacuated. He looked over at the smoldering rubble of the farmhouse and then glanced at Toofan, lying in the chopper, this so-called high-value target.

How high could his value be?

High enough to balance out the lives of the men he'd lost?

He spit on the parched ground and climbed in, his men silently making room for him on a low metal bench. One of his boots was touching Mike's dead body. The other was touching Toofan's live body.

John called out to the pilot, "Get us the fuck out of here."

The next morning Emily awoke early and was surprised John was already up, dressed and washing in a basin. He didn't want to talk about being drunk out of his mind or anything else and she didn't press him. She knew where he wanted to go.

The arrangements had been made.

Led by Garibaldi and Forneau and protected by a garrison of soldiers, the procession left the palace and made its way along the Seine to the demolished royal forge. John and Emily rode alone in one wagon, Simon, Brian, Alice, Loomis, and Caravaggio in another.

In the flat, gray light of morning, the caved-in and smoking mountain of bricks was a sad sight. A small army of French and Italian workers had already begun the painstaking task of shifting bricks and timbers and stacking them on a flat parcel of land for their eventual re-use. Immediately after learning of the blast, Garibaldi had declared his intention to rebuild and expand the forge as a blast furnace and foundry to produce the Bessemer steel he would need to make his brave, new world.

"From this disaster, we will grow stronger," he had said. "From this sorrow, we will triumph."

John jumped off the wagon and helped Emily down. He stood, watching the men clear debris, and suppressed a sob.

Emily said something to him but he said he'd be all right. Then the two of them went to Garibaldi.

"John, it might be days before we find Kyle's remains," Garibaldi said.

"I should stay," John said, "but I can't."

"I will treat him like my own brother," Garibaldi said. "We will give him a hero's burial. Was he a religious man? Perhaps we can find a man or woman who remembers what to say?"

"I don't think he was religious," John said. "You might want to bury him with a jug of beer though."

"He deserves a full barrel," Garibaldi said. "I should mention we found his killer, the Russian, Antonov. Well, the French found him hiding in an inn in the city last night, awaiting his chance to escape. They revenged the forge workers who were destroyed by chopping him into small pieces and throwing them into the river. I would have preferred to have him interrogated but I believe we already know his motives and whom he worked for."

"You've got to deal with the elephant in the room, Giuseppe."

"Ah, the elephant," Garibaldi said with a pained smile.

John shook his head. "All the AK-47s lost. The molds lost. The primers lost. And we gave a rifle to Stalin. Our plan backfired."

"Hardly," Garibaldi said, gesturing toward Loomis. "You found your man."

"I left a broken up AK rifle somewhere in the woods on the German side of the border. I'm not sure I could even find it."

"Never mind, John."

"It'll take Stalin a while to mass produce the guns and figure out the primers but when he does he'll have an enormous advantage over you."

"We will find another way," Garibaldi said. "You have your own battles to fight, John. Turn your attention away from our poor plight. Forneau and I must return to the palace. Queen Mécia and her generals await us for a war summit. We will do well to attack Stalin before he has the rifles. A great battle is coming."

"I'd like to stay a while longer, Giuseppe," John said, throwing his arms around the king. "I'll come by a little later to say goodbye."

Emily took a few steps back and left John to be alone with his brother's memory. When she heard the poignant words to Kyle flowing from his mouth she retreated further afield so he wouldn't become distracted by the sound of her uncontrollable sobbing.

"I didn't think I'd get a second chance to change your mind," John said.

They were in the main courtyard of Robespierre's palace and John was towering over Brian paying lip service to a task he knew would be unsuccessful.

"Well, I appreciate the effort and all but I haven't changed my mind," Brian said. "I'll be staying here to fight the good fight."

"I'm not surprised," John said. "Had to ask."

Emily was having the same conversation with Alice and she too was not budging.

"We're in love, you know," Alice said of Simon. "I had to come a very long way but now I've found love I'm not giving it up. I see the way you look at John. You know what I mean."

"I do," Emily said, giving her a hug.

Caravaggio approached Emily and stole a kiss while John had his back turned to them.

"I lose you yet again," he said. "Would that you could see your portrait when completed."

"Please take care of yourself," she said, "and never stop painting."

"How could I? It is as much a part of me as your beauty is a part of you. Remember, if you should ever return to our sad world without your Signore Camp, I will care for you as if you were a rare flower or a delicate songbird. I will worship the ground whereupon you tread. You will be my princess, I your slave."

"Such a charmer," she laughed.

"Do not tell John I say these things. He will punch my face and make it resemble a turnip."

Forneau assembled his personal troop of crack soldiers to accompany them to Calais and loaded one of the wagons with the gold John needed to pay their passage back to Brittania.

Before Loomis climbed onto a wagon Emily said to him, "Paul, I'm not going to renege on my promise. We will take you to Britannia but please tell me what you know in case something should happen to you along the way."

He apologized but said he was holding firm.

"Don't you trust me?" she said.

He mounted the wagon and said, "Don't take it personally, Emily. I don't even remember what trust is anymore."

John came over to her. "Ready?" he asked.

"Ready."

"Look." He pointed at a palace balcony where the red-shirted Garibaldi was waving a farewell. "I almost wish we could stay to help him."

30

Their wagon broke an axle early in the morning and they had no choice but to tackle the final few miles on foot. Along the way Trevor scanned the woods, his crossbow cocked. Each of the boys, even Andrew, clutched a sword in a fist, and Angus opted for a two-fisted approach with a sword in one hand and Bess's pistol in the other.

They were close to Sevenoaks and safety. Trevor didn't want to lose one more lad. He wished he could have rescued all of them. Four were dead. Six were on him.

A river to their north corresponded to the River Darent on his silk map.

"Almost there," he said to himself. "Keep it together."

Angus picked up his pace to draw alongside Trevor. They walked in silence but it was clear enough the boy wanted to talk.

"All right, then?" Trevor asked.

"Yeah."

"We're getting close."

"That's good."

"Look, Angus, I know you've been through a lot and it's going to take a lot of time to sort things out but if you've got something on your mind, I'm a pretty good listener."

The boy raised his pistol hand. "It's just that …"

"Just what?"

"I, you know, I shot her."

"It was self-defense. She shot your mate. She would've shot you next."

He repeated himself robotically. "I shot her in the face."

"You did what you had to do," Trevor said firmly but gently. "You were a hundred-percent in the right. When you came here you were a boy. You're leaving here a man. I'll be sure to tell your father about your bravery."

"Did you talk to him?"

"I did. Just before we left."

"Was he worried?"

"More than worried, I'd say. Not that he said as much. But I could tell."

"I don't really know him that well. I only see him on term breaks and summer hols but he's always away."

"What about your mum?"

"I suppose I don't know her too well either. I had nannies."

"Brothers and sisters?"

"I'm an only child."

"I had the opposite problem. My mum and dad were all over me up to the time I went into the army. I couldn't talk on the phone to a girl or leave the house to chill with my mates without them wanting to know all the details."

"You turned out all right," Angus said shyly.

Trevor smiled and patted his back. "Different paths to greatness, I reckon." He turned his head back to the road. When he spoke his tone was suddenly businesslike, "Get the lads into the woods. That way. Now."

Ahead, maybe half a mile away, a large group of Hellers were congregating on the road, their backs to them.

Angus shooed the boys into the forest and Trevor crept a little closer to the Hellers along the tree line. It was hard to tell how many there were but it was at least a hundred, possibly many more. Some were on wagons, some on horseback. They were stopped on the road as if they had encountered a roadblock.

Trevor rejoined the boys and told them they needed to travel the rest of the way through the woods.

Andrew began to whimper. "Are we going to die?"

Trevor was about to reassure him but Angus stepped in. "Listen to me, Andrew, we're not going to die. We're going to walk through the woods a ways, piece of cake, then we're going to meet up with the SAS and then we're going to go home."

The slender boy said, "Are you sure?"

"Yeah, I'm sure. Look at that ruddy great sword in your hand. Danny, stay close to Andrew, all right?"

Danny nodded.

"Why not me?" Nigel asked.

Angus grinned. "Because you're going to protect me, you big oaf."

They got going and Trevor whispered to Angus, "You're a born leader, know that?"

"You think?"

"I know."

When they got close to the Hellers milling on the road they veered further south to give them a wide berth. But Trevor didn't want to lose contact with the road completely. After trekking for about a mile he told the boys to stay put beside a giant oak and proceeded to reconnoiter to the north.

He crept up to the road and crouched low. To the west he saw the other side of the Heller crowd. His estimate of a few hundred was probably low. To the east he saw something altogether more appealing. Two SAS squaddies from Marsh's A Group were pacing the road with their AK-47s, facing the Hellers off.

Trevor started to backtrack to pick up the boys. His plan was to keep going through the woods until they were inside the SAS perimeter.

"What was that?" Kevin said.

"I didn't hear anything," Nigel said.

"There it is again," Kevin said.

"I heard it too," Danny said.

It was a faint cry like a baby's, scratchy and high-pitched.

Kevin, the young outdoorsman, suddenly looked alarmed. "Shit. I know what that is. It's a bear cub."

The mother, the size of a small car, lumbered into their midst and roared.

Danny began to wave his sword furiously but Kevin whispered for him to stop. "Everyone, just freeze," Kevin said.

They heard another cub crying from behind the oak tree.

The brown bear reared up on her hind legs until she was eight feet tall.

Andrew began to run.

Kevin shouted for him to stop.

The bear got back on all fours and began to give chase. It was a race she was going to win.

BOOM

Trevor heard it.

The Hellers heard it.

The SAS soldiers heard it.

Trevor got there first.

The bear was a yard from Andrew, lying on its side and bleeding from a flank wound. Angus had the smoking pistol in his hand.

Trevor didn't have time to give praise or complicated instructions. They could hear Hellers coming through the woods toward them.

"Follow me!" he shouted.

They began running as fast as they could, jumping over roots and vines, dodging saplings and bushes. Trevor lost his bearings. He wasn't sure where the SAS picket line was; he didn't want to undershoot it. When he felt they'd gone far enough he angled to the north.

They burst out onto the road at a bend. Trevor couldn't see the SAS soldiers any longer but on the other side of the road, to the north, he picked up the familiar sight of the Sevenoaks rotting room.

There was a rifle crack. A bullet cracked into a tree trunk, just to the left of Trevor's head.

"Cease fire! Cease fire, goddamn it."

It was Captain Marsh's voice.

Members of A Group, dirty and heavily bearded, emerged from hiding places in the grass and bushes.

Marsh came running toward Trevor. He would have been unrecognizable were it not for his shiny bald head, his features hidden by mountain-man facial hair.

"Jesus, Jones," Marsh called out. "You actually found them."

"Come on, boys," Trevor said to the lads. "Meet the good guys."

There were more rifle shots to the west.

Marsh's sergeant, who was one of the road sentries, came running around the bend, shouting, "They're breaking through."

"Set up a new perimeter," Marsh shouted to his men. "Jones, bring them this way!"

They began running toward the hot zone. Marsh came alongside Trevor and said, "I thought there were ten of them?"

"There were ten."

"Shit."

"How's it been?" Trevor asked.

"We've got three KIAs. Ammos' running low. But we've got the bastards at a stalemate. Or we did."

Trevor glanced over his shoulder to make sure the boys were keeping pace. Andrew and Kevin had abandoned their swords and were pumping their arms as if a PE teacher were yelling at them to sprint to the finish line.

"I've got to take the boys through," Trevor said. "Has the hot zone expanded?"

"Definitely. One of the Hellers snuck past two days ago and disappeared in an area we thought was safe. Any idea how long we've got till we're recalled?"

"No clue, sorry."

"We'll keep going if we have to use the fucking rifles as clubs," Marsh said. "I'm stopping here to cover you. Keep moving in that direction."

Trevor stopped to shake Marsh's hand and give him his crossbow and bolts. The boys pulled up.

"Lads, this is Captain Marsh, 22 SAS Regiment, the best fighting men in Britain."

"Glad you made it," Marsh said.

Puffing and out of breath, Angus said, "Captain Marsh, I'm Angus Slaine. My father is ..."

"I know who he is. Tell him we're almost out of ammo. Now go!"

Trevor told the boys carrying weapons to drop them. He led them at a dead run.

He heard Marsh and others yelling at them to keep going, keep going, then all of a sudden it was quiet.

The rough fields were gone, replaced by overgrown but tame lawn grass. In the distance were redbrick buildings with slate roofs and football practice grounds.

From behind he heard small voices.

The six boys were blinking and pointing.

"It's Belmeade," Kevin said. "We're back."

Trevor wasn't going to let his guard down. They were in the hot zone. There could be Hellers about. For all he knew the physical rules might have changed: they could be in danger of hurtling back across the dimensional divide.

"Let's keep going till we see the authorities," Trevor said. "Stay together. Stay vigilant."

"Mr. Jones," Nigel said, "our dormitory is just over there. Do you think we could stop in and change our undershorts?"

They all laughed for the first time in a long while.

Jeremy Slaine's private secretary barged into his office at Manchester City Hall.

Slaine looked up, annoyed by his failure to at least knock.

"They're back," the secretary declared.

"Who? Who's back?"

"The boys. And Trevor Jones."

Slaine removed his reading glasses and took a slow, deep breath. "All of them?"

"Six. Trevor Jones just brought them out of the Sevenoaks zone."

"Angus?"

The secretary closed his eyes and nodded. "Yes, thank God. Angus is safe."

Slaine stood but showing the effects of lightheadedness, he quickly lowered himself back down. "I'll call his mother. Get me the details on the other five boys who are safe and the four who are not. I'll need their parents' numbers. Keep this out of the press to give me a little time. And could you get the army to bring Mr. Jones and my son up here to Manchester immediately?"

Jeremy Slaine had rented a house for him and his wife in the Manchester suburb of Hale Barns. While Jeremy possessed the storied family history, Elena, his wife, contributed the serious money and they had decamped from London with a staff. She had ordered the cook to prepare her son's favorite meal, lasagna, and with little to do, she stood at the sitting room windows staring over the broad lawn and picking at her cuticles.

Her husband's ministerial Jaguar appeared in a convoy of black SUVs and police motorcycle outriders, crunching the pebbled driveway.

"Jeremy," she called out. "He's here."

Angus and Trevor emerged from the Jaguar wearing their filthy clothes.

"Nice place," Trevor said, taking in the estate.

"Bit small by our standards," Angus said.

"You're joking, right?"

"Actually, I'm not."

Trevor expected Angus's parents to be rushing outside but it was Slaine's private secretary who emerged from the house.

"Welcome home, Angus, your parents are inside," the secretary said. "Mr. Jones, congratulations on your accomplishment."

Neither Angus nor his parents ran toward each other. The boy had to approach them where they stood in the sitting room.

His mother began to cry, "Oh, Angus, look at you."

The boy looked at a mirror and said, "Lost a bit of weight."

She gave him a quick hug and overcome by his body odor, she let go.

"Welcome home, son," his father said, reaching for a hand. "We were very worried."

"Four didn't make it," Angus said.

"So I understand. I've reached out to the boys' parents. I'll need an account of what happened, of course."

Trevor jumped in, "Bit early for that."

"Yes, when he's able," Slaine said. "Mr. Jones, I'm sure it wasn't easy to accomplish what you did."

"Yeah, definitely not easy peasy," Trevor replied, "but Angus and the lads have been through more than me. More than you can imagine."

"Well," his mother said to her son, uncomfortably, "why don't you run upstairs? First door on your right. Have a good wash and put on some fresh clothes. When you come down cook has prepared your favorite—beef lasagna."

Angus blinked a few times and began to cry.

"It doesn't have to be lasagna," his mother sputtered.

Trevor put his arm around the boy and said, "It'll be okay, Angus. Give it time. Lots of time. I'm sure you'll have people to talk to about all of this."

Jeremy Slaine looked on helplessly as another man tended to his boy.

"Will I see you again?" Angus asked.

"'Course you will. I'll give you my details and when I get back we can text and all."

"Back?"

"Yeah, I'm just going to nip over one more time. Frankly, I'm already missing the food over there."

The crying turned to laughter. Angus imitated his father and extended a hand.

"Sod that," Trevor said, giving the boy a giant hug instead.

Trevor's meeting with the prime minister and Jeremy Slaine was winding down. He had felt awkward smelling like a pig in muck and scarfing down tasty but ridiculously delicate finger food, and now he was itching to get back down south.

"So you're committed to returning," the prime minister said. "No one in Britain would fault you for standing down and having a rest. No one individual can be responsible for the success of a mission."

"You know how it is, sir," Trevor said. "When you're in the army and you're up against it, you're not really thinking about the mission so much as the man next to you. John Camp and Emily Loughty and the others are still there, still in harm's way."

"Well, it's really very admirable," Lester said.

"And you've no idea whether Dr. Loughty was able to find Dr. Loomis?" Slaine said.

"None whatsoever. As I said, the last I saw them, they were on the way to the continent."

"Well, I don't need to tell you," Lester said, "but we're in a bad way here. Hellers continue to come through via Upminster particularly, London is a no-go zone under military control, our economy is in the crapper, and morale is beyond terrible. If and when you see Loughty and Camp, please tell them that speed is of the essence."

Trevor used the latter as an excuse to say he needed to be on the move.

The prime minister said, "And thank you for bringing Jeremy's son home."

Slaine seemed surprised by the comment and said, "Yes, thank you, Mr. Jones. I may have neglected to express my gratitude sufficiently."

Boarding the helicopter on the roof of the Town Hall, Trevor asked one of the crewmen if he could use his mobile phone. He had gotten her number from one of the PM's staff and he eagerly punched it in.

Arabel answered.

"Hey, it's me. Trevor."

"Oh my lord! You're safe."

"Yeah, how are you?"

"I'm still up in Edinburgh with my mum and dad and the kids. I'm okay."

"How're they doing?"

"They still have nightmares but during the day they seem all right. Where are you? Is Emily with you?"

He told her what was happening and wished he could have been more reassuring about Emily.

"I'm going back via Dartford. I'm hoping she and John'll be along soon. I just wanted to hear your voice before I left."

"I miss you," she said.

"I miss you too."

"Please come back to me."

"The thought of that's the thing keeping me going."

The winds were favorable and the seas were calm enabling the French galleon to make the crossing in less than two days.

Captain La Rue knocked on the door to his own cabin.

"Are you awake?" he called out.

John opened the door.

"We are in the estuary," the captain said.

"So I see," John said.

"You may come topside whenever you are ready."

"I'm sure you're anxious to get your quarters back."

"And my ship," La Rue said. "You have no idea, monsieur."

John had been pleased but not shocked to find La Rue still at anchor at Calais. A bucket of gold was too much for the Breton to leave on the table. It was enough to make him one of the richer commoners in Brest. The captain's eyes had lit up as he counted the bag of coins and only then did he ask about the absence of Kyle and the two SAS soldiers.

"I am sorry for your brother," La Rue had said, "but this Hell, she is a hard mistress."

Loomis was still asleep. John hadn't loved sharing a cabin with him but they weren't about to let him out of their sight.

"Tell him it's time to shove off," John told Emily.

Emily nodded and poked his shoulder. "Paul, we're almost here."

Loomis opened his eyes. "Thank God. England."

Lance Corporal Scarlet was the first to spot the masts. He raced around the hot-zone perimeter to Captain Yates' lean-to.

"You sure it's them?" Yates asked.

"Can't be positive but it's a four-master flying the same colors."

"Have the men fall in," Yates said, pulling up his tattered trousers. "If it's them they're going to need an escort."

As the longboat was being lowered John tensed at the sound of a gunshot. His concern quickly melted away.

"Now that's a lovely sight," he told Emily.

The men of B Group had secured the riverbank and a few nearby Hellers were scattering at the warning shot.

The French oarsmen landed the boat and waited only long enough for John, Emily, and Loomis to jump off before pushing off.

Yates turned gloomy when he saw men were missing.

John pre-empted the questions. "I'm sorry, Captain. Culpepper and O'Malley didn't make it."

"And your brother?" Yates asked.

"No."

"Is this Loomis?"

"Yeah, we found him."

Emily saw him first. He'd been standing behind a taller trooper. "Trevor!"

Trevor smiled and waved then darkened when he counted heads.

He rushed forward and said, "Kyle?"

John gulped.

"I'm sorry, guv," Trevor said. "Really and truly sorry."

"Why are you here?" Emily asked, embracing him.

"I found what was left of the schoolboys and brought them home at Sevenoaks. I crossed at Dartford yesterday and here you are."

"You're mad to come back," she said.

"Well, I missed you a lot and you weren't answering your emails."

"Trevor, I'd like you to meet my old boss, Paul Loomis."

Loomis nodded at him. "Emily's told me about you," he said.

"Let's get you folks back up to our camp," Yates said. "I don't like leaving the HZ unguarded."

On the way back John walked with Yates and Trevor. He asked Yates how his group had fared. "It doesn't look like you've lost any men," he said.

"We've been fortunate. Two lightly wounded, is all. Not much ammo left though."

"Have they been attacking?"

"At first. They'd mass and try to break through this way and that. We had success taking out the ones with firearms though it's the bows and arrows that've caused us the biggest headaches. Crossbows are the worst. Funnily enough, we did well with a low-tech solution. Wooden shields believe it or not."

"I told you you'd improvise."

"So when can we pack it in and go home?" the captain asked.

"Hopefully soon. Emily's going to go back to implement Loomis' fix. We'll ask her how long it'll take when he's told her the technical details."

"You mean he hasn't told her yet?" Trevor asked.

"He's milking it."

Emily walked with Loomis. "So, here we are," she said.

Loomis looked around. "I was seized here by sweepers and taken to that loathsome man, Solomon Wisdom, who sold me to the Russian ambassador."

"Yes, well, I'd like to reminisce, Paul, but it's time you told me what I came for."

"I've been thinking about that, Emily."

"What's there to think about? We agreed to bring you to Brittania. Now we're here."

"I've decided not to tell you …"

"What?" She said it loud enough for John to turn around to see what was happening.

"Yet," Loomis said. "I'll help you but not yet."

She waved John off and said in a measured way, "Look, Paul, I've got to cross today. I've got to get this sorted."

"I'm going with you."

"Oh no you're not."

"I'm afraid I am. Listen to me, Emily; I want to see my children one last time. The day I killed their mother and took my own life was the day I turned them into orphans. They're old enough now for me to talk to them. To apologize. To see what's become of them."

She was red in the face with anger now. "I sympathize, I really do, but this is simply unacceptable. We had a deal."

"And the deal has changed."

"Do you even know how to shut the portals down?" she asked. "Is all this pathetic bullshit?"

"I absolutely do know how it must be done and I will start working with you the moment we cross back to Earth. If I'm lying, send me back straight away."

"Paul …"

"I'm sorry, Emily. I'm holding all the cards."

"I wish you'd come too," she said.

John and Emily were apart from the others, holding onto each other.

"You'll be so busy you won't even miss me," John said.

"At least you'll have Trevor watching your back. I'm frantic, but if it weren't for Trevor I'd be more frantic."

"We'll pick up Professor Nightingale in Richmond, see if we can get a quick bead on the MAAC people, and cross over with or without them."

"I'm sick about Matthew and David and all my people but we both know they may be already dead. Please don't spend too much time looking for them. If and when we're able to shut down the portals there'll be enormous pressure to do it. Hellers will be trapped on Earth. Earthers will be trapped here. I don't want you and Trevor to be among the lost. I couldn't bear it."

"We'll move fast. At least Loomis told you how long his mystery process would take."

"A week, maybe a little more if we can believe him. His credibility's shot."

"If he pulls any horseshit, kick his ass for me."

"Believe me, I will."

They kissed tenderly.

John ended the embrace and added, "Because I know you're the best ass-kicker in both universes."

Yates and his men took them as close to the perimeter as they dared and cut them loose.

Emily and John locked eyes one last time. Then she and Loomis began walking toward Dartford village. At the moment they disappeared in between one heartbeat and another, John let out a deep, melodic sigh and told Trevor it was time to hit the road.

31

Gazing upon the new, massive chimneystack, Cromwell admitted he was surprised.

He told William the forger, "Your progress is most impressive, Master William."

"Do not look to me, look to this man."

Campbell Bates acknowledged the compliment. Throughout the process he had taken to calling himself the Alec Guinness of Hell after the actor's portrayal of the twisted, bridge-building colonel in *The Bridge on the River Kwai*.

"When will the great furnace be ready to produce steel?" Cromwell asked.

"It's hard for me to say," Bates replied. "There's still much work to be done."

"Well, keep at it, man," Cromwell said. "When next I return I would see great slabs of molten metal emerging from the flames."

Bates cleared his throat. "I've been asked by my colleagues to inquire as to the health and well-being of the women who've remained in London? We are very anxious to see them again."

Cromwell pursed his lips. "You may tell your colleagues that they are well."

Bates pressed on, "We would respectfully ask to return to the palace for a few days, maybe a week, to see them for ourselves."

"You may return once your work here is done, not before."

"Then could I ask whether there have been any sightings of the men who were sent to bring us home? We've all talked among ourselves and are prepared to reassure you that we will stay to finish the blast furnace. Then we would ask to be united with the soldiers who are looking for us."

Cromwell turned and with his back to the American said, "Do you take me for a fool? Return to your labors."

Trotter had been listening to the exchange and took the opportunity to catch up with Cromwell.

"You were right not to trust them," Trotter said.

Cromwell ignored him as one might ignore a passing insect.

"They've been plotting, plotting, plotting," Trotter said. "When they're not working they're trying to figure out how to escape but they're not exactly men of action. They're scared of your soldiers. They've asked me to help them because they know I am a man of action but I will not give them any assistance."

Cromwell stopped walking. "Why are you telling me this?"

"Because I've accepted what they cannot accept. We are not going to be rescued. We're going to be here for the rest of our lives. We have to adapt, make the best of it, try to be useful."

"Is that what you think?"

"It is. I'll venture that your army has already defeated the soldiers sent here. Am I right? Did Suffolk find them at Leatherhead?"

"Suffolk is a more accomplished talker than warrior," Cromwell said. "He withdrew, neither the winner nor the loser, having lost the most able field commander in the army, the Duke of Oxford. If Suffolk did not enjoy the support he does at court I would have already replaced him. But it is of no consequence. We will wait them out. Their supply of shot will dwindle and when they have no more, we will overwhelm them. I have received reports this has already happened in Upminster town where there is another Earther garrison."

Trotter raised his eyebrows at the news. "Really? Upminster, you say?"

"Good day to you," Cromwell said, resuming his walk toward the river.

Trotter took after him again. "You need me," he blurted out.

"I need you for what?"

"I can eliminate Suffolk for you."

Cromwell stopped again. His curious expression seemed to invite more.

"Henry's been missing for a considerable time but you still haven't declared yourself the new king. Why is that, I've asked myself?"

"And what answer did you provide?" Cromwell said with a smirk.

"Suffolk isn't half the man you are," Trotter replied, "but he's got friends—a lot of friends among the nobility. I'm going to guess the two of you are at a stalemate. You'd like to get rid of him and he'd like to do the same to you. But if either one of you is seen to be the aggressor you'd have a civil war on your hands. Am I correct?"

"Go on."

The non-denial had the effect of infusing Trotter with confidence. "I'll do your dirty work. Take me back to the palace. I'll tell my people you agreed to let me check on the women so they'll be none the wiser. When I get settled in I'll ask to see Suffolk and tell him I can help him defeat you. I'll play the double game. Believe me, I'm a master at it. It's what I do for a living."

Although no one was within earshot, Cromwell lowered his voice, a conspiratorial sign that caused a smile to flicker across Trotter's face. "And once such confidence is gained, then what?"

"I'll neutralize him."

"I do not know this word."

"What is it you say here? Destroy? I'll destroy him."

"How?"

"I don't know yet. Poison maybe. Do you have poisons?"

"Of course, but Suffolk has food and drink tasters as do I."

"I'll figure something out."

"After you have done the deed, what would prevent me from declaring you the culprit and—neutralizing you? We know you Earthers cannot be trusted. The court would see my hands were clean. Surely a man as clever as you claim to be would see this coming?"

"You won't do it because you'll find me useful," Trotter said. "Once you're the king you'll need a chancellor. You will find me free of any other loyalties. I'm the new man. No entanglements. I'll serve you and no one else. And you'll find out quickly enough that I'm a ruthless son-of-a-bitch."

Cromwell laughed. "I believe I already know this."

It had taken a day to find a boat to steal but once they set sail, the journey to Richmond was fast. The one-masted, flat-bottomed riverboat smelled so strongly of fish that a chance encounter with another vessel near London did not lead to their undoing. A barge headed the opposite direction loaded with soldiers, propelled at speed by downstream currents, pulled alongside. A line was cast and a man shouted for them to heave to.

Yates had given John and Trevor one of his group's AKs and a precious full magazine of ammo. John slid his hand under the burlap sack concealing it. They had both taken coarse tunics from two of A Group's victims before setting off.

"You talk," John told Trevor. "You've got the right accent."

The king's men were hungry and wanted to confiscate their catch. The men did wrinkle their noses but it was the pungency of the rotting fish guts not their Earther smell that was the trigger. Trevor said he was sorry but they had just sold their catch. The soldiers grumbled but let them sail on.

They arrived near Richmond in the early evening but waited until it was mostly dark to land the boat at the village. John took the rifle and led Trevor to the tiny cottage of Mrs. Eugenia Smith where he knocked on the door.

A fearful voice called out, "Who is there?"

"Mrs. Smith, it's me, John Camp. I've come for Mr. Nightingale."

The door slowly opened. With a crooked finger she invited them inside.

The only light was from a single log glowing in the hearth but that was enough for them to see that Nightingale wasn't there.

"Where is he?" John asked.

"I'll show you," she said.

She used a stick to transfer a flame to a nubbin of a candle and took them outside to the back of the cottage. There was a fresh mound of earth.

"He passed on not one week ago," she said. "He was so sick, he was. I didn't know what I could do other than keep him company and try to lift his spirits. He was a lovely man, he was, and such a gentleman. He was thankful all the time and kept saying he wished he could pay me. I was happy to listen to his marvelous stories about modern times and be there at his hour of need. I haven't seen a man die for a very long time. I thought I'd never see it again. Before he passed I told him I didn't recall no prayers but he said he didn't want that anyway. I dug a grave for him. Least I could do."

John had held onto a few of Forneau's gold pieces and he gave her one.

She held the candle up to the coin and said, "My stars! I'm rich."

"You did a good thing," John said.

"Did I?" she asked. "I suppose I did."

They left her and climbed the hill toward the forge. John felt he ought to tell William about Kyle's death.

There wasn't much light but there was enough to see that the forge had been transformed. A huge, new chimneystack cut into the gray-black sky.

"Something big's been happening here," John said.

"You sure we ought to carry on?" Trevor asked.

"Maybe not."

A gruff voice called out, "Who goes here?"

A soldier with a musket stepped out of the darkness to confront them. When he cocked and raised the rifle John fired once at point-blank range. The heavy AK-47 round lifted the soldier an inch off the ground before he fell with a thud.

A shot from the darkness whizzed past Trevor's ear.

"Get low," John hissed. "Let them come to us."

From a prone position in the grass, John stared down the iron sights into the darkness looking for targets to acquire.

Voices in the darkness gave away the enemy's tactics.

"How many are there?"

"I saw two men."

"Only two?"

"Only two."

"Then we'll overwhelm them. All of you, charge! Those with guns, fire at will."

The soldiers came running down the hill stupidly bunched together. The furnace wasn't lit but a few campfires were casting shadows. John saw moving shapes before he saw fully articulated men and he fired once at each gray mass, judging his accuracy by grunts and shouts of pain. Half a dozen shots came their direction but the soldiers must have been firing blindly because all were high or wide. John had started counting backwards from thirty at his first trigger-pull to track the rounds left in the mag. When he got to eighteen he stopped.

"You see anymore of them?" he asked Trevor.

"No."

All they heard was the groaning of wounded men.

John cautiously rose and gave a hand signal to Trevor to follow. They found the bleeding soldiers scattered before them and kicked weapons away from their bodies. The last man they found, highest up the hill, looked by his uniform to be an officer. He was lying on his side. When John used his foot to turn him on his back he saw a pistol coming around at him. John pulled the trigger and the threat ended. Trevor helped himself to the officer's gun.

The familiar voice of William came from the forge entrance. "We're not armed. Whoever you are, leave us in peace."

John shouted, "It's John Camp. Are there any more soldiers up there?"

"None," William replied. "You may safely show yourself."

John and Trevor slowly closed the distance to the forge but didn't relax until they saw William's smiling face.

"Good to see you, John who isn't from here," William said. "Have you dispatched the king's men?"

"Those that fired at us, yes."

"They were itching for action," William said, "and it seems they found it."

John said, "Meet a friend of mine who's also not from here. Trevor Jones."

"You never know who you'll meet these days," William said. "Where is Kyle Camp?"

John's head drooped. "He didn't make it."

"Sad news, sad news indeed. A fine man he was. Well, I would like to give you gladder news. Come inside. This building used to be a forge. Now it is called a blast furnace. I think those that built it will give you some cheer."

They stepped inside and in the candlelight John saw a gaggle of familiar faces, William's crew of skinny forge workers. These men stood aside and when they parted John saw a second group of men who had been cowering at the gunfire.

John and Trevor looked into their stunned faces.

Campbell Bates. Henry Quint. Matthew Coppens. David Laurent. Leroy Bitterman. Another bunch of young scientists they recognized by sight only.

Bitterman staggered forward. "Thank God, we're saved."

John smiled and warmly shook his head. "We're glad we found you but you're not saved yet."

"How many of you are there?" Quint asked.

"Here? Just the two of us," Trevor said.

"Just two? What about our guards?" Bates asked.

"I think we got them all, at least I hope so," John said. "What are you doing here? Where are the others?"

"The rest of us are being held in London. We haven't seen them in a while. They've kept us busy here," Bates said.

Bitterman shot them a wry smile. "Ever hear of slave labor?"

The stocky Duke of Suffolk undid the brass buttons of his tunic and eased himself onto the high-backed chair of his dining table. The acts of sitting and gorging would have placed an inordinate strain on the buttons.

"Sit, Trotter, sit," he said, pointing to the chair opposite him. "Wine?"

"Of course," Trotter said. A young manservant poured claret from a decanter.

"Has it been tasted?" Suffolk asked the servant.

"Of course, my lord," the young man replied.

"Go ahead, Trotter, see what you think."

Trotter smelled the wine, swirled it, and tasted it, all the rituals of a connoisseur.

"Like it?" Suffolk asked.

"It's quite good. I hear you have an excellent cellar."

"I do, but it is not here. I've been dipping into King Henry's offerings. I hope he will forgive the trespass."

"That implies you think he might return," Trotter said.

"I have no idea. We are in strange times. Witness my dining with a living man." Suffolk sampled the wine himself, declaring it acceptable. "Tell me, Trotter, why are we dining?"

"I wanted a chance to speak to you privately."

"About what? The forge or blasted furnace or whatever it is called?"

"Not that." He leaned across the table and whispered, "Can I speak freely in front of your servants?"

Suffolk dismissed them and told them to return with the quail.

"I trust few at court," Suffolk said. "I have stayed in fair health for a long time by exercising caution. I have some loyal servants, my tasters, some military aides but not this lot."

Trotter had more wine. "Well I don't think Henry is returning."

"No? Why?"

"My government will want to keep him. I'm not so sure they'll want to make his presence known publicly but they might. He'll be the greatest celebrity in history. He'll break the Internet."

"Excuse me?"

"Nothing, nothing. What I mean to say is, because he's the most famous of all the English monarchs, he'll be the object of intense fascination and study. He'll be worth a fortune. Not to mention, if he's given a choice, he'll probably want to stay."

"I cannot fathom what may or may not happen in a world I do not understand," Suffolk said with some irritation. "Tell me what this has to do with me?"

"I have no illusion as to my own circumstances," Trotter replied. "I won't be going home. We're not going to escape from here. I'm the only one who's a fighter, not an egghead. They'll figure out how to wall off the connection between our worlds. I'll be trapped here until the day I die." His mouth twitched and he added, "And maybe forever."

Suffolk seemed to understand and chuckled.

"So, for my own benefit, I need to back the man whom I think will replace Henry. It's pretty clear to me it's a two-horse race."

There was a knock on the door and the manservant poked his head in. Suffolk told him to serve the food and when the plates were full and they were alone he had Trotter continue.

"As I see it, Cromwell is a good political type. He's clever but he's a thinker, not a doer. A king has to be a man of action and in your world that means a military man. You're a soldier. You're decisive. It's obvious to me that you've got a lot of support in the court. That makes you the man to wear the crown. I want to help you get it."

Suffolk speared a whole bird and delivered it to his mouth at the end of his knife where he chomped on it. The oozing grease stained his white beard.

Speaking while chewing he said, "I rather thought you were Cromwell's toadie. Why should I trust you?"

"You don't have to trust me. You only have to see if I deliver on my promise."

"What promise is that?"

"To send Cromwell to the rotting room."

"How would you do that?"

"If you can provide me with poison, I'll make it happen."

"He has tasters. Not so easy to accomplish. Believe me, I have considered this."

"Leave it to me. I'll find a way that doesn't implicate you. It'll seem like a disease and when he's destroyed, well ..."

There was another knock on the door. This time the young manservant was empty-handed.

"Chancellor Cromwell asks to see you on a matter of great urgency."

"Is he here?" Suffolk asked.

"He is in his rooms," the man replied.

"I am having my supper! Do you know why it is so urgent?"

"His man tells me he is in his bed, my lord, quite ill."

Suffolk pushed back his chair and began buttoning his tunic. "Trotter, remain here. I shall return. Our conversation has, perhaps, been prescient. I may not need your special services after all."

With Suffolk gone, the manservant stood against the wall with his hands folded at his waist.

"It's all right," Trotter told him. "Go about your business and let me eat in peace."

With the servant gone, Trotter removed a vial of clear liquid from his pocket and emptied it into Suffolk's wine glass. Then he tucked into a very tasty game bird.

Trotter was undressing in his quarters when the door opened and Cromwell swept in unannounced.

"Tell me," he asked. "Is it done?"

Trotter put his trousers back on. "I put the poison in his wine and he drank all of it. Now we wait. Did he believe your story?"

"He had no reason to doubt it," Cromwell said. "I told him my body was racked with pain and burning with fire and I begged him not to commit me to a rotting room should I lapse into decrepitude. He could hardly contain his joy. This poison of yours. When should we see its effects?"

It was not a poison in Cromwell's arsenal. Trotter had given instructions on its manufacture. The product was methanol, a distillate of fermented wood shavings.

"He'll be fine for a day and then the problems will start," Trotter said. "Abdominal pain, headache, vomiting, blindness, organ failure, and coma. He's already gone but he doesn't know it." Then Trotter added two words that wiped Cromwell's perennially dour expression away. "Your Majesty."

Two days later, without warning, armed guards entered the women's dormitory and yanked away one of the young scientists, Kelly Jenkins, and for two days they had not seen her.

It was evening when a servant knocked on the door of Trotter's new, fancier rooms, and told him that one of the Earthers, Karen Smithwick desired an immediate audience. He agreed and soon she was escorted in.

"Have a seat, Karen," Trotter said. "I assume you've eaten already. Some wine?"

Smithwick looked around at the paneled walls, good furniture, and plush animal skins draped on the settee. She could hardly contain her contempt. "We heard you were back, Anthony. Nice of you to come by and see us."

"I've been busy. Why don't you sit and relax?"

"I'll stand. Where are the men?"

"Still in Richmond, beavering away."

"Yet here you are."

"I have been given different work."

"Is that so?"

"It seems I've climbed the organizational ladder rather quickly. Cromwell has made me chancellor."

"I thought he was chancellor?"

"I suppose you didn't get the memo," he said. "Suffolk took ill, rotting-room ill, and Cromwell is now king. I got promoted to his old job."

"From stooge to bigger stooge."

"How unkind."

"You've become quite the Quisling, haven't you?"

He stopped playing verbal games. "What do you want, Karen?"

"Kelly Jenkins has been taken away. Do you know where she is?"

"Refresh my memory. Which one is she?"

"Dark hair, pretty, but I'm sure you know that."

"That one. Who took her?"

"Palace guards. Where is she?"

"I have no idea."

"I don't believe you. You're too plugged in."

"I'm sorry you don't. Tell you what. I'll make some inquiries in the morning."

She pressed on. "I want you to tell me what's happened to Kelly."

"I'll let you know what I find out. Best I can do."

Smithwick aimed an accusatory finger at him. "I swear to God, Tony. I'm going to do everything in my power to ruin you."

He opened the door, summoned a guard in the corridor, and whispered something to the man. "Good night, Karen," he said. "By the way, lose the attitude. You're no longer a cabinet minister."

Trotter went into his bedchamber and unlocked an adjacent door.

The young, black-haired woman manacled to the bedframe, stared at him with hateful eyes. One of her cheeks was swollen and bruised.

"Hello, Kelly," he said, "Did you miss me?"

32

What was strangest was its familiarity.

From their vantage point across the empty parking lot, the MAAC complex looked as it might on an ordinary Sunday. Emily had come into work on so many Sundays when she was alone or nearly alone at her workstation, and for the briefest moment, she felt like it was one of those days. Loomis broke the spell. Shielding his sensitive eyes from the sunlight he said, "We're really back, we're really here."

"Come on," she said, scouring the surrounding area, "there could be Hellers around."

"You're standing next to one."

They ran across the parking lot and up to the main entrance where they found the doors locked. Emily couldn't find anything nearby to break the glass and she declined Loomis's offer to kick through telling him she didn't want him to cut himself. They decided to try other doors.

All the entrances were locked but just when they were deciding to use a rock they came across a shattered lower pane in the door across from the tennis court.

"There could be someone inside," Emily said, crouching to crab-walk through. "Keep an eye out."

The windowed hallways concentrated the sunshine. Loomis could hardly stand the brightness. He followed Emily through the seemingly empty complex until they reached her office, an interior space without windows. She switched the overhead lights on.

"Can you shut those?" he asked, squinting in pain.

"Sorry. I wanted to see if the power was on."

She booted up her desktop computer and checked the telephone for a dial tone.

"I'm glad you got my old office," he said, sitting down and looking at the walls that were covered in mementos of her life, not his.

She sighed.

"Now what?" he asked.

"Now you start talking, Paul."

"I'd like to see my children first."

He seemed genuinely taken aback by the fury of her reaction. She sprang up and stood over him, her fists ready, screaming at the top of her lungs. "Don't you dare! Don't you fucking dare! Men have died so I could get your information. You have strung me along for days. You are not going to string me along for one minute longer." She reached for a brass letter opener. "I will hurt you, Paul. I swear to God, I will hurt you."

She heard him wheeze and the wheezing turned into a paroxysm of coughing. There was a half-filled bottle of water on her desk from the last time she'd been there. She handed it to him and he drank thirstily.

He gave her a little smile and she tossed the letter opener down.

Calmer, she said, "Honestly, Paul, please start talking."

He finished the water and said, "Here's the thing, Emily. As soon as I tell you what you want to hear, I've lost all my leverage. I need some assurances first."

She sat back down behind her desk, suddenly exhausted. "What assurances?"

"First, as I said, I want to see my children."

"You know how this works, Paul. We've talked about it. Once we're in the hot zone we stay in our dimension. If we leave it, we won't be able to get back to the MAAC. We'd cross to the other side. You tell me if I'm wrong but we're going to need to do things inside the collider."

"You're not wrong."

"And your children can't come here for the same reason."

"Of course. We have a videoconference facility here," Loomis said. "I'd like for them to be taken to a videoconference facility so I can see them. After I clean up a bit."

"Let's do this once work on a fix is underway," she pleaded.

"I want to do it now," he insisted.

"All right," she said. "There's something new since you left. It's called Skype. It allows videoconferencing between any two devices. I'm sure your kids have it on their phones or tablets. I'll make a call, try to make it happen, but it's going to be traumatic for them."

"I'm aware of that but I want to do it anyway."

"All right, is that it?"

"One more thing. I want to stay here until I die again. I'll gladly remain in prison. As long as I can see my children periodically."

She started to boil over again but she dialed it back and managed to say with equanimity, "That's not a decision I can make."

"I'm sure not. I want it in writing from the prime minister, whoever that may be."

"A letter from the prime minister," she mumbled. "Anything else?"

He shook his head. "No, that's everything."

She tried to run her hand through her hair but it was too tangled. Searching her desktop she found Ben Wellington's business card and dialed his mobile.

"Wellington."

"Mr. Wellington, this is Emily Loughty."

There was a long pause on the line. "Christ," he finally said. "You're calling from a number inside the MAAC, aren't you?"

"I am."

"Did you find Dr. Loomis?"

"He's sitting across the desk from me."

It took an hour but Ben pulled off a minor miracle, persuading the children's grandparents, or more specifically, the parents of Loomis' murdered wife, to have them Skype him from their home in the Midlands. The story he used was going to be congruous with the story Loomis would tell the teenagers: he hadn't really killed himself that fateful day. He had been held in a government prison *in communicado* because of the vital national secrets and expertise he possessed. And now that he was being called upon to work on the present crisis he had renewed his long-standing demand to speak with the children. For the sake of the country, could the couple agree to this?

Paul had gone to the washroom and had used up all the paper towels scrubbing the grime from his face and neck and washing his hair. He used a hairbrush of Emily's to complete the job and returned to her office.

While he was washing, Emily had made her own personal call, to her parents and Arabel. She had told them she was safe and back in Dartford but she deflected questions about her intentions.

"I can't come up to Scotland just now," she had said. "I've got some things to do down here first."

"Can you make this better?" her father had asked.

"I hope so, dad, I really do."

"We're worried sick but we're proud of you. We've always been proud of you."

Arabel was at the playground with Sam and Bess. Emily had told her parents to tell her she'd just been with Trevor and that he was well.

"I'll ring you back when I can," she had said. "I love you both very much."

Paul came in and took her seat in front of the computer. "How do I look?" he asked.

"You look fine."

He didn't really. He looked like a hollow-cheeked, stooped old man. Since the last time he'd sat at this desk he'd lost teeth. His hair was now patchy and gray. He'd been rather robust and fit. Now he was emaciated.

She checked the wall clock. "I'll connect now," she said, bending over and clicking the mouse.

Two scared teenagers, a boy and a girl, stared into the camera of their laptop. It was clear there was no recognition of the man they saw and it was equally clear that Loomis was struggling, reconciling the memories of the small children he left behind seven years ago with the two youngsters on Emily's screen.

"Is that really you?" Loomis said, the tears running freely. "Harry? Mary?"

The boy spoke first in a blunt monotone. "They said you're our dad. Our dad's dead." In the background Loomis heard his in-laws sobbing.

"That's what you were told. It was for your own good. I did a bad thing and I've been punished for it. But I wanted to see you again, to see what became of you."

"You want to know what became of us?" the boy said. He flashed a middle finger. "This is what became of us. Fuck off and go back to being dead."

The boy's face disappeared but the girl's remained.

"You killed our mum," she said.

Loomis could hardly speak. "I wish I could take it back. It was a moment of madness. I'm so sorry, honey."

"Don't call me that," she said angrily. "I'm not your honey. I'm nothing to you and you're nothing to me."

The girl looked behind her toward her out-of-frame grandparents.

"Mary, please can we chat for a short while?" Loomis asked. "I just want to hear about your life, your school, what you like to do."

The girl's hand approached the keyboard and the picture disappeared.

"What happened?" Loomis asked.

"She disconnected," Emily said.

"Can you get them back?"

"Perhaps later, Paul. You can see how hard this was on them. Surely you can understand. For their sakes."

He rose and made some weak, random steps before Emily took him by the arm and sat him down at her conference table.

She had a small electric kettle on her sideboard that she'd filled from the women's washroom.

"I think both of us can use a cup of tea."

"Tea?" he blinked. "Yes, that would be marvelous."

When the water was hot she poured it into mugs and added teabags.

"I'm afraid I haven't got any milk at the moment. I can have a tramp around."

"No, don't worry."

"Sugar?"

He eagerly nodded, wiping away the last of his tears.

She watched him close his eyes and savor the moment he tasted the sweet tea.

"They'll come around," he said.

"Excuse me?"

"In time, they'll want to see me."

Her desktop chimed with a new email. She clicked on it and sent a job to the printer.

"Here it is," she said, handing the page to him. "The letter from Prime Minister Lester."

He read it and put it down to concentrate on his mug of tea.

"Uranium," he said.

Emily looked up. "What did you say?"

"Uranium. The U-238 isotope, I should think. What we need to do is produce much higher collision energies than lead ions can produce."

She was already on her feet and at her whiteboard, writing equations as fast as her hand could travel.

"That's right, there you go," Loomis said. "You made strangelets at 30 TeV. They're still resident within the collider complexed with gravitons. To obliterate them we're going to need to vastly exceed 30 TeV."

She said excitedly, "Uranium is heavier than lead. I didn't see this. No one did. We didn't think about obliterating energies."

"It's not just the mass of uranium, it's the shape of the ions," he added. "U-238 is football-shaped. Uranium-uranium collisions ought to produce a denser quark-gluon plasma than any other ion species. It's theoretical, of course, but it should work."

"No, Paul, it's more than theoretical. The Brookhaven RHIC collider used uranium ions in 2012 and achieved phenomenal collision energies."

"Unless it's been vastly upgraded, Brookhaven's a pygmy compared to MAAC," he said, "Whatever they achieved should be logs higher here."

She nodded and continued to scribble on the board. After several minutes she put her marker down and the two of them checked her work.

"At full power we can achieve 300 TeV," she said. "Do you think that will do it?" she asked.

"At that energy the strangelets will be smashed into their component quarks and the graviton-strangelet complexes will fall apart. That ought to slam shut the doors to Hell."

"Are you ready to get to work?" she asked.

He pressed the heating button on the kettle and said, "I think we've already begun, don't you?"

33

Emily and Loomis were so intently involved in their equations that the ringing of her office phone startled them.

"Dr. Loughty, it's Ben Wellington. In all the excitement I rather forgot something."

Emily took Loomis with her; she wasn't about to let him out of her sight and there was safety in numbers. Along the way she opened a fire door and removed the metal axe.

"You look rather fearsome," Loomis said.

"You have no idea, Paul."

They crept down the hallway with Emily and her axe at the fore. The first sounds that registered were so incongruous she didn't trust her ears. She thought she heard cartoons. The closer they got to the open door, the more certain she was.

Tom and Jerry.

And then, full-throated laughter.

"Did you see the way the little mouse crashed the cat?"

"Burnt 'im to a crisp."

Emily stood at the doorway staring at the two young men lying side-by-side on the bed. The small room was littered with cereal boxes and candy wrappers and empty tubs of ice cream.

Dirk saw her first and fell off the bed in shock.

"Duck, look! It's Miss Emily!"

The last time they'd seen her was the moment she crossed over from Dartford village at the last MAAC restart.

"She's got an axe, Dirk," Duck said.

"Don't be mad at us," Dirk pleaded. "We only stole the grub 'cause we was 'ungry."

"I'm not mad at you," she said. "Tell me, have you seen anyone else inside the building since you've been here? Any other Hellers?"

"Just us," Duck said. "We've only 'ad ourselves for company. Well, we've 'ad the cartoon vids too if they count as company. Dirk likes 'em as much as me."

"I do," Dirk said. "Duck likes the Ariel fish-girl the best. I like this one with the cat and mouse."

"And you've been in this room for all this time watching cartoons?" she asked.

"Not only this room, Miss Emily," Dirk said. "There's another room what's got the grub. There's plenty left if you're 'ungry too."

"And we go to the room where you can press the silver bar and make your shits disappear," Duck said.

"Who's the chappie there?" Dirk said, pointing at Loomis. "I reckon 'e's one of us."

"I am one of you," Loomis said. "Few more IQ points but one of you, nevertheless."

"He's a friend," Emily said.

"Is Miss Delia going to come see us?" Duck asked. "I miss 'er, I do. She was always kind to me."

"I don't think she's coming right now," Emily said. "I think we'll leave you to your cartoons now. My friend and I have some work to do. Perhaps we'll come by later to say hello and get some of the food."

"If you like, you can watch some vids with us," Duck said. "We'll let you sit on the bed while we sit on the floor."

"It's a marvelous offer," she said with a smile. "The best offer I've had in a good while."

During unguarded moments, it felt like old times, Emily and Loomis working side-by-side, grinding through equations and computer simulations, laying cables, descending into the MAAC tunnels from the subterranean level near the old control room to check and modify hardware settings on the particle guns.

Right from the start, they collaborated with the technical staff at the Large Hadron Collider in Geneva to work through the software and hardware modifications they needed to convert MAAC from accelerating lead protons to uranium protons. These were Emily's colleagues; some were also close friends. Most had been made aware of her situation after the veil of secrecy was lifted and they had been tasked with trying to come up with a solution. Seeing her for the first time on videoconference had been an emotional experience. But many of the Geneva scientists had also been friends and colleagues of Paul Loomis and though they had been prepared in advance, their shock on seeing him had been visceral.

He had rehearsed a small speech but when the time came he broke down in tears and Emily had been left to fill in. She had said that it was obviously a strange and emotional time for everyone but they couldn't let their emotions get in the way of the important tasks ahead.

The Brookhaven National Laboratory on Long Island was the only facility in the world with an ample supply of the right kind of uranium gas. Brookhaven was contacted by the Geneva staff to prepare a large canister of U-238 gas. When it was ready, it was choppered to the Hanscom US Air Force base in Massachusetts and flown by jet to RAF High Wycombe for onward staging.

After several days of around-the-clock work, an exhausted Emily declared they were ready to receive the gas and fill the particle guns. They had endlessly discussed how to get the canister delivered on site. The options were limited, so limited in fact that the consensus was that there was only one imperfect solution. The gas couldn't be transported on the ground or via air into the MAAC complex without the transporting personnel getting shunted to Hell. Drone delivery was ruled out because the canister was too heavy, not to mention hazardous if there was a mishap.

That left the tunnels.

Outside of the Dartford complex, the MAAC tunnel was sealed. There were no routine or emergency access points anywhere else along the one hundred eighty kilometer oval running under the M25 motorway.

The preparatory work began three miles southwest of Dartford along a stretch of the already-blockaded M25. A squadron of Royal Engineers dug a shaft to a depth of one hundred fifty meters beneath the motorway. Once they reached the concrete envelope of the tunnel a team of experts from Geneva supervised breaching the concrete and accessing to the oval.

On the appointed day Emily and Loomis descended into the tunnels and used the best information available to get close, but not too close to the boundary of the Dartford hot zone.

Wearing miner's hats they made their way west approximately one hundred meters from the old control room.

"This is as far as I'm comfortable with," Emily said, stopping and shining a torch further west. "If we go one step too far we may not get back in."

"Worse mistake for the men coming the other direction," Loomis said.

For them, entering Hell wouldn't be the worst of their problems. They'd be arriving there deep underground where it would be a short race between being crushed to death or suffocated.

Her walkie-talkie crackled to life.

"Dr. Loughty do you read? This is the delivery team," an engineer said.

"I read you. What is your name, please?"

"Corporal Kessel here. Are you in position?"

"Yes, as close as we dare," she said. "What's your position?"

"We've covered about five kilometers from our entry point in Darent."

"Well please be careful," she said. "Don't get too close to the HZ."

"No kidding. Wish the GPS worked down here."

"Quite. How many are you?"

"One other engineer besides me and a French scientist from Geneva who's making sure we don't break any of your gear. We're going to need line of sight."

"I'm shining a torch," Emily said. "Do you see it?"

"Negative. Tell you what, could you switch off the walkie-talkie for a sec and give us a good loud shout?"

She produced a loud hello. A moment later she heard a hello coming back at them.

Back on walkie-talkie, the engineer said that he reckoned they were within a half mile.

"How close do you need to get?" she asked.

"We can send line out five hundred meters. We're on the move."

"Again, please be careful," she implored.

In a few minutes they saw a faint light approaching.

"I see your light." She waved her torch. "Can you see ours?"

"Yeah, just about."

"Are you close enough to fire?"

"Not quite. Don't want to come up short, do we? I'd prefer to have a visual on your position."

Emily turned to Loomis and told him she was nervous.

"Makes two of us," he said.

"There you are!" the engineer said over the radio. "I can just see the two of you. Close your eyes. I'm going to shoot you with a laser to get your distance." In a few seconds he said, "Five hundred fifty meters. I'm going to get a little closer."

"Be careful, please."

"No worries."

She was relieved when he told her he was in position but he wanted them to retreat twenty or thirty meters to avoid getting hit by the projectile. The engineer put down his handset and shouted out the rest of it.

"All right, I'm ready to fire the line thrower. Stand by in three, two, one, fire!"

There was a loud, echoing blast from the smoothbore shotgun. They heard the brass projectile rattling against the concrete floor and coming to rest only a short distance from their position.

Emily scrambled for it. The brass rod was attached to a nylon line.

"Got it!" she shouted.

A different voice cried out, "No!"

"What's wrong?" she yelled.

"Kessel took one more step forward and he's gone! For fuck's sake, he's gone!"

Emily dropped to her haunches in shock. "My god, Paul, how awful."

Loomis took the brass rod from her clenched hand and said to her coldly, "People die all the time. Where I come from that would be considered an unimaginable blessing." Then he shouted down the tunnel, "Is the line attached to the canister trolley?"

"Yes!"

He began pulling.

34

The soldiers guarding the gates at Whitehall Palace were astonished by the sight and began shouting as the group drew closer.

Campbell Bates and the rest of the men raised their hands to demonstrate they were unarmed.

Bates called out to the guards, "Would you kindly inform Chancellor Cromwell that he has visitors?"

One of the soldiers replied. "He's not chancellor no more. He's the king."

All of the blast-furnace brigade were there: Bates, Quint, Bitterman, Laurent, Coppens, and the other male scientists who had been sent to Richmond to transform the forge into a steel-making colossus. But nestled among them were John and Trevor, trying not to draw attention.

"Don't make eye contact," John warned Trevor. His AK-47 was hanging from his neck concealed by William the forger's cloak.

"I'm looking at my feet, guv," Trevor replied.

When one of Cromwell's aides was summoned to the gate he asked Bates a few questions and allowed the men to pass inside. Walking through the extensive palace corridors on the way to a reception room, Matthew Coppens, according to plan, surreptitiously led John and Trevor down a different corridor from the rest of the group.

Bates and the others nervously milled around the guarded reception room until Cromwell came in, not grandly and confidently as a king might, but with his same mincing gait. His mannerisms and demeanor were those of the bureaucrat he had been for centuries, not a monarch of a great state. The only nod to his elevated status was a heavy gold necklace draped over his chest.

He eschewed the throne and stood before them.

"Why are you here?" he demanded.

Bates, as their spokesman, said, "Because you sent for us."

Cromwell looked astonished. "I did no such thing."

"Well, that's what we were told."

"Who told you this?"

Bates continued with his lies. He had told John that his background as a lawyer and FBI Director made him perfect for the assignment. "The fellow—I suppose he was a soldier—who came to the forge."

Cromwell searched the large room. "What was his name? Where is he now?"

"I didn't catch his name," Bates said. "He sailed us to London downriver. He left us at the docks and told us to go directly to the palace, which we did."

"Were you accompanied by the forge guards?"

"This fellow told them to stay there."

Cromwell sent one of his ministers to organize an immediate investigation. "Go to the docks. Find this man. Bring him to me."

The usual pair of guards was stationed outside the door of the Earther dormitory. They stiffened at the approaching men but relaxed a tad when they recognized Matthew. John took his man with a lightning takedown and a neck-breaking hold while Trevor resorted to a less artful knockout punch to the temple. Matthew opened the door and as the prisoners gathered around, John and Trevor dragged the guards in.

George Lawrence stumbled toward them, wrapped in a blanket and weak as a kitten from dysentery. "My God. Have you come for us?"

"Yes, sir, we have," John said as he did a fast headcount. "Some of you are missing."

Stuart Binford had also been ill. His clothes hung loosely and he'd taken on the appearance of a bearded scarecrow. "Brenda Mitchell's dead," he said dully. "Suicide. Kelly Jenkins is missing. We're thinking she was taken for the same reason Brenda was."

John and Trevor looked at each other in disgust.

"Karen Smithwick also disappeared a few days ago," Binford said.

"That leaves Anthony Trotter," Lawrence said. "He among us has fared well. The guards tell us that Cromwell declared himself king after the Duke of Suffolk took ill. One guess who's the new chancellor."

"Unbelievable," John said. "Okay, everyone, get your shoes on. We're getting you out of here."

"Is it just you two?" Chris Cowles asked.

"Just us here," Trevor said. "But the SAS is waiting for us in Dartford."

"Did you say the SAS?" Binford asked, sounding animated for the first time in weeks.

"Yeah," Trevor said. "The heavy mob."

Matthew had been keeping watch by the door.

He slid into the room and whispered, "Someone's coming."

John and Trevor dragged the guards' bodies behind the privy screen and hid there with them. They heard the forge brigade entering and greeting their companions then heard one of the guards who escorted them ask what happened to the men guarding the door.

"Why are you asking us?" Chris answered defiantly. "We're the prisoners, you're our bloody keepers. I am so bloody tired of the incompetence of you lot ..."

She continued haranguing them while Binford made his way behind the privy screen and flashed three fingers.

The three guards, distracted and bemused by Chris's tirade, didn't see John and Trevor coming. A frenzied attack left the men groaning on the floor. The youngest guard escaped serious injury and when he saw the broken bodies of his two mates beside him, he begged for mercy.

"Please don't crash me worse," he moaned.

John stood over him and told him not to move. "If you don't want your neck broken help us find two of our women."

"One's in the dungeons," the man croaked.

"Which one?" Chris said.

"The old bag."

"Can you take us there?" John asked.

"If you promise not to hurt me worse."

"It's a deal."

"Where's the younger one?" Chris demanded. "Her name's Kelly."

The guard winced and pushed his hand against his broken ribs. "I don't know nothing 'bout a young one."

John helped the guard to his feet. "Is there a way out of the palace from the dungeons?" he asked.

"Yeah, goes straight to the river."

Without warning, Trotter opened the unguarded door and took a step into the dormitory where he froze.

"If it isn't the chancellor," Lawrence said contemptuously.

Trotter's eyes darted around the room and he seemed to be struggling to come to grips with the situation. It reminded John of the old flashing tube computers that needed a good while to spit out the answer to a complex calculation.

"Are you alone?" John asked.

"Yes."

"Then close the fucking door."

Trotter shut the door behind him and licked his lips. "I heard that you lot came back from the forge. I didn't expect to see you here."

"Disappointed?" John asked.

"Hardly," Trotter said. "Can you get us back to Earth?"

"That's the plan," Trevor said.

Campbell Bates stepped forward. "We're not sure if you're one of us or one of them."

Lawrence started to say something but was racked with a paroxysm of coughing. When he recovered he said, "Ask me what I think."

"Don't be ridiculous," Trotter said. "I'm one of you. I've been working tirelessly behind the scenes to improve everyone's circumstances. I've been your channel to Cromwell. I know there's been some misunderstanding of my role but no one wants to get out of here more than I do."

Chris came right up to Trotter and stuck a finger in his chest. "Where is Kelly Jenkins?" she asked.

"I have absolutely no idea. I've made multiple inquiries and can only assume that Cromwell had something to do with her disappearance. He's a man of appetites."

"How did you know she was missing?" Binford asked. "You haven't even been around here lately."

Trotter didn't miss a beat. "Karen Smithwick told me. Where is Karen?"

"You don't know?" Lawrence said.

"I don't," Trotter insisted. "She came to see me a few days ago asking for help in finding Kelly. I told her I'd do my best and she left in the presence of a guard. Last I saw of her. She didn't return?"

"We know where she is," John said, "and we're going to get her on our way out of here."

"Where is she?" Trotter asked.

The young guard winced again as he talked. "In the dungeons."

John lifted his cloak and unslung his rifle.

"An AK-47," Trotter said. "Brilliant move. Bravo, Camp."

"Thanks for your endorsement," John deadpanned. "All right everyone, stick together like glue." Then he said to the young guard, "You're going to take us to the dungeons in a way that avoids your friends. If not, the first bullet that comes out of this big, black gun is going in your brain." Finally he whispered to Trevor, "Keep tabs on Trotter. I don't trust him."

The guard led them down a back staircase to the ground level and past some storerooms to a flight of winding stone stairs that were almost too dark to navigate. The air in the lowest level of the palace was fetid and damp. The stone walls of the corridor were cold and slimy.

"Just around the corner," the guard whispered to John.

"How many guards will we find?" John asked.

A shrug brought on a gasp of pain from his cracked ribs. "Not sure."

"You go first," John said. "I'll be right behind you. The rest of you, stay back."

Trevor made sure Trotter saw his blackpowder pistol. "Behave yourself," Trevor said.

"Don't worry, we're on the same team," Trotter replied.

Halfway down the next corridor, four burly soldiers were hunched over playing dice. At first they waved at the young guard and called for him to come but as soon as they saw John they reached for their swords and charged.

John berated himself for needing six rounds to put the four of them down. He reached for a ring of keys on the belt of a stricken man. The young guard pulled his fingers out of his ears. When John asked him which was the cell, he led him there. The rest of the group followed.

Each cell was crammed with pathetic, starving men, too weak to even grasp the bars or call for help. But one cell had a single occupant, a woman curled in a fetal position on a bed of dirty straw.

"That's her," the guard said.

John began trying keys. While he worked he told the others to check the other cells for Kelly. When the lock turned he motioned for Chris to help him.

John gave Trevor the rifle and he went inside with Chris.

The woman knelt beside Smithwick and said, "Karen, it's Chris. We've come to get you out of here. We're going home. We're going back to Earth."

Smithwick turned her head toward them and Chris fell backwards at the sight. Her lower face and neck were swollen beyond recognition and covered in dried blood.

John dropped to his knees to have a closer look. "Karen, it's John Camp. What did they do to you?"

Smithwick tried to speak but she could only make guttural sounds. He told Chris to bring a candle burning on a table by the guard station and by its light he gently opened Smithwick's mouth.

"My God," he said.

"What is it?" Chris asked.

"They've cut out her tongue."

Chris choked back tears while John told Smithwick he was going to help her up. It was clear she was too weak to walk so he gently lifted her over his shoulder.

In the hall the others looked on in shock as Chris passed the word what had happened to her.

"Trevor, take the point," John said. "There're eleven rounds left in the mag."

"What about me?" the young guard asked.

"Which way out?" John asked.

"Just down there."

"I can lock you in," John said.

"I'll be tortured when I'm found. I hate to say it but I'd be grateful if you'd shoot me in the arm and leave me lying with those lads. By the look of them they'll be telling no tales."

Trevor laid the guard down on the pile of writhing bodies and put a round through his triceps muscle. The young man yelped in pain and then gave him a grateful nod.

"Let's go," John said.

Chris piped up, "We didn't find Kelly."

"I'm sorry," John said. "She could be dead. She could be anywhere. It's a big palace. She could have even been sold off to someone on the outside. We've got to get out of here. Then we'll need to find a boat big enough for all of us."

Trotter said, "Cromwell keeps his barge on the docks."

At the sound of Trotter's voice, John felt Smithwick squirming on his shoulder. He made sure he had a good purchase on her and began walking. No one but Trotter saw the bug-eyed way she stared at him and no one could understand the stream of guttural sounds that began to spill from her swollen mouth.

35

Trevor tiptoed along the dock. What he saw sent him hurrying back to the shadows of the warehouse building where the others were waiting.

"The barge is crawling with soldiers," he told John.

"What are they doing?"

"Drinking by the sound of it."

"Can we take them?"

"Not without casualties, guv. Too many of them."

There were shouts coming from near the palace.

"Search the area!"

"Find them!"

As calmly as possible John told the frightened Earthers that they'd have to find a place to hide. He had put Karen Smithwick on the ground where she had curled into a fetal tuck, and now he lifted her to his shoulder again.

"You should leave her," Trotter hissed.

"Not going to happen," John said.

"You'll slow us down."

"Go fuck yourself."

With Trevor on point the group of men and women began running along a dark alley into the rabbit warren of London streets. It was late and the streets were deserted. Trevor searched for somewhere to shelter and led them away from the river, further into the medieval city. George Lawrence was frail and having trouble keeping pace but Matthew Coppens and David

Laurent helped him along. The voices of soldiers looking for them were not fading. Their pursuers were keeping pace.

They ran past a long, low building. Trevor paused to try a large double door. It creaked open. Inside, a man began screaming, "Get out! Get out! I have a pistol!"

He quickly shut the door and kept going.

He made a random turn down a very narrow alleyway and checked the others. The group snaked single-file behind him. A foul, pungent odor began to fill their nostrils. From the way she was squirming on his shoulder, John could tell it was bothering Smithwick and it bothered him too. He wondered if there was a rotting room nearby, but as the odor got stronger it seemed to be different from the stench of decaying flesh. In some ways it was worse, more acrid and burning.

Midway along the alley a small door was wide open. The building was a ramshackle, timber-framed structure. It seemed the door had been left open for ventilation because the stench was pouring from it like gas from a swamp.

Trevor stopped and holding his breath, peered in.

"We're not going in there!" Stuart Binford gagged.

They heard one soldier shouting to another, too close-by for comfort.

"Yeah, 'fraid so," Trevor said. "Tell the others to cover their faces best they can."

"I don't think I'll need to tell them that," Binford said.

As they shuffled into the dark building, Leroy Bitterman retched and asked, "What is this place?"

John answered, "It's not a rotting room."

"Thank God for that," Bitterman said.

"It's worse, I reckon," Trevor said, pointing his rifle into a space that was all blackness except for a faint glow coming from across a seemingly large expanse.

"Surely we can't stay here," Campbell Bates said.

John put Smithwick down gently and propped her against a wall. She gagged and sputtered. "Does someone have a cloth to put around her face?"

he asked.

Chris had a washcloth she carried with her and tied it into a mask.

John did some shrugs to ease his cramped shoulder. "I think it's a good place to hide because of the smell. If I were one of Cromwell's soldiers making slave wages I wouldn't stick my face in here."

"Being chased by the king's men, are you?"

The voice came from the darkness.

"Who's there?" Trevor challenged.

"Shouldn't I be asking you lot that question?"

"Show yourself," Trevor said. "We're armed and I will shoot."

"Calm yourself, matey. If you're not rovers nor militiamen then I'm not your enemy and you're not mine."

The faint glow got closer until they saw it was a candle held by a small man with a leather apron hanging over a bare, muscular chest. When he was some thirty feet away Trevor told him to stop. That's when they realized there were half a dozen more men behind him.

"We've no weapons," the man said. "This is my place. These are my men. We work here. We live here. Are you recents?"

John answered. "You might say that."

"Might I?" the man asked. "What else might I say?"

"You can't smell us?" John asked.

"That's a laugh. We can't smell nothing no more which is much to our advantage."

"We're not dead," John said.

The men whispered to each other and their boss said, "There's been all sorts of rumors flying 'bout some door to the other side's that opened allowing Earth dwellers to come to our blighted land."

"The rumors are true," John said. "We're trying to get home."

"And the king's men don't wish for you to do so," the man said.

"Something like that," John said. "What is this place?"

"It's a tannery."

"That explains it," Lawrence gasped. "I thought I recognized the stench. It's like the tanneries I visited in Morocco. Rotting flesh, ammonia, pigeon shit."

They heard the soldiers coming down the alley.

"Best come to the rear," the tanner said. "Christopher, take the candle and lead them. Is she sick?" he asked pointing at Smithwick.

"They cut out her tongue," Chris said.

"Sounds like their methods," the tanner said.

John picked up Smithwick and followed the candle around the mosaic of tanning vats dug into the floor. The tanner stood by the open door and waited.

"Think he's going to shaft us?" Trevor whispered to John from the back of the tannery behind a bunch of barrels.

"We'll find out soon."

A party of soldiers pulled up panting beside the open door of the tannery.

"Out for an evening stroll?" the tanner asked.

"Have you seen anyone fleeing us?" one of the soldiers asked.

"Why would anyone wish to flee the likes of you?"

The soldier was a dullard. "They're alive."

"If I were alive I'd be fleeing you too, I'm quite sure," the tanner said.

"You've seen no one?"

"Only my own shadow but you fine men may enter and search my premises if you so desire."

The soldier wrinkled his nose. "I'd sooner have my supper inside a rotting room," he said, continuing his search along the alley.

The tanner came to the rear and lit another candle.

"Thank you," John said. "What's your name?"

"It is John. John, the tanner."

"My name's John too."

"But you are no tanner."

John smiled. "Why are you helping us?"

"I despise the king's men. They steal from me, they beat me, they threaten to drown me in my vats. I spit on them."

John reached into his pocket and produced one of Garibaldi's gold coins. "Like I said, thank you."

The tanner took the coin and bit down on it. "Well, I should be thanking you. It's a fine piece of metal."

"We'll need to stay till tomorrow night," John said.

"You'll be wanting food then."

John sniffed the air. "I don't think food's high on our list right now."

The tanner chuckled. "Before long, you won't even notice the smell. You'll be thinking you're in a flowering garden. We'll be back to our beds. In the morn we'll bring you some bread. This lovely barrel's got beer in it. Don't recommend you drink the water in here. There's a slop trench over there."

"What else could a man want?" John said.

"What else indeed?" the tanner replied.

Most of them slept fitfully in the miasma of noxious vapors but John and Trevor resolved to stay on guard. To keep sleep at bay they talked quietly into the night.

"If we get out of this what are you going to do with yourself?" Trevor asked.

"When, not if."

"Yeah, all right, we'll keep it positive."

"Emily and I've talked about it. She says she wants to do something different, maybe teaching physics at a university."

"And you?"

"Drinking beer, watching sports, and waking up every morning next to her—that'll do me. Actually I thought about maybe opening a school for martial arts, you know, self defense."

"You'd be good at it."

"What about you?" John asked.

Trevor stifled a yawn. "I'm not a big planner, guv, never have been. I tend to follow my nose. That's how I came to be working for you if I recall. But right now my nose is leading me to Arabel and her kids. I feel a serious case of domestication coming on."

John buried his face in his hands.

"What?" Trevor said.

"Is that going to make us brothers-in-law?"

Trevor showed a bit of mock horror. "It doesn't work that way, does it?"

"Even if it doesn't we could be having Sunday dinners and Christmases together."

"I'm a 42," Trevor said.

"Huh?"

"My shirt size. If you get it right the first time, I won't have to exchange the pressie."

When daylight came the tannery workers got to work stirring up gut-wrenching smells from their vats. Those Earthers who'd managed to swallow their rations of bread struggled to keep the food in their stomachs.

Everyone spent the day huddled behind the barrels, tapping into the beer to keep from getting dehydrated. "Can you eat at all, luv?" Chris asked Smithwick.

The miserable woman was almost unresponsive.

"Can you drink a bit? You've got to drink some. You're dehydrated."

Chris detected a flicker of interest and spent the rest of the day patiently doling out tiny sips of beer.

Since half the Earthers had been away at the forge for several weeks, there was a good deal of catching up to do and everyone took part, everyone but Trotter who sat as far away from the rest of them as he could pretending not to hear when his name came up.

In the afternoon John woke from a nap and sat beside Bates and Lawrence who were locked in an animated discussion about Trotter. It grew loud enough that Trotter decided to get up and find a piece of wall to lean against closer to the front of the tannery.

"Want to help?" John the tanner said to him, offering up his vat paddle.

"No I do not," Trotter replied, folding his arms.

John came over and sat beside the intelligence chiefs. "So what's his story?" John asked.

"Trotter?" Bates said. "He's a snake-in-the-grass, first degree. Before we were sent to the forge he ingratiated himself to Cromwell and the Duke of Suffolk—a real creep, he was—and managed to get himself private quarters, better food, lord knows what. When we were sent to build the blast furnace he wouldn't do a stitch of work. Saw it as beneath him. I can't stand the guy."

Lawrence nodded. "Karen took to calling him Hell's Quisling and she was absolutely right. We suspected he was complicit in the suicide of Brenda Mitchell, a nice young lady who was snatched away by Suffolk for his personal enjoyment, if you know what I mean. Then Kelly, another nice young girl went missing and, well, the suspicion fell on Anthony."

"Any evidence?" John asked, glowering at Trotter across the tannery.

"Well, not really," Lawrence said, "but Karen was convinced. The night she went missing she went to confront him. He maintained she never arrived. Frankly it beggars belief and poor old Karen can't tell us what happened to her. If I survive this, I intend to destroy him."

"I'll be right by your side, George," Bates said.

At nightfall John the tanner agreed to have a quick walkabout to look for patroling soldiers. When he reported that the streets were quiet, John and Trevor made a run to the river to check on Cromwell's barge.

They returned a short while later, dispirited. The craft was still crawling with soldiers.

John produced another gold coin and gave it to the tanner.

"Can we enjoy your hospitality another day?" he asked.

"If you pay at this rate, you can stay a year," the tanner said, pocketing the loot.

"Did you live in London? Before, I mean," John asked.

"I did. Not far from here."

"When?"

"Oh, I passed away in 1820 or thereabouts. Touch of the plague."

"Were you a tanner?"

"I was. All I ever knew, except for drinking and raising Cain which is what landed me here."

"I'm sorry."

"Don't be. It's a funny thing, really, but ever since I was a lad my mother always told me I was going to Hell so I sort of expected it. Didn't quite have the right notion of it though, did I? I expected fire and brimstone and got an eternity of pigeon shit instead."

Trevor came over and offered to take the first night's watch. John didn't debate him. He was beyond exhausted. Seconds after he curled up in the corner he was out cold.

The flat plain of the Helmand Province was somewhere below them hidden by the blackness of night. Staring out the open door of the Black Hawk MH-60, John could feel the wind against his face. The rotor action vibrated through his body.

No one in the squad had said a word since lift-off. Most of the men were fighting back tears. John wasn't. He was too angry.

"Ten mikes to touchdown at Leatherneck," the pilot called out.

It was impossible to look at Mike Entwistle's body bag without looking into the swollen face of the man who'd killed him. Fazal Toofan was on his side, wrists and ankles zip-tied, moaning. He slowly came to, his eyes blinking open. He tried to lift his head and one of the weapon's sergeants pushed it down with the sole of his boot.

"Keep your fucking head down, motherfucker," the sergeant shouted.

The shouting seemed to clear the cobwebs away and the Taliban commander said crisply, "Where are you taking me?"

"Don't talk to him," John raged.

"Are you the one in charge?" Toofan asked.

John said nothing.

"What are you, Seals? Marines?"

The sergeant said, "Green Berets, motherfucker."

"For the last time, I said don't talk to him, goddamn it!" John shouted.

"And you, shut the fuck up!"

But Toofan wouldn't shut up. "This one, the one in the bag. Is he the asshole I shot? Are those the asshole's brains on my leg?"

John rose as high as the helicopter ceiling would allow.

He didn't say a word as he grabbed Toofan by the hair.

He didn't say a word as he lifted Toofan to his knees.

And he didn't say a word as he threw him out the open door into the blackness of the Afghan night.

The pilot and co-pilot swiveled at the sound of Toofan's fading screams.

John sat back down, breathing hard.

"Turn your asses around," the sergeant yelled at the pilots. "Nobody saw anything, you understand? You understand? He was never on this chopper. That's the end of it. It's the fucking end of it."

That's when John began to cry.

John awoke in a cold sweat to see Trotter sitting near him, staring.

"You were talking in your sleep," Trotter said.

"Oh yeah?"

"Sounds like quite the nightmare."

John sat up. "I don't remember my dreams."

"Everyone has their demons."

John had half a cup of beer by his side. He drank the rest of it. "What are yours?"

"I don't think we know each other well enough for me to bare my soul. Perhaps when we get back to London, the real London, we'll have a few drinks."

"That's not going to happen."

Trotter feigned offense. "Really? Do you have something against me?"

"Yeah, maybe. At best you're a greasy little shit. At worst you're, well …"

Trotter wouldn't let him finish. He was on his feet saying, "Let me tell you something, Camp. I don't like Americans. Never did. I work with the CIA on a regular basis and I'd say it's the absolute worst part of my job.

Give me the Germans, the Poles, anyone, even the bloody Turks any day of the week. I leave a meeting with Americans and I generally want to vomit. I hate your pseudo-Boy Scout rectitude, your black-or-white simplistic worldview, your appalling lack of subtlety and class. I'm going to sit by the stinking vats now, Camp. The air is fresher over there."

Trevor came to the rear of the tannery and handed John the rifle.

"Two of you getting into it?" he asked.

"Not really," John said, "but I've got a feeling he and I are going to have a reckoning one day."

The following night John and Trevor tried again. Creeping up on the barge they saw only a handful of soldiers onboard.

"This might be as good as it's going to get," John whispered.

"I agree, guv."

John pulled a knife and said, "Use the rifle as a club but no shooting."

Most of the Earthers were near the front of the tannery anxiously awaiting John and Trevor's return. Leroy Bitterman looked around and noticed that Trotter wasn't with them.

Stuart Binford and Matthew Coppens went looking for him, circling around the tannery from opposite directions. It was Matthew who found him standing over Smithwick.

"What are you doing?" Matthew asked.

Trotter palmed his knife and said, "I thought I heard her choking. No one was about and I was trying to help."

"She seems all right to me."

There was a small commotion near the door as John announced they'd secured the barge. He came to the rear of the forge to get Smithwick and on the way he called John the tanner out of his bunkroom.

"We're off now," he said. "You're a good man, John."

"Not half as good as you are," the tanner said.

John gave him his last gold coin.

"I haven't earned this one," the tanner said, though he quickly pocketed it.

"Sure you did. We drank all your beer."

36

Emily reviewed the latest computer simulations from Geneva and looked away. "I think we should be operational by tomorrow morning."

Loomis drank his tea. Even after a week, he let it be known that each sip was marvelous, something to be savored. "You don't seem happy," he said.

"You know why."

He nodded. "I'm concerned about the modifications we've made to the particle guns," he said. "Bit of a chewing gum and Sellotape job."

"Of course it is," she said. "If we were using uranium gas in the normal course of business, we'd have spent a year or two in design and manufacture with input from dozens of experts."

He clenched his fists then rapidly dealt out his fingers while turning his palms upwards. It was a magician's gesture. Presto! She'd forgotten he used to do it all the time. "We'll just have to push the button and see," he said.

She got up from her workstation. They were in the new, makeshift control room set up in the recreation center.

"Maybe we should hold off until we've done more prep work," she said.

"Emily, I realize you're worried about John but you've heard the powers-that-be on the conference calls. They want this done and they want it done now."

"Yes, but I'm the one who has to push the button, as you say. If I refuse to do it there's nothing they can do."

"Is that really the way you wish to play it?" he asked. "Personal good over the greater good?"

"That's ripe coming from you, Paul, for God's sake."

She stormed out and went to the washroom where she splashed her face and stared into the mirror trying to calm herself.

When she returned, Paul had something in his hand.

"What are these doing here? I found them on the floor," he said.

"A few of the people in the control room were armed the day of the last restart. The MI5 guards, Anthony Trotter too, I think. There's metal and synthetics all over the place, all of it left behind."

She took the guns and slid them under a table in the corner.

Then she apologized to him but Loomis said she was right to point out his hypocrisy.

"Selfishness has become a way of life for me," he said. "I wasn't always like this. I hope you can remember the man I used to be. I suppose I changed the moment that I madly and selfishly killed my wife, depriving my children of their mother and her parents of their daughter. And then I compounded it by selfishly taking my own life."

"Paul, please ..."

"No, let me finish. Unfortunately, I've become an expert on the subject. You can't survive in Hell unless you have a laser-like focus on your survival and creature necessities. I was luckier than most. I was quickly dealt to Stalin and though I was essentially a slave, I was a high-class slave because what I carried in my head wasn't viewed as a commodity. I could have refused to work for this monster who wanted me to be an engine for weapons manufacture, weapons which would cause pain and misery on a mass scale. I could have made a dogged effort to escape. But I didn't. I protected my own hide. Why tell you this? It's because you're not like me. You're a wonderful, altruistic person without a selfish bone in your body. To save the world from doom you will push the button, even if it means trapping your lover in Hell."

"You're correct when you say I'll do the right thing. But you're wrong about the universality of selfishness in Hell. I saw people there who transcended their narrow survival concerns for the greater good. My first time there I was rescued by a group of women who survived by looking after each other. And I'm inspired by Garibaldi and the people who've cast their lot with him to try and bring a modicum of humanity to Hell. Yes, there are terrible people doing terrible things, and yes, that may be the status quo, but I'd like to dwell on the goodness that can exist even inside people who've done evil. Are you hearing me, Paul? You've got so much goodness still inside."

He broke down and put his head in his hands, a weeping mask. She came over and put her arms around his chest and held him for a long time.

"I'll try to make you proud of me," he said. "I'll try to make my children proud. I know it won't be easy with them. With a bit of luck I'll have twenty, perhaps thirty years of life ahead of me before I die and have to return. Even if all of it is spent in prison, I'll try to do some good, in my work, in my writings. I'll figure it out."

"I know you will."

As was their habit, they joined Dirk and Duck for lunch in their unlocked cell, microwaving some frozen foods for them. They sat eating with chairs drawn up beside their bed, a muted Disney video playing on the TV.

Emily brought up the subject foremost on their minds. "I did speak to Mr. Wellington about your plea to remain here."

"What did 'e say?" Duck asked, inhaling a baked, stuffed shell.

"He said it was the government's policy to repatriate as many Hellers as they could prior to breaking the connections."

"What's that mean?" Dirk said.

"I'm afraid it means you can't stay."

"But we don't want to go back!" Duck said. "We like it 'ere. Did you speak to my Delia?"

"Not directly, no," Emily admitted, "but according to Mr. Wellington, she did put in a good word for you."

Dirk pointed his plastic spoon at Loomis. "But you don't 'ave to go back, do you?"

"No," he said, "I was able to make a deal."

"Paul has some very special skills which gave him the ability to make a bargain," Emily said.

"We've got skills," Duck said. "Dirk can make the best beer in Dartford and I can, I can, well, I can 'elp him do it."

Emily smiled at them. "Look, I'm making no promises but we're going to be very busy tomorrow, so busy we might not have the time to make sure you leave the building and make it to the soldiers at the edge of the hot zone."

"I always 'ave difficulty fathoming your meaning, Miss Emily," Dirk said.

Duck hit him with one of his sharp elbows. "She's saying we can stay!"

Emily didn't sleep that night; she didn't want to. To give her body a break she lay down on one of the mattresses she and Paul had dragged from the jail cells to the control room, but she stayed awake, straining her ears for any sign John had returned.

At six o'clock she woke up Paul, made some tea, and checked on the cooling status of the twenty-five thousand magnets arrayed inside the MAAC tunnel like a giant string of pearls. Super-cooled liquid helium had taken the magnet temperature down overnight to 4.5 K, or -268.7°C. If the schedule held, in two hours she and Paul would have to initiate the final cooling protocol to achieve 1.7 K, preciously close to the absolute-zero temperature needed to accelerate uranium protons to their maximal collision energy.

"No sign of him," Loomis said, leaning over her workstation.

She shook her head and started calling out checklist items for them to implement.

At seven o'clock the video link with Geneva opened and the full team at the Large Hadron Collider began mirroring the activities at MAAC and lending many pairs of virtual hands.

At eight o'clock Emily logged onto a videoconference with Prime Minister Lester and his Cobra group in Manchester, Ben Wellington and his people at MI5, army personnel at SAS headquarters in Credenhill, and the Drone Warfare Centre at RAF Waddington.

"Dr. Loughty, are we on schedule?" the prime minister asked.

"We can be," she answered. "If we have a final go decision we can fire the particle guns in two hours."

"Is it going to work?" he asked.

"I don't know," she said wearily. "As I've explained, we can't be sure the rather primitive modifications we've made to the injection system and particle guns will work with the uranium gas. If it does work, we can't be sure we'll be able to obliterate the strangelets. It's all based on hypothetical modeling."

Lester gave her a grim nod and said, "At least you've been consistent, but I was rather hoping for an answer of, yes, Prime Minister."

"I wish I could be more positive," she said.

The prime minister looked to his cabinet and asked, "Well, are there any objections to green-lighting this? No? MI5? No? What about Credenhill? Are your people in position?"

Major Gus Parker-Burns, the Officer Commander of 22 SAS Regiment, said, "Yes, we are in position, Prime Minister. We have three, three-man extraction teams on the fringes of the Leatherhead, Dartford, and Sevenoaks hot zones. It is our continuing assessment that the group deployed to Upminster was likely over-run by Hellers three weeks ago and sending an extraction team into Upminster would, unfortunately, neither be safe nor productive."

"RAF Waddington, what say you?" Lester asked.

The Brigadier General in charge replied, "We have Greater London blanketed by our full contingent of Reapers and Predators supplemented by the twenty on loan from the United States. We are intensely monitoring the known HZs."

Lester asked, "In the event the MAAC start-up does not have the intended result but, in fact, exacerbates the problem, are all the drones fully armed?"

"Yes, sir," the general answered. "Brimstone missiles on the Reapers,

Hellfires on the Predators."

"Mr. Wellington," the prime minister said, "I know you've had the burden of authorizing missile strikes. At this point I feel I ought to shoulder that responsibility personally."

Ben sounded relieved when he said, "Of course, Prime Minister."

"And, Mr. Wellington, has your package been delivered to Leatherhead?"

"It has. It is in the hands of the SAS extraction team."

"And finally," Lester said, "we all know that in the event that the procedure today does successfully break the connection between our world and theirs, that we will have hundreds, perhaps thousands of Hellers permanently trapped in London. We'll need to capture each and every one of them and determine their fate. However, that will be a problem for another day. Right, does anyone else have anything to say?"

Emily nodded a few times. "I would just like to point out that we haven't seen John Camp or Trevor Jones or any of the MAAC staff or visitors transported at the onset of the present crisis."

The prime minister stared gravely into the monitor; the videographer in Manchester zooming in so close that Emily could see the luminous blue of his eyes. "We know nothing of the fate of the others but we are very much aware of the heroism of Mr. Camp and Mr. Jones. I do know the implications of our decision this morning and so do you. So I ask you, Dr. Loughty, do you have an objection to initiating the final two-hour countdown?"

She closed her eyes. "None," she said. "We'll initiate the sequence immediately."

On the outskirts of Leatherhead the sergeant in charge of the extraction team rapped his knuckles against the tinted window of the Land Rover.

Malcolm Gough got out and went around to open the other rear door. The SAS team knew the nature of the package but they nevertheless seemed awestruck by the sight of King Henry in his doublet and cloak.

"These men will be your escort, Your Majesty," Gough said.

Henry surveyed the scene. To the west was a mass of army and emergency services vehicles and personnel. To the east, the town.

Turning toward the River Mole Henry said, "So this is the present-day town."

Gough said, "Yes. I believe you'll be taken across that bridge."

"That's correct, sir," the sergeant said, staring at Henry with saucer-eyes.

"I wonder what I shall find on the other side of that bridge?" Henry said.

"You've been away for a good while," Gough said.

"Indeed. I do not think I shall still be king. I venture that Cromwell and Suffolk have fought for my crown like two rats in a bag. I wonder, will the victor fight me when I seek to reclaim it or meekly place it upon my head?"

The professor said, "I'd really like to know the answers to your questions." Then he smiled, "But not enough to come with you."

"I believe you will miss me, Gough," Henry said.

"I will, Your Majesty. More than you know. It has been the privilege of my life to spend this time with you."

"If you ever stray from the virtuous life of a scholar then perhaps I will see you again at the end of that life."

"I hope not, Your Majesty."

The three-man SAS team closed in and began walking the king toward the bridge.

The professor recorded video on his mobile phone and kept recording until the soldiers and king reached the bridge and vanished halfway across.

Then he called his wife and said, "I'm coming home."

37

John pointed toward a spot on the riverbank. “There. That’s where we need to land.”

John had anointed Campbell Bates as skipper when he learned the FBI director was an avid sailor with a fifty-footer on Chesapeake Bay. But John knew the river and the two of them successfully navigated the boat through the darkness and into the dawn.

The barge made a hard landing under full wind power, jolting the Earthers on board. John and Bates quickly lowered the sails, while Trevor jumped off, pulling a line.

When they were disembarking, John passed Smithwick’s limp body to some of the men. Last off, he watched the barge drift downstream.

“Not a bad vessel,” Bates said. “Hope we don’t need it again.”

“You got that right,” John said. With Smithwick back on his shoulder, he shouted, “Everyone, follow Trevor and me.”

They were less than a mile from the hot zone but something ahead disturbed John. By the standards of Hell the day was bright and he squinted to better define what he was seeing in the marshlands and bulrushes.

“Is that a crowd?” he asked Trevor.

“Looks like it, guv.”

John swore and said, “We may be screwed.”

"Is the temperature stable?" Emily asked.

A scientist in Geneva remotely monitoring the MAAC magnet temperature came on one of the video screens and said, "Holding at 1.7 K."

"All magnets online?" she asked.

Geneva reported the schematics looks good.

"We're ready to initiate injection of the particle guns," she said. "Paul, I've begun a one-minute clock."

Loomis was hunched over a workstation and replied, "On your mark."

As the clock ticked off the seconds, she looked increasingly brittle. "Begin injection," she said.

Loomis checked the injection pressures and announced, "Uranium gas is flowing, boosters are functioning, the synchrotron appears to be filling normally."

"Please let me know when filling is complete," Emily said.

A minute later Loomis made the call and Geneva concurred.

Emily glanced at the control-room doors, hoping against hope they would fly open but they did not. "Fire the particle guns, Paul."

Trevor was staring at the Hellers blocking their way. "Maybe we can go around them," he said.

John grunted. "Maybe. Let's get a closer look."

Matthew Coppens had found a large crowbar onboard the barge and he was carrying it in both hands. He caught up with John and asked if they were going to have to fight their way through.

"We'll see."

Matthew kept up with him, stride for stride. "I'm ready if we do," he said.

"You ever fight anyone before?" John asked, smiling at his crowbar.

"Never, but now might be the time to start." Then he added with an air of desperation, "I've got to get back to my wife and son."

"Good man. Stay close."

There were dozens of Hellers between them and the hot zone, all with their backs to the approaching Earthers. They seemed to be watching and waiting, edging, but not rushing forward.

The ground to the south, nearer to Dartford village, was slightly elevated and as they got within a hundred yards of the Hellers John and Trevor spotted someone waving furiously at them a hundred yards past the crowd.

"Think that's one of the good guys?" Trevor asked.

A shot rang out, the distinctive big-boy sound of an AK-47. One of the Hellers screamed in pain and the cordon surrounding the hot zone moved back a few yards.

"Music to my ears," John said.

In the distance there was more waving and another shot was fired. Indistinct shouts from the SAS men came their way on the morning breeze.

The Hellers still had their backs to them, unaware of their presence.

"I think our guys want us to make our way through," Trevor said.

"They'd help by letting a lot more lead fly," John said.

"Maybe they don't have the ammo," Trevor said.

"You may be right." John stopped and with his free hand motioned for everyone behind him to halt.

"What's the plan?" Bates asked.

"We're going to try to ram our way through," John said. "When I give the signal, you all need to run like, you know, hell. Stuart and Matthew, help George. Leroy, you going to be able to hoof it?"

"Like Seabiscuit," Bitterman said.

"I'm not sure I like this plan," Trotter complained.

"You're overruled," John said. "You don't like it, go back to your friends at the palace."

Trotter sneered but kept quiet.

"Okay, Trev, concentrate your fire, make each shot count," John said, getting a tighter grip on the moaning woman on his shoulder.

Trevor raised his rifle. "You know I've only got ten rounds, guv."

"I know."

Ben Wellington had choppered into Dartford that morning and was at the military staging area to the west of the hot zone monitoring two channels of chatter on a headset. One channel covered military operations, the other, a feed from the MAAC control room. In Manchester, the prime minister and Cobra were doing the same.

The radio came to life with an army report from Sevenoaks. "I see them! There they are! They're coming through on the Belmeade playing fields. They're making their way toward our position."

"Are you sure it's the SAS?"

"Got to be them. Standby, please. Standby …"

Ben heard the prime minister's voice. "Did he say the SAS are coming through?"

"I can confirm now. Captain Marsh is here. This is A Group. He reports that all surviving men and the evac team have come through."

Ben was breathing heavily. "Ben Wellington, here. Any sign of John Camp or Trevor Jones?"

"Negative. That's a negative. Only SAS."

Dispirited, Ben switched to the MAAC comms channel.

Emily looked at the elliptical map of MAAC displayed on the screen. Two dots, one red, one green, representing uranium proton streams traveled in opposite directions, making the circuit around London at near light speed. If all was going according to plan, evidence of proton collisions would begin to accumulate.

Loomis had moved to the muon spectrometer workstation and was studying the data feeds.

"What's the strangelet activity, Paul?" Emily asked.

"No change. They're still within the system at elevated, baseline levels."

A technician in Geneva called out, "Approaching 20 TeV."

"That's the level that got us into this mess," Emily muttered.

"Sorry, what did you say?" Loomis asked.

"Nothing. What are you seeing, Paul?"

From Geneva: "You've exceeded 20 TeV, now 30 TeV and rising."

"I'm seeing collision tracings, lots of them," Loomis said. "Hold on, Emily, this is bad. I'm seeing a big spike in strangelet formation."

Ben heard the prime minister ask what the spike in strangelets meant. Someone in Manchester, presumably a scientist-advisor, said, "It means the connections between the two dimensions are likely to increase in size and perhaps in number."

Trevor aimed his first shot at a broad-shouldered man in a brown coat. The bullet tore through his back, swiftly dropping him. Hellers turned at the gunshot and began shouting. Trevor calmly walked toward them firing twice more until there were three bodies on the grass.

John was keeping track. Seven rounds left.

He heard another shot, this one coming from the SAS. Another Heller fell onto the pile.

"They're going to help as much as they can!" John shouted to Trevor. Then he turned to the others, "Get ready to run when I run!"

Another SAS round hit home.

John bellowed, "Okay, Trev, charge!"

Emily felt her chest tighten as the collision energies rose to levels she thought she would never see.

40 TeV

50 TeV

60 TeV

"Paul?"

He clearly knew what she was asking. "Strangelets are off the charts."

Ben heard the prime minister announcing that he was being advised to order all personnel surrounding hot zones to immediately move back from their positions.

A colonel at the Leatherhead HZ asked for specific instructions. “How far?” he said.

“How far?” Lester asked someone in his conference room.

A voice said, “I have no idea. How about two hundred yards for a start?”

The colonel in Leatherhead started to give the order but stopped. “We’ve got activity here. Men coming through. Men approaching. Hang on. SAS coming through. It’s Gatti. It’s C Group.”

Ben listened until it was confirmed that all surviving members of the group and the evacuation team were accounted for before asking about John and Trevor, only to be told they were not present.

The army colonel in charge of the Dartford HZ ordered a pullback and Ben began following the retreating personnel.

All of them were running, following Trevor who kept up a slow but steady rate of fire. John counted three more shots coming from the SAS side then no more.

They were thirty yards from the Hellers cordon. Some of them were armed with swords but they didn’t look like soldiers, just ordinary men lured by the promise of crossing to Earth. They couldn’t go forward toward the SAS gunfire or backwards toward Trevor’s so they scattered laterally but not fast enough to make a clean corridor. There were still a half dozen Hellers standing their ground near the growing pile of writhing bodies.

John lost count of how many rounds Trevor had left. Two? Three?

Trevor fired at close range and one of the remaining men fell.

He fired again and dropped another one.

He was ten yards away when he pulled the trigger again but nothing happened. On empty and five yards away, all he could do was scream at them at the top of his lungs.

Two men ran one way, two the other and Trevor hit the gap running.

John turned, and shouted for the others to keep up. George Lawrence had stumbled. Henry Quint lifted him partway and Matthew and Stuart finished the job. They began running, one on each side, transporting him in a seated carry.

Captain Yates was running toward them with some of his men, shouting, "Come on! Move it! Move it!"

Trevor reached Yates first. "You guys out of ammo?" he said.

"We are now," Yates said. "Are those the MAAC people?"

"Yeah," Trevor panted.

"Christ, we've got to hurry. We're being evacuated. They've got the fix in the works."

John arrived next and took up the offer to transfer Smithwick to a couple of troopers.

"Help that man too," John said pointing toward Lawrence.

A soldier hustled over and got Lawrence on his shoulder.

"Run!" Yates shouted, heading toward the hot zone. "For God's sake, run!"

From Geneva: "You're at 220 TeV."

Emily was standing behind Loomis now, watching the flood of spectrometer data and every few seconds, glancing toward the doors.

"Paul …"

"I see it," he said. "The strangelet activity has stabilized. It's high but it's definitely plateaued."

"220 … 240 … 260 …"

"I think the levels are falling," Emily said.

"I agree," Loomis said.

"270 … 280 … 290 …"

"Oh, John," she whispered.

"300 TeV. Maximum energy level."

She stared at the doors.

"Look!" Paul said. "Are you seeing this?"

She turned back to the screen. The strangelet activity had dropped to zero.

"It worked?" she asked.

Loomis got up and hugged her. "Yes! It worked! It actually worked!"

Ben heard the prime minister asking for confirmation. "Are we sure this has been effective?" he asked several times. "Call directly into the control room. I need confirmation."

From his new position, Ben didn't have good visual lines on the MAAC complex.

"Does anyone have eyes on the Yates group?" he asked.

No one did.

Then he heard Lester's side of a phone conversation with Emily.

"You're saying the strangelet activity is zero? They're all gone? Permanently? Yes, I suppose that would be premature. But are the connections severed? Is that the only way to tell? Really? All right, keep me informed, and Dr. Loughty, congratulations. Yes, pass that on to Dr. Loomis as well."

Ben listened to the prime minister address his cabinet and heard Jeremy Slaine say, "If the only way of finding out if the connections are severed is to enter the hot zone then we'll need a volunteer."

Ben didn't think it through. He didn't think about his wife or his children. He didn't think about himself. "I volunteer," he said into the headset.

"Who is speaking?" Lester asked.

"This is Ben Wellington. I'm at Dartford."

"Are you sure, Ben?" the prime minister asked.

"I'm sure." He started walking. "I'm heading toward the MAAC complex now, approaching from the west."

Five minutes passed, then ten.

Emily sat collapsed in her chair, a depression as black as she had ever felt, enveloping her in a shroud of sorrow.

"It's still zero," Paul said. "I think it's over." He looked at her and when he saw her anguish he said, "I'm sorry, Emily. I really am."

"I can't believe he's gone," she said. "I can't go on without him."

Loomis stood and came over to her. "You're young," he said, "you've got your whole ..."

The doors swung open.

Emily looked up, her momentary hopefulness dashed by seeing Ben Wellington come through, the doors closing behind him.

"I walked directly into the hot zone," he said to her. "I didn't wind up in Hell. I wound up here."

"Then it's really over," Emily said. Her voice was not much more than a whisper.

"But I found something along the way," Ben said, opening the doors again. "I found this."

John came through.

In an instant she was transformed. She sprang up and threw herself at him. He caught her in midair and held her against him.

"Never," she whispered to him.

"Never what?"

"Never leave me again."

Trevor was next through, then Bates, Bitterman, Quint, all of them, followed by Yates and what was left of B Group.

"You found them, you really found them," Emily said to John. "Stay there. I'll be right back."

She began tearfully hugging her people, Matthew, David, Chris, all the techs.

When she got to Henry Quint he couldn't make eye contact with her.

She still despised him for exceeding the approved energy levels and causing all this misery, but she said, "I'm sorry you had to go through this, Henry."

All he could do was mumble, "Most people would say I got what I deserved."

No one noticed Trotter slinking off on his own.

"Where's Brenda? And Kelly?" she asked.

Chris shook her head. No more needed to be said.

"Trevor," Emily said, hugging him too. "You must ring Arabel right away."

His smile lit up the room. "That's exactly what I'm going to do."

"Excuse me?" one of the troopers, the group medic, called out. "Is there a first-aid kit about? This woman needs attention. She's dangerously dehydrated."

Emily said, "It's over there, in that cabinet."

Smithwick was laid onto the floor. After a few tries, the medic found a vein and began pouring saline into her.

The next five minutes were a blur.

The technical people crowded around Paul Loomis and the spectrometry workstation, happily losing themselves in data.

Ben had, what he hoped would be his last call with the prime minister for a long time, and when he was finished he called his wife and told her the ordeal was almost over. Then he told her what she really wanted to hear—that he loved her.

Bitterman and all the VIPs picked up available phones and began making tearful calls to loved ones in England and America.

Captain Yates used Ben's headset to debrief his superior, Major Parker-Burns, then passed the headset from soldier to soldier, so they could get patched into their loved ones.

Trotter spent the time scouring the control-room floor, looking for something. He eventually found it where Emily had slid it under a table.

And Emily and John sat against a wall, just holding hands. They didn't need to talk. There was time for that.

Yates made an announcement that everyone needed to stay put for a few more minutes until an army medical and extraction team arrived.

On her second bag of saline, Karen Smithwick blinked and began looking around. She tried to sit but the medic told her to lie still. From her vantage point, she searched the room and saw Trotter.

Emily and John heard her loud, insistent grunts and got up to see what the matter was.

"Is she all right?" Chris asked.

The medic said her vital signs were improving.

"She's trying to tell us something," Chris said.

Emily saw she was making hand gestures, one hand moving over her palm and asked her, "Do you want to write something?"

Smithwick nodded vigorously.

Emily got her a pen and notebook.

When Smithwick finished writing she waved the notebook at Emily who quickly read the scrawl.

"My God," Emily whispered.

"What's she saying?" John asked.

Emily read it, loud enough for everyone in the control room to hear it. "Anthony Trotter did this to me. He is responsible for Brenda's death. I think he killed Kelly."

John saw red.

He spotted Trotter across the room and went for him, screaming, "You fucking bastard!"

"John, leave him," Trevor shouted. "He's not worth it."

But John kept coming and cornered him, wrapping his big hands around Trotter's fleshy neck.

Trevor and Ben both ran over to break things up before John killed the man but an ear-splitting gunshot rang out.

John loosened his grip around Trotter's neck and took a step back before kneeling.

Trotter was holding his gun, left behind on the control-room floor weeks earlier.

"John!"

Emily ran to him and caught his body in her arms as he collapsed all the way to the floor. His shirt was red with spreading blood.

"Help him!" she shouted.

The medic got to John the same time Trevor and Ben got to Trotter. They wrestled the gun away from him and took him down to the floor. Trevor punched him over and over and would have killed him if Yates hadn't pulled him off.

"Get me those," Yates shouted, pointing at a pack of zip ties the MI5 agents had left behind the day of their transfer.

Ben kicked the pistol aside and after binding Trotter hand and foot, he collapsed on the floor and put his head in his hands.

The medic ripped John's shirt open and saw the wound, just below his sternum. He tried to put pressure on it but the blood kept coming.

"I used both bags of fluid on her," the medic said helplessly.

Yates grabbed the headset and said, "This is Captain Yates. We've got a gunshot victim. We need emergency services. What's your ETA? That's not good enough. We need a trauma team now."

Emily was kneeling beside John. He lifted an arm and made a small gesture for her to come closer.

"Emily," he whispered, "I love you."

Through her tears she said, "I love you too. More than you'll ever know."

"I'm dying," he said weakly. She had never heard his voice so small.

"No you're not."

"I am. I need to tell you something."

"No!"

"Please."

She nodded.

"I'm going there."

"Where?"

"I'm going to Hell. I killed a man. In Afghanistan."

"You were a soldier," she whispered desperately. "Soldiers in wars don't go to Hell. You know that."

"It was murder. I murdered a man. I threw him out of a helicopter. I'm definitely going. I'm …"

He stopped talking, his eyes were still looking into hers but they saw nothing.

"John!" she screamed. "No!"

The medic put his ear to John's chest, straining to hear a heartbeat. He shook his head.

"Oh Jesus," Trevor wailed. "Oh my God!"

No one but Trotter saw Emily stumble toward the spot where Ben had kicked the pistol.

No one but him saw her pick up the gun.

When he shouted "No, don't!" it was too late for anyone to stop her putting a bullet into Trotter's brain.

And it was too late for anyone to stop her from putting the gun to her own temple and pulling the trigger.

38

They were in Dartford village in the middle of the muddy road just outside Dirk and Duck's cottage.

John looked at Trotter and he looked at Emily.

"What did you do, Emily?" John shouted. His eyes filled with tears. "Tell me what you did?"

"I did what I had to do," she said. "I did what I wanted to do."

Trotter pushed himself up from the mud. He opened his mouth a few times, gasping like a fish pulled from the water.

Then he ran.

John caught him in a few strides and began to strangle him.

"You're not going to die. You know that, don't you?" John shouted as he crushed his throat. Trotter's face turned the color of a bruise and his eyes bulged. "I'm going to leave you in a fucking ditch. The animals and the bugs are going to eat your flesh. You're going to suffer and suffer and suffer and suffer."

John's hands were shaking with the exertion and when he let go, Trotter fell face first into a muddy puddle.

John went to Emily and held her. "Why did you do this? Why did you throw your life away?"

"I didn't want a life without you."

"But this?"

She kissed him. "At least we'll be together forever."

He repeated the word. “Forever.” Then he said, “Come on, let’s go.”

“Where to?”

“We’ll get some of those AK-47s our soldiers left behind.”

“And then?”

He took her hand and they began walking toward the river.

“Then we’ll find our friends in Francia and help Garibaldi win his war. After that, I don’t know. We’re going to have to figure that out together.”

Interested in reading other books by Glenn Cooper?

Try the following titles:

~ The Down trilogy ~

Down: Pinhole

Down: Portal

~ Stand alone books ~

The Tenth Chamber

The Resurrection Maker

The Devil Will Come

Near Death

~ The Library of the Dead trilogy ~

The Library of the Dead

The Book of Souls

The Keepers of the Library

Printed in Poland
by Amazon Fulfillment
Poland Sp. z o.o., Wrocław